BLACK
ICE

BECCA FITZPATRICK

BLACK ICE

SIMON & SCHUSTER BFYR

NEW YORK LONDON TORONTO SYDNEY NEW DELHI

An imprint of Simon & Schuster Children's Publishing Division

1230 Avenue of the Americas, New York, New York 10020

This book is a work of fiction. Any references to historical events, real people, or real places are used fictitiously. Other names, characters, places, and events are products of the author's imagination, and any resemblance to actual events or places or persons, living or dead, is entirely coincidental.

SIMON & SCHUSTER BFYR is a trademark of Simon & Schuster, Inc.

For information about special discounts for bulk purchases, please contact Simon & Schuster Special Sales at 1-866-506-1949 or business@simonandschuster.com.

The Simon & Schuster Speakers Bureau can bring authors to your live event. For more information or to book an event, contact the Simon & Schuster Speakers Bureau at 1-866-248-3049 or visit our website at www.simonspeakers.com.

Book design by Lucy Ruth Cummins

The text for this book is set in Seria Pro.

Manufactured in the United States of America

2 4 6 8 10 9 7 5 3 1

Library of Congress Cataloging-in-Publication Data

Fitzpatrick, Becca.

Black ice / Becca Fitzpatrick.

pages cm

Summary: Britt goes hiking in the Grand Tetons of Wyoming with her ex-boyfriend Calvin, but trouble arises when she is caught in a blizzard, taken hostage by fugitives, finds evidence of murders, and learns whom to trust and whom to love.

ISBN 978-1-4424-7426-0 (hardback) — ISBN 978-1-4424-7428-4 (eBook)

[1. Survival—Fiction. 2. Hostages—Fiction. 3. Love—Fiction.] I. Title.

PZ7.F5777Bl 2014

[Fic]—dc23

2014004913

For Riley and Jace,
who tell me stories

ACKNOWLEDGMENTS

This book was shaped by many hands.

Thank you to my editor, Zareen Jaffery, for your wisdom and dedication. You deserve credit for some of the best parts in this book.

Christian Teeter and Heather Zundel, a writer couldn't ask for finer first readers, or finer sisters. I was never worried that you wouldn't tell me exactly what you thought of *Black Ice*. After all, you've been telling me what you think of my clothes, hair, boyfriends, and taste in music and movies since we were little. You're the bestest.

I can't fail to mention Jenn Martin, my assistant, whose brain works quite differently from mine: Hers is organized. Jenn, thank you for handling all the other stuff, so I can focus on writing.

To my friends at Simon & Schuster, including Jon Anderson, Justin Chanda, Anne Zafian, Julia Maguire, Lucy Ruth Cummins, Chrissy Noh, Katy Hershberger, Paul Crichton, Sooji Kim, Jenica Nasworthy, and Chava Wolin: I couldn't have handpicked a better publishing team myself. High fives and hugs all around.

Katharine Wiencke, thank you for copyediting *Black Ice*.

As always, I appreciate my agent Catherine Drayton's business acumen and foresight. Speaking of agents, I also happen to work with the best foreign-rights agent in the industry. Thank you, Lyndsey Blessing, for putting my books into the hands of readers around the world.

Erin Tangeman at the Nebraska Attorney General's Office deserves a shout-out for answering my law-related questions. All errors are mine.

Thanks to Jason Hale for coming up with the fly-fishing slogans for the bumper stickers on Britt's Wrangler.

I know Josh Walsh gets tired of having his name mentioned in my books, as a humble man would, but your pharmaceutical knowledge is much appreciated.

Finally, dear reader, this book is ultimately in your hands because of you. I can't thank you enough for reading my stories.

APRIL

The rusted Chevy pickup truck clanked to a stop, and when Lauren Huntsman's head thumped the passenger window, it jolted her awake.

She managed a few groggy blinks. Her head felt strewn with broken memories, shattered fragments that, if she could just piece them together, would form something whole. A window back to earlier in the night. Right now, that window lay in pieces inside her throbbing head.

She remembered the cacophony of country music, raucous laughter, and NBA highlights on the overhead TVs. Dim lighting. Shelves displaying dozens of glass bottles glowing green, amber, and black.

Black.

She'd asked for a drink from that bottle, because it made her dizzy in a good way. A steady hand had poured the liquor into her glass a moment before she'd thrown it back.

"Another one," she'd rasped, plonking the empty glass down on the bar.

She remembered swaying on the cowboy's hip, slow dancing. She stole his cowboy hat; it looked better on her. A black Stetson to match her itsy-bitsy black dress, her black drink, and her foul, black mood—which, mercifully, was hard to hang on to in a tacky dive like this, a rare gem of a bar in the noses-up, la-di-da world of Jackson Hole, Wyoming, where she was vacationing with her family. She'd sneaked out and her parents would never find her here. The thought was a bright light on the horizon. Soon she'd be so tipsy, she wouldn't remember what they looked like. Already their judgmental frowns streaked in her memory, like wet paint running down canvas.

Paint. Color. Art. She'd tried to escape there, to a world of splattered jeans and stained fingers and soul enlightenment, but they had yanked her back, shut her down. They didn't want a free-spirited artist in the family. They wanted a daughter with a diploma from Stanford.

If they would just love her. Then she wouldn't wear tight, cheap dresses that infuriated her mother or throw her passion into causes that offended her father's egoism and stiff, aristocratic morals.

She almost wished her mother were here to see her dancing, see her slinking down the cowboy's leg. Grinding hip-to-hip. Murmuring the wickedest things she could think of into his ear. They only paused dancing when he went to the bar to get her a fresh drink. She could have sworn it tasted different from the others. Or maybe she was so drunk, she imagined the bitter taste.

He asked if she wanted to go somewhere private.

Lauren only debated a moment. If her mother would disapprove, then the answer was obvious.

The Chevy's passenger door opened and Lauren's vision stopped seesawing long enough to focus on the cowboy. For the first time, she noticed the distinct crook in the bridge of his nose, probably a trophy from a bar fight. Knowing he had a hot temper should have made her want him more, but oddly, she found herself wishing she could find a man who exercised restraint instead of reverting to childish outbursts. It was the sort of civilized thing her mother would say. Inwardly lashing herself, Lauren blamed her irritatingly sensible attitude on tiredness. She needed sleep. Stat.

The cowboy lifted the Stetson off her head and returned it to his own crop of messy blond hair.

"Finder's keepers," she wanted to protest. But she couldn't get her mouth around the words.

He lifted her off the seat and balanced her over his shoulder. The back of her dress was riding up, but she couldn't seem to command her hands to tug it down. Her head felt as heavy and fragile as one of her mother's crystal vases. Bewilderingly, the very moment after she had the thought, her head miraculously lightened and seemed to float away from her body. She couldn't remember how she'd gotten here. Had they driven in the truck?

Lauren stared down at the heels of the cowboy's boots tracking through muddy snow. Her body bounced with every step, and it was making her stomach swim. Bitterly cold air, mixed with the sharp smell of pine trees, burned the inside of her nose. A porch swing creaked on its chain and wind chimes made soft, tinkling music in the darkness. The sound made her sigh. It made her shudder.

Lauren heard the cowboy unlock a door. She tried to pry her eyelids open long enough to get a dim sense of her surroundings. She would have to call her brother in the morning and ask him to come get her. Assuming she could give him directions, she thought ironically. Her brother would drive her back to the lodge, scolding her for being careless and self-destructive, but he'd come. He always did.

The cowboy set her on her feet, grasping her shoulders to balance her. Lauren glanced sluggishly around. A cabin. He'd brought her to a log cabin. The den they stood in had rustic pine furniture, the kind that looked tacky everywhere but in a cabin. An open door on the far side of the den led to a small storage room with plastic shelving along the walls. The storage room was empty, except for a perplexing pole that ran from floor to ceiling, and a camera on a tripod that was positioned to face the pole.

Even through her haze, fear gripped Lauren in a vise. She had to get out of here. Something bad was going to happen.

But her feet wouldn't move.

The cowboy backed her against the pole. The moment he let go, Lauren sagged to the floor. Her stilettos twisted off as her ankles slid out from under her. She was too drunk to scrabble back onto her feet. Her mind whirled, and she blinked frantically, trying to find the door leading out of the storage room. The more she tried to concentrate, the faster the room spun. Her stomach heaved, and she lurched sideways to keep the mess off her clothes.

"You left this at the bar," the cowboy said, dropping her Cardinals baseball cap on her head. The hat had been a gift from her brother when she'd been accepted to Stanford a few weeks ago. Their parents had probably put him up to it. The gift had arrived suspiciously soon after she'd announced she wasn't going to Stanford—or any college. Her dad had turned so red, so stopped of breath, she was positive steam would blow from his ears like a cartoon caricature.

The cowboy lifted the gold chain hanging around her neck clear of her head, his rough knuckles scraping her cheek.

"Valuable?" he asked her, examining the heart-shaped locket closely.

"Mine," she said, suddenly very defensive. He could take back his smelly Stetson, but the locket belonged to her. Her parents had given it to her the night of her first ballet recital, twelve years ago. It was the first and only time they'd approved of anything she'd initiated. It was the one reminder she had that deep down, they must love her. Outside of ballet, her childhood had been governed, pushed, and molded by their vision.

Two years ago, at sixteen, her own vision had raged to life. Art, theatre, indie bands, edgy, unscripted modern dance, rallies with political activists and intellectuals (not dropouts!) who'd left college to pursue alternative education, and a boyfriend with a brilliant, tortured mind who smoked weed and scribbled poetry on church walls, park benches, cars, and her own hungry soul.

Her parents had made their distaste for her new lifestyle clear.

They responded with curfews and rules, tightened their walls of confinement, squeezed life's breath from her. Defiance was the only way she knew to fight back. She'd wept behind locked doors when she quit ballet, but she had to hurt them back. They didn't get to pick and choose pieces of her to love. Either she was theirs unconditionally, or they lost her completely. That was her deal. At eighteen, her resolve was steel-like.

"Mine," she repeated. It took all her concentration to push the word out. She had to get her locket back, and she had to get out of here. She knew it. But a strange sensation had stolen into her body; it was as if she were watching things happen without feeling emotion.

The cowboy hung her locket on the doorknob. His hands free, he looped scratchy rope around her wrists. Lauren winced when he jerked on the knot. He couldn't do this to her, she thought, detached. She'd agreed to come with him, but she hadn't agreed to this.

"Let—go me," she slurred, a sloppy, unconvincing demand that made her cheeks burn with humiliation. She loved language, each word tucked inside her, beautiful and bright, carefully chosen, empowering; she wanted to pull those words from her pocket now, but when she reached deep, she found snipped thread, a hole. The words had tumbled from her muddled head.

She threw her shoulders forward uselessly. He'd tied her to the pole. How would she get her locket back? The thought of losing it made panic scratch inside her chest. If only her brother had returned her call. She'd left a message about going drinking tonight, as a test. She tested him constantly—almost every weekend—but this was the first time he'd ignored her call. She'd wanted to know that he cared about her enough to stop her from doing something stupid.

Had he finally given up on her?

The cowboy was leaving. At the door, he tipped the black Stetson up, his blue eyes smug and greedy. Lauren realized the enormity of her mistake. He didn't even like her. Would he blackmail her with compromising photos? Was that the reason for the camera? He must know her parents would pay any price for them.

"I've got a surprise waiting for you in the toolshed around back," he drawled. "Don't go anywhere, you hear?"

Her breath came fast and erratically. She wanted to tell him what she thought of his surprise. But her eyelids drooped lower, and each time, it took longer to snap them open. She started crying.

She'd been drunk before, but never like this. He'd given her a drug. He must have slipped it in her drink. It was making her exhausted and leaden. She sawed the rope against the pole. Or tried to. Her whole body felt heavy with sleep. She had to fight it. Something terrible was going to happen when he came back. She had to talk him out of it.

Sooner than expected, his form darkened the doorway. The lights in the den backlit him, casting a shadow twice his height across the storage room floor. He was no longer wearing the Stetson, and seemed larger than she remembered, but that wasn't what Lauren focused on. Her eyes went to his hands. He yanked a second rope between them, checking that it would hold.

He walked toward her and, with shaking hands, fit the rope around her neck. He was behind her, using the rope to pull her neck back against the pole. Lights ruptured behind her eyes. He was tugging too hard. She knew instinctively that he was nervous and excited. She could feel it in the eager tremble of his body. She heard the choppy panting of his breath, growing more charged, but not from exertion. From adrenaline. It made her stomach roll with terror. He was *enjoying* this. A foreign gurgling noise filled her ears, and she realized with horror that it was her voice. The sound seemed to scare him—he swore and tugged harder.

She screamed, over and over inside herself. She screamed while the pressure built, sweeping her toward the edge of death.

He didn't want photographs. He wanted to kill her.

She would not let this horrible place be her last memory. Closing her eyes, she went away, into the darkness.

One year later

CHAPTER ONE

If I died, it wouldn't be from hypothermia.

I decided this as I crammed a goose-down sleeping bag into the back of my Jeep Wrangler and strapped it in, along with five duffels of gear, fleece and wool blankets, silk bag liners, toe warmers, and ground mats. Satisfied nothing was going to fly out on the three-hour drive to Idlewilde, I shut the tailgate and wiped my hands on my cutoffs.

My cell phone blared Rod Stewart crooning, "If you want my body," and I held off answering for a moment so I could belt out the "and you think I'm sexy" part along with Rod. Across the street, Mrs. Pritchard slammed her living room window shut. Honestly. I couldn't let a perfectly good ringtone go to waste.

"Hey, girl," Korbie said, snapping her bubble gum through the phone. "We on schedule or what?"

"Tiny snag. Wrangler's out of room," I said with a dramatic sigh. Korbie and I had been best friends forever, but we acted more like sisters. Teasing was part of the fun. "I got the sleeping bags and gear in, but we're going to have to leave behind one of the duffels: navy with pink handles."

"You leave my bag, and you can kiss my g-ass money good-bye."

"Should've known you'd play the rich-family card."

"If you've got it, flaunt it. Anyway, you should blame all the people getting divorced and hiring my mom. If people could kiss and make up, she'd be out of a job."

"And then you'd have to move. Far as I'm concerned, divorce rocks."

Korbie snickered her amusement. "I just called Bear. He hasn't started packing yet but he swears he's gonna meet us at Idlewilde before dark." Korbie's family owned Idlewilde, a picturesque cabin in Grand Teton National Park, and for the next week, it was as close to civilization as we were going to get. "I told him if I have to clear bats out of the eaves by myself, he can count on a long, chaste spring break," Korbie added.

"I still can't believe your parents are letting you spend spring break with your boyfriend."

"Well—" Korbie began hesitantly.

"I knew it! There is more to this story."

"Calvin is coming along to chaperone."

"What?"

Korbie made a gagging noise. "He's coming home for spring break and my dad is forcing him to tag along. I haven't talked to

Calvin about it, but he's probably pissed. He hates it when my dad tells him what to do. Especially now that he's in college. He's going to be in a horrible mood, and I'm the one who has to put up with it."

I sat on the Jeep's bumper, my knees suddenly feeling made of sand. It hurt to breathe. Just like that, Calvin's ghost was everywhere. I remembered the first time we kissed. During a game of hide-and-seek along the riverbed behind his house, he'd fingered my bra strap and shoved his tongue in my mouth while mosquitoes whined in my ears.

And I'd wasted five pages recording the event ad nauseam in my diary.

"He'll be back in town any minute," Korbie said. "It sucks, right? I mean, you're over him, right?"

"So over him," I said, hoping I sounded blasé.

"I don't want it to be awkward, you know?"

"Please. I haven't thought about your brother in ages." Then I blurted, "What if I keep an eye on you and Bear? Tell your parents we don't need Calvin." The truth was, I wasn't ready to see Calvin. Maybe I could get out of the trip. Fake an illness. But it was my trip. I had worked hard for this. I wasn't going to let Calvin ruin it. He'd ruined too many things already.

"They won't go for it," Korbie said. "He's meeting us at Idlewilde tonight."

"Tonight? What about his gear? He won't have time to pack," I pointed out. "We've been packing for days."

"This is Calvin we're talking about. He's, like, half mountain man. Hold up—Bear is on the other line. I'll call you right back."

I hung up and sprawled in the grass. *Breathe in, breathe out.* Just when I'd finally moved on, Calvin was back in my life, dragging me into the ring for round two. I could have laughed at the irony of it. He always did have to have the final say, I thought cynically.

Of course he didn't need time to prepare—he'd practically grown up hiking around Idlewilde. His gear was probably in his closet, ready at a moment's notice.

I rewound my memory several months, to autumn. Calvin was five weeks into his freshman year at Stanford when he dumped me. Over the phone. On a night when I really needed him to be there for me. I didn't even want to think about it—it hurt too much to remember how that night had played out. How it had ended.

Afterward, taking pity on me, Korbie had uncharacteristically agreed to let me plan our upcoming senior spring break, hoping it would cheer me up. Our two other closest friends, Rachel and Emilie, were going to Hawaii for spring break. Korbie and I had talked about spending our break with them on the beaches of Oahu, but I must have been a glutton for punishment, because I said adios to Hawaii and announced that in six months we would be backpacking the Tetons instead. If Korbie knew why I'd chosen the Tetons, she had the sensitivity not to bring it up.

I'd known Calvin's spring break would overlap ours, just like I'd known how much he loved hiking and camping in the Tetons. I'd hoped that when he heard about our trip, he'd invite himself along. I desperately wanted time with him, and to make him see me differently and regret being stupid enough to give me up.

But after months of not hearing from him, I'd finally gotten the message. He wasn't interested in the trip, because he wasn't interested in me. He didn't want to get back together. I let go of any hope of us and hardened my heart. I was done with Calvin. Now this trip was about me.

I closed my mind to the memory and tried to think through my next steps. Calvin was coming home. After eight months, I was going to see him, and he was going to see me. What would I say? Would it be awkward?

Of course it would be awkward.

I was ashamed that my next thought was so incredibly vain: I wondered if I'd gained any weight since he'd last seen me. I didn't think so. If anything, the running and weight lifting I'd done to prepare for our backpacking expedition had sculpted my legs. I tried to cling to the idea of sexy legs, but it wasn't making me feel any better. Pretty much, I felt like throwing up. I couldn't see Calvin now. I'd thought I'd moved on, but all the pain was surging back, swelling in my chest.

I forced a few more deep breaths, composing myself, and listened to the Wrangler's radio playing in the background. Not a song, but the weather report.

"... two storm systems set to hit southeastern Idaho. By tonight, the chance of rain will rise to ninety percent, with thunderstorms and strong winds possible."

I perched my sunglasses on top of my head and squinted at the blue sky stretching from one horizon to the other. Not a wisp of cloud. Just the same, if rain was coming, I wanted to be on the road before it hit. Good thing we were leaving Idaho and driving ahead of the storm, into Wyoming.

"Daddy!" I hollered, since the house windows were open.

A moment later he came to the front door. I craned my neck to look at him and put on my best little girl pout. "I need money for gas, Daddy."

"What happened to your allowance?"

"I had to buy stuff for the trip," I explained.

"Hasn't anyone told you money doesn't grow on trees?" he teased, observing me with a patronizing shake of his head.

I jumped up and kissed his cheek. "I *really* need gas money."

"Of course you do." He opened his wallet with the softest of sighs. He gave me four faded, rumpled twenties. "Don't let the gas tank drop below a quarter full, you hear? Up in the mountains, gas stations start to thin. Nothing worse than getting stranded."

I pocketed the money and smiled angelically. "Better sleep with your cell phone and a tow rope under your pillow, just in case."

"Britt—"

"Only kidding, Daddy," I said, giggling. "I won't get stranded."

I swung into the Wrangler. I'd dropped the top, and the sun had done a fine job of warming my seat. Sitting taller, I checked my reflection in the rearview mirror. By the end of summer, my hair would be as pale as butter. And I'd have added ten new freckles to the ranks. I'd inherited German genes from my father's side. Swedish from my mother's. Chance of sunburn? One hundred percent. Lifting a straw hat off the passenger seat, I squashed it on my head. But dang it all, I was barefoot.

Perfect attire for 7-Eleven.

Ten minutes later, I was in the store, filling a cup with Blue Raspberry Slurpee. I drank some off the top and refilled it. Willie Hennessey, who was working the register, gave me the evil eye.

"Good grief," he said. "Help yourself, why don't you?"

"Since you offered," I said cheerfully, and stuck the straw between my lips once more before refilling.

"I'm supposed to keep law and order in here."

"Two little sips, Willie. Nobody's going bankrupt over two sips. When did you become such a crank?"

"Since you started pilfering Slurpee and pretending you can't operate the gas pump so I have to come out and fill your tank for you. Every time you pull in, I want to kick myself."

I wrinkled my nose. "I don't want my hands smelling like gas. And you are particularly good at pumping gas, Willie," I added with a flattering smile.

"Practice makes perfect," he muttered.

I padded barefoot through the aisles looking for Twizzlers and Cheez-Its, thinking that if Willie didn't like pumping my gas he really should get another job, when the front door chimed. I didn't even hear footsteps before a pair of warm, calloused hands slipped over my eyes from behind.

"Guess who?"

His familiar soapy smell seemed to freeze me. I prayed he couldn't feel my face heat up under his touch. For the longest moment, I couldn't find my voice. It seemed to shrink inside me, bouncing painfully down my throat.

"Give me a clue," I said, hoping I sounded bored. Or mildly annoyed. Anything but hurt.

"Short. Fat. Obnoxious overbite." His smooth, teasing voice after all these months. It sounded familiar and foreign at the same time. Feeling him so close made me dizzy from nerves. I was afraid I'd start yelling at him, right here in the 7-Eleven. If I let him get too close, I was afraid I might *not* yell at him. And I wanted to yell—I'd spent eight months practicing what I'd say and I was ready to let it out.

"In that case, I'll have to go with . . . Calvin Versteeg," I sounded carelessly polite. I was sure of it. And I couldn't think of a bigger relief.

Cal came around me and leaned an elbow on the aisle's endcap. He gave me a wolfish smile. He had nailed the whole devilishly charming thing years ago. I'd been a sucker for it back then, but I was stronger now.

Ignoring his handsome face, I gave him a bored once-over. By the looks of it, he'd let his pillow style his hair this morning. It was longer than I remembered. On the hottest days of track practice, when sweat dripped off the tips, his hair had turned the color of tree bark. The memory made something inside me ache. I shoved aside my nostalgia and eyed Calvin with cool detachment. "What do you want?"

Without asking, he bent my Slurpee straw sideways and helped himself. He wiped his mouth on the back of his hand. "Tell me about this camping trip."

I yanked my Slurpee out of his reach. "Backpacking trip." I felt it was important to make the distinction. Anyone could camp. Backpacking required skill and moxie.

"Got everything you need?" he went on.

"And a few wants, too." I shrugged. "Hey, a girl needs her lip gloss."

"Let's be honest. Korbie will never let you leave the cabin. She's terrified of fresh air. And you can't say no to her." He tapped his head wisely. "I know you girls."

I gave him a look of indignation. "We're backpacking for one full week. Our route is forty miles long." So maybe it was a teensy exaggeration. In fact, Korbie had agreed to no more than two miles of hiking per day, and had insisted we hike in circles around Idlewilde, in case we needed quick access to amenities or cable TV. While I'd never truly expected to backpack the entire week, I had planned to leave Korbie and Bear at the cabin for a day and trek off on my own. I wanted to put my training to the test. Obviously now that Calvin was joining us, he was going to find out about our true plans soon enough, but at the moment my biggest priority was impressing him. I was sick of him forever insinuating that he had no reason to take me seriously. I could always deal with any flak he might give me later by insisting that I'd wanted to backpack the whole week and Korbie was holding me back—Calvin wouldn't find that excuse far-fetched.

"You do know that several of the hiking trails are still covered in snow, right? And the lodges haven't opened for the season, so people are sparse. Even the Jenny Lake Ranger Station is closed. Your safety is your own responsibility—they don't guarantee rescue."

I gazed at him with round eyes. "You don't say! I'm not going into this completely in the dark, Calvin," I snapped. "I've got it covered. We'll be fine."

He rubbed his mouth, hiding a smile, his thoughts perfectly clear.

"You really don't think I can do it," I said, trying not to sound stung.

"I just think the two of you will have more fun if you go to Lava Hot Springs. You can soak in the mineral pools."

"I've been training for this trip all year," I argued. "You don't know how hard I've worked, because you haven't been around. You haven't seen me in eight months. I'm not the same girl you left behind. You don't know me anymore."

"Point made," he said, flipping up his palms to show it was an innocent suggestion. "But why Idlewilde? There's nothing to do up there. You and Korbie will be bored after the first night."

I didn't know why Calvin was so set on dissuading me. He loved Idlewilde. And he knew as well as I did that there was plenty to do there. Then it hit me. This wasn't about me or Idlewilde. He didn't want to have to tag along. He didn't want to spend time with me. If he got me to drop the trip, his dad wouldn't force him to join us, and he'd get his spring break back.

Digesting this painful realization, I cleared my throat. "How much are your parents paying you to tag along?"

He made a big deal of looking me over in mock critical evaluation. "Clearly not enough."

So that's how we were going to play this. A little meaningless flirtation here, a little banter there. In my imagination, I took a black marker and drew a big X through Calvin's name.

"Just so we're clear, I argued against having you come. You and me together again? Talk about uncomfortable." It had sounded better in my head. Hanging between us now, the words sounded jealous and petty and mean—exactly like an ex-girlfriend would sound. I didn't want him to know I was still hurting. Not when he was all smiles and winks.

"That so? Well, this chaperone just cut your curfew by an hour," he jested.

I nodded beyond the store's plate-glass window toward the four-wheel-drive BMW X5 parked outside. "Yours?" I guessed. "Yet another gift from your parents, or do you actually do more than chase girls at Stanford, such as hold down a respectable job?"

"My job is chasing girls." An odious grin. "But I wouldn't call it respectable."

"No serious girlfriend, then?" I couldn't bring myself to look at him, but I felt immense pride over my oh-so-casual tone. I told myself I didn't care about his answer one way or another. In fact, if he'd moved on, it was yet another flashing green light telling me I was free to do the same.

He poked me. "Why? You got a boyfriend?"

"Of course."

"Yeah, right." He snorted. "Korbie would have told me."

I stood my ground, arching my eyebrows smugly. "Believe it or not, there are some things Korbie doesn't tell you."

His eyebrows furrowed. "Who is he?" he asked warily, and I could tell he was thinking about buying my story.

The best way to remedy a lie is not to tell another lie. But I did anyway.

"You don't know him. He's new in town."

He shook his head. "Too convenient. I don't believe you." But his tone suggested he might.

I felt an overpowering urge to prove to him that I had moved on—with or without closure, and in this case, without. And not only that, but that I'd moved on to a much, much better guy. While Calvin was busy being an oily womanizer in California, I was not—I repeat, not—moping around and pining over old photographs of him.

"That's him. See for yourself," I said without thinking.

Calvin's eyes followed my gesture outside to the red Volkswagen Jetta parked at the nearest gas pump. The guy pumping gas into the Jetta was a couple years older than me. His brown hair was cropped, and it showed off the striking symmetry of his face. With the sun at his back, shadows marked the depressions beneath his cheekbones. I couldn't tell the color of his eyes, but I hoped they were brown. For no other reason than that Calvin's were a deep, lush green. The guy had straight, sculpted shoulders that made me think swimmer, and I had never seen him before.

"That guy? Saw him on my way in. Plates are Wyoming." Calvin sounded unconvinced.

"Like I said, new in town."

"He's older than you."

I looked at him meaningfully. "And?"

The door chimed and my fake boyfriend strolled inside. He was even better-looking up close. And his eyes were most definitely brown—a weathered brown that reminded me of driftwood. He reached into his back pocket for his wallet, and I grabbed Calvin's arm and hauled him behind a shelf stacked with Fig Newtons and Oreos.

"What are we doing?" Calvin asked, staring at me like I'd sprouted two heads.

"I don't want him to see me," I whispered.

"Because he's not really your boyfriend, right?"

"That's not it. It's—"

Where was a third lie when I needed it?

Cal smiled devilishly, and the next thing I knew, he had shaken off my hand and was ambling toward the front counter. I trapped a groan between my teeth and watched, peering between the two top shelves.

"Hey," Calvin said affably to the guy, who wore a buffalo-check flannel shirt, jeans, and hiking boots.

With barely a glance up, the guy tipped his head in acknowledgment.

"I hear you're dating my ex," Calvin said, and there was something undeniably wicked in his tone. He was giving me a taste of my own medicine, and he knew it.

Calvin's remark drew the full attention of the guy. He studied Calvin curiously, and I felt my cheeks grow even hotter.

"You know, your girlfriend," Calvin prodded. "Hiding behind the cookies over there."

He was pointing at me.

I straightened, my head surfacing above the top shelf. I smoothed my shirt and opened my mouth, but there were no words. No words at all.

The guy looked beyond Calvin to me. Our gazes locked briefly, and I mouthed a humiliated I *can explain*. . . . But I couldn't.

Then something unexpected happened. The guy looked squarely at Calvin, and said in an easy, unruffled voice, "Yeah. My girlfriend. Britt."

I flinched. He *knew my name?*

Calvin appeared similarly startled. "Oh. Hey. Sorry, man. I thought—" He stuck out his hand. "I'm Calvin Versteeg," he stammered awkwardly. "Britt's . . . ex."

"Mason."

Mason eyed Calvin's outstretched hand but didn't take it. He placed three twenties on the counter for Willie Hennessey. Then he crossed to me and kissed my cheek. It was a no-frills kiss, but my pulse thrummed just the same. He smiled, and it was a warm, sexy smile. "I see you haven't gotten over your Slurpee addiction, Britt."

Slowly I smiled back. If he was game for this, then so was I. "I saw you pull in, and needed something to cool me off." I fanned myself while gazing up at him adoringly.

His eyes crinkled at the edges. I was pretty sure he was laughing on the inside.

I said, "You should stop by my house later, Mason, because I bought a new lip gloss that could use a test run. . . ."

"Ah. Kissing game?" he said without missing a beat.

I shot a covert glance at Calvin to gauge how he was handling the flirting. Much to my enjoyment, he looked like he'd caught a mouthful of lemon peel.

"You know me—always spicing things up," I returned silkily.

Calvin cleared his throat and folded his arms over his chest. "Shouldn't you be heading out, Britt? You really should get to the cabin before dark."

Something undecipherable clouded Mason's eyes. "Going camping?" he asked me.

"Backpacking," I corrected. "In Wyoming—the Tetons. I was going to tell you, but . . ." Ack! What possible reason could I come up with for not telling my boyfriend about this trip? So close to pulling this off, and I was going to blow it.

"But it seemed unimportant, since I'm heading out of town too, and we won't be able to spend the week together anyway," Mason finished easily.

I met his eyes again. Good-looking, quick on his feet, game for anything—even pretending to be the boyfriend of a girl he'd never met—and a frighteningly good liar. Who *was* this guy? "Yes, exactly," I murmured.

Calvin cocked his head at me. "When we were together, did I ever take off for a week without telling you?"

You took off for eight months, I thought snidely. And broke up with me on the most important night of my life. Jesus said forgive, but there's always room for an exception.

I said to Mason, "By the way, Daddy wants to have you over for dinner next week."

Calvin made a strangled noise. Once, when he'd brought me home five minutes after curfew, we'd pulled into the driveway to see my dad standing on the porch tapping a golf driver in his palm. He'd marched over and smacked it against Calvin's black

Ford F-150, leaving a nice round crater. "Next time you bring her home late, I'll aim for the headlights," he'd said. "Don't be stupid enough to need three warnings."

He hadn't meant it, not really. Since I was the baby of the family and the only girl, my dad had a grouchy streak when it came to the boys I dated. But actually, my dad was a lovable old bear. Still, Calvin never broke curfew again.

And never once had he been allowed to come to dinner.

"Tell your dad I could use a few more fly-fishing tips," Mason said, continuing to hold up our charade. Miraculously, he'd also correctly guessed my dad's favorite sport. This entire encounter was starting to feel . . . eerie. "Oh, and one more thing, Britt." He combed his hand through my hair, pushing it off my shoulder. I held perfectly still, his touch freezing my breath inside me. "Be safe. Mountains are dangerous this time of year."

I gawked with amazement at him until he pulled out of the gas station and drove off.

He knew my name. He'd saved my butt. He knew *my name*.

Granted, it was printed across the chest of my purple orchestra-camp tee, but Calvin hadn't noticed that.

"I thought you were lying," Calvin told me, looking stupefied.

I handed Willie a five for my Slurpee and pocketed the change. "As satisfying as this conversation has been," I told Calvin, "I should probably go do something more productive. Like key that Bimmer of yours. It's too pretty."

"Just like me?" He waggled his brows hopefully.

I filled my cheeks with Slurpee, miming that I intended to

spit it at him. He jumped clear and, to my satisfaction, erased his cocky grin at long last.

"See you tonight at Idlewilde," Calvin called after me as I pushed out of the store.

By way of answer, I gave him a thumbs-up.

My middle finger would have been too obvious.

As I passed Calvin's BMW in the parking lot, I noticed the doors were unlocked. I glanced back to make sure he wasn't watching, then made a split-second decision. Climbing through the passenger door, I knocked his rearview mirror out of alignment, dribbled Slurpee on the floor mats, and stole his vintage CD collection from the glove box. It was a petty thing to do, but it made me feel a smidge better.

I'd give the CDs back tonight—after I'd scratched a few of his favorites.

CHAPTER TWO

A few hours later, Korbie and I were on the road. Calvin had taken off before us, and I had Korbie to blame. When I'd rung her doorbell, she had been packing yet *another* bag, languidly pulling shirts from her closet and handpicking lipsticks from her cosmetics case. I'd sat on her bed, trying to speed things up by stuffing everything into the bag.

I'd really hoped to beat Calvin to Idlewilde. Now he'd get first dibs on a bedroom, and his stuff would be spread around the cabin by the time we arrived. Knowing him, he'd lock up behind himself and force us to knock, like guests. Which was infuriating, since this was *our* trip, not his.

Korbie and I had the top down, to enjoy the warmth of the valley before the cold mountain air hit. We had the music cranked. Korbie had made a mixtape for the trip, and we were listening to that song from the—seventies? eighties?—that went, "Get outta my dreams, get into my car." Calvin's smug face was still floating around in the back of my mind, and it was bothering me. I firmly believed in the adage "Fake it till you make it," so I pasted on a smile and giggled as Korbie tried to hit the high notes.

After a quick stop for more Red Bull, we left behind the horse pastures and green farmlands, with tidy rows of corn seedlings whizzing by in a blur, and climbed to higher elevation. The road narrowed, lodgepole pines and quaking aspens crowding up against the shoulders. The air rushing through my hair felt cool and clean. White and blue wildflowers burst from the ground, and the world smelled sharp and earthy. I bumped my sunglasses higher on my nose and grinned. My first trip without my dad or my big brother, Ian. No way was I going to let Calvin spoil it. I wasn't going to let him ruin my mood on the drive, and I wasn't going to let him ruin my week in the mountains. *Screw him. Screw him, and have fun.* It seemed like a good mantra for the week.

The sky was such a dazzling blue it hurt my eyes, the sun glinting off the windshield as we came around a bend. I blinked to sharpen my vision, and then I saw them. The white glacial horns of the Teton Range jutting up in the distance. Sharp, vertical peaks soared into the sky like snow-tipped pyramids. The view was mesmerizing and overwhelming—the sheer vastness of trees, slopes, and sky.

Korbie leaned out the window with her iPhone to take the best shot. "I had a dream last night about that girl who was killed by drifters in the mountains last summer," she said.

"The white-water rafting guide?" Macie O'Keeffe. I remembered her name from the news. She was really smart and had a full ride to Georgetown. She disappeared sometime around Labor Day.

"Aren't you freaked out something like that could happen to us?"

"No," I said sensibly. "She went missing really far from where we'll be. And there was no proof that drifters killed her. That's just what everyone assumes. Maybe she got lost. Anyway, it's too early for drifters to be camping by the river. Plus, we'll be up in the mountains, where the drifters don't go."

"Yeah, but it's kind of creepy."

"It happened last summer. And it was only one girl."

"Yeah? What about Lauren Huntsman, the socialite who was on every news channel last year?" Korbie argued.

"Korbie. Stop it. Seriously. Do you know how many thousands of people come to the mountains and make it home safely?"

"Lauren disappeared very close to where we'll be," Korbie insisted.

"She disappeared from Jackson Hole, miles from where we'll be. And she was drunk. They think she waded into a lake and drowned."

"On the news they said people saw her leave the bar with a cowboy in a black Stetson."

"One person saw that. And they never found the cowboy. He probably doesn't exist. If we were in any danger, my dad wouldn't have let me come."

"I guess," Korbie said, sounding unconvinced. Thankfully, a few minutes later she seemed to have shed her apprehension. "T minus two hours and we'll be roasting marshmallows at Idlewilde!" she cheered at the blue dome of sky.

The Versteegs had owned Idlewilde as long as I could remember. It was more of a lodge than a cabin in the woods. Three stone chimneys jutted from a gabled rooftop. Idlewilde had six bedrooms—seven if you counted the sofa bed in the basement next to the foosball and pool tables—a wraparound deck, a stunning bank of south-facing windows, and nooks and crannies galore. While the Versteegs occasionally spent Christmas at Idlewilde—Mr. Versteeg had his pilot's license and had bought a single-engine helicopter to get up the mountain, since most roads were snow-packed and closed until springtime—they used it almost exclusively as a summer home, and had installed an apron of lawn with a hot tub, badminton court, and fire pit nestled between lounge chairs.

Two Christmases ago, I'd spent my vacation at Idlewilde with Korbie's family, but not this past Christmas. Calvin had gone to the home of one of his college roommates for the holiday, and Korbie and her parents had gone skiing in Colorado, leaving Idlewilde vacant. I'd never visited Idlewilde without Mr. and Mrs. Versteeg. I couldn't picture it without Mr. Versteeg's watchful eye following us like a shadow.

This time, it was just us kids. No adults and no rules. A year ago, being alone with Calvin for a week would have seemed forbidden and dangerous, a secret fantasy come true. Now I didn't know what to expect. I didn't know what I was supposed to say to him when we bumped into each other in the hallway. I wondered if he was dreading this as much as I was. At least our first awkward run-in was out of the way.

"Do you have any gum?" Korbie asked, and before I could stop her, she opened my glove box and Calvin's CD collection tumbled out. She picked it up and eyed it quizzically. "Isn't this my brother's?"

I'd been caught; might as well own it. "I took it from his car this morning at the gas station. He was being a jerk. I was totally justified. Don't worry, I'll give it back."

"Are you sure you're okay with the whole Calvin thing?" Korbie asked, clearly finding it strange that I'd stolen his CDs. "He's just a butt-face to me, but I keep reminding myself that you guys were, like, together. Or whatever. We can talk about it as much as you want—just don't bring up kissing. The thought of anyone swapping spit with my brother, especially you, is vomit-inducing." She shoved her finger down her throat for emphasis.

"Totally over him." What a big fat lie. I was not over Calvin. The fake boyfriend I felt compelled to make up proved it. Before this morning, I really believed I'd moved on, but when I saw Cal, my repressed emotions had boiled to the surface. I hated that I still felt something for him, even if it was intense negative emotion. I hated that I was still giving him power to hurt me. I had so many bad memories inextricably linked to Calvin. Did Korbie not remember that he broke up with me the night of homecoming? I had a dress and dinner reservations at Ruby Tuesday, and I'd paid my and Calvin's portion of the limo rental. And I was up for homecoming queen! I had dreamed countless times of what it would feel like to stand on the football field wearing a crown, beaming as the crowd clapped and cheered, and how it would feel afterward, dancing in Calvin's arms.

We'd planned to meet at my house at eight, and when eight thirty rolled around with still no Cal, I actually worried he'd been in an accident. I knew his flight wasn't delayed—I'd tracked its progress online. The rest of our group had left in the limo, and I was on the brink of tears.

And then the phone rang. Calvin hadn't even left California. He'd waited until the last minute to call, and he didn't bother to fake an apologetic tone. In a smooth, unconcerned voice, he told me he wasn't coming.

"You waited until now to tell me?" I exclaimed.

"I've had a lot on my mind."

"This is so typical. You haven't called me in weeks. You haven't returned any of my calls in days." Calvin wasn't the same person since leaving for college. It was like he got a taste of freedom, and everything changed. I was no longer a priority.

"I should have known you'd do something like this," I snapped. I was trying so hard not to cry. He wasn't coming. I didn't have a date for homecoming.

"You're monitoring the frequency of my calls? I'm not sure how I feel about that, Britt."

"Seriously? You're making me out to be the creep? Do you know how much you're letting me down right now?"

"You're exactly like my dad, always whining that I'm not good enough," he said defensively.

"You're an asshole!"

"Maybe we shouldn't be in a relationship," he said stiffly.

"Maybe we shouldn't!"

The worst part was, I could hear loud music and sports broadcasts in the background. He was in a bar. I'd placed so many expectations on this night, and he was getting drunk. I slammed the phone down and burst into tears.

These memories were starting to make me grumpy. I really wished I didn't have to talk about Calvin. It was chipping away at my determination to keep a positive attitude. It would be much easier to fake happy if I didn't have to waste energy convincing the whole world that I was peachy, just peachy.

"It's not going to be weird with him around?" Korbie pressed.

"Don't be ridiculous."

She narrowed her eyes speculatively. "You're not going to use this opportunity to hook up with him again, are you?"

"Gross. Please never ask me that again." But the thought had occurred to me. It totally had. What if Calvin made a pass at me? It wasn't hard to imagine. Korbie and Bear would be all over each other. Which left Calvin and me. It wouldn't surprise me if he tried something. Which meant I had to decide right now if I was going to let him.

Maybe, if I thought he'd really moved on, I could forget about him. But the way he'd looked at me at the 7-Eleven? When I was flirting with Mason? If that wasn't regret, I didn't know what was.

But this time, I decided, I was going to make him work for my attention. He'd humiliated me, and he had a lot of making up for it to do. I wouldn't take him back until he'd sufficiently suffered. A little groveling with a cherry on top. Calvin knew I wasn't a cheater, which would work to my advantage. I'd have some fun with him and then dump him, claiming guilt over cheating on my fake boyfriend.

You know what they say about payback? Pretty soon, Calvin was going to know too.

Glad that I finally had a plan, I settled deeper into my seat, feeling smugly triumphant and ready for the long week ahead.

Korbie unzipped the CD case, but before she could flip through the CDs, she noticed a folded paper in the front of the case. "Wow, check this out."

I glanced sideways. She was holding a topographic map of Grand Teton National Park—the kind you get from a park ranger station—but this one had notes jotted everywhere in Calvin's handwriting. It folded in thirds, and then again in half, and the coloring was faded, the edges frayed. Calvin had clearly made good use of it.

"Calvin's marked all the best hiking trails," Korbie said. "Look how far he's hiked—there are notes everywhere. It must have taken him years to make this. I know I always teased him for being such an outdoor nerd, but this is kind of cool."

"Let me see." I took the map, flattening it to the steering wheel and glancing between it and the road. Calvin had marked more than hiking trails. The map was riddled with notes detailing snowmobile trails, unpaved roads, emergency shelters, a ranger station, scenic points of interest, hunting grounds, unpolluted lakes and streams, and wildlife crossings. Idlewilde was also marked. To a hiker stranded in the mountains, the map would be a useful survival tool.

We were still too far away to find our location on Calvin's map, but I was seriously considering trading it for Mr. Versteeg's inferior notes once we got closer.

"You definitely have to give Calvin the map back," Korbie insisted.

I refolded the map, tucking it into the back pocket of my shorts. A map this painstakingly detailed would be worth something to Calvin. I'd return it. But first I'd make him sweat a little.

Thirty minutes later, the mixtape came to an end with "Every Day Is a Winding Road" by Sheryl Crow. The road had steepened, and we zigzagged up the mountain on switchbacks. The shoulders of the road fell away sharply, and I leaned forward over the steering wheel, concentrating around each hairpin curve. One misguided turn would send us careering over the mountainside. The realization was as thrilling as it was heart stopping.

"Do those look like rain clouds to you?" Korbie asked, frowning as she pointed at a cluster of dark clouds sprouting above the treetops to the north. "How is that even possible? I checked the weather before we left. Idaho was supposed to get rain, Wyoming wasn't."

"It will pour for a couple minutes and then the sky will clear." If you don't like the weather in Wyoming, hang around five minutes. So the saying went.

"It had better not rain a single day we're up here," Korbie huffed with more indignation. I wondered if she was thinking about Rachel and Emilie sunbathing on Waikiki Beach. I knew how much Korbie had wanted to go somewhere tropical for spring break. I thought it said a lot about our friendship that she was with me now. We fought, sure, but we were solid. Not many friends would give up the beach for hiking in the mountains.

"I read in a guidebook that rain has something to do with the warm and cold air up here always bumping together," I murmured idly, keeping my eyes glued to the road. "At this altitude, water vapor can turn to ice, which has a positive charge. But rain has a negative charge. When the charges build up, they create lightning and we get a storm."

Korbie lowered her sunglasses down her nose and gawked at me. "Do you also light fire with sticks and navigate by the stars?"

I let go of the steering wheel long enough to give her shoulder a shove. "You should have at least glanced at some of the guidebooks your dad bought you."

"You mean the guidebooks that taught me that a human can subsist on rabbit droppings if faced with starvation?" She wrinkled her nose. "That was the first and last time I picked up a guide. Anyway, reading a guidebook would have been a waste, since my brother will take charge and boss us around."

Calvin wasn't going to be in charge. Not this time. I hadn't trained this long and hard just to hand over control.

Soon after, the sky glowered a dark, dirty gray. The first drop of rain splashed like ice on my arm. Then another. Three more. In a matter of seconds, the rain was pattering down steadily, splattering the windshield with tiny pinpricks of water. I stopped the Wrangler in the middle of the road, since there was nowhere to pull off.

Korbie swatted the raindrops like they were mosquitoes.

"Help me put the top up," I said, jumping out. I raised the soft top, indicating that she should latch it down. Opening the tailgate, I unrolled the window and fastened the straps. By the time I finished, I was thoroughly wet, the hairs on my arms standing stiff from cold. I slicked water out of my eyes and zipped up the side windows. Finally, I secured the Velcro seam and leaped back inside the car with a violent shiver.

"There's your negative charge," Korbie deadpanned.

I pressed my cheek to the cold window and peered up at the sky. Violent gray storm clouds stretched in every direction. I could no longer see any blue, not even a crack of it on the horizon. I rubbed my arms for warmth.

"I should call Bear and give him the heads-up," Korbie said, speed-dialing him on her phone. A moment later she slumped back in her seat. "No phone service."

We'd only made it another couple of miles before the rain broke from the sky in a torrent. A stream of fast-moving water gushed down the surface of the road. Water splashed up over the tires and I worried about hydroplaning. The windshield wipers couldn't remove the water fast enough; the rain beat down so furiously, I couldn't see where I was going. I wanted to pull over, but there wasn't a shoulder. Instead, I steered as far to the right of my lane as I could, parked, and turned on my hazard lights. I hoped if anyone drove up behind us, they'd be able to see the lights flashing through the downpour.

"I wonder what the weather's like in Hawaii," Korbie said, using her sleeve to clear the fog accumulating on her window.

I tapped my nails on the steering wheel, wondering what Calvin would do in my shoes. It would brighten my mood tremendously if, tonight, I could report to him that I'd weathered the storm, no problem.

"Don't panic," I murmured aloud, thinking it sounded like a good first step toward success.

"It's downpouring, we have no cell phone service, and we're in the middle of the mountains. Don't panic. Sure," Korbie said.

CHAPTER THREE

The rain didn't let up.

An hour later, it continued to stream down the windshield, thickening to slush. It wasn't quite snow. A few more degrees, though, and it would change. I was still parked in the road, and I'd left the engine running almost the whole time. Every time I turned it off to conserve gas, both Korbie and I started shivering violently. We'd changed into jeans and boots, and put on our winter coats, but the extra clothing hadn't kept off the chill. For better or worse, nobody had driven up behind us.

"It's getting colder out," I said, chewing my lip nervously. "Maybe we should try to turn back."

"The cabin can't be more than an hour away. We can't turn back now."

"It's coming down so hard I can't make out the road signs." I leaned against the steering wheel, squinting through the windshield at the yellow diamond-shaped sign ahead. The black markings were completely illegible. It had gotten dark awfully fast. The clock showed after five, but it might as well have been dusk.

"I thought the Wrangler was made to go off-road. I'm sure it can handle the rain. Just give it a lot of gas and get us up this mountain."

"Let's wait ten more minutes, see if the rain stops." I didn't have a lot of experience driving in a downpour, especially one this severe, with gusting wind. The growing darkness only compounded the low visibility. Right now, driving, even at a crawling pace, seemed dangerous.

"Look at the sky. It's not stopping. We have to keep going. Do you think the windshield wipers will hold up?"

It was a good question. The rubber was wearing away from the metal skeleton, which etched into the glass with a soft squeak.

"Maybe you should have replaced them before we left," Korbie said.

Good of her to point that out *now*.

"On second thought, I'm worried this weather might be too much for your car," Korbie continued in a smoothly concerned voice.

I kept my mouth shut, afraid I'd say something I'd regret. Korbie's digs were always like that—under the carpet. She had the whole guilelessly undermining thing down to an art.

"They've really improved off-road vehicles over the years, haven't they?" she added just as sleekly. "I mean, the difference between your Wrangler and my SUV is remarkable."

I felt my back go up. She was turning this into a competition, like always. I would never tell Korbie, but last summer, during a sleepover, I'd peeked in her diary. I thought I'd find secrets about Calvin, things I could playfully tease him about later. Imagine my surprise when I found two side-by-side lists comparing Korbie and me. According to her, I had better legs and a more defined waist, but my lips were too thin, I had too many freckles, and therefore I was only *generically* cute. She had the better bra cup size, better eyebrows, and she weighed ten pounds less than me—of course, she failed to mention she was three inches shorter! The list took up two pages, and I could tell by the changes in ink color that it was ongoing. She'd given each feature a point rating, and added up our score totals. At the time, she had me beat by a safe ten points. Which was ridiculous, since she'd given her manicure five points more than mine and we'd gotten matching ones at the same salon.

I thought of her secret list now, and felt more determined than ever to defend the Wrangler. I would get us up this mountain to keep from giving her yet another victory on her stupid list. (Better car? Check.) I knew this game shouldn't matter, it was rigged, and I knew she'd never let me beat her, but I wanted to. Badly.

Oddly enough, I'd gone through the same charade in my relationship with Calvin, trying excessively hard to convince everyone around me, especially Korbie, that Calvin and I were perfect. *Forever.* I had never thought about it so consciously before, but I felt an overpowering need to show Korbie how great my life was. Maybe because of the list. Maybe because it annoyed me to think she was keeping score, when that was the sort of game enemies, not best friends, played.

"Did you put snow tires on this thing before we left?" Korbie wanted to know.

This thing? It was times like this when I had to stop and remind myself why Korbie and I were friends. We'd been inseparable as far back as I could remember, and even though we'd started drifting in different directions, especially this past year, it was hard to let go of a relationship that had been years in the making. Plus, when I really stopped and thought about it, I couldn't count how many times Korbie had thrown herself in the road for me. Starting when we were little girls, she'd paid for things I couldn't afford and whined until her parents let me come on family vacations. She made sure I was never left out. Big personality or not, Korbie's small acts of kindness had endeared me to her.

Still.

We were definitely more like sisters than friends: We loved each other, even if we didn't always like each other. And we were always there for each other. Rachel and Emilie hadn't chosen hiking in the Tetons over a beach for spring break, though they knew I needed it. But Korbie hadn't hesitated. Well, had barely hesitated.

"It wasn't supposed to snow," I fired back. "Your parents told us the roads would be clear to Idlewilde."

Korbie exhaled a long, pouty sigh and crossed her legs impatiently. "Well, now that we're stuck here, I guess we'll wait for Bear to come rescue us."

"Are you implying it's my fault we're stuck? I can't control the weather."

She turned on me. "All I said is 'We're stuck,' and now you're blowing it out of proportion. Even if I *was* implying the Wrangler can't handle the weather. It is true, isn't it? You're just mad that I'm right."

My breathing came a little faster. "You want to see the Wrangler make it up this mountain?"

She gestured grandly out the windshield. "I'll believe it when I see it."

"Fine."

"Go ahead. Be my guest. Put the pedal to the metal."

I blew hair out of my eyes and gripped the steering wheel so hard my knuckles went white. I didn't want to do this. I didn't trust the Wrangler to swim upriver—that's practically what I would be asking it to do.

"You're such a faker," Korbie said. "You're not gonna do it."

I had to do this. I hadn't left myself a choice.

I put the Wrangler in gear, summoning bravado, and steered tentatively into the water that gushed over the road. I was so scared, I felt a bead of sweat trickle down my spine. We hadn't even made it to Idlewilde, and already we were running into problems. If I screwed this up, Korbie would never forgive me for dragging her here. Worse, she'd tell her brother, who'd point out that I shouldn't have attempted a rigorous backpacking trip if I couldn't maneuver my car through bad weather. I *had* to get us through this.

The back tires jerked and skidded but finally grabbed the road and we started climbing. "See?" I said proudly, but my chest still felt cinched in a knot. My foot was frozen on the gas pedal, and I was afraid if I made the slightest adjustment, the Wrangler would slip or slide—or worse, skid over the mountain edge.

"You can pat yourself on the back when we reach the top."

Enormous snowflakes flew at the windshield, and I turned the barely usable wipers up a notch. I could only see a few feet in front of the Wrangler. I switched on the high beams. Not much better.

We kept up our crawling pace for another hour. I couldn't see the road anymore—only fleeting glimpses of black pavement beneath blinding white. Every few feet, the tires skidded and locked. I gave the Wrangler more gas, but I knew I couldn't inch my way uphill forever. It was one thing to save face in front of Korbie. It was something else to kill us both needlessly.

The Wrangler stalled out. I restarted it and eased my foot down on the gas. C'mon. Keep going. I wasn't sure if I was coaxing the car or myself. The engine whined and stalled again. The steep grade, compounded by the icy road, made driving any farther impossible.

I couldn't see where on the road I'd stopped, and it scared me. We could be inches from the edge. I turned the hazard lights back on, but it was snowing so heavily no one was going to see them until it was too late.

Pulling out Calvin's map, I tried to orient myself. But it was useless. I couldn't see any landmarks through the whiteout snow.

We sat in silence several minutes, our breath clouding the windows. I was glad that for once, Korbie didn't offer commentary. I couldn't handle arguing with her right now. I kept going over our options. We didn't have food—it was at the cabin. Mrs. Versteeg had had her assistant bring it up last weekend so we wouldn't have to. We didn't have cell phone service. We had sleeping bags, but was camping here in the road tonight really an option? What if a truck plowed into us from behind?

"Holy crap," Korbie said, wiping away the vapor on the windows and gawking at the whiteout. Never had I seen snow fall this hard and fast. It covered the road, piling higher.

"Maybe we should turn back now," I said. But that wasn't really an option either. Going downhill on ice seemed far more dangerous than climbing on it. And I was already exhausted from the concentration I'd put into getting us this far. A dull headache scraped my skull.

"We're not turning back. We're going to stay here," Korbie said decisively. "Bear is probably an hour or two behind us. He'll pull us out with his truck."

"We can't sit in the middle of the road, Korbie. It's too dangerous. There has to be a turnout somewhere up ahead. Get out and push."

"Excuse me?"

"We can't park here. We're in the middle of the road." I didn't know if we were in the middle of the road. The ground, the trees, and the sky blurred white. There was no telling where one ended and another began. And while I didn't really think we should try to move the car—not when we couldn't see—I was tired of Korbie's stupid, thoughtless suggestions. I wanted to give her a reality check. "Get out and push."

Korbie's eyes widened, then narrowed. "You can't be serious. It's, like, snowing out there."

"Fine. You drive. I'll push."

"I can't drive stick."

I knew this, and making her admit it didn't improve my mood like I'd hoped. We were stuck and I had no idea how to get us out. A strange feeling fluttered in my throat. I was suddenly afraid we were in worse trouble than either of us understood. I pushed aside the chilling thought and shoved myself out of the car.

Immediately, the wind and snow buffeted my skin. I dug through my coat pockets for my wool ski hat. Five minutes in the snow and it was going to look like a wet dishrag. I had a backup hat, a ball cap that Calvin had given me last summer, buried somewhere at the bottom of my pack, but it wasn't waterproof. The whole reason I'd brought it on the trip was for the satisfaction of giving it back to him and sending a clear message that I was over him.

Wrapping my red scarf around my neck, I hoped it fared better than my hat.

"Where are you going?" Korbie shouted through the open door.

"We can't sleep here. If we leave the Jeep running all night, we'll run out of gas. If we don't run the heater, we'll freeze." I held her eyes, making sure she registered what I was saying. I barely understood it myself. The idea that we could be in danger seemed to drift aimlessly at the back of my mind. It wasn't sinking in. I kept thinking of my dad. Did he know it was snowing in the mountains? He could be in his truck now, coming for us. We weren't in real trouble, because my daddy would save us . . . but how would he find us?

"But it wasn't supposed to snow!" Korbie argued shrilly.

If my dad had seen this coming, he wouldn't have let me leave. I'd be home now, safe. But the thought was a waste of time. I was here, it was snowing, and we had to find shelter.

"You're suggesting we sleep out there?" Korbie pointed into the forest, dark and haunted-looking in the swirling snow.

Stuffing my hands into my armpits to keep them warm, I said, "We can't be the only people up here. If we walk around, we should be able to find a cabin with lights on."

"What if we get lost?"

The question irritated me. How should I know? I was hungry, I had to use the bathroom, and I was stuck on a mountainside. I was abandoning my car to look for better shelter, and I didn't know if I'd find any. My phone didn't work, I had no way of reaching my dad, and my heart was beating so fast it was making me dizzy.

I shut the driver's-side door and pretended I hadn't heard her question. I pushed "getting lost" far down on my list of things to worry about. If my dad couldn't get up the mountain, if Korbie and I stayed the night in the Wrangler, if we didn't find a cabin, we were going to freeze to death. I hadn't told Korbie, but I wasn't even sure where we were. She had a worse sense of direction than I did, and had put me in charge of reading Mr. Versteeg's instructions. The freezing precipitation had iced over the road signs, making them unreadable, and even though I'd pretended to be confident, I wasn't sure the last turn I'd made had been right. There was one main road up the mountain, but if I'd branched off too early, or too late . . .

Bear was following us in his truck, but if we were on the wrong road, he'd never find us. Idlewilde could be miles from here.

Korbie met me at the rear of the Wrangler. "Maybe I should stay here while you go look. That way one of us knows where the Wrangler is."

"The Wrangler isn't going to do us any good if this storm lasts through the night," I pointed out. Snow clung to her hair and coat. It was coming down harder. I wanted to believe it would let up soon. I also wanted to believe Bear was close behind. But a feeling of panic deep in my chest told me I couldn't count on it. "We should stay together," I said. It seemed like a good idea. It seemed like the sort of thing Calvin would say.

"But what if we miss Bear?" Korbie protested.

"We'll walk around for a half hour. If we don't find anyone, we'll come back."

"Promise?"

"Of course." I tried to keep my voice neutral. I didn't want Korbie to know how worried I was. If she figured out I didn't have everything under control, she would flip. Reasoning with her would be out of the question. I knew her well enough to know she'd either break down crying or start yelling at me.

And then I wouldn't be able to think. And that's what I had to do. Think. Think like someone who knew how to survive. Think like Calvin.

I grabbed a small flashlight from the gear and led us into the storm.

We waded through the snow for thirty minutes. Then forty-five.

I followed the road to keep from getting lost, but it had grown so dark, and was snowing so heavily, it was easy to get disoriented.

We were coming up on an hour, and I knew I was pressing my luck—Korbie would start whining to go back soon. "A little farther," I said, not for the first time. "Let's see what's up there, behind those trees."

Korbie didn't answer. I wondered if she was finally as scared as I was.

The snow bit into my skin like sharp teeth. Every step hurt, and my brain started shifting to another plan. There were sleeping bags and blankets in the Wrangler. We couldn't sleep in the car, not while it was parked on the road, but if we put on our layers of clothes, dug into a snowdrift, and slept close to conserve heat . . .

Light. There. Ahead.

It wasn't a mirage. It was real.

"Lights!" I said, my voice thin with cold.

Korbie started crying.

I grabbed her hand and together we trudged through the trees, over ground soft and soggy with snow. It clung to my boots, making each step heavier. A cabin. A cabin. We were going to be all right.

The windows cast enough light for us to see an old, rust-colored truck buried under inches of snow in the driveway. Someone was home.

We ran to the door and I knocked. I didn't wait for an answer; I started knocking louder. Korbie joined me, fists pounding the door. I didn't let myself think *what if* no one answers, *what if* they've gone and left the truck behind, *what if we have to break in*—I was pretty sure I would break in, if it came to that.

A moment later, footsteps sounded on the other side of the door. Relief crashed inside me. I heard a muffled exchange of arguing voices. What was taking them so long? *Hurry, hurry,* I thought at them. *Open the door. Let us inside.*

The porch lights burned to life suddenly, glaring down on Korbie and me like spotlights. I flinched, trying to adjust my vision. We'd been walking in darkness so long, the brightness stung my eyes.

The bolt slid and the door opened with a soft creak. Two men filled the doorway, the taller one withdrawn a few steps. I recognized him right away. He was wearing the same buffalo-check shirt and rugged boots from earlier. Our eyes met, and for one moment, there was nothing but stark surprise blanking his face. He stared at me, and as recognition dawned, his features hardened.

"Mason?" I said.

CHAPTER FOUR

"Twice in one day," I said, smiling at Mason through chattering teeth. "That's either a really big coincidence, or fate is trying to tell us something."

Mason continued to stare down at me, his lips pressed tight, his eyes dark and uninviting. Snow swirled through the open door, but he didn't ask us in. "What are you doing here?"

The guy leaning on the door frame beside Mason split a curious glance between us. "You know her?" He looked about the same age as Mason, early twenties. But he was shorter, and built straight up and down like a board, his fitted T-shirt revealing a flat, rawboned chest. Shaggy blond hair fell over his forehead, and behind a pair of round black poet's glasses, his eyes were arctic blue. What held my attention longest was his crooked nose. I wondered how he'd broken it.

"How do you know each other?" Korbie asked, nudging me expectantly.

I couldn't believe I'd forgotten to tell her about Mason. If I weren't so cold, I might have laughed at the memory of Calvin's jealous expression when Mason and I had convinced him that we were together. I would have to tell Korbie before we got to Idlewilde, so I could recruit her help in carrying out my charade in front of Calvin.

"We met—" I began, but Mason cut me off.

"We don't know each other. She was in line with me when I filled up for gas this morning." Those warm, sexy brown eyes from earlier were cold and hooded now. His tone was curt and irritated. It was hard to imagine he was the same guy I'd flirted with hours ago. I didn't understand why he was being so closed-off now. And why, suddenly, he wasn't interested in keeping up our charade. What had changed?

Our eyes met again, and if he could tell I was confused, he didn't seem to care. "What do you want?" he repeated more harshly.

"What does it look like?" Korbie hugged herself for warmth and danced impatiently on her toes.

"We're st—stranded," I stammered, thrown off by his hostility. "We got caught in the snowstorm. We're freezing. Can we please come in?"

"Let them in," Mason's friend said. "Look at them—they're soaking wet."

Without waiting for further permission, Korbie rushed inside and I followed. As Mason's friend shut the door behind us, the heat seeped into my skin, and I gave a great shudder of relief.

"They can't stay here tonight," Mason said immediately, positioning himself to block the hallway leading deeper into the cabin.

"If we don't stay here tonight," Korbie said, "we'll turn into human ice cubes. You don't want that on your hands, do you?"

"Sounds serious," Mason's friend said, a sparkle of amusement in his eyes. "And no, we definitely don't want to be held accountable for human ice cubes. Especially ones that look much better in their warm-blooded form."

In reply to his flirting, Korbie bobbed a curtsy and flashed a shameless smile.

"Where's your car?" Mason demanded. "Where did you park?"

"Out on the main road below your cabin," I said. "We walked an hour to get here."

"The car is probably buried under a snowdrift by now," Korbie added.

"Unbelievable," Mason muttered, glowering at me. Like this was my fault. Well, excuse me for not controlling the weather. Excuse me for asking for a little help, a little hospitality.

"Are you alone?" Mason's friend asked. "Just the two of you? I'm Shaun, by the way."

"And I'm Korbie," she returned in a velvety voice.

Shaun shook Korbie's hand, then reached for mine. I was too cold to pull it out of my pocket. Huddling into my coat, I nodded my acknowledgment instead. "Britt."

"Yup, just the two of us," Korbie said, answering his question. "You have to let us stay. It'll be fun, promise," she added with a coy, perky smile.

I ignored Korbie's flirting and watched Mason closely. I didn't understand why he was acting so strangely. He'd bent over backward for me earlier. I glanced around his large frame, deeper into the cabin, looking for a clue to explain his sudden coldness. Had Korbie and I interrupted something? Was there something—or someone—he didn't want us to see?

As far as I could tell, Mason and Shaun were alone. Evident by the two men's coats drying on hooks across the foyer.

"It'll be fun, the four of us holed up here together," Korbie assured them. "We can snuggle close to conserve body heat," she added with a giggle.

I shifted my irritation to Korbie. What an asinine thing to say. We didn't even know these guys, not really. And she seemed to have completely forgotten that, up until a few minutes ago, we thought we were going to freeze in the mountains. I was still shaken from the scare, and watching her turn on her charm for Shaun made me want to shake her. I'd been terrified in the forest. Really terrified. What was the matter with her, that she could flip a switch and go from sobbing to giggling in the same breath?

"We'll only stay one night," I told Mason and Shaun. "We'll take off first thing."

Shaun draped his arm over Mason's shoulder and said, "What do you think, buddy? Should we help these poor girls out?"

"No," Mason answered automatically, shrugging off Shaun's arm with a scowl. "You can't stay here," he told me.

"We can't stay outside either," I shot back. I found it ironic that I was begging for a place to stay. Because the more we talked, the less I wanted to be inside the cabin with Mason. I didn't get it. There was no trace of the easygoing, playful guy in the man standing before me now. Why had his attitude shifted?

"Sometimes you have to ignore Mase the Ace," Shaun explained to us with a strange smile. "He's good for a lot of things, but friendliness isn't one of them."

"News flash," Korbie said under her breath.

"C'mon, Ace. Could be worse," Shaun said, clapping Mason on the back. "Take for instance . . ." He scratched his cheek thoughtfully. "Actually, I can't think of anything better than waiting out this storm in the company of two attractive girls. In fact, these girls wandering in is the best thing that could have happened to us."

"Can I talk to you alone?" Mason asked in a low, tight voice.

"Sure, after we warm up these girls. Look—they're freezing. Poor things."

"Now."

"Oh, get over it," Korbie told Mason exasperatedly. "We're not ax murderers. I'll even pinkie promise to it," she added playfully to Shaun.

Shaun grinned at Mason, punching him lightly in the chest. "Hear that, buddy? She'll pinkie promise."

All this back and forth was testing my patience. I was so numb with cold, I was tempted to barrel past Mason toward the fire I could see burning in the hearth. It cast lively shadows on the walls of the den at the end of the hallway. I imagined sitting close enough to feel its heat and finally warm up.

"One night isn't going to kill anyone, is it, Ace?" Shaun went

"Why not?"

I waited for him to answer, but he merely continued to eye me in that dark, fierce way.

Coolly, I said, "We didn't exactly have a choice. I guess it's too much to ask you to save my butt twice in one day."

"What are you talking about?" he said irritably.

"You helped me save face in front of my ex, remember? But keeping me from freezing to death is obviously too big a burden."

"What's with the whispering?" Shaun hollered from the den. He and Korbie sat together on the plaid love seat, and her legs were crossed toward him. It almost looked like the toe of her boot was touching his leg. Clearly she'd gotten over waiting for Bear to rescue her. "Get in here where it's warm."

Mason lowered his voice, speaking with quiet urgency. "Is it as bad as you say? Is your car really stuck? If I take you to it later tonight, can we dig it out?"

"Anything to keep me from staying here?" I asked testily. I didn't deserve to be treated like this. Not after what we'd shared earlier. I wanted an explanation. Where was the Mason from before?

"Just answer the question," he said in that same low, hurried voice.

"No. The road is too icy and the grade is too steep. The car isn't going anywhere tonight."

"You're sure?"

"Quit being such a tool." I stepped around him, even though he didn't make it easy. He stayed rooted to the spot; I brushed his arm as I squeezed between him and the wall.

Halfway down the hallway, I glanced back. He still had his

on. "What kind of men are we if we turn these girls away?"

Mason said nothing, but the muscles in his face visibly tightened. He couldn't have made his feelings more clear. He didn't want us in the cabin. Shaun, on the other hand, was more than happy to let us stay as long as we needed. Had the two argued before Korbie and I arrived? I could feel the tension between them crackling like a live wire.

"Can we please talk this over in front of the fireplace?" Korbie asked.

"Good idea," Shaun said, leading the way. I watched Korbie follow him down the hall toward the den, unraveling her scarf as she went.

Left alone with Mason, I saw his face go slack with defeat. The look was gone in an instant, his expression hardening. With anger? Animosity? His gaze cut into mine, and I thought maybe he was trying to tell me something. There was an intensity to his eyes that seemed to indicate a deeper meaning.

"What's your problem?" I muttered, attempting to step around him. Mason stood directly in front of me, blocking the hallway, and I expected him to step aside at my approach. He didn't. He kept me boxed in the doorway, his body uncomfortably close.

"Thanks for the warm welcome," I said. "So warm, I've almost thawed."

"This isn't a good idea."

"What isn't a good idea?" I challenged, hoping he'd tell me why he was acting so bizarrely.

"You shouldn't be here."

back to me, and was scrubbing his hand roughly over his cropped hair. What was bothering him? Whatever it was, it was making me antsy too.

Even though Korbie and I were out of the storm, I didn't feel completely safe inside the cabin. Other than from my run-in with him this morning, I didn't know Mason. I knew Shaun even less. And while Korbie and I were no longer in danger of freezing to death, we were staying the night with two guys we didn't know if we could trust. It was unnerving. For now, I had no choice but to keep my guard up and hope the snow stopped soon.

I met Shaun and Korbie in the den. "Thanks again for letting us crash here," I said. "This weather sucks."

"I'll drink to that," Shaun said, raising a plastic cup of water.

"Do you have a land line?" Korbie piped up. "Our cell phones aren't getting service out here."

"No phone. But we do have chili and beer. And an extra bed. Where were you planning to crash tonight? Before the storm hit, I mean," Shaun asked us.

"At my family's cabin," Korbie answered. "Idlewilde."

Shaun's face didn't register recognition. Which meant I'd probably taken a wrong turn and we were nowhere close to Idlewilde.

"It's the really big, beautiful cabin with stone chimneys," I added, hoping to stir his memory. Idlewilde sat alone on the lake and was a landmark in and of itself.

"How far is your cabin from here?" Mason cut in, his voice preceding him down the hallway. He stopped in the den's entrance. "I can walk you there."

Shaun shot a brief, displeased glance at Mason, subtly but firmly shaking his head no. In response, the line of Mason's mouth tightened and I felt a strain in the black look they shared.

"Might want to check the road conditions before you commit to that," Korbie chimed in. "Envision a layer of mud, several inches deep. And then imagine eight inches of snow and growing on top of it. Nobody is going anywhere tonight."

"You got that right," Shaun said, rising from the love seat. "Can I offer you girls a drink? We've got water and hot chocolate mix, though I can't vouch for its freshness. And two bottles of beer."

"Water, please," I said.

"You got it. Korbie?"

"Same," she said, folding her hands on her knees and flashing him a winning smile.

"Ace, buddy?"

Mason hovered near the entrance to the den, a clouded, almost uneasy look on his face. He must have been thinking hard about something, because after a few seconds' delay, he jerked. "What?"

"Drink?"

"I'll get it myself."

When Shaun disappeared into the kitchen, Mason stuffed his hands in his pockets and leaned against the wall, never peeling his eyes off us. I cocked my eyebrow at him in a challenging way. I told myself I was better off ignoring him, but I couldn't help it. Curiosity was tearing away inside me. What was with the moody act? Where was the friendly and, dare I say it, sexy guy from this morning? Because I wanted that guy back. In a way I couldn't explain, I wanted that guy more than I wanted Calvin right now. Which said a lot.

"This place is so adorably rustic," Korbie said, her eyes tracing the exposed timbers along the ceiling. "Which one of you does it belong to?"

Korbie and I looked at Mason when he failed to answer.

With an exasperated sigh, Korbie pushed off the love seat, crossed to Mason, and snapped her fingers in his face. "It's called English. Use it."

Shaun came back into the room at that moment. "It's Ace's cabin," he said. "His parents recently passed and they gave it to him in their will. This is our first time up here since the funeral."

"Oh." I swallowed. "It must be really hard—the memories, I mean," I stammered diplomatically. Mason didn't appear to hear me, or chose not to. His eyes were fastened on Shaun, his eyebrows drawn, his gaze inflamed.

"Ace doesn't like to talk about it," Shaun explained easily, with an almost humorous twitch of his lips. "He's an atheist. Death always makes him shifty. Doesn't believe in the afterlife. Right, buddy?"

None of us said anything. I cleared my throat, finding Shaun's insensitivity a bit much, even if I was so over caring about Mason's feelings.

Shaun broke the tension with a disarming laugh. "You girls are too gullible for your own good. You should see your faces right now. The cabin is mine, not Ace's. And before you ask, his parents are perfectly healthy retirees living in Scottsdale, Arizona."

"You're worse than my brother," Korbie groaned, tossing a sofa pillow at Shaun.

Shaun's grin split his face. "This is the price you're gonna have to pay for sleeping here tonight—putting up with my twisted sense of humor." He rubbed his hands together. "So, tell me. What are you girls doing up here in the mountains alone?"

"Starving," Korbie announced bluntly. "It's dinnertime. Can we eat and then talk? I swear I lost ten pounds hiking here."

Shaun looked at me and Mason, then shrugged. "Fair enough. I'm gonna make you girls the best damn-good chili of your lives, wait and see."

"Go work your magic," Korbie encouraged him, with a shoo of her wrist. "But you're on your own. I don't do manual labor, cooking included. And don't bother asking Britt for help either. She's even worse at cooking than I am," she said, eyeing me in a way that warned, Don't you dare help him—he's mine.

I knew Korbie's reasons for not wanting me alone in the kitchen with Shaun. But I was surprised to see Mason stand alert suddenly, as if he intended to jump in and intervene should I decide to leave the room with his friend. He stared me down, and it looked a lot like a warning. I found the whole thing bizarrely comical. He didn't want me here. Or there. Or anywhere. He especially didn't want me alone with Shaun. Well, too bad. If that's what it took to goad him back, I wasn't going to pass up the opportunity.

"Korbie's right, I am an awful cook," I confessed to Shaun. "But just because I'm bad at something doesn't mean I'll refuse to do it," I added, a subtle dig at Korbie. "I'd love to help you cook dinner."

Before anyone could stop me, I strolled into the kitchen.

CHAPTER FIVE

The kitchen was fully furnished, with a knotty pine table, a Navajo rug, and framed pictures of the Teton Range in various seasons. Aluminum pots and pans dangled from a hanging rack above the island. A layer of dust dimmed the pots' luster, and cobwebs hung like silvery streamers from the rack. Obviously Shaun didn't make it up here often.

A fire blazed in the double-sided fireplace that shared a wall with the den. The room smelled pleasantly of smoke and wood. I was in awe that Shaun could afford such a place. It wasn't anywhere as nice as the Versteegs' cabin, but Korbie's mom had been a successful divorce attorney for years.

"What do you do for a living?" I had to know. Had he graduated from college already? Was he a cutthroat investment banker, some kind of financial genius?

He flashed me an easy but self-deprecating smile. "I'm a ski bum. I'm putting college on hold until I know what I want to do with my life. Technically, this place belongs to my parents. But they don't ski anymore, so they handed it off to me. I'm up here all the time."

He must order out a lot, I thought. The pots hadn't been used in ages. "You're pretty far from the resort, though, right?"

"I don't mind the drive."

I washed my hands in the sink, but since there wasn't a dish towel, I dried them on my jeans. "Where should I start? I have mean can-opening skills." Before Shaun could stop me, I went to the pantry and opened the door. To my surprise, except for two cans of chili and a faded canister of Swiss Miss hot chocolate mix, the shelves were completely bare.

Shaun came up behind me. "We forgot to go shopping before we came up," he explained.

"There's no food," I said, dazed.

"The snow will stop by morning and we'll hit the store then."

The closest general store was miles away. We'd passed it on our way up. "You didn't buy any food on your way into the mountains?"

"We were in a hurry," Shaun said almost sharply.

I didn't push the issue, because his tone made it clear he didn't want to discuss it. But his lack of preparation struck me as alarming. Shaun said he came to the cabin often to ski, but it almost seemed like no one had been living here for a long time. There was something else bothering me. Something about Shaun was a little off. He was charming and friendly, but not necessarily warm or genuine.

Or maybe I was just being paranoid because I was stuck in a cabin with two guys I didn't know. The truth was, Shaun had invited us in. He was cooking us dinner. I needed to relax and accept his hospitality.

I opened the cans of chili slowly, feeling the urge to preserve them, knowing they were the only food we had to outlast the storm, and if it grew into something much worse, this might be all we had to stay alive for days. I had granola bars in the Jeep, and wished I'd grabbed them. Almost hesitantly, I passed the cans to Shaun, who'd turned up the heat under a large pot on the stove.

Out of habit, I checked my cell phone for new texts. Maybe Calvin had tried to call. He knew we were supposed to arrive at Idlewilde around six, and it was almost nine now.

"Until you get down to lower elevation and out of the trees, your cell phone is nothing but dead weight in your pocket."

I groaned lightly. Shaun was right. "I swear I can't go five minutes without checking it. A bad habit. I feel so useless without it."

"What about you?" he asked. "You come up here often?"

I waved my phone high over my head, but no signal bars magically appeared. "Sure," I said absently.

"Do you know the area pretty good?"

"Better than Korbie." I laughed. "And yes, that was a note of pride you detected, since she's the one with the family cabin. I always had the better sense of direction." Except that mine hadn't been very reliable on the drive up, in the rain. But I kept that to myself.

"And Korbie plays the better damsel in distress."

I didn't bother telling him that usually I played that gig better too, since the tone he used in referring to Korbie wasn't particularly flattering.

"So, are you guys up here for spring break?" he went on. "Let me guess—girls' weekend at the cabin? Lots of Christian Bale movies, ice cream, and gossip?"

"Swap James McAvoy for Christian Bale, and you could pretty much go into business as a psychic," I quipped.

"Seriously, I really want to know what you're doing up here. You know about me, now it's my turn to find out about you."

I wanted to point out that I knew next to nothing about him, but I was more than happy to talk about myself. "Korbie and I are backpacking the crest of the Teton Range. Forty miles. We've been preparing for this trip all year."

His brows arched in admiration. "The entire crest? Impressive. Don't take this the wrong way, but Korbie doesn't strike me as the outdoorsy type."

"Oh, she doesn't know about the forty miles part yet."

That earned me a loud, resonating laugh. "Wish I could see her face when you break the news."

I smiled. "It'll be memorable, I'm sure."

"I bet you've got a lot of sweet gear in your car."

"Top of the line." Korbie had put her mom in charge of buying our gear, and Mrs. Versteeg had passed the assignment off to her assistant, who had no problem spending her boss's money. Everything had arrived Next Day Air from Cabela's. I wasn't going to complain about our windfall, but there was one tiny red flag. I knew Mr. Versteeg had made Calvin pay for his own gear over the years. If Cal found out that his parents had paid for ours, he would blow into a rage. He constantly complained that they sheltered Korbie, and when we'd dated, he'd nursed resentment that his parents didn't even try to make things fair between him and his sister. I doubted much had changed since he'd left for Stanford. For the sake of keeping the peace, I'd have to remind Korbie not to mention anything about our gear to Calvin.

"I'll bet you're an expert on the area," Shaun said.

He had opened the door with a little flattery, and I found myself diving headlong through it. "I come up here to hike often," I said, the white lie out before I could stop it. "I've been doing shorter hikes on the weekends to prepare for this trip." At least that much was true. "I wanted to go into this completely prepared. Most of my friends are in Hawaii for spring break, but I wanted to do something really challenging, you know?"

"And it's really only you and Korbie? Your parents aren't meeting you up here?"

I hesitated, almost mentioning Calvin and Bear, but at the last moment changed my mind. First rule of talking to a boy: Never drag your ex into the conversation. It makes you look clingy. And bitter.

"My mom died when I was young, so it's just my dad now." I shrugged, cool as can be. "He trusts me. He knows I can handle myself. I told him I'd see him at the end of the week. If I'm in trouble, he knows I'll get myself out of it." Now I was really exaggerating. My dad had never witnessed me digging myself out of trouble. The idea was unthinkable. My dad was a model of indulgent parenting. I suspected it was because I was a girl, and the baby, and because I'd lost my mom to cancer before I was old enough to remember her. My dad was always standing by, ready to save me from even the most minor inconveniences. The truth was, I was comfortable being dependent on him—and every other man in my life. It had worked out well for me . . . until it had led to my heart being broken.

Shaun smiled in a funny way.

"What?" I asked.

"Nothing. I'm just surprised. I had you and Korbie pegged as silly high school girls. The stereotypical giggling, helpless, awkward type."

I batted my eyes. "I don't know what to do with all this flattery."

We both laughed.

"I amend my statement," he said, lowering his voice to keep our conversation from drifting out of the kitchen. "I knew Korbie's type from the minute you guys came knocking. But you were harder to peg. You're good-looking and smart, and it threw me. Most pretty girls I've met don't have the complete package. They're crazy, sure, up for adventure, but not like this. Not up for hiking the crest of the Tetons."

His response could not have been more perfect. I wanted Calvin to hear his words, all of them. I wanted Cal to see that an older boy, older even than Cal, was interested in me and believed in me. I gave Shaun a coy smirk. "Are you flirting with me, Shaun?"

"I think the honor of biggest flirt goes to Korbie," he answered.

I wasn't expecting that, and it took me a moment to think up an equally cagey response. "Korbie's good at what she does."

"And what about you?" He took a step closer. "Do you ever flirt, Britt?"

I hesitated. I hardly knew Shaun. What's more, Korbie had called dibs on him. But she was the one with a boyfriend. If anything, I should have dibs.

"At the right moment," I said with a shrewd smile. "With the right boy."

"And this moment?" He stood so close now, his husky whisper was directly in my ear. "This moment is headed somewhere, and we both know it."

I wondered if his pulse was thrumming like mine. I wondered if he kept stealing glances at my lips, the way I shamelessly watched his.

"What about Korbie?" I said in a soft voice.

"What about her?"

"She likes you."

"And I like you." He poured us each a plastic cup of water, then raised his to mine in a toast. "To the snowstorm. For trapping you here with me."

I tapped my cup to his, grateful to have found Shaun, because for a minute there, I'd thought I was going to have to save myself. Instead, I'd wandered into the protective care of a sexy older man.

I dared any of my friends to return from spring break with a better story.

A few minutes before the chili finished simmering, Korbie and I went to the bathroom to tidy up for dinner.

"Did you have fun cooking with Shaun?" she asked, her tone testy.

"It was okay," I said neutrally, giving away nothing. A petty part of me liked keeping her in suspense. Payback for her shots at the Wrangler.

"You left me alone with Frankenstein."

"Frankenstein is the name of the doctor. I left you alone with Frankenstein's monster. And anyway, you didn't have to stay in the den. You could have come in and helped me and Shaun."

"Not after I said I don't cook!"

I shrugged as if to say, *Your problem.*

"What did you and Shaun talk about?" Korbie grilled me.

"Why do you care? You have Bear."

"Shaun's here, Bear's not. Well? What did you talk about?"

I finished rinsing my hands, but since there wasn't a hand towel in the bathroom, either, I had to dry them on my jeans again. "Oh, you know. Typical stuff. Mostly we talked about our backpacking trip."

Korbie looked relieved. "That's it? Just the backpacking trip? You didn't try to flirt with him?"

"And what if I did?" I said defensively.

"I have dibs."

"You have Bear."

"Bear and I are going to different colleges in the fall."

BECCA FITZPATRICK

"So?"

"So we aren't forever. What's the point of being completely loyal when I know our relationship is going to end? And I don't really appreciate your self-righteous attitude. You and Calvin were hardly the exemplary couple."

I turned, backing myself against the countertop to face her head on. "What are you talking about?"

"He kissed Rachel. At my pool party last summer."

I gasped. "Rachel Snavely?"

Korbie raised her brows superiorly. "Nobody's perfect, Britt. Get over it."

The idea of Calvin kissing Rachel made me squeeze the ledge of the counter hard between my fingers. Calvin and I had started dating in April, a year ago. Korbie's pool party had been in July. I'd been faithfully devoted to Cal until he broke up with me in October, but obviously he hadn't returned the gesture. Was Rachel a onetime slip-up? Or had he cheated on me several times? And what about Rachel? How had she justified going behind my back? "And it only now occurred to you that I might want to know?"

"You need a reality check. We have the rest of our lives to be committed. Right now, life is about having fun."

Is that what Calvin told himself while kissing Rachel? That having fun overrode his commitment to me? And how had Rachel justified her actions? I couldn't wait to ask her. Scratch my earlier plans. There was no way I was hooking up with Calvin over spring break.

"Dinner's ready!" Shaun hollered from the kitchen.

Korbie grabbed my sleeve before I could march out of the bathroom. "I have dibs," she repeated more firmly.

I glanced down at where her fingers curled tightly into my shirt.

"You only want him because I do," she went on, irrationally angry. "You always want what I have. And it's tiring. Stop being so fake. Stop trying to be me."

Her words burned, but not because they were true. I hated when she turned on me like this. At these moments, our relationship seemed so dysfunctional, I questioned why we even stayed friends. I almost brought up the secret list in her diary—almost asked, if I was trying so hard to be her, why was she taking note of every little thing I did, said, and had, and making sure to top it? But doing so would mean admitting I'd looked in her diary, and I had more pride than that. Plus, if I revealed I knew her secret, she'd make sure I never got a chance to look in her diary again, and I wasn't going to forfeit that opportunity just yet.

I pulled on a patient smile, knowing it would infuriate her. She wanted to drag me into a fight so I'd spend the night sulking, and I wasn't going to lose this game. I was going to flirt my ass off with Shaun. "I think we should go to dinner; the boys are waiting," I said in a light, unruffled tone. I left the bathroom ahead of Korbie.

Before I reached the kitchen, I heard Shaun and Mason arguing in low, tense voices.

"What were you thinking? Are you even thinking?" Mason demanded.

"I've got everything under control."

"Under control? Are you serious? Take a look around, man."

"I'm gonna get us off this mountain. We're fine. I've got this."

"No one wants off this mountain more than me," Mason hissed.

Shaun chuckled. "You're stuck with me, buddy. Damn unlucky weather. Whatcha gonna do?"

I frowned, wondering what exactly they were arguing over, but neither one said more on the subject.

Mason didn't join us for dinner. He retreated to the far side of the kitchen, propping one shoulder on the window frame and shifting his steely gaze between the three of us. He looked almost as morose as the stuffed buck head hanging over the mantle in the den. Every few minutes he raked his hand through his short hair, or rubbed the back of his neck, but otherwise he kept his hands shoved deep inside his pockets. Shadows pooled in the hollows of his eyes, but I couldn't decide if they were from fatigue or worry. I didn't know why he was so upset, or why he didn't like having Korbie and me in the cabin, but it was clear he wanted us gone. If Shaun weren't here, he'd probably boot us out. Right into the storm. At that moment, he looked up and found me staring at him.

He gave a subtle shake of his head. I didn't know what it meant. If he had something to tell me, why didn't he come right out and say it?

"Hungry, Ace?" Shaun asked him. Shaun placed bowls, spoons, and napkins on the table, then began opening cabinet doors and drawers at random. It struck me as odd that he didn't know his way around his own kitchen. Then again, my brother, Ian, was always hunting for kitchen utensils, and we'd lived in the same house our whole lives. At last Shaun found what he was looking for: He pulled a trivet from the drawer beside the oven and laid it at the center of the table.

Mason, who'd been peering out the window into the darkness, dropped the curtain. "No."

"More for us," Korbie said. I could tell she didn't like Mason. I didn't blame her. He'd hardly said anything, and his expression—when he had one—fell somewhere between sullen and menacing.

"Still snowing?" Shaun asked him.

"Heavily."

"Well, it can't go on forever."

Shaun ladled chili into three bowls, and the moment he sat down, Korbie plopped herself in the chair next to him. "So," she said to Shaun. "What are you boys doing up here? You never told us."

"Skiing."

"The whole week?"

"That's the plan."

"But you didn't bring any food. I looked in the fridge. It's empty. Not even milk."

Shaun shoveled a spoonful of chili into his mouth. He grimaced. "This is the worst chili I've ever had. Tastes like rust."

Korbie took a bite and made a face. "No, it tastes like sand. It's gritty. Did you check when the cans expired?"

Shaun gave an aggravated snort. "Beggars can't be choosers."

She pushed the bowl away. "Well, I'd rather starve than eat that."

"It can't be that bad," Mason said, and we all looked up. Mason's eyes flickered warily between Shaun and Korbie, like he anticipated something bad was about to happen.

"Says the guy who hasn't tried it," Korbie returned snidely. "I'd give anything for a fillet of salmon right now. My family always eats salmon at our cabin. Salmon with jasmine rice and steamed green beans. In the summer we eat salmon with arugula and pine nuts. Sometimes my mom makes this incredible mango chutney to go with it."

"Well, go on," Shaun said, setting his spoon down harder than necessary. "Tell us what you had to drink, and what you ate for dessert."

"Are you making fun of me?" she said, pouting.

"Just eat the chili," Mason said from across the room, and I wondered why he'd gotten involved. He'd made it clear he wanted nothing to do with us. There had to be a long list of things he'd rather be doing than skulking around the dinner table.

"The botulism risk is looking pretty high," Korbie said snobbishly. "I'll pass. This is what you get for asking Britt to cook with you. I warned you she's awful in the kitchen."

Shaun chuckled under his breath, but it seemed to carry a harsh undertone. I was sure I'd imagined it until he said in a stiff, eerie voice, "Don't be ungrateful, Korbie."

"I see how it is. You can make fun of the chili but I can't? Isn't that kind of shallow?" Korbie teased him. "Besides, I was blaming Britt."

"Eat the damn chili." The soft, threatening way Shaun said it made the hairs on my arms stand up.

"This is why you should have brought fresh food," Korbie said, turning up her nose.

"Give him a break," I murmured to Korbie, who was evidently still bemused and not feeling the tense charge in the air.

"If we wake up with stomach cramps in the middle of the night, we'll know who to blame," she said, eyeing me blackly. I wasn't sure Korbie understood that even though she was targeting me, she was inadvertently being rude and ungrateful to Shaun. And it was clearly digging under his skin. I wished she'd get over her anger at me long enough to see that she was making things very strained for everyone.

I glanced at Shaun. His face had transformed to rigid angles, his blue eyes snapping. I squirmed in my seat. My heart beat faster, but I was more uncertain than afraid. Again, that feeling that something wasn't right. The whole room felt alive with voltage, but surely Shaun wasn't upset over the insults. That was just Korbie. She never knew when to shut her mouth. And even when she did know better, it didn't stop her—her mouth was on autopilot. She had to have the final say. Hadn't he figured that out by now?

"Give me the chili," Mason said, striding over and breaking the tension that seemed to crackle around the table like electricity. He scooped up Korbie's bowl, but not before giving her a dark, berating look.

Korbie blinked at him, too stunned to respond.

After a moment, Shaun tipped his chair back on its hind legs

and laced his fingers behind his head. He grinned at us in turn, as if nothing had happened. "Ace, I think we should probably get down to business."

"If we're talking about washing dishes, I'm out," Korbie said. "I vote Mase the Ace does them," she added with a vengeful glitter in her eyes. "He seems quite enamored with my bowl. He's cradling it almost affectionately in his hands. Let him play out his romantic fantasy a couple more minutes. You like them when they don't talk back, right, Ace? You like them about as mannered and conversational as yourself?"

I snickered behind my hand. Partially out of nervousness, and partially to defuse whatever was going on. The tension in the air was thick enough to touch.

"What gear did you bring?"

It took me a moment to realize Mason was addressing me. He'd carried Korbie's bowl to the sink, and had asked the question without bothering to turn around and face me.

"Your car. What gear did you pack?" he repeated. "What did you bring to the mountains?"

"Why?" I didn't see what our gear had to do with anything.

"Sleeping bags, tents, nonperishable food? Anything useful?"

"Useful to who? You already have a furnished cabin."

"We have sleeping bags, a tent, first aid, and some food," Korbie said. "But everything's stuck in the car. Which is stuck in the road. Which is why we came here." She spoke each word slowly, implying that we'd already gone over this and Mason wasn't very quick on the draw.

Ignoring Korbie, Mason asked me, "Matches?"

"No, a fire starter."

"Compass and map?"

"Compass." For whatever reason, I left Calvin's map out. It was still tucked in my back pocket.

"Flashlights?"

"Yes, and headlamps."

"Ice axe?"

"No." I'd thought about bringing one, but didn't think I'd get a chance to use it—not with Korbie's definition of backpacking.

"Why does any of this matter?" Korbie interjected, exasperated.

"Because," Shaun said, rising to his feet, "Ace and I are stuck here too, waiting out the storm. Only we didn't bring gear, because we didn't plan on staying long. If we're going to get out of here before the snow melts and the roads clear, we'll need your gear. And that's exactly what we're going to do—get off this damn mountain as soon as possible."

It took me a minute to register that the object he pulled from the waistband of his jeans was a gun. He waved it indolently at me, and a strange urge to laugh bubbled in my throat. The picture I was seeing and the picture in my mind weren't matching up. A gun. Pointed at me. The reality of it floated just out of reach.

"Shaun?" I asked, believing this had to be a joke, his quirky sense of humor.

He didn't acknowledge me.

"Both of you, in the den," he directed in a cold, detached voice. "We can do this the easy way, or the way that gets you killed. And believe me, if you scream or fight or argue, I will shoot."

I stared back, my body numb. That bizarre urge to laugh continued to tickle my throat. And then I saw Shaun's eyes. They were cold and unfeeling, and I wondered how I'd missed it before.

He said, "If there's one thing you need to know about me, it's that I don't bluff. Your bodies won't be found for days, and by then Ace and I will be through the mountains and far from here. We've got nothing to lose. So, girls." He watched us. "What's it gonna be?"

CHAPTER SIX

Icy fear fluttered in my veins, but I did exactly as he directed.

Rising from the kitchen table, I numbly allowed Shaun to corral me out of the room. Korbie was directly behind me, and I heard her sniffling. I knew what she was thinking, because it was the same thought racing through my own mind: How long until Calvin realized we were in trouble and came looking for us?

And when he did, how would he find us given the snow, the possibility that I'd taken a wrong turn, and the fact that we'd hiked a good distance from the car? There was no logical way for him to find us.

Shaun marched us through the den and opened a door, revealing a small, unfinished storage room with empty plastic shelves lining the walls. At first I thought it was a water pipe running from the floor to the ceiling, but when he flipped on the light, I saw that it was a solid metal pole. Something about the pole only made the room more terrifying. There were nicks along the shaft, nicks that could have been made by friction from a chain. The rank smell of urine and wet dog permeated the enclosed space. I had to will myself not to speculate further.

Shaun told Mason, "Keep Korbie here. I want to talk to Britt alone."

"You can't do this!" Korbie shrieked. "Do you know who I am? Do you have any *idea* who I am?"

The last word had barely escaped when Shaun smacked the gun across her face. A red welt sprang up in its path.

I gasped. My dad never touched me roughly. He never raised his voice to me. Outside of television and movies, I had only seen a man strike another person once. Years ago, I'd been invited to sleep over at Korbie's, and in the middle of the night, I'd crawled out of bed for a drink. In the shadows of the hallway outside her bedroom, I watched Mr. Versteeg give a sharp blow to Calvin's head, knocking him flat on his back. Mr. Versteeg barked for Calvin to get up and take his discipline like a man, but Calvin lay there, unmoving. I couldn't tell if he was breathing. Mr. Versteeg pried open his son's eyelids and felt his neck for a pulse. Then he carried him to bed. I hurried back to Korbie's bed, but I didn't fall asleep. I didn't know if Calvin was okay. I wanted to check on him, but what if Mr. Versteeg returned? I never told Calvin what I saw. I spent years trying to scrub that memory from my mind.

Korbie whimpered, clutching her cheek.

Just like that night outside Korbie's bedroom, I felt hot and sick, and I wanted to cry, even though Korbie was hurting, not me.

I caught a flash of something dark and loathsome in Mason's eyes, but he blinked it away and obediently guided Korbie into the storage room while Shaun steered me down the hall to the bathroom with a rough prod of his gun. He jerked his head at the toilet seat. "Sit."

He left the door ajar, a crack of light spilling into the room. I waited for my eyes to adjust to the shadows. Slowly, his face took shape, his eyes becoming dark holes that watched me, judging, calculating, evaluating.

"The cabin isn't yours, is it?" I asked quietly. "It doesn't belong to you."

He ignored me, but I already knew the answer.

"Did you break in?" I continued. "Are you and Mason in trouble?" If the police were searching for them, I worried what it meant for Korbie and me. We could identify them. We knew other information too, like what cars they drove. I could direct police to the security cameras at the 7-Eleven and show them exactly what Mason looked like. Korbie and I were a liability. There was nothing stopping Shaun from killing us.

He laughed, the sound sharp and cruel. "Do you really think I'm going to answer your questions, Britt?" He braced a fist against the wall, leaning over me. "The gear you told us about earlier. We need it."

"It's in my car."

"Can you find your way back?"

I was about to give a surly no when the faintest worry scratched at the edge of my mind. Instinctively, I said, "Yes, I think so."

BECCA FITZPATRICK

He nodded, his gun-hand relaxing, and I knew I'd given the right answer. "How far?"

"In the snow, we could walk it in about an hour."

"Good. Now tell me the best way out of the mountains on foot. No roads or trails. I want to stay in the woods."

I flinched. "You want to go on foot? Through the trees?"

"We leave tonight. As soon as we get the gear and supplies."

Shaun was definitely in trouble. If we were going through the forest, it was to avoid being seen. I couldn't think of a single other explanation. Hiking through the forest—at night, in a storm—was dangerous. I didn't need Calvin's expertise to know that. By now, several inches of snow blanketed the ground. Trekking through it would be bitterly cold and slow. If we became stranded, no one would discover us.

"Do you know the way or not?" Shaun asked.

The thought that had been scratching wildly at the back of my brain broke through at that moment and made me see with clarity what Shaun was doing. This was a test. I was up first, followed by Korbie. He'd weigh our answers. He needed to know we could navigate him off the mountain. Otherwise, we were worthless to him.

Forcing myself to be brave, I looked at him squarely. "I've been coming to these mountains for years. I know my way around. I've backpacked parts of the Teton Crest Trail multiple times, and I've hiked all over the mountain range. I can get you off it. It will be a lot harder traveling through a snowstorm, but I can do it."

"This is useful, Britt. Good work. I need you to take us

somewhere where I can lift a car. What do you say to that?" Shaun leaned in close, resting his hands on his knees. His face was level with mine, and I could see his mind working rapidly behind his eyes. If I blew this, it was over.

"I'll take you through the forest to the highway. It will be one of the first roads they plow." I didn't know where the highway was in relation to us. I didn't even know where we were. But I had Calvin's map. If Shaun left me alone for a few minutes, I might be able to use it to determine our location and figure out which direction we should travel. I *wanted* to take Shaun to the highway. A highway meant cars. People. Help.

"How far to the highway?"

"Six miles," I guessed. "But we won't be taking a direct route. Maybe seven?"

"That's my girl." He stuck his head out the door and hollered to Mason, while I shut my eyes in relief. I'd passed this portion of the test. I'd kept us alive a little longer. Granted, the hardest part— convincing them I knew what I was doing once we were hiking through the trees—was yet to come. "Time to switch. Korbie's up next."

Korbie and I didn't speak as we passed. Our eyes met briefly, and I saw that hers were red and glassy. Her nose was swollen, and her bottom lip trembled. My own fingers started to shake, and I squeezed them into fists. I gave her a nod; a secret message passed between us. *Calvin and Bear will find us.*

But I didn't fully believe it.

BECCA FITZPATRICK

Outside, the wind pushed big, wet snowflakes against the storage room window. The snow swirled, making me think of schools of tiny white fish.

Choosing a spot farther down the wall, so that the pole wasn't directly in my line of vision, I leaned back and hugged my knees to my chest. The iciness outside seeped through the cement walls, and I immediately jerked ramrod straight.

"I'm cold," I told Mason, who stood between me and the door, guarding it. The picture was almost comical. Did he think I was going to barrel past him? And go where—into the storm?

"Can you at least bring me my coat?" I persisted. I had my red scarf, which I'd worn all evening, but it wasn't enough against the chill. "I think I left it in the kitchen."

"Nice try."

"What do you think I'm 'trying'?"

He didn't respond.

"It would be tragic if I ran off into the forest and got lost, wouldn't it?" I went on, feeling angry suddenly. "Then you'd have no one to help you off the mountain. Are you and Shaun in trouble? What did you do? Are you running from the police? That's it, isn't it?"

Mason remained closemouthed.

"What happened at the 7-Eleven earlier?" I'd intended to sound tough and accusatory, but my voice broke on the last syllable, revealing my hurt. "If you're really a cold-hearted criminal, why did you help me?"

He glanced at me with cool detachment. At least he'd acknowledged me. It was halfway to a response.

"You played along," I continued. "You tricked my ex-boyfriend. You knew my name. Who was that guy?"

"Your name was printed on your T-shirt."

"I know that," I said tersely. "The point is, you took the time to read it and care. You were a different person. You helped me. And now you're holding me hostage. I want an explanation."

His face returned to impassive.

"Do you and Shaun really think you can pull this off? The storm will blow over, and people will fill the mountainside again. You won't be able to hold Korbie and me hostage and keep it a secret. People will see the four of us in the forest together—hikers and campers and park rangers. They'll want to talk, because that's what people do in the mountains. They're friendly and observant. They'll know something is wrong."

"Then keep us far away from those people."

"The deeper I take you into the forest, the greater the chance we'll get lost."

"Don't get lost."

"I know you're not like Shaun," I said, refusing to give up. "You didn't want to let us inside the cabin tonight. It's because you knew this would happen, didn't you? That Shaun would take us hostage. And you tried to prevent it."

"Even if that were the case, it didn't work."

"Do you really think Shaun will kill us? Why won't you tell me what's going on?"

"Why would I do that?" he said crossly. "I'm in this for myself. If you're worried about what's going to happen to you, start focusing on getting us off the mountain. Do that and we'll let you go."

"How do I know that?"

He merely looked at me.

"You're lying," I whispered, my voice suddenly hoarse. "You're not going to let us go."

The contours of his face tightened. I feared I had my answer.

A wild idea shot into my brain. It was risky, but if Korbie and I were going to die, I had to do something. Mason and Shaun didn't need both of us to get them off the mountain—they only needed me. Shaun already believed Korbie was useless. She hadn't prepared for this trip the way I had, and it showed. I didn't think I could get us both out of this mess, but I had a shot at getting Korbie out safely. I just had to reaffirm in Shaun's mind that she was worthless and nonthreatening. And that he was better off leaving her behind.

I swallowed hard. I had never considered myself brave. I was the spoiled daddy's girl. If I went through with this, it meant leaving Korbie. I didn't know if I had the courage to hike into the forest alone with Shaun and Mason.

But I didn't see any other choice.

"Korbie has type one diabetes," I said. "She has to take insulin. Without it, she'll go into a coma. If it lasts long enough, it's fatal." Once, at summer camp, Korbie and I convinced our camp counselor that Korbie had diabetes and wasn't feeling well enough to help out with the service project. While the rest of the girls picked up trash along the river, Korbie and I stole ice cream sandwiches from the kitchen and ate them in our cabin. If Shaun or Mason quizzed Korbie about having diabetes, I was confident Korbie would remember our ruse, know I was planning something, and go along with it.

"You're lying."

"She takes Humalog and Lantus daily. She has to keep her blood sugar level as close to normal as possible." I knew about type 1 diabetes because my older brother, Ian, had it. If Mason pressed for more information, I had an abundance of it. I could sell this story.

"Where's her medication?"

"In the car. It's frozen by now, which means it has to be thrown out. She isn't going to last long without insulin. This is serious, Mason. You have to let her go. I can tell Shaun doesn't care if we live or die, but you don't want Korbie's death on your hands, do you?"

Mason studied me closely. "You haven't been here that long. The medication might not be frozen. Tell me how to get to your car. I'll get the insulin."

"We've been here two hours. That insulin is frozen solid."

Something undecipherable flitted over his features. Before I could nail down the emotion, a shadow moved in the doorway, and I realized Shaun was standing there. I didn't know how much he'd heard, but his eyes appeared sharp and attentive. A ponderous frown tugged at his mouth.

"Insulin? That doesn't sound good," he said at last.

"I'll get it," Mason told him. "And I'll grab their gear while I'm at it. I'll take Britt with me. She can show me the way."

My heart leaped at this sudden turn of events. If I went with

Mason, I could try to find Calvin. He had to be looking for Korbie and me by now, searching the roads near Idlewilde. How many wrong turns could I have made? One? We had to be close to Idlewilde. Five miles away at most.

"No," said Shaun. "Britt stays here. I don't want to risk anything happening to her, since she's our ticket off this mountain. Britt, tell Mason where to go. No games. If he's not back in two and a half hours, I'm gonna have to assume you lied." His frown deepened. "Believe me, you don't want to lie to me."

I had to convince Shaun to let me go outside. "You won't know what you're looking for," I told Mason. "Have you ever seen insulin or an insulin pen before?"

"I'll figure it out."

"I don't remember exactly where I packed them—"

"It's a car." Mason cut me off. "It won't take long to search the whole thing. You drive an orange Wrangler, right?"

I flinched. "How do you know that?"

"The gas station," he replied brusquely. Before I could press, he continued, "How do I get to your car from here?"

"It would be easier if I went with you."

"No," Shaun repeated firmly.

Sweat dampened my skin. My chance was slipping away. If I didn't find Calvin before we hiked into the forest, I would probably die out there. Just as worrisome, Shaun was going to figure out I'd lied about the insulin. The whole story was unraveling.

I could give Mason the wrong directions to the Wrangler, but if I sent him wandering for hours, Shaun would know I'd tricked him. I didn't have any option but to tell him where the car was.

And devise a backup lie. When Mason returned without the insulin, I would say that I must have forgotten to pack it. I would suddenly remember having left it on my kitchen counter at home. Maybe it was better this way. If they didn't think they had the medication to save Korbie, they'd be more likely to leave her behind. Especially if they believed she was going to die anyway. In fact, Shaun might think that he wouldn't be pinned for Korbie's murder if she died of natural causes.

"If you're facing the cabin, we approached from the left," I said. "Cut through the trees until you reach the main road. Follow it downhill to my car."

"I should be able to follow your footprints most of the way," Mason said. "Snow's coming down hard, but I'll be able to tell where it's been disturbed."

After Mason left, Shaun pointed a warning finger at me. "Stay here and don't make noise. I need to think."

He turned the storage room light off, but left the door cracked. I stood alone, willing myself not to cry. My breath came in short, erratic pants, and I bit down on my fist to muffle the sound. A far-off worry was beginning to creep into the back of my mind. What if I couldn't convince Shaun to leave Korbie behind? If he dragged her along, she'd never make it. Even if she could withstand the rigorous and dangerous hike to the highway, I feared her personality would push Shaun to lash out violently.

I blinked my eyes dry, sniffling until I felt composed. I had to be smart. My best tool now was my brain. I had to use this time to evaluate my situation.

I went over everything I knew about Mason and Shaun. Shaun had a gun. That meant he was the ringleader. Or did it? Mason didn't seem the lackey type. I didn't have a good read on their friendship. I felt a strained push-and-pull between them, an unwilling juggle of power. Most of the time Mason let Shaun have his way. But not out of fear. I saw the way Mason watched Shaun when Shaun wasn't looking. The icy glint in his eyes ran deeper than contempt. Derision, maybe. And I could be imagining it, but he seemed to calculate Shaun's every move, almost like he was hunting for weaknesses and storing the information to use later. But why?

Through the door, I caught glimpses of Shaun as he paced in front of the dying fire. He'd put on a black cowboy hat, a Stetson, tilting it to shade his eyes. Maybe it was a reach, but I couldn't help remembering that Lauren Huntsman had supposedly disappeared from Jackson Hole with a cowboy wearing a black Stetson. The idea that Shaun could be that man caused a violent chill to shudder through me.

I watched Shaun march back and forth, chewing at a hangnail on the thumb of his left hand. His shoulders were hunched, his legs stiff, the muscles of his jaw clenched in concentration. He looked tightly wound.

Like he might snap at any moment.

CHAPTER SEVEN

I'd drifted asleep.

Rolling slowly to my knees, I cringed at the soreness spiking along my shoulder, down through my hip. The cement floor provided no comfort or warmth. Wiping drool at the corner of my mouth, I shivered violently. The storage room door had been shut, leaving me in darkness. A frigid draft from the thin windowpane prickled my skin. Snow was still coming down, but not the big, swirling flakes of earlier; now tiny grains drilled into the window like hurled sand.

I didn't know how much time had passed, but the sky was full dark. I didn't hear Shaun pacing the den. I didn't hear Korbie's quiet sobs from the bathroom.

To keep my mind busy, and not focus on how scared I was, I mentally went over the cabin layout, what I'd seen of it anyway, and took stock of escape routes. The front door was the only exit I knew of to the outside, and it was at the opposite end of the cabin. I'd have to run down the hall and get Korbie, then backtrack through the den and down the entryway hall, all without Shaun hearing or seeing me. Plus, I didn't know where Shaun had put our coats. We wouldn't last long in the storm without them. And even if we made it outside, where would we go? No one would be driving in these conditions—there would be no one to help us.

I wondered if Shaun had gone outside to look for Mason. Or maybe he'd fallen asleep. I wondered if I should take my chance and run now.

I was about to press my ear to the door and listen for Shaun, when it opened.

Shaun held a metal folding chair in one hand and a beer bottle in the other. He sank into the chair and stared at me, his face twisted into a scowl.

"What's wrong?" I asked.

He pointed his finger at me, his lips twitching in anger. "Don't you talk to me."

Any chill I'd felt vanished; immediately, sweat popped out on my skin. Shaun's mouth formed a downward seam, and those slotted eyes. They were glazed with hatred. He flung the door shut, and my heart started pounding so hard I was sure we'd both hear it.

He took a slug of beer and continued to glare at me. "Mason's not back."

I hesitated, not sure he really wanted me to speak. "How long has it been?" I asked carefully.

"Over three hours. It's after one in the morning. Did you lie to me, Britt? Did you lie about where you left your car?"

"Maybe he got lost," I quickly offered. "Maybe the gear is heavy and it's slowing him down."

"He took a sled. The gear's not the problem."

"If you had let me go with him—"

Shaun was out of his chair so fast I didn't see him coming. His hand lashed out at my throat, propelling me backward. He shoved me against the wall. I was so startled, it took a few moments for the pain to sink in. As I scratched frantically at his hand, his knuckles dug harder into the soft underside of my jaw, cutting off my airway. The room blurred at the edges.

"You lied."

He eased up enough for me to gasp air. It wheezed down my throat. I shook my head no, no, no.

"If Mason's lost, it's because you sent him the wrong way. He's out there looking for a car that's miles away. Isn't that right, Britt? Thought you'd level the playing field? Take him out so it's you and Korbie against me? Maybe you're stupider than I thought, pulling something like that."

I wrenched at his hand, trying to tear it off my neck. I couldn't breathe. I didn't know if he'd kill me. I was terrified he might.

"You took Mason away from me, maybe I should take Korbie away from you."

My eyes widened with alarm.

"If we're playing games, I know a few." His face was close enough that I could make out the blue stones of his eyes. Rage burned at the back of them. "That's right, Britt. You played your hand, now it's my turn, isn't that how it works?"

He loosened his grip, and I choked down a breath. As soon as I swallowed air, he pushed my neck to the wall again. "Did you send Mason in the wrong direction? If you did, I won't like it. But if you tell the truth right now, that's something we can work with. Nod if you understand."

Light-headed, I nodded.

"You're ready to start telling the truth?"

Yes, yes, I nodded. Pain raked inside my lungs. It felt like I had a cement block sitting on my chest.

Shaun's hand eased up, and I cried out in relief.

"Another half hour, give Mason that, please," I begged. "It's still snowing. It's deep, and it will take him time to get to the car and back, plus he's dragging the gear. He's okay, he's just moving slower than we thought."

I waited to see if Shaun would fly into a rage.

The storage room door rattled in its frame, as though the pressure in the cabin had changed suddenly. Not a moment later, a blast of arctic air shot under the door. Immediately, Shaun and I both turned in that direction. The front door closed with a heavy slam, and footsteps carried across the wood floors of the den.

"Ace?" Shaun called out. "That you, buddy?"

The storage room door opened. Shaun's hand dropped

innocently to his side, and I recoiled, pressing my back into the corner, wishing I could disappear through the wall.

Mason patted the wall inside the door until he found the light switch.

"What's going on?" he asked, his gaze shifting between us. His face was ruddy from cold, beads of melted snow glistening on his hair and eyebrows. The shoulders and arms of his coat bore a thick dusting of snow.

"Just having a chat," Shaun said in the most ordinary voice. "Isn't that the case, Britt?"

I didn't answer. My breath came in choppy spurts. The air seemed to scrape my throat as I drew it in. Gingerly, I fingered my neck, my eyes filming at the bruises that burned under my skin.

I looked at Shaun, and a disturbing smile inched across his face. I nearly threw up. I felt the lingering steel of his hand vising my neck. When I shut my eyes, it only made his hate-filled eyes glow that much more vividly.

"You got the gear?" Shaun asked Mason.

Panicky, irrational thoughts bombarded my mind. I had to get out. I had to run. Maybe I wouldn't freeze in the forest; maybe I'd survive. I'd risk it, to get away from Shaun. I would run and run, until I was safe.

"The gear looks decent? It'll work?" Shaun prompted Mason.

Mason didn't answer right away. I felt his gaze continue to press down on me. I wanted to burrow through the wall and run into the forest. The first chance I got, I had to take it, because I might not get a second one.

"What happened to her neck?" Mason asked.

"I caught her tying her scarf around it like a noose," Shaun said with a chuckle, motioning at my red scarf on the ground. I'd taken it off before falling asleep. I'd rolled it into a ball and cuddled it against my chest for something comforting to hold. "Would you believe it? Another couple minutes alone, and she'd have killed herself. Gonna have to put this one on suicide watch."

I flinched when his cold hand patted my cheek. "No more tricky stuff, Britt. You might know these mountains better, but your friend is turning out to be the better houseguest. Maybe I'll change my mind about you."

"Can I talk to Korbie?" My voice was a thin, hoarse whisper.

"What kind of question is that?" Shaun said irritably. "What do you think I'm going to say?"

"I want to make sure she's okay."

"She's okay."

"Can I please see her? I won't try anything, I promise." I had to tell her we were going to run. First chance we got. There was no saying what Shaun would do as the hours wore on.

"I don't know that," Shaun said. "You already tried to kill yourself. The only thing I know is that I can't trust you."

Mason hadn't spoken in a long time, and I looked over to find him turning my scarf in his hands. His sharp brown eyes fixed on the fabric. Maybe I was imagining it, but his body seemed to draw taut and the set of his jaw appeared to harden. Did he believe Shaun? I wasn't sure. If the rift between him and Shaun widened, it might help Korbie and me. Maybe we could turn Mason to our side. Maybe he'd help us escape.

Once again, I tried to untangle Shaun and Mason's mystifying relationship. Shaun had lied to Mason to cover up his own actions. It seemed like another clue. More proof that Shaun didn't hold all the power. Did he fear Mason would retaliate if he hurt me? I knew nothing about Mason, definitely not enough to trust him, but I did know that I was less frightened of him than of Shaun. Whatever happened, I had to stay close to Mason. If I was right about him, he wouldn't let Shaun hurt me again.

"We should inventory the gear," Mason finally told Shaun. "Figure out what we need and what we can leave behind."

"You shouldn't have brought any gear we don't need," Shaun criticized.

"I was freezing and grabbed everything in a hurry," Mason snapped. "Have you looked out the window? The snow is coming down hard. It took me twice as long to get there and back because of it. We can sort through the gear now."

Shaun grunted his compliance. "Fine. We've got time. We're not taking off until the snow stops."

As Mason followed Shaun out, he glanced over his shoulder, as if he'd had an afterthought. His brown eyes met mine briefly. "By the way, I found Korbie's insulin. It wasn't frozen. Looks like I got to it just in time."

CHAPTER EIGHT

Alone in the storage room, I stood frozen in place, my heart skipping erratically. I dragged my back down the wall and sat on the floor. This time, I didn't care about the cold bleeding through the concrete. My mind reeled. There wasn't any insulin. Because Korbie wasn't diabetic. Mason had to have figured that out. He'd found the gear, so he must have searched the Wrangler. He'd lied about finding the insulin, but I couldn't figure out why.

I considered what Mason was trying to tell me.

I reviewed his exact words, the tone of his voice, his body language. With one hand resting on the doorknob, he'd raised the issue of the insulin casually, but deliberately. As if he'd needed to ease my mind on the subject. *Your secret is safe with me. For now.*

I felt a sudden necessity to get Mason alone. I had to find out why he was covering for me, what he wanted in return. I rubbed my forehead with the heel of my hand. I also had to prepare.

When the snow stopped, we were leaving. We'd strap our gear to our backs and I would lead us down a mountainside I'd never hiked. I pulled out Calvin's map, careful not to tear it along the worn folds. Then I crouched by the ribbon of light at the bottom of the door. I studied the markings on the map carefully. Off-trail hiking routes, caves, streams, abandoned huts once used by fur trappers—every place Calvin had explored and carefully recorded.

I quickly located Idlewilde and the highway—Calvin had labeled both. The longer I studied the map, the more certain I became of our current position. Calvin had marked a cabin to the south of one of the bigger lakes, far off the main road, and jotted the note "vacant/furnished/electricity." If the cabin was in fact our current location, I'd driven too far. I'd overshot Idlewilde by approximately five miles.

I stopped. What if instead of leading Shaun and Mason to the highway, I tricked them into following me to Idlewilde? But Idlewilde was at a higher elevation, and they would be immediately suspicious if I led them uphill. For now, I would have to guide them downhill toward the highway. Away from Idlewilde and farther from Calvin.

Staring through the window, I told myself that when the snow stopped, and the clouds cleared, the stars would come out and the darkness wouldn't seem so encompassing or hopeless.

I traced my finger over the frosted glass. H-E-L-P. The letters streaked through the condensation before evaporating. I wondered where Calvin was. I wanted to believe he'd found the

Wrangler and was piecing together our next steps. I had to hope it was possible. But would he find us before we left? I closed my eyes and said a desperate prayer. *Guide his steps, and quickly.*

Calvin knew the mountains better than anyone. And he was ingenious. He could outsmart Mason and Shaun—if he found us. He'd gotten average grades in school, but only because he hadn't tried. Mostly to goad his dad, I knew. Calvin had coasted through high school, doing the minimum required work, and the more Mr. Versteeg tried to punish him, the more lax Calvin became about school. Once, after a really bad report card, Mr. Versteeg kicked Calvin out of the house. Calvin checked into a hotel for three days, staying until Korbie convinced her dad to let him come home. When Calvin scored a 31 on his ACT, followed by an astounding 2100 on the SAT, instead of being proud or relieved, Mr. Versteeg was infuriated that Calvin had proved him wrong—that he could get into a top-tier university like Stanford his own way.

A rumor had circulated in school last year that Mr. Versteeg had donated a substantial amount to Stanford and bought Calvin's admittance, but Korbie swore it wasn't true. "My dad would never help Calvin, especially not after the way he went about getting into Stanford," she told me privately.

I paced the tight quarters of the storage room, trying to battle the cold manifesting itself in hundreds of goose bumps springing up on my arms. At the far end of the room, I was about to turn and march back, when my eye landed on a large antique toolbox sitting on the lowest tier of the plastic shelving. I'd been so distracted and scared, I hadn't noticed it before. Maybe there was something I could use as a weapon inside.

Careful not to be heard, I dragged the distressed toolbox, mottled with rust, out onto the concrete floor. I opened the latches and raised the lid.

Familiarity enveloped me like a cold, damp cloud.

My mind tried to make sense of the shapes inside the box. Long, pale shafts and a sphere with two large sockets below the curve of the brow, and a third hole, a nose, centered below them. The limbs were bent at the joints to fit in the box. Hard, leathery skin and connective tissue held the largely decomposed body together.

Paralyzed, I gasped feebly. Logically, I knew that it—they—she, judging by the soiled black cocktail dress, couldn't hurt me. The body was a remnant of a departed life. It was more the knowledge that someone had died in the storage room that I found horrifying. Someone like me, trapped here. It was as if a window appeared in my brain and I looked through it to glimpse my own fate.

I squeezed my eyes shut. When I opened them, the dead body was still there. The skull's toothy grin seemed to jeer at me. *You're next.*

I shut the lid. I backed away. A scream stuck in my throat.

I could not tell Mason or Shaun what I'd seen. They likely knew about the body. They had probably put it there. I didn't need another secret of theirs to keep. My life was already in the balance enough.

Pushing the image of the body deep down, I bit my quivering lip, and tried not to think about death.

CHAPTER NINE

I've heard that when people are close to death, memories flash before their eyes. While I was waiting to see what fate Shaun and Mason had in store for me, my mind brought up memories of Calvin, who I desperately hoped was on his way to find us.

The first time I went camping with the Versteegs, I was eleven years old and Calvin was thirteen. It was July, and the mountains were a cool relief from the heat of town. Korbie and I were finally old enough to sleep outside alone, and Mr. Versteeg helped us pitch a tent on the deep green lawn behind Idlewilde. He promised to leave the kitchen door unlocked, in case we needed to use the bathroom in the middle of the night.

Korbie and I had tubes of lipstick and colorful tubs and pots of blush and eye shadow spread on the tent floor, and we were taking turns giving each other Katy Perry makeovers. When we finished, we were going to film our own music video of "Hot N Cold." Korbie had aspirations of fame, and couldn't wait to get started.

Korbie was applying Candy Apple Red to my mouth when we heard fake ghost noises coming from outside. A beam of light danced erratically through the tent fabric.

"Leave us alone, Calvin!" Korbie yelled.

"Calm down," he said, unzipping the tent and crawling inside. "I'm dropping off the flashlight. Mom said you forgot it."

"Fine," Korbie said, yanking the flashlight out of his hands. "Now get out. Go play with Rohan Larsen," she added in a mocking tone.

Calvin bared his teeth at her like a dog.

"What's wrong with Rohan?" I asked. Korbie had invited me on the camping trip, and Calvin had invited Rohan. I thought Calvin and Rohan were friends.

"My dad made Calvin bring Rohan," Korbie announced with smug superiority, "but Calvin can't stand him."

"My dad likes Rohan because he's good at tennis and he's smart, and his parents are loaded," Calvin explained to me. "He thinks Rohan will rub off on me. He won't even let me choose my own friends. I'm in junior high, and he's arranging playdates for me. It's stupid. He's stupid."

I looked worriedly at Korbie. "Did he make you invite me?" I couldn't stand the thought of Calvin and Korbie snickering at me behind my back.

"He only does stuff like that to Calvin," Korbie assured me.

"Because you're his princess," Calvin said in a dark, loathsome voice. "He doesn't care what you do."

"Get out," Korbie snapped, leaning forward so her face was nose to nose with her brother's.

"Sure I will. But first, you guys know what tonight is, don't you?" Calvin said.

"Friday," I answered.

His eyes glittered. "The thirteenth."

"Friday the thirteenth is a stupid superstition," Korbie said. "Get out before I start screaming. I'll tell Mom you were trying to look at Britt's underwear. She'll ground you from video games all weekend."

Calvin looked at me and I blushed. I was wearing my old white underwear with holes under the elastic. If he did see them, I would die of embarrassment.

"Britt wouldn't rat on me, would you?" he asked me.

"I'm staying out of this," I muttered.

"If Friday the thirteenth is just superstition, how come hotels don't have a thirteenth floor?" Calvin asked his sister.

"Hotels don't have a thirteenth floor?" Korbie and I echoed at the same time.

"Nope. Too unlucky. That's where the fires, suicides, murders, and kidnappings happened. Finally, people got smart and cut out the thirteenth floor."

"Really?" Korbie asked, wide-eyed.

"Not with a saw, stupid. They relabeled the thirteenth floor. They all became 12A. Anyway, there's a reason you should be scared of Friday the thirteenth. It's when ghosts rise from the grave and deliver messages to the living."

"What kinds of messages?" I asked, feeling the skin at the back of my neck crawl with delight.

"Even if we believe you, which we don't, why are you telling us this?" Korbie demanded.

Calvin reached through the tent door and dragged a blue duffel inside. I could tell by the way the fabric strained that something with sharp angles was zipped inside. "I think we should see if the ghosts have a message for us."

"I'm gonna tell Mom you're trying to scare us on purpose," Korbie said, glancing warily at the duffel before rising to her feet.

Calvin grabbed the sleeve of her pj's and dragged her back down. "If you'd shut up for five seconds, I'd show you something cool. Really cool. Wanna see?"

"I do," I said. I glanced at Korbie and knew I'd said the wrong thing, but I didn't care. I wanted to keep Calvin in the tent as long as possible. His skin was golden brown from spending days at Jackson Lake, and he'd grown almost as tall as his dad. Korbie told me he'd started doing push-ups and sit-ups over the summer, and it showed. He was way better-looking than any of the boys in the fifth grade. He looked like a man.

Calvin then pulled a wooden board from the duffel. The alphabet was printed in swirling black font on the face of the board. The numbers one through ten were printed below the alphabet. I knew right away it was a Ouija board. My dad wouldn't let me or Ian play with them. In Sunday School, my teacher told me the Ouija board had the power of the devil. A shudder tiptoed up my spine.

Calvin then pulled a small, triangular device with a window

encased at the center from the duffel and set it on the board.

"What is it?" Korbie asked.

"A Ouija board," I answered. I glanced at Calvin, and he nodded his head approvingly.

"What does it do?"

"It uses mediums—spirits—to answer your questions," Calvin said.

"Don't you have to hold hands when using the Ouija board?" I asked, hoping the rumors I'd heard were true, and that I'd look knowledgeable in front of Calvin.

"Kinda," Calvin said. "Two people place their fingers on the pointer. I guess there's a chance your fingertips could touch."

I scooted closer to him.

"I'm not touching your gross, sweaty hand," Korbie told him. "I'll start smelling like your jockstrap. I've seen you with your hand down your pants when you think no one's looking."

Korbie and I covered our mouths in a fit of giggles, but Calvin simply said, "You guys are so immature. I can't wait until I can hold an actual conversation with you."

Me too, I thought dreamily.

"Ready?" Calvin asked us, gazing earnestly into our faces. "There's only one rule: No pushing the pointer. You have to let it move on its own. You have to let the spirits guide it, because only they can see the future."

"Do you think there's a ghost in here?" Korbie stage-whispered, while muffling more giggles.

Calvin shone the flashlight around the tent, into the corners. It wasn't a big tent, but he wanted us to see that we were completely alone. If the pointer moved, it would be by preternatural means alone. "Ask it anything," he told us. "Ask it about your future."

Will I marry Calvin Versteeg? I thought.

"If this really works, I'm gonna pee my pants," Korbie said.

I was scared of the Ouija board, and scared my dad would find out I'd played with it, so I was grateful when Calvin said, "I'll go first."

In a quiet, ceremonious voice, he asked the Ouija, "Of the three of us, who is going to die first?"

I swallowed, staring nervously at the pointer. My heart felt tight in my chest, and I realized I'd stopped breathing. Korbie had been joking about wetting her pants, but I felt like I actually might.

At first the pointer didn't move. I met Korbie's eyes, and she shrugged. And then, slowly, the device began to glide toward the black letters.

C.

"I'm not pushing it, I swear," Korbie said, glancing anxiously at Calvin.

"Quiet," Calvin chided. "I never said you were."

A.

"Oh, gosh," Korbie said. "Oh, gosh. Oh, gosh!"

L.

"I'm scared," I said, covering my eyes. But I couldn't stand the suspense, and splayed my fingers, peering through them.

"How does Calvin die?" Korbie whispered at the board.

R-O-P.

"Rop?" I said, unsure if this was a real answer. "Does it mean 'rope'?"

Calvin vigorously motioned me to be quiet.

"Who kills me?" he asked, his brow furrowing.

D-A-D.

Something happened in the tent then. A muscle in Calvin's jaw jumped, like he was clamping his teeth together real hard. He rocked back on his haunches, and his brows tugged together as he gazed almost hatefully at the Ouija board.

"Dad would never kill you," Korbie insisted softly. "It's just a game, Calvin."

"Don't be so sure," he murmured at last. "He handpicks my friends and decides which sports I can play. He reviews every homework assignment and makes me redo most of them. He'll probably choose where I go to college and who I marry. Britt was right—the Ouija meant 'rope.' And dad's doing a great job of strangling me already."

It wasn't a pleasant memory, but I couldn't focus on anything good while I was trapped in the storage room with a dead body. The thought of Cal all those years ago reminded me to cut him some slack. He'd never had it easy growing up. He may have cheated on me, and hurt me when he'd ended things between us, but he wasn't a bad person.

And if he saved us, I promised myself I would forgive him for everything.

CHAPTER TEN

The body in the toolbox still haunted my thoughts when the last of the snow fell. I was curled on the floor, trying to fall asleep so I'd forget about how cold I was, when Shaun opened the storage room door. The blackness in the room was so complete that the shaft of light coming through the door seemed to pierce my eyes.

"Get up. We're leaving."

I was in that groggy in-between place, caught halfway between sleep and wakefulness. He ground his boot into my ribs, and I bolted upright.

"Where's Mason?" I asked automatically.

"Getting Korbie. They're meeting us outside." He dropped my coat and a large bundle at my feet. "Strap this on."

I tried to keep the despair off my face. He was bringing Korbie. I had taken a huge risk in lying about the insulin, but it hadn't been enough to convince Shaun to leave her behind. I had to accept that she wasn't going for help. No one would find us now. I felt the nightmare rising over my head.

After dressing in my outerwear, I hoisted the backpack onto my shoulders, the weight of it throwing off my center of balance. I was glad I'd practiced carrying my pack for months, gradually increasing the weight over time. I'd have to find a way to slip a few of Korbie's supplies into my pack. Otherwise, I was sure she'd never last—she hadn't trained with me, since she'd been counting on Bear to carry the heavy gear.

"You've got two sleeping bags, ground mats, toilet paper, and a few layers of clothing Ace grabbed from the duffel in your car," Shaun said. "Ace and I have the granola bars from your car, water, the fire starter, headlamps and flashlights, canteens, blankets, and compasses—yours, and one Ace already had." His eyes pierced mine with menacing effect. "Run off, and you won't last long."

"What time is it?"

"Three."

Three in the morning. I'd slept a little, then. Hopefully, Korbie had too. We were going to need energy to hike over the rough terrain. "I have to use the bathroom."

"Make it fast."

In the bathroom, I reviewed Calvin's map one more time. I closed my eyes, letting the landmarks sink deep. Then I folded the map and tucked it away, inside my shirt, pressed against my heart, where I'd feel him with me. I wrapped my red scarf around my head, improvising something of a ski mask out of it. As the soft fabric rubbed my cheek, I thought of my dad, who had given the scarf to me. I tried to remember if I had hugged him hard, making it last, before I'd said good-bye.

Shaun and I trudged outside into the darkness. The snow came to the tops of my boots—and the surrounding trees looked as if they'd been painted with ice. The wind had died and a full moon was out, casting eerie, smoky-blue light on the glittering snow. I could hear the crunch of it with every step; the top layer was frozen, but beneath that my boots sank easily into the powder.

My breath clouded when I spoke. "Where are Mason and Korbie?"

"They got a head start. We'll catch up."

"They know the way to the highway?" I asked, puzzled. I thought that was why Mason and Shaun needed me.

"We're testing the compasses. Just follow me."

Shawn cradled a compass in the palm of his hand, but something wasn't right. Testing compasses? Separate from each other? Frowning, I said, "We should have stayed together as a group."

"You," he said, spinning abruptly and pushing his face close to mine, "don't give the orders."

I shrank back in alarm. He continued to glare at me, then cut through the tense silence with an uncanny chuckle. I didn't want to travel alone with Shaun, but I didn't have a choice. Right now, my best option was to stay out of his way. We'd meet up with Mason and Korbie soon. With Mason close by, I didn't think Shaun would hurt me. It wasn't that I'd decided to trust Mason. But he'd lied about the insulin to cover for me, and that had to mean something.

We continued our slow, steady pace down the mountainside. Shaun's gaze flickered between the compass and the tunnel of darkness ahead. If the snow didn't start up again, we'd leave a path leading away from the cabin. I prayed Calvin would find it.

Minutes later a shadowy form emerged from the trees ahead. At first I thought I'd imagined it, but the shape of a man became more distinct the closer he got. My heart soared at this sudden turn of events. Someone else, someone who could help me. Shaun must have seen the man too, because he swung his headlamp in that direction, bathing the man in a cone of light.

"You found us," Shaun called in good spirits.

My heart dropped as Mason shielded his eyes from the glare of the headlamp. "Lower your light."

Shaun held his compass side by side with Mason's, comparing them. "Looks like they're both working now. Crisis averted."

Mason glanced at me. "The generator at the cabin was causing your compass to reverse. But it appears to be working now."

"Where's Korbie?" I asked, searching the woods behind Mason, waiting for her to appear out of the black backdrop.

Mason and Shaun exchanged a look, but neither answered.

"Where is she?" I tried again, feeling the first scratch of hope—and panic. Mason's eyes shifted, avoiding mine. What weren't they telling me?

"She's back at the cabin," Shaun finally said.

I blinked in confusion. "What?"

"We're short on supplies," he said harshly. "We only brought what we need. And we don't need her. Especially if she's sick."

His words hummed inside me, leaving me excited but cautious. I didn't want to hope too soon. "But you said we were all going together."

"I know what I said, but that's changed. Korbie's staying at the cabin. She doesn't know the mountains like you do and she's a liability."

I came to a halt. My whole body vibrated with hope and relief. They'd left Korbie behind. If she could last a day without food, until the snow melted, she'd make it out all right. She could go for help. Even better, Calvin might see the cabin lights and find her. She'd tell him everything, and he'd come for me. I just had to be brave a little longer.

And react to this change in program in a way that Shaun would expect. I couldn't let him know I'd hoped for this, that I had a secret plan.

"We have to go back!" I said. "I'll get you off the mountain, but first we have to get Korbie. We ate the last of the food. If the pipes freeze, she'll run out of water. It could take days for someone to find her. We have to go back."

From the corner of my eye, I saw Shaun drag his gun from the pocket of his parka. His expression was uncaring. "The faster you get us out of the mountains, the more time you'll have to come back and save your friend."

I looked him head-on, even though he frightened me. My stomach curled as I recalled wanting to kiss him. I'd never been so wrong about a person in my life. A warm, sour taste rose in my throat. I'd been so desperate for attention, to prove something to Korbie, I'd actually fallen for this monster's act.

Now I was beginning to see the situation with true clarity. Shaun believed he'd left Korbie for dead. And he felt no remorse. Once I helped him and Mason off the mountain, there was nothing stopping him from dealing me the same fate. I'd saved Korbie, but there was no guarantee on my own life.

I bent sideways and emptied my stomach.

"Leave her alone," Mason told Shaun. "You're making it worse. We need her focused."

Mason kicked snow over my mess, and handed me a wad of toilet paper from his coat pocket. When I didn't take it right away, he gently wiped my mouth dry.

When he spoke, I expected his voice to sound curt, but instead his words were underscored with weariness. "Take a minute to pull yourself together, Britt. Then get us to the highway."

CHAPTER ELEVEN

Calvin Versteeg was my first crush. My childhood love for him grew and grew over the years and was sealed on his tenth birthday. I remembered that magical, woozy feeling of knowing with certainty that he was the one.

Even though Calvin was two years older than me, he was only one grade level ahead. He had an August birthday, and his parents had held him back a year before kindergarten to give him an extra year of growth and a better shot at excelling in sports. It was a good move. By sophomore year, Calvin had earned a spot on the boys' varsity basketball team. Junior year, his name was on the starting roster.

We drove to Jackson Lake in the Versteegs' Suburban. Calvin and his two friends called dibs on the back row. Korbie and I were stuck in the middle row, closest to her parents. Every time we turned around to eavesdrop on Calvin and his friends, he would grab our heads and knock them together.

"Mom!" Korbie howled. "Calvin's hurting us!"

Mrs. Versteeg looked over her shoulder. "Leave your brother alone. Talk to Britt, or play with your My Little Ponies. They're in the case under your seat."

"Yeah," Calvin snickered under his breath. "Play with your ponies. I bet they have a surprise for you."

Korbie snatched up the case and flung it open on her lap. "Moooom!" She screeched so loud it made my eardrums vibrate. "Calvin cut off my ponies' hair!" She flipped around in her seat, color flooding her cheeks. "I'm gonna kill you!"

"What's the big deal?" Calvin said, grinning devilishly. "Mom will buy you new ones."

I remembered thinking Calvin was the meanest big brother ever. Worse than my brother, Ian, who hid in my closet, then jumped out and yelled "Boo!" after I turned out the light. Being scared was a lot better than having bald My Little Ponies.

Of course, Calvin made up for it halfway through the day. After spending the afternoon water-skiing, he and his friends caught frogs by the lake, and Calvin let me name his frog. Even though I picked a stupid name—Smoochie—Calvin let it stick.

Later that night, when we were lined up to use the bathroom before the long drive home, I whispered in Calvin's ear, "You're not so bad."

He tweaked my nose. "Don't you forget it."

As we piled into the Suburban, nobody called dibs on seats. We were too tired. Somehow, I ended up sitting next to Calvin. I fell asleep with my head on his shoulder. He didn't nudge me away.

CHAPTER TWELVE

"You sure we're going the right way?"

Careful not to be seen, I folded Calvin's map along the worn seams and tucked it down my neckline and into my bra. I shut my eyes briefly, blocking out the distraction of Shaun's voice carrying through the trees as I committed the scribbled notes and topography to memory. The farther we hiked, and the more landmarks we passed, the more certain I was that I knew where we were.

Zipping up my jeans, I stepped out from behind the pine tree that had served as my privacy screen, and answered stoically, "You tell me. You've got the compasses. Are we heading south?"

"The scenery isn't changing any," Shaun complained, flicking open his compass to make sure he'd kept us on course. "It doesn't seem like we're getting anywhere."

He was right. We'd been traveling for hours, but it was all about perspective. On Calvin's map, we'd hardly eaten up a few millimeters.

"I thought the highway was southeast of the cabin," Mason said, frowning slightly.

A tremor of fear shot through me, but I pulled on an unflustered face. "It is. But we have to skirt a small lake. We'll turn east once we're around it. I thought you didn't know the area."

"I don't," he answered slowly. "But I glanced over a map at the gas station yesterday." His frown deepened, a look of concentration and recall shadowing his expression. "I could be remembering wrong."

"Well, which way is it?" Shaun snapped. "One of you is right."

"I'm right," I said confidently.

"Ace?" Shaun prompted.

Mason rubbed his jaw in a thoughtful, considering way, but said nothing more. A whole minute must have passed before I was able to breathe easy. Because Mason was right. The fastest way to the highway *was* to travel southeast. But now that I knew where we were, I wasn't taking them to the highway. According to Calvin's map, if we shifted our course due south, we'd run into a ranger patrol cabin.

Based on my calculations, we'd be there before sunup.

The moon had been out most of the night, but shortly before dawn, a new embankment of clouds rolled in, leaving us once again in that indescribable shade of wilderness black. The wind had picked up again too, whipping through the trees and chafing our faces.

We resorted to headlamps, even though Mason had made it clear we needed to conserve the batteries. The package instructions said each headlamp had only a three-hour life span.

My back ached from the weight of my pack. My legs, stiff with cold, moved over the snow in shorter and slower strides. Except for a brief nap at the cabin, I hadn't slept in almost twenty-four hours. My vision slid in and out of focus as I tried to concentrate on the monotonous carpet of crystalline white extending in every direction. I fantasized what it would feel like to lie in the snow, shut my eyes, and dream myself somewhere else, anywhere else.

"I have to go to the bathroom again," I said, coming to a stop and catching my breath. We weren't moving quickly, but the continuous weight of my pack and the jarring impact of hiking down the steep, rugged slopes were taking their toll.

"You're giving her too much water," Shaun complained to Mason. "She's pissing every hour." He turned on me. "Make it quick."

Mason helped me out of my backpack and rested it against a tree before shrugging out of his own pack. He did a few shoulder rolls, and I knew the weight was starting to get to him too.

"Ignore him," he told me, and while there wasn't kindness in his voice, it wasn't filled with contempt, either. More matter-of-fact. He handed me his headlamp. "Take five."

I walked a short distance, then stepped behind a pine tree. I switched off the headlamp and peered back through the branches, watching them. Shaun was relieving himself in the open, and Mason leaned his forearm on a tree, cradling his face in the crook of his elbow. If a person could sleep standing up, it would look like that, I thought. Of the three of us, Mason was the most powerfully built, so it took me by surprise that he seemed to be handling the hike the worst. He peeled off a glove and rubbed his eyes, looking increasingly exhausted.

I wondered, if five minutes stretched to ten, would either of them notice I hadn't come back? I could run. It was an option, flickering like a loose lightbulb at the edge of my mind. I had promised myself I'd take the first chance I got. I could hike back to Korbie and we could go for help together. But if Calvin's map was right, we'd see the ranger patrol cabin as we came over the next slope. I could run now, and face the wilderness alone. Or I could stay, and pray there was a ranger at the patrol cabin.

I played out the scenario a step further. When the ranger patrol cabin came into view, Mason and Shaun wouldn't be expecting it, and I would have to mirror their surprise. I'd have to convince them I hadn't planned to run into it, and I'd have to talk them into knocking on the door. Then I would need to covertly communicate to the ranger that I was in trouble—we both were. Because if I led Mason and Shaun to the ranger patrol cabin, I was dragging the park ranger into this. Whether I wanted to or not. The difference, I told myself, was that the park ranger was trained to handle the worst.

Confirming that Mason and Shaun weren't coming to check on me, I pulled Calvin's map out and examined it closely under the headlamp. Some distance behind the ranger patrol cabin was a small, narrow lake. Calvin had scribbled "clean water source" next to it. I filed away this information before heading back to Mason and Shaun.

"How long before we rest?" I asked them. "We can't go forever without sleep."

"We'll rest after the sun comes up," Mason said. "We have to get to the highway by the time they plow the roads."

So you can steal a car before the police find you, I thought.

"There's an uncontaminated lake nearby, but it will take us about an hour off course," I said. "It's our last chance at clean water."

Mason nodded. "Then we'll refill at the lake, set up a temporary shelter, and catch a quick nap." He held out my backpack, and he must have seen me grimace, because a brief, apologetic smile flickered at his mouth. He lowered his voice, keeping his next words between us. "I know it's heavy, but we're almost there. A couple more hours."

I took the backpack skeptically, unsure how to interpret his small gesture of kindness. He was holding me hostage. How did he expect me to respond? With a smile of my own? Remembering the dead body back at the cabin, I tried to reconcile this considerate version of Mason with the one who might be a killer. Was his kindness genuine? Would he kill me if he had to?

"A couple hours," I echoed.

I didn't tell him, but if things went my way, we'd be stopping much sooner.

Not thirty minutes later, as we approached the basin of the slope, our path slanting diagonally through the trees to catch the softer edge of the mountain, I got my first glimpse of the ranger patrol cabin. It was small, two or three rooms at most, with a low roof and a tiny porch.

Up until this point, I'd kept my hope nailed down, afraid I wouldn't find the patrol cabin, but suddenly my heart swelled, burning in my chest. My relief smacked me with more force than the bitterly cold wind. The patrol cabin, just ahead. With a ranger inside, I was sure of it. After everything that had gone wrong, I was finally catching a break. The nightmare was coming to an end.

Beside me, Mason halted. He grabbed my arm and yanked me behind a tree. Shaun jumped the other way, concealing himself behind a tree a few feet away. I could hear Mason's breath coming in hard, choppy pants.

"The shelter down there. Did you know about it?" he demanded in a low, harsh whisper.

I shook my head no. I didn't trust my voice not to give me away. A strange, delicious hope thudded in my chest, and I was afraid Mason would hear it in my voice.

"So it's a coincidence?" he said, not sounding like he believed it.

"I didn't know, I swear," I said, wide-eyed. "Think about it. The shelter is minuscule compared to the vastness of the forest. It would be easier to miss than to hit. I'd have to have a map to find it in the dark. It's a coincidence, just bad luck."

Shaun pointed a threatening finger at me. "If you knew about this, if you led us here on purpose—"

"I didn't know, I swear. You have to believe me." I was so close. The ranger patrol cabin was a short distance down the hill. I couldn't blow this now. "You chose the direction, you told me where you wanted to go. You've had more control over our direction than I've had."

Mason steepled his gloved hands over his mouth, thinking. "No one can see us from the structure in this light. We haven't been seen. Nothing's changed."

"Then we take the long way around," Shaun said. "We walk a mile out of the way, if that's what it takes."

"What if it's empty?" I said. "If the pipes haven't frozen, it will have running water. Probably food and other supplies too. If we fill up here, we won't have to go out of our way to find the lake I told you about. It will save us a lot of time."

Mason studied me. "You're suggesting we raid the shelter?"

"We aren't going to make it to the highway on what we've got. We need to restock. Especially on water."

"Look around," Shaun said, kicking snow at me. "We got an endless supply of water."

"It's thirty degrees out," Mason said curtly. "How are we going to melt the snow? Britt is right. The shelter should have running water."

"I don't like it," Shaun muttered, folding his arms moodily over his chest. "We agreed: no people. Going down there is too risky."

"I'll go down first," I offered. "I'll look in the window. I'm not going to run away—I've already had enough chances. Where would I even go?"

"If anyone's going, it's me," Shaun said. "I have the gun."

At the reminder, I drew a silent intake of air. Would the ranger have a gun of his own? I didn't know. I hoped I knew what I was doing. I hoped, when this was over, I still thought leading us here was a good plan.

Mason gave his friend a nod of consent. "See what you can find."

Gun in hand, Shaun ran in a crouch downhill, making his way toward the dark, sleepy-looking patrol cabin dwarfed by dense evergreens whose tips seemed to sweep the sky.

"He'll be back soon," Mason said, as if the thought should comfort me.

"When are you going to tell me who you're running from and why?" I asked as soon as we were alone.

He merely looked at me. I couldn't decide if the root of his silence was arrogance or carefulness. He seemed like the kind of guy who weighed each word, each movement. Carefulness, I decided. Because he had a lot to hide.

"It's the police, I know it is, so you can stop pretending like you don't know what I'm talking about. You did something illegal. And now you're only making things worse by kidnapping me."

"Do you think your dad knows you never reached the cabin?" he asked, avoiding the subject. "Were you supposed to call him and check in when you got there?"

"I told him I'd call," I admitted, wondering what Mason was getting at.

"Your dad won't be able to get up here in this weather, and even if he could, he won't know where to look for you, but do you think he's called the park and notified them that you never made it to the cabin? Or were you telling the truth when you said your dad thinks you can get yourself out of trouble?"

I regarded him warily. "I told Shaun my dad knows I can handle myself, but I didn't tell you. When Shaun and I were in the kitchen cooking, were you eavesdropping?"

"Of course I was listening," he said, covering up any embarrassment with a tone of annoyance.

"Why?"

"I had to know what you told Shaun."

"Why?"

He gave me a long, considering look, but he didn't answer.

"Were you spying on me . . . or Shaun? Are you and Shaun even friends?" I was suddenly prompted to ask the question because of the strange tension I sensed between them. Maybe I'd been wrong this whole time. Maybe they weren't friends. But then, why were they together? One thing I knew for sure. I was far more afraid of Shaun. I would never ask him these questions, or even take this tone with him.

"What makes you think we're not?" he said in that same clipped, irritated voice.

"He lied to you. He told you I tried to kill myself, but he made the marks on my neck."

I could tell by the lack of surprise in his expression that he knew Shaun had been the one to hurt me.

"Was he afraid of what you'd do to him? Does he know you don't want me to get hurt? Is that why he lied?"

"Do you really think I'd step in and stop him from hurting you?" he demanded curtly. "Why would I do that?"

I recoiled at the hot contempt flashing in his eyes.

"You girls are all the same," he muttered with disgust.

"What does that mean?"

"You think I'll save you." He said it accusingly, bitterly. His eyes found mine, and even in the cold, pink light of dawn, I could see deep pain broiling in his gaze.

The back of my throat felt slippery. Any remaining fragment of hope seemed to crumble inside me. He wouldn't help me. I'd been wrong about him; he wouldn't soften. He was as useless to me as Shaun.

I wanted to turn away in indignation, to show him he couldn't treat me this way, but I couldn't afford to waste the time I had alone with him. Pushing down my despair, I focused on the questions I needed to ask. "Why did you lie about finding Korbie's insulin?"

"To cover for you. Shaun would have known you played him. How do you think he would have handled that? Think about it, Britt. I need you to get me off this mountain. You're no good to me dead."

"You lied to help yourself."

"I've seen the way you look at me. You think I'll protect you. You think when it comes down to moral obligation, I'll do the right thing. I'm not the same as Shaun, but I'm not good." He wasn't looking at me anymore, but rather off in the distance. He had the ragged, unpredictable look of someone haunted by old ghosts. An uneasy chill crept inside me. I began to believe he might be more dangerous than Shaun. That he was biding his time, playing Shaun's game with Shaun's rules, until the moment he was ready to make his move. . . .

The crunch of snow alerted us to Shaun's return. I jerked toward the sound, my eyes immediately going to the gun in his grip. He hadn't used it—I would have heard the shot. Even so, the way he held it, a natural, practiced extension of his hand, made my spine stiffen.

He grinned. "All clear. It looks like a park ranger outpost. No one has been there in days."

The hope I'd been clinging to seemed to deflate inside me. Empty? For days? I was so heartsick, I wanted to kneel in the snow and sob.

"Even better, there's lots to loot. Canned food, bedding, and dry firewood under a tarp around back," Shaun continued, with a greedy gleam in his eyes.

Beside me, Mason relaxed. "We'll refuel and crash here for a couple hours."

We hiked down to the patrol cabin. At the door, Shaun showed us how he'd gotten inside; he waved the key with a display of entitlement. "Found it under the doormat," he explained. "Stupid, trusting fools."

Mason held the door for me, and I stepped inside, not taking in the whole cabin at once, but searching for specific signs that Shaun had missed something, that a ranger had been here recently and might return soon.

The stale air was thick with dust. There were no dishes on the kitchen counters, no lingering smells of coffee. No wet, muddy footprints on the linoleum. A bar separated the kitchen from the living area. One corduroy sofa, a southwestern rug, and a beat-up trunk that served as a coffee table. No dishes there either, and no newspapers. Nestled into the corner beside the fireplace was an antique rocking chair that bore a fine layer of dust. A door at the end of the living room led to a small bedroom with a sloped roof.

Mason went to gather firewood, and soon after, dumped an armful of wood near the fireplace and started building a fire. Shaun kicked off his boots, tucked the gun into the back of his jeans, and ambled to the bedroom. He flopped facedown on the mattress.

"Keep an eye on her, Ace," he called through the doorway. "I'm beat. I'll take the next shift."

Casually, I began opening kitchen drawers and cupboards. Shaun was right; we'd eat well today. Canned corn, peas, sloppy joe sauce, powdered milk, rice, kidney beans, and vegetable oil. Sugar, flour, cornmeal, vinegar. I crouched in front of the sink and peered into the cabinet. I stared at the gallon-size clear plastic bag filled with first aid supplies . . . *and a pocketknife.*

"Fire's going," Mason said from above, and I immediately shut the cabinet and stood up. The kitchen bar separated us, and I hid my hands in my pockets to keep Mason from seeing that they were shaking.

"That's good," I responded automatically.

His bleary eyes instantly came alert with suspicion. "What are you doing?"

"Figuring out what to cook. I'm starving."

He continued to watch me, his look pure calculation. He came around the bar, slowly opening cabinet doors. His gaze shifted between the contents of each cupboard and my face, as if my reaction might clue him in on what I was up to. There was a knife block with steak knives on the counter, and he immediately seized it, studying me distrustfully.

He finished checking the bank of cupboards over the stove and moved down the counter toward me. In a matter of seconds, he'd open the door under the sink.

"You'll have to show me how to work the stove," I said, fiddling with the knobs. "I can cook something for us once the stove is on. We have a gas stove at home, so I'm not used to electric," I added, trying to keep my voice neutral.

With one final, searching look at me, Mason turned his attention to the stove top. He twisted one of the greasy, worn knobs. Immediately, a sweet, pleasant burning smell filled the kitchen, and when I held my hand over the coils, I felt rising heat.

"A good sign," I said.

He nodded in agreement. "Power's not out—yet."

"Sleep first or eat first?" I asked.

"Your call," he said, making it sound like the decision was up to me and he didn't care either way. In one of those rare moments, though, he made the mistake of shooting a split-second look of longing at the sofa. I felt a small victory in noticing. It meant Mason wasn't perfect after all—he could slip up and give away his secrets. And that gave me hope.

"Let's nap first," I said, turning off the stove burner. "We're exhausted."

After he fell asleep, I'd come back for the pocketknife.

I sank into the rocking chair near the fireplace, and Mason

stretched out on the sofa. The heat from the fire tingled my skin, and I pulled a wool blanket up to my chin. A warm smokiness filled the ranger outpost, making my thoughts drowsy. I sighed, already feeling stiffness in my muscles from the long hike here. I wished I never had to move again.

Long after I shut my eyes, I felt Mason watching me. I knew he wouldn't sleep until he was sure I'd fallen asleep first. To keep my mind alert, I counted time. I was exhausted, but I could outlast him. I had to, if I wanted the pocketknife.

The fire burned down, smoldering quietly in the grate. At long last, I heard Mason shift, rolling to face away from me. His breathing slowed, and when I stole a quick glimpse, his long legs were relaxed in sleep.

CHAPTER THIRTEEN

It was a bleak, drizzly afternoon in March of my junior year, and the Wrangler was in the shop with a blown gasket. My brother, Ian, had promised to hang around after school—I had Key Club—and give me a ride home. After ten minutes of waiting, I left a distress call on his voice mail. After thirty minutes, my messages turned hostile. After an hour, the janitor kicked me out and locked up for the night.

Within seconds, my hair was plastered over my ears and my dress clung to my figure. Rain dripped off my eyelashes. My lips felt stiff with cold, and to keep them from freezing, I muttered every swear word I could think of, in every possible combination. I was going to punch Ian. The minute I got home, I was going to shove my fist into his nose, and I didn't care if it got me grounded from Korbie's party the following weekend.

Halfway home I kicked off my silk polka-dot ballet flats and hurled them furiously into the gutter. Ruined. I hoped Ian had eighty dollars sitting around, because that's how much they were going to cost him.

I was about to jaywalk across the street, when a black truck honked and I jumped back onto the curb. Calvin Versteeg rolled down the passenger window and hollered, "Get in!"

I threw my books in the backseat of his extended cab and boosted myself inside. I felt rivulets of water running down my thighs and pooling in the leather seat. When I glanced down, I could see skin peeking through the lavender fabric of my dress. I couldn't remember what color underwear I'd put on that morning. A mortifying thought struck me. Had my underwear been showing through my dress the whole walk home? I folded my hands self-consciously in my lap.

If Calvin noticed, he had the decency not to comment. He grinned. "I ever tell you the story about the girl who tried to take a shower outside?"

I punched him in the shoulder. "Shut up."

He reached into the backseat, groping blindly. "I bet I can scrounge up some soap in my gym bag. . . ."

I giggled. "You are the dumbest boy ever, Calvin Versteeg."

"Dumb but chivalrous. Where to?"

"Home, so I can strangle Ian with my bare hands."

"A no-show?" Calvin guessed.

"With a death wish."

Calvin cranked the heat. "You should have called me."

I looked at him, perplexed. Calvin was my best friend's older brother, but aside from that, we didn't have a relationship. I'd dreamed for years that he would see me in a new light, but the truth was, calling Calvin for a ride would have been the same as calling any other guy at school.

"I guess I didn't think of that," I said, bewildered by his offer.

He turned on the radio. Not loud and blaring; a steady melody to chase away the silence. I don't remember what we talked about the rest of the ride. I stared through the window, thinking, I'm in Calvin Versteeg's truck. Without Korbie. Just the two of us. And he's hitting on me. I couldn't wait to tell someone. And then it dawned on me. For the first time, I couldn't run straight to Korbie. She didn't want me flirting with her brother. She would brush it off, telling me he was just being nice. But he wasn't. He was hitting on me, and it was the most flattering thing that had ever happened to me.

Calvin pulled into my driveway. "We should do this more often," he told me as I climbed out.

I smiled back, unsure. "Yeah. That would be nice."

I was about to shut the door when he said, "Hey, you forgot this," and he offered me a folded scrap of paper.

It wasn't until he'd backed onto the street that I thought to open the paper. If I'd ever wondered what his handwriting looked like, now I knew.

Call me.

CHAPTER FOURTEEN

A loud bang at the patrol cabin door jolted me fully alert.

Mason was kneeling beside me in an instant, muffling my cry of surprise with his hand. He raised his finger to his lips, signaling me not to make another sound.

Shaun moved swiftly into the room, gun drawn, aiming it at the shadowy silhouette showing through the café curtain over the window in the front door.

Another, harder rap sounded. "Anybody home?" a man's voice called out.

I wanted to scream, Help! I'm here! Oh, God, please help! The words were right there, exploding inside me.

"Answer it," Shaun ordered in a gruff whisper. "Tell him you're fine. Tell him you're waiting out the storm. Get him out of here. One false move, Britt, and you're dead, both of you are." He clicked off the gun's safety for emphasis, the sound echoing in my ears as loud as the toll of a bell.

I walked to the door, each step stiff and weighted. I wiped my hands on my thighs. My face was bathed in sweat. Shaun crept along the outer kitchen wall, keeping the gun trained on me. At my sideways glance, he nodded, but it wasn't a sign of encouragement. He was reminding me that he meant every word.

I unlocked the door and cracked it enough to see out. "Hello?"

The man wore a brown parka and cowboy hat, and seemed startled at the sight of me. He collected himself and said, "I'm Deputy Game Warden Jay Philliber. What are you doing here, miss?"

"Waiting out the storm."

"This is a park ranger patrol cabin. You don't have permission to be here. How did you get in?"

"I—the door was unlocked."

"Unlocked?" He sounded doubtful and tried to peer behind me. "Everything okay in there?"

"Yes," I said in a dry, papery voice.

He shifted to see around me. "I need you to fully open the door."

In my head, I could hear myself saying, *They have a gun, they're going to kill me.*

"Miss?"

A strange buzzing filled my ears. I was light-headed; his voice rolled through me like a slurred rumble, but I couldn't make out the words. I squinted at his mouth, trying to read them.

"... get here?"

I licked my lips. "I'm waiting out the storm." Had I said that already? Out the corner of my eye, I saw Shaun wave the gun impatiently. It rattled my nerves further. I couldn't remember what I was supposed to say next.

". . . transportation?" the game warden asked.

I felt an overpowering urge to run. I pictured myself through the door, in the woods. I was so disoriented that for one moment, I thought I'd really done it.

"How did you get here?" he asked again, his eyes watching me carefully.

"I hiked."

"By yourself?"

Absurdly, I wondered if Calvin was thinking about me right now. Had he slept last night? Had he found the Wrangler and set off into the forest, searching for Korbie and me? Was he worried about me? Of course he was. "Yes, by myself."

The game warden held up a grainy, enlarged black-and-white photograph. It was taken from a security video, and showed the inside of a Subway sandwich shop. There were two men in the photo. The cashier stood behind the counter, his palms raised to shoulder level. The man facing him, the man aiming the gun, was Shaun.

"Have you seen this man?" the game warden asked, tapping his finger against Shaun's blurry, two-dimensional profile.

"I—" Red lights popped behind my eyes. "No. He doesn't look familiar."

"Miss, you're not all right. I can see that plainly." He was taking off his hat. He was going to step inside. The hum in my ears rose to a deafening whine.

"I'm fine," I blurted. I looked around desperately. Shaun's eyes blazed into mine, hot with rage.

"Please stay outside," I said, panicking. I kneaded the heel of my hand into my forehead. I'd said the wrong thing.

The game warden brushed past me. At the same time, there was movement in the corner and Shaun was out in the open, gun drawn.

The game warden's face went white with fear.

"Kneel down." Shaun barked the order. "Hands on your head."

The game warden obeyed, murmuring that Shaun should rethink, he was an officer of the law, they could talk this out, Shaun should hand over his weapon.

"Shut up," Shaun spat. "If you want to live, you'll do exactly as I say. How did you find us?"

The game warden tilted his head, giving Shaun a long, challenging look. At last he said, "I'm not out here alone, son. We've got the whole damn US Forest Service looking for you boys. Sure, we're slowed down by the storm, but so are you. And there's more of us. You aren't getting off this mountain. If you want to come out of this alive, you need to lower your weapon right now."

"Give me the gun, Shaun. Take Britt and start packing our things."

Mason's icily calm voice cut through the tension like a whip. He stepped up to Shaun's shoulder and extended his hand expectantly.

"Stay out of this," Shaun growled, visibly tightening his grip on the gun. "If you want to make yourself useful, go to the win-

BECCA FITZPATRICK

dow and figure out what he drove here in. I didn't hear a truck approach."

"Give me the gun," Mason repeated, so softly his voice barely carried. Despite his quiet tone, it was laced with authority.

Clearly not wanting to give them the chance to plot secretly, the game warden spoke up. "You boys robbed a Subway sandwich shop and shot a police officer while trying to get away. You put a teenage girl in the hospital after you hit her and ran. You're lucky she's alive. You're lucky the officer you shot is also alive, but nobody in the criminal justice system is going to look kindly on it. Things aren't looking good for you, but they're gonna be a helluva lot worse if you don't lower your weapon immediately."

"I said shut up," Shaun barked.

"Who are you?" the game warden asked me. "How do you know these boys?"

"I'm Britt Pheiffer," I said in a rush before Shaun could prevent me. "They're holding me hostage and forcing me to guide them to the highway." Finally! Law enforcement would know I was in trouble. They'd send a search party. Someone would tell my dad what had happened. I was so overcome with relief I nearly cried. And then my heart sank. This was possible only if the game warden got away. If Shaun didn't shoot him.

Shaun gave me a rake of his cold blue eyes. "You shouldn't have done that."

"If we tie him up, he won't be found for a day or two," Mason reasoned with Shaun. "He'll live, but it will buy us time to get off the mountain."

"And if he escapes?" Shaun challenged, plowing a hand through his hair. His eyes were wide and wild, showing bloodshot whites around blue orbs. He squeezed his eyes shut, reopening them and blinking hard, like he was struggling to focus.

"Killing him isn't going to help," Mason repeated in that same steely, authoritative tone.

Shaun squeezed the bridge of his nose. He wiped his free arm across his damp forehead. "You gotta stop ordering me around, Ace. I'm in charge. I make the decisions. I brought you along to do one job; stay focused on that."

"We've been working together for almost a year," said Mason. "Think of everything I've done for you. I want what's best for you—for us. Now lower the gun. There's rope in the storage trunk on the back porch. If we tie him up, it buys us a day at least."

"We've already shot one cop. There's no turning back. We have to see this through, do whatever it takes." There was something irrational and frantic in the way Shaun's eyes darted back and forth, unfocused. After saying the words, he swallowed and nodded, like he was trying to convince himself this was his best option.

Mason said more sternly, "We're going to leave him here and keep pushing toward the bottom of the mountain."

"Stop yelling at me, I can't think!" Shaun roared, rounding on Mason and aiming the gun briefly at him before swerving back to point it at the game warden. More beads of sweat sprang onto Shaun's brow.

"No one's yelling," Mason said quietly. "Lower the gun."

"This is my call," Shaun growled. "I'm calling the shots. And I say we cut loose ends."

A spark that was equal parts fear and understanding flared in Mason's eyes. In one convulsive movement, he lunged for the gun. Shaun didn't appear to notice; his eyes were fixed on the game warden's kneeling form. Before Mason was able to stop Shaun, a blast of noise exploded in my ears. The game warden's body sagged to the ground.

I was screaming. I heard the sound splitting my head, filling the room.

"How could you?" I cried. There was blood everywhere. I'd never seen so much blood. I turned away dizzily, afraid I'd pass out if I looked at it any longer. My whole body vibrated with shock. Shaun had shot him. Killed him. I had to get out. I couldn't worry about the storm—I had to run.

"What was that for?" Mason's heated voice erupted at Shaun. Mason looked shocked and sickened, and immediately crouched over the game warden's body, feeling his neck for a pulse. "He's dead."

"What was I supposed to do?" Shaun yelled back. "Britt didn't sell the story, and he was onto us. We did what we had to. We had to kill him."

"We?" Mason repeated. "Are you hearing yourself? We didn't kill him. You killed him." His eyes burned with hot wrath and seemed to reflect his thoughts—I didn't sign up for this. He stared at Shaun with guarded, watchful disgust, and from that single searing look, I realized something. At one point, they had been two criminals with a common predicament and goal. Not anymore. As Shaun grew increasingly unstable and unpredictable, I felt Mason peeling away. His desire to break from Shaun was written plainly on his face.

Shaun snatched the photograph of himself at the Subway shop and ripped it multiple times. He flung the pieces against the wall. Then he rifled through the game warden's pockets, taking out a small, curious-looking key and slipping it into his own coat pocket.

"They're onto us. We have to keep moving," he said, suddenly speaking far more rationally, like shooting the game warden had released the tightly wound coil inside him. "They're gonna be crawling all over the mountain soon. Looks like he got here on a snowmobile. The wind is so loud, we didn't hear the engine. He almost got us. But now we've got the snowmobile, and good thing—it will help us get over this damn snow faster. Grab one of his arms, Ace. We gotta hide the body."

"Give me the gun." Mason held out his hand, his tone uncompromising.

Shaun shook his head. "Grab an arm. Hurry up. We gotta move."

"You're not thinking clearly anymore. Hand over the gun," Mason repeated.

"I just saved your butt. I'm thinking straight; you're the one who's letting the heat get to you. We gotta do what we gotta do. We never should've come to the outpost. We should've done what I said and kept walking toward the highway. From now on, I call the shots. Grab an arm."

Mason glowered at him, but grabbed one of the game warden's limp arms. They dragged him out the front door, and before I knew what I was doing, I walked into the kitchen, took my coat off the back of the chair, and put it on. I opened the cupboard beneath the sink. My mind was in a fog, but the rest of my body acted with controlled deliberation, as if a switch had flipped and it had taken over. I ripped open the plastic bag and stuffed the pocketknife into my coat pocket.

I had to be ready to run. My chance was coming, I could feel it. I would find Calvin in the forest. Even if I failed, I would rather freeze out there than stay here with Shaun.

When I straightened, Mason and Shaun had rounded the outside corner of the cabin and were crossing in front of the window. At that moment, Mason caught my eye. His gaze fell on my pocketed hand. He watched me for several thick beats, his sharp brown eyes assessing.

Mason spoke to Shaun, and they set the body down. Right away, I knew Mason was coming back. I walked to the far end of the kitchen, out of the view of the window, and fumbled the knife out of my pocket. I stuffed it the only safe place I could think of—down my pants.

Mason crossed the threshold. "Take off your coat."

"What?"

He yanked on the zipper and wrenched the coat off himself. He searched through the pockets, both inside and out.

"What did you put in your pocket?"

"You're crazy," I stammered.

"I saw you hide something in your pocket."

"I'm cold. My hands are cold." If he felt them, he'd see it was the truth. My whole body felt frozen with fear.

He patted my arms, across the back of my torso, down my legs, and dug inside the elastic of my socks. "What are you hiding, Britt?"

"Nothing."

He glared down at me, his eyes shifting momentarily, suspiciously to my chest. My bra was one of only two places he hadn't checked. Immediately, he looked uncomfortable that he'd even had the thought, and averted his eyes.

"In the bathroom," he ordered. "Strip down and wrap a towel around yourself. You've got one minute. Then I'm coming in to search your clothes. Don't bother trying to stash anything in the vanity, the toilet, or down the drain—I'll search them too. I'll search the whole room."

CHAPTER
FIFTEEN

"I'm not hiding anything." My throat was dry with terror. If he searched me, he'd not only find the pocketknife; he'd discover Calvin's map too. If they had the map, they wouldn't need me. They'd kill me.

"Damn weather!" Shaun cursed loudly, his voice carrying through the patrol cabin's open front door. "It's snowing again. Get out here, Ace, and help me dump the body!"

More snow? I looked to the window to confirm it. Large, wet flakes flurried down. How was I going to escape if the weather worsened?

"I can't believe you're going to dump his body in the woods," I told Mason. I said it in hopes of pricking his conscience, but also to shift his focus away from searching me. "Think of his family. He deserves better. What Shaun did was awful."

If Mason planned on defending himself, he didn't get his

chance. A gale of bitterly cold wind rushed into the cabin, slamming the front door back against the wall, jarring us out of the conversation.

With one final torn look between me and the snowflakes flying through the doorway, Mason made his choice. He marched outside, banging the door closed behind him.

I went to the window. Shaun pointed at the game warden's body, then at the snowdrifts at the edge of the trees. They were going to shovel snow on the body and hope no one stumbled across it until they were out of the mountains.

I closed my eyes, calming the dizziness creeping in from the corners of my brain. I had the knife and the map. I would run. Tonight, while they slept. If I stayed with them to the highway, Shaun would kill me. I knew it as surely as I knew that snow was cold and fire was hot.

I would have one chance. If they caught me trying to escape, Shaun would either kill me on the spot, or let me live just long enough to wish he had.

I sat on the sofa, rocking back and forth, partly to keep warm and partly to steady my nerves. As cold and unfeeling as it was to do so, I had to push the game warden's death from my mind and rationally plan my next move. He was dead, I was alive. There was hope for me, but I could do nothing to change his fate.

I thought these words, but the image of his body pitching forward eclipsed everything. For the first time, I looked down through my splayed hands at my jeans. They were splattered with his blood. A dreamlike sensation floated inside me. It was like standing in the ocean's tide as it pushed and pulled; that strange, tipsy realization of being powerless against a much stronger force.

The cabin door slammed. Mason and Shaun peeled off their wet coats, hanging them to dry on the backs of the kitchen chairs. The fingers of their gloves bore sleeves of ice from digging in the snow.

"What are you looking at?" Shaun sneered at me on his way to the fireplace. He shoved a log into the flames, sending angry sparks flying from the grate. "Maybe the snow isn't such a bad thing," he said to Mason. "It will cover our tracks. It'll clog the main roads again, and it'll take time for them to plow. If we can't travel, they can't either. It buys us time. For now, we hang out here and wait for the snow to stop."

In the evening, Mason heated three cans of corn on the stove. He and Shaun ate at the kitchen table and I sat by the fire, soaking up heat before I braved the forest alone tonight. I ate the food but hardly tasted it. I chewed slower and slower. I tried to shut out their voices in the background and lose myself in another memory of Calvin, a new one, one I hadn't already played over and over in my mind to keep from going crazy here in this awful place.

Calvin had hurt me, and I hadn't forgotten that he'd kissed Rachel behind my back, but during the trauma of the past twenty-four hours, I'd curiously forgiven him. I couldn't focus on the negative right now. I had to stay positive and hopeful, even if that meant clinging to the good memories and blocking everything else. I needed a beacon to fix my sights steadfastly on. Right now, that beacon was Calvin. He was all I had.

When Mason came to collect my bowl, I saw a shadow of sympathy in his eyes. I looked away, purposefully rejecting his compassion. I would not ease his conscience. I would not let him think any of this was okay. It made me feel better to treat him with frigid hostility. I wanted to hurt him more than I wanted to hurt Shaun. Despite his protests, he was the better of the two, and that made me expect more from him.

Icy snow pelted the ranger patrol cabin throughout the evening. Even though the fire had warmed the three small rooms, I stayed bundled in my coat, boots, gloves, and scarf. It would save time later, when I would have to run at a moment's notice. I also had the knife stowed in my pocket. I hoped I'd know when it was the right time to use it.

I figured that when Mason and Shaun discovered I had escaped, they would expect me to head straight for Korbie, which ruled out going back for her. It wasn't an easy decision to come to, but if I wanted to keep us alive, I had to go for outside help. I wished there were some way to let Korbie know I was coming, that she just had to be patient. I could only imagine how isolated and terrified she must feel.

In the bathroom, I studied the map. I wouldn't have a compass tonight, not unless Shaun or Mason left one of theirs out in the open where I could easily grab it, but Calvin had detailed the map with enough landmarks that I could connect the dots to the ranger station, roughly six miles away. I could do this. I had to do this.

I rehearsed my plans, standing quietly by the window. It was only a surface calm. Deep down, I grew more and more frightened. How long could I last in the freezing woods without water, food, and shelter?

Shaun yawned loudly and closed himself in the bedroom, leaving me alone in the living room with Mason.

"I found a pair of wool socks in the bedroom," Mason told me, extending a pair of black Wigwam ski socks. "You might want to swap out the ones you're wearing so your feet stay dry."

"You found them—you take them," I said, snubbing him.

"I thought I'd offer them to you."

"Why would you do that?"

"Because I know how uncomfortable wet feet are."

"I don't want the socks." But my feet *were* damp and cold, and I would have given almost anything for fresh socks—almost. Just not my self-respect, in accepting a gift from the man who held me captive.

"Have it your way," he said with a shrug.

"If I had *my* way, I wouldn't be here with you."

"Take the sofa tonight," Mason offered, ignoring my biting tone. He threw his blanket in the rocking chair, claiming it, and peeled off his fleece jacket, leaving on his fitted gray thermal shirt. Next he took off his belt, presumably so it wouldn't grind into his hips while he slept. It was a harmless action, but somehow his undressing made the air in the room feel thicker.

Mason rotated his arms in wide circles, releasing tension in his shoulders. I didn't want to watch him, in case it gave the wrong impression, but when he didn't seem to notice me, I continued to study him in quick, stolen glances. He was taller than Calvin and more muscular. Not in a bulky, gym-rat way, but it was obvious he was athletic. His tight shirt revealed sculpted arms and a broad chest that tapered to a hard, flat stomach. It was difficult to recall what I'd first thought of him at the gas station, yesterday. Before I knew who he really was. That first meeting felt so very long ago. And I'd been so very wrong about him.

Finally, a more recent memory of Cal. It dropped into my head after I'd given up, and wasn't that the way it always happened? It was a good one. Our first trip to Jackson Lake as a couple. I'd been stretched out on a towel on the shore, reading *People* magazine. Calvin and his friends were taking turns racing jet skis around the buoys. I'd only finished one article when lake water, icy cold, dripped on my back.

I rolled over, startled, as Calvin flung himself playfully onto my towel and pulled me close to cuddle. He was soaking wet. I shrieked, trying halfheartedly to squirm away. The truth was, I loved that he'd left his friends to spend time with me.

"You didn't jet-ski very long," I pointed out.

"Long enough to keep the guys happy. Now I get to keep you happy."

I kissed him, slow and deliberate. "And how do you plan on doing that?"

He wiped a smudge of wet sand off my cheek with his thumb. We were propped on our elbows, facing each other, gazing into each other's eyes with an intensity that made my blood feel like it had been lit on fire. Just before he leaned in to kiss me back, the moment seemed to hold its breath, and I remembered thinking how perfect he was. How perfect we were.

I could have lived in that moment forever.

"Take first dibs on the bathroom," Mason told me, transporting me back to the thick of the nightmare. I tried to block him out. My mind was desperately fishing for more of the memory. I wanted to replay that perfect moment over and over.

Mason stopped stuffing his pillow into a laundered pillowcase and gave me a funny look, and I knew I hadn't erased the nostalgic, faraway expression from my face fast enough. He kept his emotions locked away, and I wanted to be equally self-controlled. But this time I'd slipped.

"You're thinking about him? The guy from 7-Eleven?" he asked gently.

I felt a flash of anger—not because he'd been perceptive enough to guess the truth, but because he'd brought up Calvin. I was stuck in this awful place and the only thing keeping me from losing it was Calvin, the memories of him and, yes, even the hopes, because as imperfect as our relationship had been, I still had hope for us. Things would be different this time. We knew each other better. We knew *ourselves* better. We'd grown up during the last year, and our maturity would show. Until I was far from this place, and back with Calvin, he was my secret life jacket, my sanctuary, the one thing Mason and Shaun couldn't take. If I lost Calvin, I lost everything. The nightmare would swallow me whole.

"I don't have to use the bathroom," I said curtly, again rejecting his kindness. I did have to pee, but thinking about my bladder would keep me awake through the night. The worst that could happen now would be to fall asleep and miss my chance. "And I'll take the rocking chair," I said coldly. "I slept fine in it earlier."

Mason appeared doubtful. "It doesn't look comfortable. Really, you can have the sofa. I'll feel better if you do." He shot me a brief, disparaging smile. "This is your chance to make me bear my load of the pain."

"Why does my comfort suddenly matter to you?" I lashed out. "You're holding me here against my will. You're forcing me to hike in exhausting, frigid, dangerous conditions. Am I supposed to believe you're suddenly worried how I feel? Because this is how I feel: I hate it here. And I hate you. More than I've ever hated anyone!"

A spark of emotion flickered over his face before it turned stoic again.

"I'm keeping you here because there is a blizzard outside. You wouldn't make it on your own. You're safer here with me, even though you don't believe it."

I was seized with rage. "I don't believe it. That's exactly the kind of lie you want me to believe to keep me passive and obedient. You're keeping me here because you need me to get you off this mountain, end of story. I hate you, and I'll kill you if I get the chance. Would love to, in fact!" They were strong words, and I realized I'd probably never carry out their threat. Even if I got the opportunity, I didn't believe myself capable of killing another human, but I wanted to make myself perfectly clear. None of this was okay.

I was angry and frustrated, but the truth was, the more I spent time with Mason, the harder it was to believe he was capable of killing another human. I'd seen the shock and horror on his face when Shaun brutally shot the game warden. And even though I'd originally suspected Mason had been involved in the death of the girl whose body I'd found at the cabin, I was starting to think he didn't have anything to do with it. He might not even know about the body.

"Just please take the sofa," Mason said one last time, his voice infuriatingly calm.

"Never," I breathed wrathfully. With a pointed look at him, I brushed his blanket onto the floor and sat in the rocking chair as grandly as if it were a throne. The curved bars dug into my back and the hard, wooden seat didn't have a cushion. I wouldn't be able to sleep twenty consecutive minutes. Every time I shifted, I'd be jarred awake. Meanwhile, Mason, who had to be exhausted, would sleep soundly on the sofa.

"Good night, Britt," Mason said uncertainly, clicking off the lamp.

I didn't respond. I didn't want him to think I was softening, or that I was letting him in. I wouldn't crack. As long as he kept me here, I would hate him.

I woke up damp with sweat. For several disoriented seconds, I couldn't remember where I was. The walls flickered with shadows, and I turned to find the source—the fire, which had died down, but gave off heat. As I stretched my legs, the rocking chair creaked, and that's when I remembered how vital it was that I not make a sound.

Mason stirred at the noise, but after a pause, his breathing resumed droning softly through the darkness. He lay sprawled on the sofa, his cheek pressed into the cushion, his mouth parted slightly, his too long legs and arms draping over the edges. He looked different with the firelight dancing on his face and a pillow hugged to his chest. He looked younger, boyish. Innocent.

His blanket had fallen off in the night, and as I walked silently past, I stepped over it, listening to the quiet rise and fall of his breathing. The air felt almost solid as I pushed my way toward the front door. Barely breaking stride, I greedily picked up a headlamp and canteen, which, to my great fortune, one of them had left on the kitchen bar. The canteen was full. An even better stroke of luck.

I put one foot in front of the other, eyes boring into the door handle, which seemed to slide out of reach with every step.

A heartbeat later, it was in my hand. My stomach somersaulted, part joy, part fear—there was no turning back now. I twisted the knob by the tiniest degrees. It reached the end of the rotation. All I had to do was pull. The pressure in the cabin would change slightly when I opened the door, but Mason wouldn't notice. He was deep in slumber. And the fire would chase away the cold draft I let in.

Suddenly I was on the porch, inching the door shut behind me. I half expected to hear Mason bolt to his feet and chase me, shouting for Shaun to wake up. But the only sound came from the bitterly cold wind striking snow, as fine as sand, at my face.

The woods were abysmally dark; I'd only made it one hundred

paces from the patrol cabin when, in a single backward glance, I could no longer see it. The night enveloped it in velvety blackness.

The wind whipped through my clothes and lashed at any patches of skin I hadn't managed to cover, but I was almost grateful for it. I was wide-awake from cold. And if Mason and Shaun came looking for me, it would be impossible for them to hear my movements above the fierce whistle hissing down the slopes. Bolstered by this line of thinking, I wrapped my coat more tightly around me, shielded my eyes from the blowing precipitation, and picked my way carefully up the steep slope riddled with rock fragments and tree stumps that hid beneath the snow. The rocks were jagged enough, and hard enough, that if I fell at the right angle, I could break a bone.

An owl hooted overhead. The sound carried into the midnight-black woods, mingling with the howl of wind tearing through the branches and clacking them together with haunting effect. I tried to quicken my pace, but the snow was too deep, and I continually sank forward on my knees, nearly dropping the canteen and headlamp in my arms. As tempted as I was to switch on the headlamp, I didn't dare yet. Until I was a safe distance from the patrol cabin, it would act like a beacon for Mason and Shaun to follow.

By the time I reached the summit, my climbing pace had lagged, and my breathing was labored. My legs trembled with exhaustion, and knots of stress seemed to ball like fists in my lower back. The anxiety of the past twenty-four hours had taken a toll—I'd never felt so sucked of energy, so small and powerless in the shadow of the treacherous mountains.

According to Calvin's map, I needed to get over this pass and down into the basin, which I could follow to the park ranger station. But there was no clear path, and as I waded through the snow, it crept higher up my boots, making each step increasingly heavy.

An itchy warmth prickled along the inseams of my clothes and under my arms. I'd broken a sweat, a mistake. Later, when I rested, the sweat would cool and freeze against my skin, rapidly lowering my body temperature. I'd have to worry about it when it happened. The park ranger station was miles away. I had to keep moving. But to be safe, I slowed my pace further.

Compacting snow between my gloves, I made a slushy ball, and pushed it into my mouth, letting the icy mixture melt down my throat. It was painfully cold, but invigorating. If I was sweating, I needed to drink. It seemed impossible that I could dehydrate in such cold weather, but I trusted the guidebooks and my training.

A hazy beam of light bobbed spottily in the woods ahead. Instinctively, I dropped behind a tree. I ground my back into it, forming a frantic, rapid conclusion. The light originated behind me, not very far away. I strained my ears, listening. A man's voice, shouting. The wind distorted his words, but he was hollering my name.

"Britt!"

I couldn't tell if it was Mason or Shaun, but I almost prayed it was Shaun. I stood a chance of escaping him. The forest was a vast maze; he'd never be able to track me.

"Britt! Not . . . hurt you. Stop . . . run!"

I wasn't above the tree line, but the dense woods sheltering the bottom of the mountain had thinned. I didn't have the cover

I needed, and though indeed it was indescribably dark, he had a flashlight. The minute I stepped into the open, he'd see me. I was trapped.

The light swerved away. With a moment to think, I decided to make a run for it. Breaking into the open, I lunged toward the next cluster of trees, using my free arm to propel myself faster. Far short of my target, I tripped, hands shooting out as I sprawled on the snow a split moment before the flashlight glided back, illuminating the darkness above my head. I army-crawled several more feet, dragging my supplies behind me and taking cover behind an outcropping of rock that jutted like an iceberg above the sea of snow.

I watched the beam from his flashlight scatter intermittent light through the branches ahead.

He was closer, moving up the mountainside far faster than I had. Squeezing the canteen and headlamp to my chest, I pushed to my feet and ran to another patch of trees.

". . . help each other!"

Help each other? I had the sickening urge to laugh. He thought I'd fall for that? He wanted off the mountain; as soon as I helped him, he'd kill me. I stood a better chance at survival facing the forest alone.

I set my provisions in the snow beside me. Planting my gloved hands on my thighs, I leaned forward, giving my upper body a moment's rest. I was breathing so loudly, I was sure he'd hear it. Each gulp of air scraped painfully down my throat. I was so light-headed, I feared I might pass out.

"Britt? It's Mason."

Damn, damn, damn.

He called out to me in a reassuring voice, but I wasn't going to let it fool me. "I know you can hear me," he continued. "You can't be far. There's another storm coming; that's why the wind has picked up. You can't stay out here. You'll freeze to death."

I squeezed my eyes shut against the gusting snow. *He's lying, he's lying!* I shouted the words at myself, because I felt my resolve weakening. I was frightened and desperate and cold, and to my amazement, I actually wanted to believe him. I wanted to trust that he'd help me. That scared me most of all. Because deep down, I knew the minute I moved out from behind the tree, I was dead.

From my hideout, I watched him kneel a short distance away and observe how my tracks had disrupted the snow. Even if I tried to run, it was inevitable. He'd catch me now or in five minutes.

"Think about it, Britt," Mason called. "You don't want to die out here. If you can hear me, call out my name."

Never, I thought at him.

I watched him pick up my trail and start jogging toward my hideout. I knew what was coming, but knowing my fate didn't dim the deeply embedded need to survive. I pushed to my feet and ran as hard as I could.

"Britt, stop!" he shouted.

"No!" I said, whirling around to face him. "*Never.*" I bit off the word. I would not go back. I would fight. I would die fighting rather than let him drag me back.

He started to shine the flashlight on me, thought better, and instead of blinding me, asked, "Are you okay?"

"No."

"You're hurt?" There was evident alarm in his voice.

"Just because I'm not hurt doesn't mean I'm okay."

He hiked uphill, approaching me cautiously. He circled me, scrutinizing me for injuries. His eyes fell on the ground, to my stolen provisions.

"You took a canteen and headlamp," he said, sounding almost impressed. Which made me feel a strange mix of pride and irritation. Of course I'd grabbed what I could. I wasn't helpless.

And then his voice turned serious, admonishing. "Three hours. That's how long you would have lasted out here on your own, Britt. Less, if this storm turns severe."

"I'm not going back." I sat in the snow, cementing my position.

"You'd rather die out here?"

"You're going to kill me anyway."

"I'm not going to let Shaun kill you."

I snapped my chin up. "Why should I believe you? You're a criminal. You belong in prison. I hope the police catch you and send you away for life. You didn't stop Shaun from killing the game warden or shooting that cop. Or from killing that girl in the cabin," I went on, before I could stop myself. I hadn't meant to tell Mason that I knew about the dead body, but it was too late for secrets now.

Mason's brows pulled together. "What girl?"

His confusion seemed genuine, but he was a good liar. And

damned if I was going to let him fool me again. "The storage room at the cabin, the one you forced me to stay in. There was a large toolbox with a dead body inside. You really expect me to believe you know nothing about it?"

A brittle pause.

"Did you tell Shaun about the body?" Mason asked, his voice unnaturally cool and calm. But his whole body had gone rigid, tight as a knot.

"Why? Did you kill her?" Cold dread trickled into my veins.

"You didn't tell Shaun."

"And I don't know why I didn't!" I fired back, as nervous as I was distraught. Had Mason killed her? I'd seen glimpses of a nicer guy, but maybe I'd been wrong. Maybe all along I'd let a few kind gestures distract me from seeing his true character. "You were never going to let me live, not from the first moment."

"I meant what I said; I'm not going to kill you. And neither is Shaun—I won't let him."

"Really," I breathed wrathfully. "Do you hear how stupid and empty that promise sounds? Shaun has the gun. He's in control. You're—nothing more than his pathetic lackey!"

Instead of taking offense, Mason watched me closely, as if trying to figure out my true frame of mind.

"Stand up," he said at last. "Your clothes are getting wet and your body temperature is going to drop."

"So? Let me die. I'm not going to help you off the mountain. I'm done helping you and Shaun. You can't force me to do it. I'm useless to you. Just let me go."

Mason hoisted me to my feet, swatting snow off my clothes. "Where's the tough little girl from before? The girl who wanted to backpack the Teton Range, damn the odds stacked against her?"

"I'm not her anymore. I want to go home," I said, my eyes filming. I missed my dad and Ian. They must be so worried about me.

"Pull yourself together," Mason instructed me. "You've been tested physically—now you have to be mentally tough. We're going back to the outpost. We're going to pretend like nothing happened. We won't tell Shaun. In the morning, you're going to get us off the mountain, and then we'll let you go."

I shook my head no.

"I'll carry you if I have to, but I'm not letting you die out here," Mason said.

"Don't touch me."

He flipped his palms up. "Then start walking."

"You're really not going to let me go, are you?"

"Go where? Into the forest, during a blizzard, where you'll freeze to death? No."

"I hate you," I said miserably.

"Yeah, you said that. Let's go."

CHAPTER SIXTEEN

The walk downhill to the ranger patrol cabin should have been far easier than the climb I'd just made, but each step felt heavier than the last. I had failed. Mason promised to keep my secret, but what assurance did I have that Shaun wouldn't be pacing the floor with his gun when we made it back? I could be marching to my own slaughter.

I'd witnessed Mason trying to stop Shaun from shooting the game warden—I was sure that was his intent when he lunged for the gun—and maybe he was a better person than I was giving him credit for. But it didn't matter where Mason drew the line between right and wrong. Shaun had the gun.

And there was the girl's body back at the first cabin. I didn't know who had killed her, but the way Mason had reacted when I'd told him about it didn't sit well with me. He was keeping something from me, and from Shaun too, it seemed.

At last the patrol cabin appeared out of the darkness. I was almost to the front porch, when I found myself flying backward as Mason yanked me toward him. His gloved hand clamped over my mouth, and for one wild moment, I thought he was trying to suffocate me. His breath panted in my ear, his body a stiff wall at my back.

The patrol cabin's front door was open, Calvin's voice drifting through it.

My heart accelerated. Calvin. Here. He'd found me!

"Where are they?" Calvin demanded from out of sight.

"I don't know what you're talking about," Shaun answered sulkily.

Mason scooped me up, immune to my kicking and thrashing, and hauled me silently to the top of the porch steps. We could view both men through the kitchen window. Calvin must have surprised Shaun in his sleep, because he held him at gunpoint. I didn't recognize the gun. Calvin must have brought it with him from Idlewilde; I knew the Versteegs kept guns at the cabin. Shaun's gun was nowhere in sight. To my dismay, a lamp had been turned on in the living room, making it impossible for Calvin to see me on the other side of the kitchen window—it was far too dark outside by comparison. If he glanced this way, he'd only see the cabin's interior reflected in the windowpane.

I tried to scream his name, but Mason's glove crushed my mouth ruthlessly. I kicked at his shins, my heel colliding with bone before he shoved me against the outer wall with shocking force. I'd sorely underestimated his strength, and found myself outmatched; his free hand captured both my wrists, and he dug his knee into the flesh at the back of my leg, until I couldn't stand the pain any longer and went limp. He took advantage of this unguarded moment to grind his body viciously against mine, trapping me between him and the cabin. My cheek was shoved up against the icy shutter, and I strained to see Calvin through the window.

"There are three bowls in the sink, three glasses on the counter!" Calvin growled. "I know Korbie and Britt were here with you." He strode to the sink, hastily inspecting the bowls with a swipe of his finger. "The food's moist. They were here recently. Where are they now?"

"Maybe I used all three bowls," came Shaun's surly reply.

Calvin hurled a glass at Shaun's head. He ducked, and the glass shattered against the wall behind him. When he faced Calvin again, he'd blanched slightly.

"Did you kill them?" Calvin's stride didn't break as he marched up to Shaun, aiming the gun at point-blank range. His voice shook with rage, but his gun hand remained steady. "Did you?"

Shaun fidgeted with his hands uneasily. "I'm not a killer," he answered, in a tone far too guileless to be believable.

"No?" Calvin said in a soft, deadly voice. "I know you. I've seen you around. At Silver Dollar Cowboy Bar. You like to get girls really drunk and take their picture like some pervert."

I watched the play of emotion on Shaun's face. His artless act drained from it, replaced with fear. "I don't know what you saw, it wasn't me, I don't take pictures of girls, I don't even own a camera, I'm never up here in the mountains. . . ."

"What kind of perverted things do you do with the pictures?" Calvin demanded. "I saw you with that girl, the socialite who went missing. Maybe I should tell the cops."

"You've—got the wrong guy," Shaun stammered.

"Where's my sister? Where's Britt? Start talking or I will tell the cops!" Calvin was yelling now. "Did you take pictures of them? Did you think you could blackmail my family? Or post the pictures online to harass my sister? Or sell them?"

Shaun visibly swallowed. "No."

"I'm not going to ask again—where are the girls?"

"You have to believe me, we never meant no harm. We took them in 'cause they were stranded and we couldn't let them freeze with the storm blowing in—"

"We?"

"Me and my buddy, Ace. He was here when I went to sleep; he must have run off with her. It's him you want—"

"'Her'? Who's 'her'?"

"Britt. He took Britt. She was here with us. I think he had a thing for her, but I never touched her, I can swear on my mother's grave to that. Check the woods. Maybe he dragged her out, wanted some privacy. Go take a look."

"What about Korbie? Where's she?"

"Ace made me leave her at the cabin, before we hiked here. He said we didn't have enough supplies for both girls. I left her food and water, even though Ace told me not to. I made sure she'd be safe."

"You left my sister alone in a cabin?" Calvin demanded. "Which cabin?"

"A few miles from here. Sits far back from the road. Blue curtains in the windows. Lawn has turned to weeds. Nobody's been up for years."

"I know the one. The snowmobile out front—where's the key?"

Shaun didn't answer right away, clearly reluctant to give up his recent windfall. "Don't know. It was parked out front when we arrived. It's not ours," he said. "Looks like its rider ran out of gas and left it here. Doubt it's worth the trouble of trying to hot-wire."

Calvin leveled the gun at him. "Don't lie to me. Give me the key. Now."

"You wouldn't shoot me. They'd figure out it was you. Nobody's up in the mountains, not with this storm. Only you, me, Ace, and the girls."

"Don't worry, I won't leave anything for them to find."

Calvin fired.

The staccato bursts pierced my ears, startling me. Behind me, Mason's body jerked forcefully—he was just as shocked. I had watched Shaun kill the game warden, I had watched pieces of human tissue spray the walls, but that had not prepared me for watching Calvin kill in cold blood.

It couldn't be happening. My mind groped through the madness, trying to find some way to justify Calvin's violence. Why hadn't he tied Shaun up and turned him over to the authorities? That he'd kill Shaun without any real evidence of Shaun's having hurt Korbie and me was unthinkable. Was he so worried about us that he wasn't thinking clearly?

I had to get to Calvin. I had to reassure him I was alive, and calm him down. Together we could leave this horrible place.

More determinedly, I thrashed against Mason's hold. His fingers dug into my skin, but any pain floated just outside my awareness. The only thought pounding clearly in my mind was of reaching Calvin. I'm here! I screamed wildly at him in my mind. I'm right outside!

Inside, Calvin kicked Shaun's lifeless form, making sure he was dead. He searched his pockets. Calmly, he took the cash from Shaun's wallet, and the snowmobile key. He strode into the bedroom where Shaun had slept, reappearing a moment later with Shaun's gun, which he tucked into his belt. In a hurried exploration of the kitchen drawers, he found a Zippo lighter.

At first I didn't understand why he lit the living room curtains on fire. And then it came to me. Shaun had been right. The police would suspect Calvin of killing him. They might even suspect Calvin of the game warden's murder. He had to destroy the evidence.

Thick black smoke poured off the sofa, which Calvin lit on fire next, and bright flames surged up the walls. I could not believe how quickly the fire caught. It rushed from one piece of furniture to the next, heavier smoke billowing to fill the room.

As Calvin strode toward the front door, Mason wrestled me into a dark corner of the porch. From our hiding spot, I heard Calvin's boots clap against the porch steps as he trotted down them.

He was leaving. Without me.

I wrenched from side to side, desperately trying to fight my way free, but Mason was too strong; his grip was steel. I couldn't run. I couldn't yell. My muffled screams were too low to be heard over the wind and crackle of the fire. Calvin was leaving. I had to stop him. I couldn't bear to stay with Mason another minute.

The snowmobile started with a rumble. In a matter of seconds, the drone of the engine faded into the distance.

Mason let go. I collapsed against the porch railing. I could feel my heart breaking, splintering into irreparable fragments. Pressing my face into my folded arms, I made a deep sound of agony. Tears streamed down my face. The nightmare was dragging me back, to a depth I had not known existed.

"Stay here," Mason said urgently. "I'm going in for our gear."

Pulling his coat up to protect his head, he darted through the open door. I could have run. At that moment, I could have raced for the trees. But I knew he would track me. And he had the gear. He was right: I wouldn't last long on my own.

Slowly, I backed my way down the porch steps, too much in shock that Calvin had left without me to be fully aware of the fire. In a haze, I watched the bright flames lick across the floor and sparks rain from the ceiling. The crackle and hiss of the fire had grown to a roar. Through the smoke, I caught fleeting glimpses of Mason thrusting whatever he could into our packs. Even from this distance, heat blasted through the doorway, drenching my face in sweat. Mason had to be sweltering.

At last he staggered through the door, coughing violently, two packs slung over his shoulders. His face was coated in black soot, and when he blinked, it made the whites of his eyes stand out. My expression must have hinted at this monstrous sight; he wiped his coat sleeve across his face, smearing most of the soot away.

Heavy snow swirled down between us, freckling the grime clinging to his cheeks.

"The storm is hitting full force," he told me. "We need to find shelter before it's too late."

CHAPTER SEVENTEEN

Mason was right. Wet, heavy snow was driving down the face of the mountain. Since the ground was already covered from the earlier storms, the snow accumulated quickly. I watched it creep up the tree trunks and sag their branches. No one was getting up the mountain now. Not the police, not my dad. We were on our own. And I could think of nothing more terrifying.

We had to get out of the weather. I knew of no nearby cabins, which left finding a fallen tree or a cave for shelter. As we slogged on, Mason took off his fleece cap and handed it to me. I'd grown suspicious and resentful of his small gestures of kindness over the past day and a half, but this time I took the hat gratefully. My socks were damp from earlier, and my teeth were beginning to clatter. I was willing to risk my pride for whatever warmth I could salvage.

"Thank you," I told him.

He nodded, his lips a bloodless blue. His cropped hair glistened with snow. I knew I should give him the hat back, but I was freezing too. So I looked away and pretended not to see.

The smart thing would have been to consult Calvin's map. It would show the closest shelter. But I didn't know how to look at the map without letting Mason see it too. If he knew about the map, he wouldn't need me. He could take the map and then it would be every man for himself. Plus, if the map got wet, the ink would probably bleed. Worse, the paper might tear or disintegrate.

We hiked for a long time, each step slow and cautious, making sure there wasn't any debris hiding beneath the snow before we put our full weight down. The storm clouds blotted out the moon, making it darker than ever, even with flashlights. My toes became numb with cold. Even when I clamped my jaw shut, I could not stop my teeth from chattering. I squinted against the arctic blasts of wind, focusing on Mason's boots ahead. Every time he took a step, I forced myself to do likewise. His height and broad shoulders blocked the worst of the wind, but it found me, penetrating my coat and licking ice over my skin. Soon, my brain shut down and I put my energy into simply moving forward.

And then my thoughts went where they always did. To Calvin.

CHAPTER EIGHTEEN

"I'm coming out," Korbie announced from behind the dressing room door at JCPenney. I heard the swish of silky fabric as she shuffled over to slide the bolt free. "Don't lie, because I'll know right away if you are."

I sat on the bench in the dressing room directly across the hallway, my door wide open. Hurrying to finish my text, I hit send and dropped my phone sneakily into my purse. As I did, I felt a squeeze of guilt. I didn't like hiding things from Korbie. "I'm offended you think I'd lie," I said—but not without a pang of conscience.

Korbie stepped out in a violet corseted gown that fluttered around her ankles as she completed a Disney-princess twirl. "Well? What do you think?"

"It's purple."

"So?"

"You told me Bear hates purple."

She made an exasperated gesture. "That's why I'm wearing it. To help him change his mind. If he sees how great I look in purple, he'll realize he loves it."

"Are you going to make him wear a matching purple bow tie?"

"Um, yes," Korbie said, rolling her eyes at the stupidity of the question. "It's prom. We have to coordinate. Our picture might end up in the yearbook."

"Yearbook photos are black and white."

"You're not making this very fun. At least try one dress on," Korbie begged, pulling on my hands in an effort to get me off my butt. "Last year we went prom dress shopping together and both of us participated. I want this year to be like last year. What is wrong with the boys at our school? I can't believe one of them hasn't asked you yet."

I didn't tell Korbie that Brett Fischer had asked me to prom and I'd turned him down. I was off the market, unofficially dating someone. I didn't know how much longer I could keep the secret, because that's what it was, a secret that I'd sworn to keep before I realized this particular secret would burn a hole in my chest.

My cell phone chimed in my purse.

"Who's texting you?" Korbie wanted to know.

"Probably my dad," I said, feigning boredom with a flick of my ponytail.

A scandalized smile spread across Korbie's face. "Do you have a secret lover, Britt, darling?" she teased.

"Yes," I deadpanned, but I ducked my head so she wouldn't see me blush.

"Well, I hope you find a date soon," she said seriously, "because I won't have any fun at prom if I know you're at home watching a movie, eating ice cream and getting fat. Oh, I know! What about that guy who always talks to you on the way out of math class?"

"Um, Mr. Bagshawe?"

Korbie snapped her fingers, whipping her arm from hip to hip like a backup dancer in a music video. "That's the one. An older, illicit lover. That's how my girl Britt rolls."

"Next dress, please," I said.

When she disappeared behind her dressing room door, I grabbed my cell phone. Calvin's text was waiting.

Can I see you tonight?

Whaddya have in mind? I texted back.

Sneak out around eleven. Bring your swimsuit. I'll be the guy in the hot tub with drinks.

The Versteegs had a backyard pool and hot tub, and as much as I wanted to be with Calvin tonight, I was tired of the extra work that went into these secretive, late-night meet-ups.

Calvin had told me that Korbie couldn't find out about us yet—no one could. He'd convinced me that keeping our relationship secret made it exciting. I wanted to tell him I was seventeen now, above secrets and games. But I worried he'd take it the wrong way. He was almost nineteen, after all. Who was I to give him relationship advice?

"I can hear you texting," Korbie singsonged through the dressing room door. I heard a zipper snag as she tried on another dress. "You're supposed to be giving me your undivided attention. Ugh! Why don't we have a real department store? I love how we have a ten-to-one McDonald's-to-people ratio but no Macy's. I'm going to have to order a dress online."

It was hard to think about prom when I knew I wasn't going. I *wanted* to go, but Calvin wasn't ready to take our romance public.

Instead of focusing on the depressing realization that I wasn't going to prom, and wouldn't be doing any of the fun, girly things that went along with it, I forced myself to think positively. I was dating Calvin Versteeg. The love of my life. In the big scheme of things, what was one silly school dance?

It had been hours since Calvin kissed me good-bye after school, when we'd slipped into an empty classroom and made out until we heard the janitor pushing his cart down the hall. I bit my lip to suppress a smile. Calvin and I had known each other our whole lives. Hardly a day had passed that I hadn't seen him. He used to yank my ponytail and call me Britt the Brat. Now he ran his finger affectionately down my cheek when we talked, and he kissed me in stolen moments and forbidden encounters.

I had to admit, it *was* kind of exciting.

Sometimes.

And then there were the other times.

Like last week when Calvin's best friend, Dex Vega, caught us making out behind the baseball diamonds, long after the team had finished practice. I'd had my back pressed to the driver's-side door of Calvin's truck, and he was leaning into me, leaving zero space between our bodies.

Dex gave us the standard "Get a room," because he wasn't very creative. He ran track with Calvin and was great at hurdles. Not so great with everything else.

"Been there, done that," Calvin told him, winking at me conspiratorially. I knew Cal wouldn't like it if I disputed this in front of his best friend, but we had *not* slept together.

Dex's eyes gave me a full-body rake. The way he grinned at me made me feel slimy. "Thought you didn't have a girlfriend, Versteeg."

I knew we'd agreed to keep our relationship quiet for now, but wasn't this the perfect opportunity to finally be open about it? Why did Calvin feel the need to lie to his best friend? Why was he asking me to lie to *my* best friend? Calvin had a reputation as a player who couldn't commit, and he'd never had a serious girlfriend, but this was different. I was different. He cared about me.

I was certain of it. I only wished I didn't sound like I was trying hard to convince myself.

"I don't," Cal said.

They laughed, slugged each other affably, then exchanged a tricky handshake.

"Dude, your hair is sticking up everywhere," Dex said.

Dex was right. I'd been mussing Calvin's thick brown hair, and the tips were pointing to the sky.

I thought Calvin would laugh it off, but he bent to look in the side mirror and said, "Damn, Britt, I have dinner with my parents after this." He tried ineffectively to smooth his hair down.

"So? You're going to shower before dinner, aren't you?" I said, growing tired of sitting quiet while Calvin and Dex made me feel invisible.

"You sound like my dad, always telling me what I should be doing next," he complained. "Stick to kissing, will you? It's what you're good at."

Dex snorted his amusement and sauntered off.

When Calvin and I were alone again, I said accusingly, "Why did you let Dex think we've had sex?"

"Because, babe," he said, slinging his arm over my shoulder, "any day now we will."

"Oh, yeah? That's funny, because I want to wait. So when were you going to tell me?"

He laughed off my question, but I wasn't joking. I really did want to hear his answer.

"Tell Mr. Bagshawe he should cut me some slack on our next unit test if he doesn't want me to dish on your secret fornication," Korbie snickered, pulling me out of the memory.

When I didn't answer, she added, "You're not offended, are you? You know I'm only kidding. I know you're not with Mr. Bagshawe. You'd never go out with a guy and not tell me."

Well, that did it. I made up my mind. No swimming tonight, I texted Calvin, hoping he didn't assume I was having my period. We'd been together for weeks, and I knew him in a way I'd never known another guy, but we weren't to the point where I wanted him bringing me ibuprofen and a heating pad for my cramps.

When am I gonna see you in a bikini? he texted back. One with strings I can undo . . .

When you come clean about us, I texted. My thumb hovered over the send button.

In the end, I deleted the text. I wasn't going to manipulate my boyfriend. I was seventeen now, above games.

CHAPTER NINETEEN

I did not know how long Mason walked with his arm under my shoulders, propping me up, urging me forward. As we plodded heavily downhill, looking for any refuge from the weather, I shook myself awake, realizing I must have been falling in and out of sleep for some time. Under other circumstances I would have recoiled from Mason, the idea of touching him repellent, but I was too exhausted to care.

He spoke in my ear. I could tell by the tone of his voice that he was excited. I lifted my drooping eyelids, taking in the endless, swirling white landscape. He pointed toward something ahead. When I saw it too, my heart surged with joy.

We hobbled over to the fallen tree with its intricate network of roots now exposed aboveground. Clumps of frozen mud filled in the gaps, and the effect was something of a cave, a secret hideaway from the weather. Mason helped me crawl under the canopy of gnarled, twisted roots, then came in after me. Protected from the snow and wind, I felt the weight of hopelessness roll away. The tree smelled of dirt and decay, but the place was dry. And compared to the buffeting winds outside, almost balmy.

Mason pulled off his gloves to blow on his hands and rub them briskly together. "How are your feet?"

"Wet." It was the lengthiest response I could manage. My teeth hurt from knocking together, and my lips had hardened into painful strips of ice.

He frowned. "I'm worried you could have frostbite. You should have—" He caught himself in mid-sentence, but I knew what he had meant to say. I should have taken the dry wool socks he'd offered when I'd had the chance.

I'd lost feeling in my feet. Even the uncomfortable tingling had gone away. It was hard to muster up concern over frostbite when I couldn't feel pain . . . and when I was so bone-weary that my brain couldn't grasp a single thought.

"Here, drink some water before you fall asleep," Mason instructed, passing me a canteen.

I took a few sips, but my eyelids were already drifting downward. In that half-conscious moment, I felt my dad and Ian praying for me. They knew I was in trouble, and they were on their knees, asking God to strengthen me. A calm warmth spread through me and I exhaled softly.

Don't give up on me, I thought across the vast distance that separated us.

It was my last groggy thought before falling asleep.

When I woke, milky light streamed through the twisted mesh of roots above. Morning sunlight. I'd slept for hours. I felt Mason stir beside me, and realized with a start that I'd slept curled against his body. I scooted backward, and immediately regretted it as cold air swarmed to fill the void where our bodies had touched.

"You awake?" he asked, his voice husky with sleep.

I sat up, my head brushing the roots. It was then that I noticed Mason had spread waterproof ground mats beneath us and covered us with blankets and the sleeping bag. I was also surprised to find Mason's boots on my feet. They were large, but he'd tied the laces tight, and my toes felt toasty warm. His own feet were covered in a thick, woolly pair of high-quality hiking socks, but I doubted even they were keeping out the biting air.

"Your socks were soaked through," he explained.

"You didn't have to give me your boots," I said, feeling very grateful he had.

"I hung your boots and socks to dry." He pointed to the drying rack he'd jury-rigged from one of the lower protected roots. "But until we get a fire started, they're going to do more hanging than drying."

"Fire," I said slowly, savoring the word. Delicious longing crept through me at the thought of real heat.

"It's not snowing right now. Good time to find wood." He reached across me and started unlacing his boots from my feet. Of course he would need his boots if he was going out to collect firewood, but the easy, familiar way that he touched me took me off guard. The only boy who'd ever touched me so intimately was Calvin.

Mason slipped the boots off my heels and put them onto his own feet. Somewhat shyly, I gave him back his fleece hat.

"How much snow did we get?" I asked.

"Several inches. Any roads up the mountain that were open are definitely closed now. We're on our own for a couple more days, until they can plow. Don't worry," he said, looking at me suddenly, as if realizing this news might alarm me. "As long as we keep our heads, we'll be fine. I've survived worse."

I felt strangely reassured by his company. But I couldn't help wondering if Mason's confidence stemmed from knowing that the roads were clogged and the police couldn't come after him. He had time to plan his next move. This seemed to boost his spirits, but made mine shred further. No one was coming to rescue me. I knew Calvin wouldn't stop looking for me—he'd find Korbie and come back for me as soon as he could—but I couldn't count on him. I couldn't count on my dad. I couldn't rely on the police. One by one, I felt rocks begin to drop on my chest.

"You're not going far, are you?" I asked Mason as he crawled out of our hideaway.

He studied me curiously for a moment; then a look of amusement flickered in his eyes. "Worried I won't come back?"

"No, it's just . . ."

Yes, that summed it up.

Oddly, only hours before, I had tried to run away from him. I hadn't trusted him then, and I wasn't sure I could trust him now. He still needed me to help him off the mountain, which was probably the only reason I was alive. Or was it? Did I really think Mason could—would—kill me? If he'd killed the girl whose body I'd found at the cabin, then he was capable of killing again. But I wasn't sure who to pin her death on. And I wasn't about to ask Mason again—it wasn't in my best interest to provoke him.

"I'm going to dig for dry twigs around the base of the trees," Mason said. "I should be back in a half hour."

"See if you can find pine pitch, too," I said.

"Pine pitch?"

"Sap. It's sticky but easy to pull off, and it burns like gasoline when ignited." Calvin had taught me the trick years ago.

A little smile of approval rose in Mason's eyes. Just for a moment, it seemed to soften his serious, closed-off expression. "Pine pitch it is."

I slept until Mason returned. I heard him crawl under the awning of roots, and even though I was stiff with cold, I scooted over to watch him light the fire. I didn't want to be a nuisance or a show-off, but maybe I could offer him a few other pointers. I hadn't expected to put my training to use in such dire circumstances, but I was suddenly immensely grateful I'd mastered at least some basic survival skills.

Mason set four smaller logs side by side, forming a platform. He wiped the sticky globs of pine pitch onto the platform, pausing only to wink at me. Then he used twigs to construct a ventilated tepee. This took time, and so did getting the twigs to ignite with the fire starter. Finally, a spark took and the twigs began to smoke, then burn.

"We'll be warm soon," he promised.

Warm. I'd almost forgotten the feeling.

"Why are you helping me, Mason?" I asked him.

He shifted uneasily, then settled into thoughtful silence. At last he said, "I know you don't believe me, but I never meant to hurt you. I want to help you. I wanted to help you from the beginning, but things got—out of hand," he said remotely.

"Were you scared of Shaun? Scared of going against him?" I'd thought Shaun was scared of Mason, but maybe I'd gotten it wrong.

Mason didn't answer.

"I'm not sorry he's dead, but I am sorry you lost him. I'm sorry you had to see him die."

Mason gave a bitter laugh, wagging his head between his knees. "Me too," he said heavily. "You have no idea."

"I didn't think he would die like—that," I added quietly, still unnerved by Calvin's heedless decision to kill Shaun.

"Forget about Shaun," Mason said, his eyes momentarily darkening with regret. He blinked, seemingly clearing away any lingering reluctance to accept that Shaun was really gone. "Just you and me from now on. A team, right?" He extended his hand.

I eyed it, but didn't clasp it. "Why should I trust you?"

"This feels like a job interview. 'Why should I hire you?' 'Why are you the best person for the job?'"

"I'm serious."

A shrug. "I'm all you've got."

"That's not a reason to trust you. If I were stuck in this tree-cave with Shaun, I wouldn't trust him, even if he were the only other human for a hundred miles."

"It's more of a burrow, really."

I resisted the urge to sigh. "Why do you need me? You know how to start a fire. You've clearly spent time in the woods—you're good at tracking. Why not leave me here and fend for yourself?"

"Is that what you want?"

"Of course not," I said quickly, shuddering at the thought of facing the immense reach and brutality of the mountains alone. "I mean, our chances of survival increase if we stick together."

"My thoughts exactly."

"So you're using me."

"No more than you're using me."

I fell silent. There was a certain relief in finally being able to ask Mason questions, but our exchange wasn't as satisfying as it should have been. I got the distinct impression he wasn't giving me straightforward answers. He gave me just enough, a nibble of bait, nothing more.

"You want a reason to trust me?" he finally said, uncannily sensing my frustration. "My name isn't Mason. It's Jude."

I flinched. "What?"

He reached into his back pocket and opened his wallet. His driver's license was tucked behind a plastic see-through inset, and he dug it out, passing it to me.

I looked at the Wyoming driver's license issued to Mason K. Goertzen.

"Looks real, doesn't it?" Mason said. "It's not." He then passed me a second driver's license, which had been carefully hidden behind the first. Only this time, he slid his thumb to hide his last name and address.

The second driver's license had the same photo as the first, but was issued in California.

"I don't understand," I said.

"I didn't want Shaun to know my real name."

"Why not?"

"I didn't want him to have anything on me, in case we had a falling-out. I didn't trust him. And while I'm not sure I can trust you, either, I'm putting myself out there. I'm hoping you'll meet me halfway. If I open up to you, maybe I can convince you to share your secrets."

"I don't have a secret identity. I don't have any secrets," I argued, wondering what kind of ploy this was, what information he wanted to lure from me now.

"That's not true. You told me that you and Korbie came up to the mountains alone."

I frowned. "We did."

"Then what's your ex doing here? Calvin, that's his name, right? The roads are closed. He must have come up before the first storm hit, two days ago. Did you know he'd be up here?"

"What if I did?" I said defensively.

"Why didn't you mention him? Back at the cabin, before you knew Shaun was dangerous, why didn't you tell us the truth?"

Because I was interested in Shaun, and didn't want to ruin my chances by bringing up my ex. It was too shameful a truth to confess, so I gave him an answer that let me live with myself.

"Maybe I didn't fully trust Shaun or you, and wanted an ace up my sleeve, just in case. Turns out I was smart—Calvin took Shaun completely by surprise." It now struck me that if I hadn't tried to escape from the ranger patrol cabin, Calvin would have taken all of us by surprise, and I'd be with him now. The realization seemed to knock me breathless, like a punch to the stomach.

"Do you think Calvin is at Idlewilde?" asked Mason.

"I don't know." But I did think Calvin was there. If he'd found Korbie, he would take her to Idlewilde.

"Can you find Idlewilde from here?"

I stared at Mason, trying to figure out what he was planning. I had Calvin's map and I could lead us to Idlewilde. But why would Mason want to help me get to Idlewilde?

"I think so," I said at last, not sure I should commit to anything until I had untangled his endgame.

"Is Idlewilde closer than the ranger station?"

"About a mile closer."

"Then I think we should go there. What kind of guy is Calvin?"

"You have to ask?" I scoffed. "He doesn't let anyone mess with him. You saw that. When you took us hostage, you had no idea what you were getting into. Calvin won't give up until he finds me. He's gone to look for Korbie, but he'll be back. You have every reason to be scared, Mason," I warned.

"Jude," he corrected.

"Is that really what you want me to call you?" I asked, with a touch of exasperation. "I've been calling you Mason this whole time. I'm not sure I can see you as anyone else."

His eyes jumped to mine, and a strange, unfathomable look passed over his face. "Try."

"Jude," I said, with even more aggravation. "Jude," I repeated, softer this time, experimenting with the sound of it. I actually believed I preferred it, though I'd never confess that to him. "It's short; I always preferred boys' names with two syllables. And it reminds me of that Beatles song. Or Jude Law, who you look nothing like," I added quickly.

He stroked his jawline in mock consideration. "True, he's got nothing on me."

In spite of myself, I laughed out loud. And immediately regretted it, when Mason—Jude—grinned back, clearly pleased with his joke. The grin seemed to open his entire face, softening the steely angles and warming his hooded, aloof eyes. For a moment, I found the picture both sexy and alluring—but I immediately resented my attraction. It wasn't real. If Stockholm syndrome existed, I was sure my attraction was an early symptom of it.

Even so. Maybe I would call him Jude after all. If we were going to work together to stay alive, it might be helpful to think of him as someone different. Not the guy who'd abducted me, but someone with a dark past. Someone who hadn't stood up to Shaun, but had wanted to. Someone who would help me, if I helped him.

"I was named after Jude the Apostle, also known as Jude, patron saint of lost causes."

I eyed him doubtfully. "Patron saint of lost causes? Is that even true?"

"Of course it's true. I'm here with you, aren't I?"

I tilted my chin up. "Are you suggesting I'm a lost cause?"

"Actually," he said, his face growing serious, "the opposite. I think you're more capable than people give you credit for. Sometimes I wonder what kind of girl you were before you came on this trip."

He wondered about me? What other things did he think about me?

He eyed me in a way that made me feel increasingly transparent—and uncomfortable—and continued, "I watched how you and Korbie interacted, and it made me wonder if, back home, in front of your friends and family, you offer a slightly different version of the real Britt. A less capable version. You're not that girl here in the mountains. I like that you face your fears. And while it's not normally something people consider as a virtue, you're a very gifted liar. How many times did you coax Shaun's hand with a convincing lie?"

I did not like the long, cool stare of his brown eyes on me, and quickly exclaimed, "If kidnapping and abduction don't pan out for you, I'm sure you could give psychic reading a try!"

He rubbed his thumb and index finger together, as if expecting money. "The least you can do is give me my first tip."

"Here's a tip: Next time, try sticking to a story that isn't so outlandish and off base; your victim might actually believe it."

This time, it was my turn to feel smugly pleased when his eyes glittered with amusement. I might be stuck in the wilderness, but hey, at least I hadn't lost my sense of humor.

"Do you think it's strange Calvin shot an unarmed man?" Jude asked, reverting back to our earlier topic.

I hesitated. I wanted to defend Calvin. I'd worked out in my head every possible way to justify his actions. He'd been frantic with worry. He'd believed Shaun had hurt Korbie and me. He had made the best move under the circumstances. I told myself these things, but I was deeply troubled by Calvin's decision.

Drawing a sharp breath, I said, "No, I don't. He knew Shaun was lying. Calvin isn't stupid. He knew Korbie and I were—are—in danger, and he knew Shaun was at least partially responsible. Anyway, Shaun was hardly innocent. How many times did he hold a gun on me and Korbie? We were unarmed. You didn't seem to care then. You're just angry because Shaun was your friend. If their roles had been reversed, Shaun would have shot Calvin without a moment's thought. You can't honestly tell me Shaun felt any remorse when he shot the game warden. And don't forget about the police officer he shot before you fled to the mountains, or the girl he sent to the hospital. Shaun had no regard for life. I'm not sorry Calvin shot him."

Jude nodded. Not in a way that made me think he agreed with me. It was more that he now understood my frame of mind, and took note of it. "I definitely think we should go to Idlewilde. Assuming Calvin can find Korbie, he'll take her there. Which means getting you to Idlewilde, and reuniting you with your friends, should be our top priority."

I stared at him curiously. For the second time I asked, "Why are you helping me?"

He leaned back against the roots, lacing his fingers behind his head and crossing his ankles, looking for all the world like a carefree lumberjack. "Maybe I'm in this for me. It's in my best interest to explain myself to Calvin. I wouldn't want him to shoot me too," he suggested lightly enough, but—perhaps I imagined it—with a touch of dark severity.

CHAPTER TWENTY

Jude and I sat on ground mats and a sleeping bag under the uprooted tree, huddled around the fire, soaking up every last ripple of heat. Jude asked a few more questions about Calvin, which made me think he *was* scared of him, but mostly we kept the conversation light.

As Jude talked, I found myself wondering about him. Why he'd left California. How he'd fallen into an uneasy friendship—or maybe "partnership" was the better word—with Shaun. I wanted to question him, but I was afraid he'd see it as a trick to get him to reveal details that I could use later to help the police identify him. Which, in part, *was* my intent. I had a moral obligation to aid the police in capturing Jude. But on a more personal level, I was growing increasingly curious about him. For reasons I didn't want to dissect.

I was beginning to doze off to the low, pleasant timbre of Jude's voice, when without warning he said, "Once we get to Idlewilde, Calvin is going to want to turn me over to the authorities. It was Shaun's idea to abduct you, but I went along with it." He frowned. "He might even try to use physical force to detain me."

Suddenly fearful that Jude would change his mind about helping me to Idlewilde, I quickly said, "We can tell Calvin that you turned on Shaun and helped me escape."

"Your story won't match Korbie's."

"We'll tell Calvin you turned on Shaun after you abducted me. That you were scared to stand up to Shaun at first, because he was the ringleader and had a gun, but when you saw how horribly he treated me, you decided to take matters into your own hands."

Jude shook his head, unconvinced. "That doesn't erase the fact that I took you in the first place. Calvin doesn't strike me as the forgiving type—for him, there's no such thing as a mistake. He'll want retribution."

No such thing as a mistake? He sounds like Calvin's dad, I thought.

"I'll talk to him," I said. "He'll listen to me."

"Really," he said in an incongruously level tone. "I didn't get the feeling Calvin listens to anyone. He definitely didn't care what Shaun had to say."

The conversation had suddenly gotten out of my hands. I had to convince Jude that Calvin wouldn't harm him, but the truth was, I didn't know how Calvin would react when we arrived at Idlewilde. Especially since he'd already killed Shaun. I didn't want to believe he was capable of shooting Jude in cold blood too, but I couldn't rule it out.

"Even in the unlikely event that you get Calvin to back down," he went on, "what about the police? You'll have to report what happened. Everything will come out, including my role in your abduction."

"No." I shook my head adamantly. "I won't tell them about you."

"Not on purpose, maybe. But you're going to have to tell them about me, Britt. They're going to ask a litany of questions, and the truth will come out. You got dragged into this mess by accident. You don't have anything to hide. You have no reason to cover for me, and we both know it."

"That's not true. Listen, it was Shaun's idea to take me hostage. If you promise to help me, I'll lie for you. I'll—do anything you want!" I finished desperately.

He turned to face me, his brown eyes locking me in a penetrating gaze. "Do you think I'm only helping you because I want something in return?"

I didn't know why he was helping me. But it only made sense that he expected some kind of payment. Up until now, I'd avoided any serious speculation about what I might have to do here in the mountains to survive, but I would make it out. I wasn't going to die up here. I'd do what I had to. If I had to send my mind to another place while I did, so be it.

Jude moved toward me suddenly, and I drew back with a frightened gasp. Too late, I realized he'd only been shifting his weight.

He gave a snort of disgust. "Think I'd hit you? Among other things? Your brain is going wild trying to imagine the sordid requests I might make of you in exchange for helping you to

Idlewilde—don't bother denying it, your revulsion is written on your face. Well, you can stop panicking. I won't force myself on you. And I'll try to look past your thinking I would. I took you hostage because I didn't see another option. I'm sorry you got dragged into this mess, but I'll remind you that I did try to stop it from happening. And while we're on the subject of my character, let me ease your conscience. I've never been with any woman who wasn't willing," he finished with thinly veiled resentment.

"I don't know you," I stammered, shaken not only by his perceptiveness but by the topic of our conversation. I didn't want to talk about sex with Jude. I only wanted to make it out of here alive. "So forgive me for doubting your motives."

Jude had a scathing comment ready to fly—I saw it in his broiling, angry eyes—but at the last moment the tension went out of his face and he settled into a gloomy silence.

I bowed my head between my knees. I wished my socks would hurry up and dry. I couldn't fully stretch out my legs in our tiny fortress without touching Jude. He sat so close, I could hear him breathing, every exhalation sounding agitated.

"Why did you break up with your ex?" Jude asked unexpectedly. He wouldn't look at me, but I could tell he was doing his best to sound friendly. Maybe not friendly. Maybe just not offended. Like me, he probably realized we were stuck here together and it was in our best interest to keep things as civil as possible. "You said his name a few times while you were asleep."

Instead of being embarrassed, I felt cheated that I couldn't remember the dream. Most of the time I dreamed that Calvin and I had never broken up. That he still lived three blocks away, that I could call him or stop by his house whenever I wanted. I dreamed we still went to school together, and that he stored his books and sunglasses in my locker. I never dreamed about the dark side of our relationship, the times when Calvin turned moody after fighting with his dad and refused to talk to me, punishing his father vicariously through me. During those times, he seemed to really believe it was him against the world. I tried to let go of those memories, especially now, when I needed something hopeful to cling to.

"He broke up with me."

"Dumb guy," Jude said, dipping his head to catch my eye. He smiled. I could tell he was only trying to make me feel better.

"He's not dumb—he's very smart. And an excellent hiker. He knows these mountains really well," I added, letting the threat dangle. *If we don't go to Idlewilde, he will find me.*

"Does he come up here often?"

"He used to. Before he left for college."

"He's a freshman?"

"At Stanford."

Jude paused, absorbing this quietly. After a moment, he let out a whistle. "You're right. He is smart."

"Smart enough to track us to the ranger patrol cabin," I shot back. "Smart enough not to be fooled by Shaun."

"Who he killed. For lying and kidnapping. He must have a temper."

"Calvin doesn't have a temper. It's more that he—" How to put it? "He has a keen sense of justice."

"Which takes the form of shooting unarmed men?"

"Shaun shot the game warden, who was unarmed, so this is really a case of the pot calling the kettle black."

"Do you by chance remember Calvin's SAT score?"

I snorted. "Why do you care?"

"Just curious if he beat me—if he's smarter than me."

"He got a twenty-one hundred," I announced proudly. *Beat that.*

Jude clapped his hands, clearly impressed. "Well, that'll certainly get you into Stanford."

"Calvin got horrible grades to get back at his dad, who placed a lot of emphasis on report cards and student rank, then aced both the ACT and SAT. That is so Calvin," I added. "He has to do things his own way. Especially when it comes to his dad—they don't have a great relationship."

"Did you visit Calvin at Stanford? Did you ever hit that restaurant downtown, Kirk's, with the green walls? They serve the best steak fries."

"No, we broke up a few weeks after Calvin left for school. How do you know anything about Palo Alto? Have you ever been there?"

"I grew up in the Bay Area."

"You're awfully far from home."

He made a dismissive gesture. "I was tired of the perfect weather. Everyone needs a blizzard now and then, a life-and-death adventure, you know?"

"Hilarious." I dug around in my pack, hoping against hope

that when Jude had grabbed clothes from my duffel in the Jeep, he'd inadvertently included—

Yes. It was here. The Stanford baseball cap Calvin had picked up when he and his dad toured Stanford last year, back when Calvin was still deciding between Stanford and Cornell. A few days before Calvin left for Stanford for good, I'd asked if I could keep the hat while he was away. I wanted something special of his, and I had no intention of giving it back. It wasn't even a fair exchange; in the end, I'd given him my heart, the whole of it. "Calvin gave me this hat right before he took off for school. It's as close to Stanford as I've been."

"Calvin gave you this?"

I held it out to him, but Jude didn't take it right away. He sat stiffly, as if he wanted nothing to do with Calvin's and my past. At last he reached hesitantly to take the hat from my outstretched hand. He turned it over and over, examining it without a word.

"Looks like you wore it painting," he commented, brushing his thumb over a yellow splatter on the top.

"Probably mustard from a baseball game." I scraped my thumbnail over the stain, flaking it off. "Calvin loves baseball. His dad never let him play—it overlapped with tennis and track seasons—but he went to the games. His best friend, Dex, was our high school's pitcher. When Calvin was a kid, he'd tell everyone he was going to play in the majors. One time, he took me to see the Bees play in Salt Lake." Unexpectedly, my voice cracked as I relived the memory. Every time the Bees had scored, Calvin had leaned over and kissed me. We'd sat in our seats, hidden by a sea of fans who shot to their feet cheering, and shared an intimate moment.

I buried my face in my hands. More than ever, I longed for Calvin. If he were here, he'd get me off the mountain. I wouldn't have to struggle to read the map anymore, because he'd lead the way. I rubbed my eyes to keep from crying, but that's what I really wanted. To let go and have a good cry.

"You miss him."

Yes, I did. Especially right now.

Jude asked, "Have you seen Calvin since he left for school? Before two mornings ago at the gas station, I mean. Did you ever get a chance to talk to him and feel closure?"

"No. Calvin never came home. Up until two days ago, I hadn't seen him in eight months."

"Not even for Christmas?" Jude asked with an upward sweep of his eyebrows.

"No. I don't want to talk about Calvin anymore, and I don't want to talk about me." I didn't want to talk about Jude, either, but that seemed safer than playing the dangerous game of wishing Calvin were here.

Jude passed me his canteen again, but I wasn't thirsty for stale water. I wanted a Coke and cornflakes and mashed potatoes with gravy and toast with real butter, not margarine. It suddenly hit me that I hadn't eaten since last night. My stomach twisted painfully, and I wondered how Jude and I were going to survive the long hike to Idlewilde with nothing but water.

Jude, always observant, guessed my thoughts. "We have three canteens of water and two granola bars, but I think we should save the food until we really need it."

"What happened to the fourth canteen? I heard Shaun say we left the cabin with four."

"I left one behind for Korbie." He pressed his finger to his lips. "Don't tell Shaun; it's our little secret."

I stared at him. His morbid humor was lost on me, but his act of generosity made my throat grow tight with emotion. I wanted to squeeze his hand and weep at the same time. "You did that?" I finally managed to say.

"I left her a canteen and two granola bars. It's enough food for her to outlast the storm. In another day or two, she'll be able to make her way to the road. She's going to be fine. I know you're worried about her, Britt, but given the two options—staying in the warmth of the cabin, lonely as that must be for her, or coming with us and risking exposure, exhaustion, and starvation—she got the better deal. When you lied about her having diabetes, you probably saved her life. I know I said I only covered for you to help myself, but I was frustrated when I said it, and in the heat of the moment, I lost my temper. The truth is, I saw what you were doing, and I was impressed by your ingenuity and your bravery. I should have told you then. I didn't, so I'm telling you now. You should be proud of what you did."

I hardly heard his praise. I was too busy concentrating on the first thing he'd said. "But . . . why would you do that for Korbie?"

"Surprised to discover I'm not entirely evil?" he said, with a jaded curve to his mouth.

This was his greatest kindness so far, and I didn't know what to say. Tempting as my initial reaction was—to snub him with chilly detachment—I was incapable of expending the energy. I was tired of building walls. Blinking away tears, I simply exhaled a shaky breath and said, "Thank you, Jude. I can't thank you enough."

He accepted my gratitude with a quick nod. The gesture hid the faintest grimace, which, I was almost certain, seemed to signify his discomfort at being heralded a hero. To save him from his embarrassment, I decided to change the subject.

"Do you think my boots and socks are dry enough? I have to go to the bathroom." I wanted to look at Calvin's map again, especially if we were taking off soon, but I also really did have to go.

After I laced up my boots, I trudged off into the snow. I didn't walk far enough to lose sight of our temporary camp, just far enough to have some privacy. Planting myself behind a tree, I pulled out Calvin's map. He had marked an old, abandoned fur trapper's hut less than a quarter of a mile away. The description read, "Semidecent roof, good wind protection." Too bad I hadn't been able to discover the hut last night, in the thick of the storm.

Calvin had made a green dot beside the fur trapper's hut. There were two other identical green dots on the map; one marked the cabin where I'd first met Jude and Shaun. The third green dot also seemed to mark a shelter. Beside this final dot, Calvin's notes merely read, "Broken windows." The shelter was probably abandoned, but it fell between our current location and Idlewilde; hopefully, Jude and I could rest there.

On the chance that I might find something useful at the fur trapper's hut, like granola bar wrappers left behind by hikers that could be used as fuel, and because I was already close by, I decided to check it out. Jude wouldn't miss me if I was gone an extra few minutes.

Using the map, I navigated my way through the trees. The branches snagged my clothes, making me think of clawing, bony fingers. I pushed the image away with a shudder, suddenly wishing I'd brought Jude.

Finally, the trees cleared to reveal a drooping, windowless, bare-bones log structure that looked well over a hundred years old. The door was so narrow and short, I would have to hunch over to pass through it.

The tiny door was not a gross miscalculation on the part of the mountain men who'd built the hut. When the first fur trappers arrived in the area, Wyoming and Idaho were heavily populated with grizzly bears. We still had them, but not in the same numbers. The trappers had built their huts' entryways too small for a grizzly bear to get through, to preserve their beaver pelts and their own lives. I owed this bit of historical trivia to Calvin, who, along with Dex, had waited out a rainstorm in what had to be a similar trapper's hut last spring on a hiking trip.

As I grew closer, a bit of yellow tape caught on sagebrush drew my eye. Police tape. A chill of familiarity tingled my spine, as if this clue should mean something to me.

The hut's door creaked in the wind.

I started to back away, suddenly cold with a bad feeling. The hairs on my scalp stood on end. I kept my eyes fastened to the door, afraid something awful would come out if I turned my back.

And that's when my brain snapped to life.

I knew this hut. It had been featured on the news last October when a local girl, Kimani Yowell, had been found murdered inside it.

CHAPTER
TWENTY-ONE

Kimani Yowell. Miss Shoshone-Bannock. The high school pageant winner who was killed last October. Her death hadn't made the news the way Lauren Huntsman's had, because Kimani wasn't from a wealthy family. She had fought with her boyfriend at a party in Fort Hall, Idaho, the night she died. She left alone, and he went after her. He drove her to the mountains, strangled her, and crammed her body inside the fur trapper's hut. If hikers hadn't stumbled across her remains, her boyfriend might have gotten away with it.

Kimani had gone to Pocatello High, my rival school, so her story had seemed especially traumatic at the time. Now it felt bone-chilling. She had died out here. In the same woods where I was fighting for my life.

The hut's door creaked again and something dark and *alive*

lumbered out, its large, clawed paws crushing into the snow. Covered in thick, oily brown fur, the animal was larger than a dog. It stopped, jerking its snout up, startled by my presence. Its beady black eyes glittered hungrily behind a silvery facial mask. Grunting, snorting sounds ground low in its throat.

I had heard stories of wolverines. They were ferocious enough to take on prey three times their size.

The wolverine walked toward me, its gait startlingly bearlike. I turned and ran.

I heard the wolverine loping across the snow behind me. In a panic, I tried to glance backward, and slipped. Icy slush seeped through my jeans and I curled my fingers into the snow, clutching for something to pull myself up. I grasped the first object I felt and stared at it in a stupor. The long shaft of the bone was picked dry and riddled with tooth marks. With a shriek, I flung it away.

I got my feet under me and started sprinting toward the blur of trees ahead. Jude's name was the one clear thought drumming in my head.

"Jude!" I screamed, praying he would hear me.

Branches whipped at my face and the deep snow swallowed my legs. I risked a second look behind me. The wolverine was a few paces back, its eyes black with raw, animal determination.

Dodging blindly through the trees, I tried frantically to orient myself. Which way was Jude? I swept my eyes over the frozen ground. Why couldn't I find my footprints from before? Was I heading even farther from him?

I screamed his name again. My voice bounced off the trees,

into the vast sky. Not one bird took flight. He couldn't hear me. No one could. I was alone.

My hands were smeared with blood from the sharp spruce needles, but I was oblivious to the pain; I was sure I felt the wolverine's razor teeth and thick, hooked claws snatch at the backs of my legs.

It grabbed me suddenly from behind. I lurched and kicked, almost as desperate to free myself as I was to stay on my feet. If I went down, it was over. I would never get back up.

"Easy, Britt, I'm not going to hurt you."

The knots in my chest unraveled at the sound of Jude's low, reassuring voice. The pressure inside me deflated, and I sagged against him. I made a whimpering sound of relief.

Jude loosened his hold on me gradually, making sure I had my footing. "I'm not going to hurt you," he repeated. He turned me to face him. His eyes searched my face, quizzical and worried. "What happened?"

I stared down at my scratched, bleeding hands. I couldn't find my voice.

"I heard you screaming. I thought a bear—" He drew a rocky breath.

Without thinking, I pressed my face to his chest. A sob hung in my throat. I just wanted to be held. Even if it was by Jude.

Jude stood stiffly, startled by my embrace. When I didn't let go, his hands moved hesitantly up to my arms. He stroked them reluctantly at first, then settled into a soothing rhythm. I was glad he didn't touch me like he thought I'd break. I needed to know he was solid and real. When he cradled my head against his chest and murmured soothingly into my ear, I couldn't fight the tears any longer. I buried my face into his coat, crying freely.

"I'm right here," he said gently. "I'm not leaving. You're not alone." He rested his chin on top of my head, and I found myself instinctively nestling closer. I was so cold. So bone-cold, so sucked of warmth, chilled to the very core. It felt good to let him hold me.

Right there, in the frigid air, Jude took off his coat and wrapped it around my shoulders. "Tell me what happened."

I didn't want to think back. How ridiculous he would think I was. A wolverine, however vicious, was nothing to cry over. It could have been worse. It could have been a grizzly. I was drawing air too quickly, and it was making my head float sickeningly.

"Take this." Jude offered me a small bottle from his coat pocket. I was so rattled, I hardly felt the liquid burn down my throat. It was cold like water, but bitter, and I sputtered and coughed as I tipped the bottle for more. Soon a certain warmth crept into my body, and my breathing relaxed.

"At first I thought it *was* a bear." I squeezed my eyes shut, hearing my breath start to hitch again. I could still see the animal's snarling lips behind my eyelids. "It was a wolverine and it charged me. I thought it was going to kill me."

"It must have heard me coming, realized it was outmatched, and bolted. It was gone by the time I found you," he said, holding me tighter.

After I composed myself, I took a long sip from the bottle and continued, "It was hiding in an old fur trapper's hut, one that I think a girl was found dead in last October. I remember seeing a very similar hut on the news when they reported finding her body, and a minute ago I saw a small piece of yellow crime-scene tape in the sagebrush outside the hut. I think it's the same one. I found a bone outside the hut. It can't be hers, can it? The crime scene investigators would have made sure to remove all her remains, right? Please tell me you don't think it was hers!"

I remembered the hollow way the bone had felt in my hand. A shell of death. It made me think of the leathery, decomposed body in the storage room of the first cabin. At that moment, I felt certain that death was pressing in from every reach of the mountains. What had ever made me want to come to this horrible place?

Jude took me by the shoulders, examining my face intently. His expression clouded and his lips pressed tight with concentration. "Which girl?"

"Kimani Yowell. Do you remember hearing about her on the news? She was a senior at Pocatello High School, and was already a concert pianist. She was invited around the country to play. Everyone said she'd go to Juilliard; she was that good. And then her boyfriend killed her. He strangled her and dragged her body up here to hide it."

"I remember her," Jude said remotely, looking off in the distance.

"What kind of guy kills his own girlfriend?"

Jude did not answer. But something dark and unpleasant darted across his features.

CHAPTER TWENTY-TWO

As we made our way back to camp, Jude walked slightly closer to me than usual. It was hard to believe that only two days ago, I'd shamelessly flirted with him at the 7-Eleven, viewing him as some kind of godsend who was saving me from humiliating myself. In two days, I'd gone from adoring him, to deploring him, to—

At this moment, I didn't know what to feel. I didn't know what to think.

Our sleeves accidentally brushed. Jude didn't pull away or apologize. In fact, he seemed so unbothered by it, I wondered if he noticed. I noticed. His closeness made a strange, slippery warmth pour through me. I stole a fleeting glance up at him. Unshaven and sleep-deprived, he still managed to look hot. Like a rugged REI model. He spent time outdoors—it showed in his coloring and the sun-lightened tips of his hair. A few faint lines fanned out from his eyes, the kind you got from squinting into the sun. And he had the faintest raccoon eyes from wearing sunglasses. Instead of corny, it looked almost sexy.

Despite exhaustion, he walked with his shoulders squared—with purpose. Beneath his dark brows, his eyes gazed out at the world with a long, cool stare. Part calculating, part discriminating, I decided. But under the surface, I detected a glimmer of uneasiness. I wondered what he was afraid of, what scared him most. Whatever his fears were, he kept them buried deep.

He saw me looking at him. Immediately, I averted my gaze. I couldn't believe he'd caught me staring. More than ever, I resented any attraction I might be feeling to him. He was my captor. He held me against my will. His recent kindness didn't change that. I had to remind myself of who he really was.

But who was he really? He and Shaun had never made sense as partners. Jude—Mason—had never been cruel. And he had tried to warn me and Korbie not to come in the cabin. I gave a conflicted sigh. Nothing about Jude added up.

"First order of business, get you warm," he said. "After that, we have to find food. It's too early for berries, so we're going to have to hunt."

The past two days I'd been wary and even suspicious of Jude's seeming concern for my well-being. This time, I found myself deeply curious about his motives. When Calvin had first started showing an interest in me, he'd showered me with compliments, teased me affectionately, and made little excuses to see me, all of which were flattering, but the biggest clue that he liked me was his sudden interest in taking care of me. When it frosted, he scraped my car windows. At the movie theater, he made sure I had a seat in the middle of the row. When my Wrangler was in the shop, he insisted on driving me everywhere. Maybe I was reading into Jude's gestures too deeply, but I wondered if his concern for me was more than plain chivalry.

Did he feel something for me?

I sternly reminded myself that it didn't matter. Because I wasn't going to reciprocate his feelings, real or imagined.

"How did you know I drive an orange Wrangler, and how did you know my dad loves fly-fishing?" I suddenly asked him, stepping over a fallen tree nearly hidden under the snow.

"There were two cars in the parking lot of the 7-Eleven. An older-model orange Jeep Wrangler and a BMW X5. When I walked into the store, I immediately pinned your ex with the Bimmer and you with the Wrangler," he explained. "It had two faded, peeling bumper stickers: 'My Other Ride Is a Drift Boat' and 'I Brake for Riffles.' I assumed the Wrangler belonged to your dad before he gave it to you."

It hadn't, but he'd caught a lucky break. Actually, the bumper stickers were one of the reasons my dad had bought the Wrangler. He felt a kinship to fishermen, and illogically trusted them over other men.

"What made you so sure I didn't drive the BMW?" I pressed, not sure if I should feel insulted or proud.

"Your sunglasses came from Target. Your ex had on Fendi. Most people who go flashy do it across the board."

I tried to think of the last time I'd been that observant about anything. "Do you always match people with their cars at the gas station?" I joked.

He shrugged. "It's a riddle. I like solving problems."

"Interesting. You're a riddle to me."

Jude's gaze cut to mine, then away.

To break the strange feeling buzzing in the air between us, I cocked my head speculatively. "So. Are you one of those genius types?"

His countenance automatically closed off, as if he had trained himself not to reveal anything in the face of personal inquiry. After a moment, his expression softened, and a faint smile played around his mouth. "Would it impress you to know my third-grade teacher had me tested for photographic memory?"

I waved an arm nonchalantly through the air. "Nah, not at all."

He scratched his head, smiling wider. "I failed. But was close enough to be considered."

I counted his strengths off on my fingers. "So you practically have photographic memory. And you have excellent survival skills. Anything else I should know? Like maybe where you go to school—you are in college, aren't you?"

"I dropped out last year."

I hadn't seen that coming. Jude struck me as a serious, studious person, not a dropout. "Why?"

"I had to take care of something," he said, shoving his hands in his pockets and hunching his shoulders uncomfortably.

"Gee, that makes everything clear."

His mouth hardened at the edges, leading me to believe I'd hit a nerve. "Everyone needs secrets. They keep us vulnerable."

"Why would anyone want to be vulnerable?"

"To keep their guard up, so they don't get sloppy."

"I don't understand."

"If you have a weakness, you have to work hard to defend it. You can't be lazy about it."

"What's your weakness?"

He laughed, but not with amusement. "You really think I'll tell?"

"Worth a shot."

"My sister. I love her more than anything."

His answer took me by complete surprise. Somehow, with that single answer, it was like a layer had been lifted and I could see a softer side of Jude. On the outside, he was a rugged and skilled man, a force to be reckoned with. But on the inside, there was a tender goodness about him.

"I wasn't expecting that," I said after a moment. "It sounds like she means a lot to you."

"My dad died when I was a baby, and my mother remarried. My sister was born a few months before my third birthday, and I remember thinking she was the worst thing that would ever happen to me." He smiled. "I got over myself pretty fast and figured out how wrong I was."

"Is she in California?"

"Haven't seen her since I left home."

"You must miss her."

Jude laughed again, and this time it was thick with emotion. "I took my role as her brother and protector seriously. I swore nothing bad would ever happen to her."

I exhaled slowly. A certain sadness and longing fluttered inside me. Jude would not know it, but I believed I understood how his sister felt. My dad and Ian had always protected me. I counted on them for everything. I felt like I was the center of their world, and I took no shame in it. They weren't here now, but Jude was. And in a strange, unexplicable way, I found myself jealous of his sister. Jealous that he was thinking of her, when I wanted him to be thinking of me.

"What about you?" Jude said. "What secrets are you keeping?"

"I don't have secrets." But I did. I was keeping one very big secret from Jude, and I wouldn't even allow myself to think it, because it was wrong. So very wrong. Suddenly I couldn't look him in the eye, afraid I'd blush if I did.

"How did you and Shaun become friends?" I asked.

"Not friends," Jude corrected. "You were right about that. We worked together, that's it."

"So you didn't like him—you never liked him?" I pressed.

"We had nothing in common."

"Where did you work?"

"Odd jobs, here and there," he answered vaguely.

"What kind of odd jobs?"

"Nothing to be particularly proud of," he said in a way that made it clear he wasn't going to divulge more on the matter. "Shaun had things I needed. And vice versa."

"What happened at the Subway store? Was that a job—a job gone wrong?"

Jude snorted. "That was a robbery. Plain and simple. After I saw you at the 7-Eleven, I met up with Shaun at our motel," he replied, startling me with his response. I hadn't expected him to be so forthcoming. Maybe he too was tired of building walls. "We had some business to take care of in Blackfoot, and we went together in his truck. On the way, Shaun wanted to stop for a late lunch—or so he told me. He went inside the Subway, held the cashier at gunpoint, then panicked when an officer arrived on the scene."

"Where were you when this happened?"

"In the truck," Jude said with thinly veiled rancor. "I heard the shot and started to climb out. I didn't know what was going on. Shaun came running and yelled at me to get back in the truck. If I hadn't gotten back in, Shaun would have taken off without me, and I would have been arrested. Plus, the gun Shaun used to shoot the officer was mine. So I got in the truck and we fled. We went through the mountains, hoping to evade the police, but then the snow hit. We were forced to wait out the storm, and that's when we met you."

"Why did Shaun have your gun?"

He uttered a loathsome laugh. "Last week, before we came to the mountains, Shaun had me go with him to collect money from a guy who owed him. It was my job to lean on the guy. We didn't give him the heads-up we were coming, but he must have gotten tipped off. We'd only been there a couple minutes when we heard sirens. We bolted for the alley, and the police followed on foot. I had to dump my gun, and Shaun saw me throw it in a garbage bin right before we split up. We lost the cops, but by the time I circled back to the garbage bin, my gun was gone. Shaun got to it first, and he wouldn't return it. I came up with a few ideas to get it back, but they all would take time. If I'd known a few days later he was going to shoot a cop, I would have worked faster."

"So you feel bad about what happened?"

"Of course I do."

"You expect me to believe you're a good guy, then?"

Jude tossed his head back with an abrupt laugh. "A good guy? Is that really what you think?"

I didn't want to tell Jude what I thought of him. He made me feel tingly and loose and hot under the skin. He'd told me—in his own words—that he was dangerous. And while his dark eyes did smolder with secrets, I had seen beyond them. I knew that buried under the surface was a gentleness, a kindness. It was as endearing as alluring. I recalled Jude's taut, disciplined body when I'd watched him undress at the ranger patrol cabin. He made Calvin look like a boy. I glanced furtively at Jude, my eyes flitting automatically to the soft, mysterious set of his mouth, wondering what it would feel like to—

I choked at the thought.

Jude regarded me peculiarly. "What's wrong?"

Fingering my neck, I said, "Must be getting a cough."

"Your face is bright red. Do you want some water?"

Why not? Clearly I needed something to cool me off.

Before he could reach for the canteen at his hip, Jude came up short. His hand instinctively gripped my arm, holding me back. He stared into the woods, a flash of panic registering in his brown eyes.

"What is it?" I whispered, my stomach squeezing instinctively.

Jude's body remained tense for several more beats, until at last his hold on me relaxed. "Timber wolves. Three of them."

I followed his line of vision. I squinted at where the shadows made strange patterns on the glittering snow, but I didn't see movement.

"They're gone now," Jude said. "They came to check us out."

"I thought wolves avoided humans." Calvin had told me stories of spotting wolves while hiking. In the time it took him to pull out his camera, they always ran away.

"They are. They won't attack unless they're sick or provoked." Jude's eyes fell on mine with a look of significance. "I'm worried about grizzly bears. They often follow wolves, then move in after the pack makes a kill. They're freeloaders. Especially in the spring, when they've been hibernating and they're hungry."

"In other words, where there's a wolf, there's a grizzly bear." I shuddered, but this time not from cold.

My stomach scraped with hunger.

I could not picture myself killing an animal, but I was also deliriously hungry. The hollow ache wore me down to where my thinking shifted, and I agreed to join Jude on the hunt for breakfast. My body had long ago burned through the canned corn I'd eaten yesterday evening for dinner, and I could not continue hiking without food. Hunger pecked incessantly at my thoughts, until it was the only thing I could think about. I wanted to get to Idlewilde as soon as possible, but there was no way we'd last the strenuous and demanding hike without eating first.

Jude prepped me on the essentials of hunting, including how to track small animals and how to set a deadfall trap using sticks and a large rock. "We'll have to make our way out of the densest parts of the trees," he said. "Animals gravitate toward water, food, and shelter. The sun doesn't penetrate this deep into the forest, which makes for little light and, subsequently, little food."

"I can find a river," I offered helpfully. At Jude's dubious glance, I added, "The same way I knew how to guide you and Shaun deliberately to the ranger patrol cabin."

His hooded eyes evaluated me carefully. "That was intentional?"

"Yup," I said, proud I could prove myself useful yet again. Unzipping my coat, I drew out Calvin's map. I wasn't sure I was doing the right thing by showing Jude the map, but it was a risk I decided to take. He still thought I was knowledgeable about the terrain—he needed me as much as he needed the map, which was a confusing jumble of Calvin's scribbled notes. Besides, if Jude were going to abandon me, he'd had several opportunities. The best plan now was to combine our resources and get to Idlewilde as quickly as possible.

I handed the map to Jude, who pondered it silently for a long time. At last he said, "Where did you get this?"

"It's Calvin's. Did you see the countless notations? Impressive, right? I told you he's an expert on the area."

"Calvin made this?"

"I took it from his car before I drove up here. Without it, I'd probably be dead by now."

Jude said nothing, only continued to search the map keenly.

"This area right here is approximately our current position," I said, pointing near one of the many smaller glacial lakes that dotted the Tetons. "Here is the ranger patrol cabin. It's less than a mile away. Can you believe, after all that time trudging through the storm, we didn't even travel a mile? And here is Idlewilde. Given how slow we've been traveling, it could take most of a day to get there."

"What do the green dots represent? They're not labeled."

"This green dot marks the fur trapper's hut. And this one farther north marks the cabin where Shaun took me hostage."

"And this green dot?"

"I think it's also a shelter, probably abandoned. We'll pass it on our way to Idlewilde. I'm hoping we can rest there, warm up, and maybe find running water."

Jude continued to ponder the map, his attention sharply focused. His hands gripped it tightly, almost greedily, and for one moment I feared he'd tear the paper. "I believed you when you said we'd stumbled across the ranger outpost by accident. You played me."

I faked an expression of superiority. "Like a fiddle."

"This map could save our lives. Can I hold on to it?" Jude asked. "For safekeeping?"

I bit my lip, unable to conceal my anxiety. I hoped I hadn't made a mistake in showing him the map.

"I'm not going to run off with it," Jude said gently. "I want to study it and see if I can find any shortcuts to Idlewilde."

"Maybe for a bit," I agreed hesitantly. "I want to study it too," I added, hoping he didn't think I was suspicious of him. Because I wasn't. At least, I didn't think I was. It was just that the map was my insurance. It was my safeguard and a physical symbol of Calvin, who I could trust completely.

"Deal." Jude tucked the map inside his coat with a strange, intense light in his eyes.

CHAPTER TWENTY-THREE

It was late afternoon before we ate. Hunting with jury-rigged tools was a painstaking and frustrating process that made me appreciate the pioneers and farmers who had settled Wyoming and Idaho, and the hours that must have gone into meeting their basic needs. If I made it home, I'd never take modern conveniences for granted again.

Jude and I trapped five rabbits, skinned them, and roasted them over the fire. I was normally a finicky eater, and thought I'd be queasy about eating an animal I had seen alive less than an hour earlier, but my hunger won out and I devoured the meat, eating until I was so full, I gave myself a stomachache.

In the forest, night fell early, and Jude and I decided to hold off leaving for Idlewilde until first thing in the morning, rather than navigate the trees after sunset. We couldn't be sure how much longer our flashlight and headlamp batteries would last, and it seemed foolish to risk the long hike when we'd likely wind up walking in utter darkness.

Jude scavenged evergreen branches and laid them under the ground mats and sleeping bags to create a more comfortable bed. One bed, which we would share.

A practical side of me knew sleeping together was the smart thing to do—it would conserve body heat—but as the evening wore on, I found myself wondering if Jude was as jittery as I was. When I caught him stealing glimpses at me from behind those long, dusky eyelashes, I tried to guess his thoughts, but his face never wavered from its pleasant, friendly mask.

"How did you learn to hunt?" I asked him, stretching out on my back. Ghostly blue moonlight filtered through the network of roots overhead. Bundled up in my coat and gloves, the night sky didn't look quite so glacial or inhospitable.

Jude rubbed his nose, smiling mysteriously down at me. "Do you have the bottle of moonshine I gave you earlier?"

Moonshine. Of course, he'd given me alcohol. I'd never drunk it before, so the taste had been foreign. But I should have guessed by the sting it left behind. My dad pushed two rules in our household. First and foremost, no sex. And second, no drinking. Those rules that had strictly governed my weekend plans through high school suddenly felt useless out here in the desolate and lawless wilderness.

I handed him the bottle and watched him take a long swig.

He closed his eyes, letting the alcohol soak in, and after a moment said, "Summer before my senior year of high school, I went to wilderness camp."

His confession caught me off guard; I threw my head back, laughing. "So you were a troublemaker, a menace to society, long before now!" I teased. "Korbie's boyfriend, Bear, also had to go to one of those camps."

"Bear? That's his name?"

I shook my head, giggling. "Bear's his nickname. His real name is Kautai. He moved to Idaho from Tonga when we were in junior high school. He didn't speak a word of English, but he was this big, surly-looking guy, so nobody teased him. And then he joined the football team. He carried the team to the National Youth Football Championships in Las Vegas. That's how he got his name—not only did he look like a bear, but he was an animal on the field. Anyway, Bear's parents sent him to wilderness camp when he got in a fender bender. His mom, who is super strict, was convinced he was drinking, and thought a few weeks at wilderness camp would dry him out. So what's your story? What did you do that was terrible enough to get you sent to bad-boy camp?"

He smiled. "It wasn't like that. I went to high school in an affluent part of San Francisco. My classmates were kids of congressmen, famous lawyers, and foreign diplomats. For most of them, summer vacation meant partying in Ibiza or Saint Barts. My mom wanted me to spend the summer before my senior year traveling in Europe with her and my sister. I grew up thinking bouncing from one European five-star hotel to the next was normal. But by the time I was seventeen, the extravagance revolted me. I told my mom I wasn't going—I'd signed up for wilderness camp. I think I wanted to prove to myself that while I couldn't help being rich, I wasn't a spoiled, lazy, entitled punk. Wilderness camp was my personal crusade to separate myself from my family's lifestyle."

I took the bottle from Jude and coughed down several sips. I knew the moonshine wasn't technically making me any warmer, but it did a good job of helping me forget how cold I was. It was also relaxing me. I wasn't even sure I wanted Calvin to rescue me anymore. I was enjoying spending time with Jude, getting to know him better. He was a mystery I wanted to solve. At least, that's what I told myself. But a voice of worry at the back of my mind dangled the idea of Stockholm syndrome. Was that what this was—a false attraction? One born out of necessity and survival?

"What did your mom say?" I asked.

Jude grinned, accepting the bottle from my outstretched hand. "You should have seen her face when I told her I wasn't going to any old wilderness program, but to Impetus."

"What's Impetus?"

"It was a cultlike wilderness program for troubled teens. They used harsh punishments, abuse, and brainwashing to correct behavior. It's no longer operational. Impetus is being sued for child abuse by former participants. In the end, they'll probably pay out around twenty million in settlements. At seventeen, it sounded like the perfect cultural backlash to me." Jude laughed nostalgically. "My parents were furious. At first my dad forbade me from going. He threatened to take away my Land Rover and told me he wouldn't pay for college. My parents didn't think I'd survive. A fair concern, since two of the kids in my group died."

I covered my mouth with my hand. "They died?"

"One from exposure, the other from starvation. We were expected to make our own shelter and hunt our own food. There wasn't a safety net. If you failed to trap a rabbit or get out of the rain, you had to deal with it."

"That's horrible. Seriously, I can't believe that was legal."

"We signed a very thorough disclosure agreement."

"I can't believe a rich little punk like you made it out okay."

"You're as bad as my parents," he said, ruffling my hair playfully. I froze. I'd sworn to deny any attraction to Jude, but when he touched me, the wall I'd built between us suddenly felt weak at the base. If Jude noticed my stiffness, he didn't show it. He went on, "I had a few close shaves, but after a rough first week, I caught on fast. I followed the best hunters in the group and watched how they built their traps. By the end of the summer, I wasn't scared of anything. I'd learned to hunt, learned how to set broken bones, which insects and plants were safe to eat, and how to build a fire with minimal resources. I'd dealt with hypothermia, infections, and freeloaders—that was the hardest, having to fight off my camp-mates to protect what I'd rightfully killed or built. Walking around for days on an empty stomach didn't faze me. Looking back, it was an impressive transformation in three short months."

He took another long drink from the bottle, then stretched out on his side next to me, propping his head on his fist. I felt a whirl of dreadful excitement at this forbidden closeness. His facial hair had a couple days' growth, and it gave him a roguish appeal. A faint smile had curved his mouth all evening, and I was going wild trying to guess his thoughts. The fire had warmed our little hideaway, and I was beginning to feel dizzy and drowsy. And daring. Very subtly, I stretched my arms over my head, then rolled closer to Jude.

"How long ago was this?"

"Four years ago. I'm twenty-one now." He smirked. "And not half so arrogant or strong-willed."

"Mmm, I'll bet. How did you go from affluent Bay Area teen to Wyoming outlaw?"

He gave a flippant laugh. "Maybe I'm a stereotype. Rich kid whose parents are never around, and who eventually goes off the deep end."

"I don't believe that."

His face turned more somber. "I got in a fight with my parents. I said things I now regret. I blamed them for a lot of the problems my family has faced, especially recently. Every family has troubles, but the way my parents handled ours—" He broke off. That long, cool stare of his wavered for a moment, showing vulnerability. "They always expected the best from me and my sister. We felt a lot of pressure. I thought if I left home for a while, I could cool down and find a way to set things right."

"Are you sure you're not running from your problems?"

"Seems that way, doesn't it? I'm sure my parents think I am. What about you? How did you get interested in wilderness back-packing?"

I could tell Jude didn't want to talk about himself anymore, and I decided to respect his privacy. "Calvin was the first person I knew to backpack the Teton Crest Trail," I said, treading carefully. It was a long, messy story, and I didn't know how much of it I wanted to tell Jude. "I always looked up to him. Even when I was young, and came up to the mountains with the Versteegs, I studied him and let him teach me his tricks, like using pine pitch in place of lighter fluid. And my dad, he'd bring me into the mountains when he'd go fly-fishing, so being up here feels a bit like hanging out in my extended backyard. To prepare for this trip, I read an entire library shelf of guidebooks, completed several shorter day hikes with my brother, Ian, lifted weights, that sort of thing. Plus, like I said before, I've backpacked all over this mountain more times than I can count, so I had that experience to fall back on," I added quickly and untruthfully.

Jude made a casual sound of agreement. I took the moonshine and forced down several burning gulps.

Jude reached for the bottle, eyed its nearly gone contents, and pocketed it.

"Hey, I wasn't done with that," I argued.

He ignored my protest and studied me with a focused, probing gaze. "Why did you tell Shaun you're an expert backpacker? Why did you lie?"

My face grew warm and a nervous feeling expanded in my chest. "What are you talking about?"

"Have you ever been backpacking before? I don't think you have."

Defensively, I said, "Just because I don't know as much as you doesn't mean I'm incompetent."

He nudged me softly. "You don't have to lie to me, Britt. I'm not judging you."

I didn't know if this was a trick or a test. Either way, if I told Jude I'd never backpacked the Tetons before, he'd realize how useless I was. He wouldn't need me. He could take the map and head out alone.

"Not judging me? Funny, that's exactly what this feels like— you asserting your position over me."

"Don't get upset," he said calmly. "You can tell me anything. We're a team now."

"If we're a team," I demanded, "why have you consistently evaded my questions? Why haven't you told me how you ended up in league with Shaun? You're nothing like he was. What could he possibly give you?"

He smiled self-deprecatingly, clearly trying to lighten the mood. "There you go again, assuming I only join forces with people who can give me something in return."

"I want a straight answer!"

The smile dissolved from his face. "I came here looking for someone. I care about them, and I made a promise to them. I'm trying to do right by that promise. I thought Shaun could help me."

"Who are you looking for?"

"It's not your business, Britt," he said with such unexpected sharpness. I found myself too startled to argue back. Instead of meeting my eyes, he stared stonily into the distance.

His sudden savagery hurt my feelings, and I rolled onto my knees, crawling out from under the fallen tree as fast as I could.

I accidentally brushed my glove over the fire's ash, singeing the fabric. I could see clear through to my finger. Cursing under my breath, I stormed out into the frosty darkness.

Behind me, I heard Jude groan.

"Britt! Wait up! I wasn't trying to make you angry. I'm sorry. Can I explain myself?"

I marched into the trees, my thoughts darting frantically. How could I salvage this? How could I convince him to stay and not leave me?

"Britt!"

I whirled around, crossing my arms tightly over my chest. "You called me a liar!"

"Just listen to me for a sec—"

"So what if I lied to Shaun? I had to! If he didn't need me, he would have killed me. Look what he did to Korbie—he left her to die! Is that what you're going to do too? Now that you realize I'm not an expert on the area and I've been relying completely on the map? Are you going to run off and leave me to fend for myself?"

Jude reached toward me, but I batted his hand away. I was breathing heavily, my heart thundering. If he left me now, I'd never make it. I'd die in this place.

"You were clever enough to trick Shaun," he said. "You were smart enough to grab supplies when you ran away from the outpost. And you were able to decipher Calvin's map, which is a confusing collection of his own scribbled notes and hand-drawn landmarks. Not everyone could have read it with the same success." He put his hands on his hips, wagging his head at the snow between our feet. "I like—" he began, then caught himself. Drawing a breath, he started again. "I like having you around, Britt. That's the truth. I'm not leaving you. Even if you were a pain in the butt, I'd stay with you. It's the right thing to do. But it turns out I find you likable and interesting, and while I'm not glad you have to go through this, I'm glad we have each other."

I stared at him, thrown off guard. I hadn't expected that. He liked having me around? Even though I couldn't give him anything in return?

He reached toward me a second time, resting his hand tentatively on my shoulder. He seemed relieved when I didn't immediately slap it away. "Truce?"

My eyes flicked over his face, which appeared sincere. I nodded, grateful our fight hadn't ended badly. I still had Jude. I wasn't alone.

He drew a deep breath and his face relaxed. "Time to get some sleep. We've got a long day of hiking, starting first thing tomorrow."

I swallowed hard. "I came on this trip because of Calvin. I wanted to impress him. At one point, I actually thought we'd get back together. I thought if I came on the trip, he'd invite himself along. I trained hard, but I always thought I'd have him to rely on. Because that's what I do—I expect the men in my life to rescue me." Tears stung my eyes. "My dad, Ian, Calvin. I've always been dependent on them, and it never bothered me. It was so . . . easy to let them take care of me. But now—" My throat closed off. "My dad must think I'm dead. No way could he imagine his little girl surviving in the wild." My lip quivered uncontrollably and my face crumpled. Hot tears dripped off my chin. "There. That's the truth. That's the pathetic truth about me." Jude said we needed secrets to keep us vulnerable, but he was wrong. I'd revealed myself to him; I'd cut myself open. If that wasn't vulnerability, I didn't know what was.

"Britt," Jude said softly. "Look around. You're alive. You're doing pretty great at surviving, and you've even saved our lives a couple times. You're going to see your dad and brother again. I'd tell you that I'm going to see to it, but I don't have to. You're going to make sure you do all on your own. Because it's what you've been doing every step of the way."

I drew my fingers under my eyes, drying them. "If I had known things would turn out this way, I would have trained harder. I would have learned to take care of myself. But I guess that's the point, isn't it? You never know what you're going to have to face, so you'd better be prepared."

Jude looked ready to agree, when his eyes drifted from my face. And then he swore under his breath.

CHAPTER TWENTY-FOUR

I heard the bear before I saw it.

Huffing and snorting, it pawed the ground only a few dozen yards away. In the moonlight, its bushy coat glistened with streaks of silver. Rising on its short, powerfully built hind legs, the grizzly sniffed the wind and angled its large head for a better look at us.

With a guttural growl, it dropped on all fours. Holding its ears back, it warned us we'd come too close. Swinging its head side to side, it snapped its teeth aggressively.

In my mind, I scanned every guidebook. Every paragraph, sentence, caption, bullet point, and chapter summary on bear attacks.

"Run back to camp," Jude told me in a low, soft voice. "Put the fire between you and the bear and make a torch if you can. I'll yell and make noise to draw him away from you."

I grappled for his hand, squeezing his fingers to keep him by my side. "No," I said in an equally low but trembling voice. Running triggers a grizzly to charge. Yelling triggers a grizzly to charge. I knew Jude was only trying to protect me, but his plan might get us both mauled or killed.

"Britt . . . ," Jude warned.

"We're going to do what we're supposed to do." *Stand still. Don't make eye contact.* I licked my dry lips. "Back away slowly. Speak in a soft, nonthreatening—"

The grizzly charged. Woofing and snorting, it ran directly at us, muscles rippling beneath its satiny fur. My stomach cramped and my throat went dry. It was hard to gauge the bear's size in the dark, but it was definitely much larger than the wolverine, which now seemed like a harmless pet in comparison.

"Run," Jude insisted sharply, shoving me away.

I squeezed his fingers tighter, pressing into him. My heart pounded so hard, I could feel blood swarming my legs. The grizzly rushed violently at us, its enormous paws kicking up snow.

With a loud bark, the grizzly made a bluff pass, but not before brushing my coat sleeve. The hairs on my scalp tingled as each bristle of fur scraped over the fabric. I shut my eyes, trying to erase the bear's bottomless black eyes.

"Turn around and face it," I told Jude, barely audibly. *Never turn your back on a bear.*

The moment we turned, it charged again, huffing and growling, eyes locked on us. This time, it stopped abruptly in front of Jude. It jerked its snout around Jude's face, picking up the scent of him. I felt Jude's body stiffen beside me. His breath came in short pants, and his face had blanched.

The bear swung its paw, knocking Jude over. As Jude fell into the snow, I bit my lip to keep from crying out. Very slowly, I lowered myself beside him, flat on my stomach, and clasped my hands over the back of my neck. I hardly felt the snow that wormed down my collar and shoved up the wrists of my gloves. The cold was a remote worry. My mind throbbed with only one piercing thought: Don't panic, don't panic, don't panic.

The grizzly let out another roar. Unable to stop myself from peering upward, I saw fangs flash in the moonlight. The bear's wild, silvery-brown coat rippled as it stamped impatiently.

Protect your head, I thought at Jude, tucking my chin and hoping he mimicked the gesture.

The grizzly's nose nudged and inspected my slightly spread arms and legs. With a single powerful swat of its massive paw, the bear rolled me over.

"If I kick him, and run in the opposite direction to lure him away, will you run back to camp?" Jude asked softly.

"Please do what I ask," I returned in a shaky voice. "I have a plan."

The grizzly roared, inches from my face. Paralyzed, I lay there while its breath blasted me like a damp gust of wind. It bounded from side to side, lifting its head up at intervals, clearly agitated.

"Your plan isn't working," Jude whispered.

"Dear God," I murmured, so softly even Jude couldn't hear me, "just tell me what to do."

A bear might bluff-charge several times before retreating. Hold position.

The grizzly swung its massive body toward Jude, repeatedly crashing its front legs down in the snow, as if challenging Jude to engage. Jude lay motionless. The bear swiped its paw at Jude, further trying to intimidate him into action. Clamping its muzzle down on Jude's leg, the bear shook him, but the bite could not have been severe; Jude remained motionless and made no sound.

And then, miraculously, either growing bored or no longer perceiving us as a threat, the bear lumbered off, disappearing into the trees.

I raised my head cautiously, peering into the darkness where it had vanished. My whole body was shaking with fright. I wiped my hand across my cheek, realizing only now that it was wet with bear drool.

Jude dragged me up to my knees and into his arms. He cradled my head against his chest and I could hear the throb of his rapid heartbeat. "I was so scared he was going to attack you," he said in my ear, his voice rough with emotion.

I slumped into him, suddenly exhausted. "I know you wanted me to run to keep me safe, but if you died, Jude, if something happened to you and I was left out here alone—" I choked off, unable to finish. The weight of that dark possibility seemed to press down, crushing me. The isolation and hopelessness, the sheer odds mounted against me . . .

"No, you were right," Jude said huskily, squeezing me tighter. "You saved my life. We're a team. We're in this together." He laughed, a short, painful sound of relief. "It's you and me, Britt."

Back at camp, in the light of the fire, Jude rolled his jeans to his knee, revealing fresh blood.

"You're bleeding!" I exclaimed. "You need first aid. Do we have a first aid kit?"

He winced, reaching for his pack. "We've got moonshine and gauze. I'll be fine."

"What if it gets infected?"

He looked directly at me. "Then I won't be fine."

"You need medical attention." As soon as I said it, I realized how pointless a remark it was. Where were we going to find a hospital, let alone a doctor?

"Given the damage the bear could have inflicted, I think I got off relatively well." He splashed the last of the moonshine over the wound, washing rivulets of blood down his leg. Next he wrapped the gauze around his leg until he ran out of it. Two pins fastened the bandage in place.

"I wish I could help," I said uselessly. "I wish there was something I could do."

Jude tossed a log on the fire. "Distract me. Play a game with me."

"Are you trying to get me to play Truth or Dare with you, Jude?" I said, attempting to be funny to distract him from his pain. For emphasis, I cocked a speculative eyebrow.

He snorted his amusement. "Tell me about the warmest place you've ever been. The warmest place you can think of."

"Reverse psychology?" I guessed.

"Worth a try."

I tapped my finger thoughtfully on my chin. "Arches National Park, Utah. My family spent a week there last summer. Picture this: An inescapable sun baking the dry, cracked land with vicious heat. The bluest sky you'll ever see domes a desert of red rocks that have eroded into arches, spires, and sandstone fins. They stab up from the earth like strange statues—it's like a scene out of a science fiction novel. People say the desert isn't beautiful. Those people have never been to Moab. Okay, your turn."

"Growing up, my sister and I would dive for abalone at Van Damme State Beach in California. It's not hot like the desert, but after diving, we'd always stretch out on the gray sand with our faces turned to the sun. We'd lie there until the sun had sapped every last ounce of energy from us. Every time, we swore we wouldn't wait until we were sick with heat to pack up and go. And every time, we'd break our vow. Delirious, we'd stagger up to the parking lot and search for my car. I'd drive us to this local joint for ice cream cones. We'd sit by the air conditioner, shivering from cold and dizzy with sunstroke." He grinned at the juxtaposition.

I tried to picture Jude with his sister, with loved ones, with a past. I had never really imagined him as a whole person before. I had only seen him as he was now, the man who had abducted me. His story opened a new door, one that I found myself wanting to peer through. I wanted to know the other versions of Jude.

"Do you feel warmer now?" I teased him. I wanted to press for more stories from his life, but I didn't want to sound too interested. I wasn't sure I was ready to hint that my opinion of him was shifting slowly.

"A bit."

"What's abalone?"

"Edible sea snails."

I made a face. I wasn't a seafood girl, especially not a slimy sea-food girl.

"No way," Jude told me, seeing my expression and giving a scolding wag of his head. "You don't get to be a food snob until you've tried them. If we get off this mountain, first thing I'm going to do is make you eat abalone. I'll even cook them myself— over an open fire on the beach, so you can experience abalone the authentic way." He spoke cavalierly, but his words caused me to swallow. If we got off this mountain, I would not be spending time with Jude. He had to know that. He was wanted by police. Whereas I—

I wanted my life to go back to normal.

"They're actually pretty difficult to harvest," Jude was saying. "The best place to look is in the deep rocks off the coast. You can try to shore-pick abalone, but we preferred breath-hold diving, which is what it sounds like—diving and holding your breath as long as you can."

"Is it dangerous?"

"Even if you know what you're doing, being trapped in the ocean's tide can be disorienting. The constant push and pull makes it challenging to find your footing or maintain your posi-tion. You're in constant motion, and a lot of divers find it hard to relax. Most people don't willingly subject themselves to a force far more powerful than they are. Lots of free divers get vertigo. That's when diving becomes dangerous. If you can't tell which way the shore is, or worse, which way is up, you're going to run into trouble fast. To make matters worse, there's bull kelp everywhere, and in the murky water, the flowing stalks look eerily like rippling hair. I can't tell you how many times I've thought there was a person floating to the side of me—only to jerk around and discover it was kelp undulating in the ebb and flow of the current."

"I've only been to the ocean once, if you can believe it. Which is why I really should have picked Hawaii over backpacking in the mountains for spring break," I added with a rueful laugh.

"Next year," he offered optimistically, his grin lighting up his whole expression.

I studied his face, bright and open, and tried to compare this version of him, the carefree diver, with the Jude I thought I knew. Despite how we had met, despite the circumstances that had trapped us together, over the past three days, he'd protected me and respected me. My opinion of him *was* changing. I wanted to learn more about him. And I wanted to share myself with him.

Without thinking, I slapped him on the thigh and said, "You know what? I *do* feel warmer." Immediately, I withdrew my hand and smoothed it through my hair, as if nothing were out of the ordinary. As if our boundaries hadn't changed.

I jolted out of sleep, panting softly as I stared up at the tangled, knurly roots overhead. A bad dream. My hairline felt sticky, and I was overly warm in my layers of clothes and blankets. I sat up and tugged off my coat, sponging my face with it before setting it aside. Then I inhaled deeply over and over, trying to regain my breath.

I rolled my head around my shoulders, attempting to come back to reality and banish any lingering memory of what it had felt like when I dreamed Jude stretched his tall, muscular body on top of mine and pushed his mouth damply against my own.

It was a dream, I knew that. But this one made me tremble and ache.

After several minutes, I settled back down with a sigh, but I didn't close my eyes. I was afraid to fall asleep. What if I went back to the dream? In some inexplicable way, I felt drawn to it with an urgent longing that made me feel both wildly alive and afraid.

With a soft groan of frustration, I rolled onto my side.

Jude's eyes were open, watching me.

In a sleep-roughened voice he murmured, "What's wrong?"

"Bad dream."

Our faces were only inches apart, and as I bent my knee to shift to a more comfortable position, I accidentally grazed his leg. Electricity seemed to sear my skin.

He rose up on his elbow and touched my arm. "You're shaking."

"The dream felt very real," I whispered.

In the darkness, our eyes connected. We watched each other silently. My pulse thrummed, strong and steady.

"Tell me about it," he said quietly.

I scooted closer, until I was on his half of the bed, sheltered under his slightly raised body. It was a daring thing to do, maybe even a bit foolish. From some far-off place, I could hear the voice of reason urging me to rethink. I didn't feel the switch, but I knew my mind had lost the fight and my body had taken over. I remembered Jude's wet, sensual kiss from my dream, and I had to know if he could elicit the same heated response in me awake.

"It started out like this," I said in that same hushed voice. With me. Under you.

He wiped a strand of hair off my cheek. He held his hand there a moment, debating. An unfathomable look flickered in his brown eyes, and I had no idea what he was thinking, or what his next move would be. I imagined running my hands up his muscular arms, but I lay scarcely breathing, second-guessing my boldness. I lost my nerve and made up my mind to roll back to my half of the bed, when his voice cut through the silence.

"Britt." His face searched mine, as if he needed to know this was what I really wanted.

I wanted this. I'd wanted it for some time. Even though it was wrong, it was the truth.

Doing this with Jude was crazy. I knew that. But there was something about almost dying that made me desperate to feel alive—and Jude's touch was the only thing that made me feel alive right now.

Jude cupped my cheek, his thumb delicately stroking the line of my eyebrow. "It was a bad dream?"

I swallowed. "A scary dream."

"Are you scared now?"

I slid my hand behind his neck, running my fingers over his short dark hair. I pulled his head down until his mouth almost

BECCA FITZPATRICK

touched mine. I could feel the deep rise and fall of his chest. I hardly dared breathe myself, feeling my heartbeat drum in a hypnotic rhythm. The moment felt dreamlike, unreal.

His voice came out hoarse. "Britt—"

I pressed my finger to his lips. "Don't talk." The instruction was meant more for myself, because if we talked, I'd start thinking. And if I thought this through, I'd realize I was making a mistake. I liked the strange, slightly tipsy sensation of having my head strewn with clouds. With my thoughts muted, I felt heady and dangerous, capable of anything.

Jude's lips grazed my mouth, and my body seemed to turn to water, hot and flashing and unstoppable. Jude deepened the kiss, scooping his arm under me, lifting me against him. I ran my hands over his chest, feeling his muscles clench as a great shudder rippled through him. Sliding my fingers to grip behind his shoulder blades, I held on tightly, losing myself in the sheer sensation of his kiss.

He brushed a kiss across my ear. Another rougher kiss to my throat. I lay there, eyes shut, feeling the ground spin beneath me. He teased me with his teeth, nipping and sucking, pushing his knee between my legs to separate them. Somewhere outside myself, I could feel the heat of the campfire. The burn was insignificant next to Jude's hands skimming fire over my body as he kneaded and caressed me with the same hungry impulsiveness that I was feeling as I dug my nails in, trapping him closer.

He dragged me up to my knees and we faced each other in the smoky darkness, pushing our mouths together, shamelessly and recklessly, until mine felt swollen and battered. I climbed onto his hips, arching against his strong hands; he held one splayed to my back while the other traced a delicate, seductive line down the length of my breastbone. He finished his invisible sketch with a kiss planted at the baseline, and I shivered with pleasure.

I unzipped his coat and shoved it down his arms, tossing it hastily aside. With it off, I teased my fingers across his flat, taut stomach and felt the cold metal button at the front of his jeans, and without warning, the gesture caused me to flash back to Calvin. To touching his body. His ghost stormed into my thoughts, and it was like he was right there, in the space with us.

Jude's mouth ground against mine, but I tore away, gasping for air. I couldn't do this. I couldn't kiss Jude and think of Calvin.

Jude's body went rigid. Immediately, I thought he'd sensed the reason for my reluctance, and I grappled for a way to explain. Cal was the first. He was the only other boy. He wasn't easy to forget.

I listened to Jude pant, his whole body stiff as he turned his head toward the open doorway of our hideaway, listening. And that's when I knew it was something else.

"What is it?" I whispered, clutching him, afraid.

His mouth brushed my ear as he spoke. "I'm going to have a look around outside. Stay here."

"Jude—What if—?" I couldn't finish the thought. My fear hung like a stone in my throat.

"I won't be gone long," he assured me, reaching for the headlamp.

I sat huddled in our hideaway as the minutes stretched on. I grew cold, but I didn't dare scoot closer to the fire. The fire was just outside the doorway—out there, where something in the darkness had scared Jude.

After what felt like a very long time, I heard the crunch of his boots in the snow. He ducked through the entrance, and right away I knew something was wrong.

"Grizzly tracks," he said soberly. "The fire must have deterred him, but I think he's stalking us."

CHAPTER TWENTY-FIVE

"We have to move camp," I said, blindly groping in the shadowy corners of our hideaway for my pack.

Jude took my wrist, gently forcing me to stop. "Whoa. It's okay, Britt. Don't panic," he said in a soothing voice. "We need to keep the fire burning. He won't cross it to get to us, no matter how curious or hungry he is. I collected extra firewood this morning; it should be enough to keep the fire going through the night. Tomorrow morning I'll follow his tracks, figure out his position, and we'll swing wide around him on our way to Idlewilde."

"I'm scared," I whispered. I'd felt tipsy and loose ever since drinking the moonshine, but even it couldn't mask the worry sloshing like ice water inside me. A grizzly bear. If the fire burned out, if it came after us, if we had to run—we would be fatally out-matched.

Jude gathered me into his arms. He reclined so that I sat with my back to his chest, his long legs drawn up on either side of mine. Cradling me against his body, he wrapped his arms protectively around me.

"Better?" he murmured into my ear.

I let my head fall back on his shoulder. "I'm glad you're here, Jude. I'm glad we have each other."

His breath ruffled my hair. "Me too."

"This may sound strange, but I almost feel . . . more capable with you around. I really do feel like we're in this together, if that makes sense."

"Perfect sense."

If Calvin were here with me instead, I wouldn't be able to say the same. I had always let Calvin take care of me. When we used to go out, even if we took my car, Calvin drove. Calvin paid for dinner. If it was raining and I'd forgotten my coat, I pestered him until he gave me his. I'd wanted him to adore me, protect me, and bend over backward for me. When he didn't measure up, I acted helpless to force him to pay attention to me. With Jude, I trusted my own ability to take care of myself. I felt a sense of security, not desperation. I believed our strengths complemented each other.

Jude swept my hair off my shoulder and kissed the nape of my neck. "Tell me what you're thinking."

I stretched my neck, inviting him to kiss me. I shut my eyes, feeling my skin tingle under the soft pressure of his mouth. "How do you know I'm not seducing you so you'll help me to Idlewilde?" I baited him. Somewhere outside myself, I could hear how flirty I sounded. But the moonshine had relaxed me and I didn't care.

He nuzzled my neck. "When you bluff, your left eyebrow twitches. It hasn't twitched all night. Besides, I already told you I'm going to get you there safely. No need for games now."

I pulled back indignantly. "My left eyebrow does not twitch."

Jude studied me with an idle smile, as if calculating the wisdom of saying more. "When you're amused, your mouth takes on a mischievous curl," he went on, as if proving his point. "When you're angry, you press your lips together and three tiny lines jump out between your eyebrows."

I rolled onto my knees and planted my hands squarely on my hips. "Anything else?" I asked hotly.

He thumbed his nose, struggling not to grin. "When you kiss, you make a purring noise deep in your throat. It's so faint, I have to be touching you to hear it."

Now I turned bright red.

"We should kiss again and see what other observations I make," he suggested.

"Fat chance, after you insulted me!"

"You want me to think you're insulted, but your left eyebrow is twitching—you're bluffing." At my exasperated look, he shrugged and spread his hands as if to say, *I can't help myself.*

I realized Jude must have been studying me *a lot* if he'd come to these conclusions. My mind traveled back to the times I'd caught him watching me. I'd assumed he'd kept his eye on me to make sure I didn't run. But now I wondered if he'd secretly been piecing me together like a puzzle, out of his own deep interest. The idea made my breath come faster.

"Fine," I said at last. "Say I do let you kiss me again." I knelt on all fours in front of him, smiling temptingly. My mind was definitely still present, but the alcohol had given me a pleasurable buzz. I felt warm and alive, and a teensy bit reckless. "First, I want to set some ground rules."

"You have my rapt attention."

"When was the first time you knew you wanted to kiss me?"

"That's your ground rule?"

"I'd like to gather some information before I lay down the law."

"My, my, but you're demanding. This, and that, and who knows what else."

My smile widened. "Answer it."

He leaned back and scratched his head, exaggeratedly struggling to recollect the exact moment.

"Take your time," I said sweetly. "The longer you take, the longer until we kiss."

"The first time I wanted to kiss you," he said thoughtfully, rubbing his chin, "was at the 7-Eleven, right after I discovered you told Calvin that you were with me now. The resentment on his face was memorable, but your expression was priceless. I've never seen someone fight so hard to hide their giddiness. You had both of us in your hand. I wanted to kiss you and, as I recall, I did."

I frowned, trying to remember. "That kiss? It was about as puritanical as a hymnbook."

"Didn't want to seem forward."

I doubted that. The more I got to know Jude, the more his veneer of modesty peeled away. I was pretty sure there were remnants of the arrogant, swaggering kid he'd claimed to have left behind in his teen years.

"I'm not the type to start up with perfect strangers," I told him. "I still don't know what brought you to Wyoming or how you got wrapped up with Shaun."

Jude studied me quietly a moment. "There are things I want to tell you but can't. I know it's not a good explanation, but it's the best I can do right now. I care about you, Britt. I want what's best for you. I'm sorry you got dragged into this mess, and I will do everything I can to get you home safely."

Neither of us brought up what would happen after that. Jude was a wanted man. An accomplice at the very least. And if Korbie had been rescued by Calvin, she may have already told the police that Jude was one of our kidnappers. We had no way of knowing how much trouble Jude was up against. Right now, I didn't want to think the worst. I didn't want to think about *after*, period.

"Do you have a girlfriend?" Jude didn't strike me as a cheater, but it was a valid question. He knew I wasn't with anyone. If I was going to make a mistake with him tonight—and against my better judgment, I was considering it—I wanted to know I wasn't dragging a third party into the mix.

"No."

"That's it? Just 'no'? No explanation?"

"You asked a straightforward question. Given the alternatives— 'yes' and 'maybe'—I thought you'd be happy with 'no.'"

"You're making fun of me."

He smiled. "I don't have a girlfriend, Britt. My last serious relationship was a year ago. I've never cheated on any of the girls I've been with. If I feel the need to cheat, something in my relationship isn't working, and if I can't fix it, I end it. I don't believe in hurting people."

"Very good answer, Mr. Jude . . . ?"

I saw him hesitate, gauging me. "Van Sant. Jude Van Sant. That's my real name." He reached for me, catching me by the wrist. He stroked his thumb in a slow circle at the base of my palm.

"Not so fast," I said, resting my finger on his lips as he bent to kiss me. "I like this new, open side of you. I want to hear more of your secrets."

"Some things you have to find out for yourself."

And he pulled me down on top of him.

CHAPTER TWENTY-SIX

Something about the morning sunlight slanting through the tree, and the moonshine's spell wearing off, made the memory of last night surge back with horrifying clarity. I lay stiffly on the ground, aghast as every detail of my actions flashed across my mind.

I'd made out with Jude. The man who'd held me captive. That he was hot and sexy and protective of me was irrelevant.

I kept my eyes shut in feigned sleep several minutes after I woke, even though I could hear Jude rustling around. I tried out icebreakers in my head. Nothing seemed appropriate. What had I been thinking, to drink moonshine? It had led me to kiss him.

No. I'd been attracted to Jude when I was 100 percent sober. I could try to convince him it was the alcohol, but I couldn't lie to myself. I made out with him because I wanted to. It was shameful, but it was the truth.

I massaged my palm into my forehead and grimaced. No choice but to get the awkward morning-after over with.

"About last night," I began, sitting up and feeling a dull headache roll across my skull. With a shock, I realized I was experiencing my first hangover. Mild, but undeniably a *hangover*. If there was a silver lining, it was that my dad couldn't see how severely I'd disappointed him. Unfortunately, I couldn't spare myself the same humiliation.

Pretending to be deeply interested in lacing my boots, I kept my eyes steadfastly on my feet, avoiding Jude's direct gaze. "What we did was stupid, obviously. A mistake." *A colossal mistake.* "I had too much to drink, and I wasn't thinking. I wish I could take it back."

Jude made no comment.

"I was half passed out when we . . . did what we did. I hardly remember what happened." *If only it were true.* In reality, my memory tormented me with a perfectly scripted blow-by-blow. "Whatever happened between us, I didn't mean it. The real me didn't do those things, I mean."

When Jude still didn't respond, I stole a nervous glance in his direction. The careful, evaluating manner in which he watched me made it hard to read him. I was sure he felt the same way. Didn't he? There were so many things I wanted to ask him, but I stopped myself. I wasn't going to dig for a way to rationalize my behavior. It didn't matter what Jude thought. What I did was wrong, period. And he was the worst possible person I could have made such a grave mistake with.

Jude sat up and stretched, languid as a cat. He rolled onto his knees, belted his jeans, and cast me a sly look. "How long did it take you to come up with that speech?"

I frowned. "It wasn't a speech. It was impromptu."

"Good. That explains why it sucked."

"Sucked? Excuse me?"

"You weren't drunk, Britt. You had a buzz, sure, but don't forget I took my half of the bottle. I'll try not to take offense that you think I'd impose myself on you while you were drunk. And if that's how you kiss when you're drunk, I can't wait to see what you kiss like when your mind is fully present."

I stared at him, mouth ajar. I didn't know how to respond. Was he teasing me? At a time like this?

"When was the last time you were kissed?" he went on easily. "And I'm not talking about the dry, noncommittal, meaningless kiss you forget about as soon as it's over."

I scrambled out of my stupor long enough to quip, "Like last night's kiss?"

He cocked an eyebrow. "That so? I wonder, then, why you moaned my name after you drifted to sleep."

"I did not!"

"If only I'd had a video recorder. When was the last time you were really kissed?" he repeated.

"You seriously think I'm going to tell you?"

"Your ex?" he guessed.

"And if he was?"

"Was it your ex who taught you to be ashamed and uncomfortable with intimacy? He took from you what he wanted, but never seemed to be around when you wanted something back, isn't that right? What do you want, Britt?" he asked me point-blank. "Do you really want to pretend like last night never happened?"

"Whatever happened between me and Calvin isn't your business," I fired back. "For your information, he was a really great boyfriend. I—I wish I was with him right now!" I exclaimed untruthfully.

My careless comment made him flinch, but he recovered quickly. "Does he love you?"

"What?" I said, flustered.

"If you know him so well, it shouldn't be a hard question. Is he in love with you? Was he ever in love with you?"

I tossed my head back haughtily. "I know what you're doing. You're trying to cut him down because you're—you're jealous of him!"

"You're damn right I'm jealous," he growled. "When I kiss a girl, I like to know she's thinking about me, not the fool who gave her up."

I turned away, humiliated that he'd guessed the truth. I could try to deny it, but he'd see right through me. The air between us felt charged and thick, and I sat there, hating him for making me feel guilty. Hating myself for letting things go this far. There was a name for people who fell in love with their captors. This wasn't real attraction; I'd been brainwashed. I wished I could take back kissing him. I wished I could take back ever meeting him.

Jude tied his bootlaces, yanking the knot. "I'm going to set a few traps and hopefully bring back breakfast. I shouldn't be gone more than a couple hours."

"What about the grizzly?"

"I just put two logs on the fire. He won't cross it to get to you."

"What about—you?" I kept my voice carefully indifferent.

He flashed me a cold smile, sharp at the edges. "Worried about me?"

Because I couldn't think of anything snide to say, I stuck my tongue out at him.

Jude wagged his head. "More tongue exercises? Would have thought you'd had enough last night."

"Go to hell."

"Sorry, love, but we're already there."

Without another word, Jude strode off into the snowy forest.

After Jude left, I decided to inventory our resources. The project would occupy my mind and keep me from analyzing my kiss with Jude. I did not want to figure out how I really felt about him. I did not want to admit that I might be in over my head.

We had a day's hike to Idlewilde, and I wanted to make sure, if a new storm rolled in or we faced some other unseen obstacle, that I knew what supplies we had. Unzipping Jude's backpack, I began organizing his belongings into three groups: bedding, food, and tools.

When I reached the bottom of the pack, I found a small canvas bag holding a few objects, but there wasn't a zipper, or any other opening that I could see. In fact, it was almost as if the bag had been entirely sewn shut. The objects' angular sides strained against the fabric, but I couldn't get to them.

It shouldn't have surprised me that Jude was hiding something—
he had gone on about the importance of secrets—but when I used
the pocketknife I'd stolen from the ranger patrol cabin to make a
neat incision along the seam, and when I saw the contents inside,
that's exactly what I was. Surprised.

No, not surprised. Shocked. Dizzy with disbelief. Sickened.

I pulled out a photograph of a girl. It was a candid shot, taken
from a distance, but the girl's eyes were eerily aware. Her wide,
haughty smile seemed to gloat at the camera, her eyes sizzling
with contempt, as if she were mentally flipping off the entire
world with a single piercing look.

Lauren Huntsman. The socialite who had disappeared last
April while vacationing with her parents in Jackson Hole.

Why did Jude have a picture of her? And not any picture, but
one taken without her permission. It was like he'd been spying
on her.

I went back to the canvas bag, this time retrieving a pair of
handcuffs. My stomach soured. Why would Jude have handcuffs?
I could think of an explanation. And it wasn't good.

I pulled out Lauren's diary next. It felt wrong to read her personal thoughts, but as I fanned through the pages, I told myself I
was only keeping an eye out for Jude's name. I had to know how
he was connected to her, but the bad feeling in my gut told me I
already knew.

Going dancing tonight. Watch out, Jackson Hole. It's gonna be one of
those nights. Plan A: Get drunk. Plan B: Do something I'll regret. Plan

C: Get arrested. Bonus points if I manage all three. Can't wait to see the look on M's face tomorrow. I'll know I've failed if she doesn't burst into tears at least once during dinner. Well, I'm off—wish me luck!

XO, Lauren

That was it. Lauren's diary ended abruptly on April 17 of last year. No mention of Jude.

It wasn't until I pulled the final item from the canvas bag that my hands started to shake in earnest. A heart-shaped gold locket. I dimly remembered watching one of the press conferences related to Lauren's disappearance on TV. Lauren's father had held up a sketch of a heart-shaped gold locket that Lauren had worn every day since she was a girl. He was adamant she would have been wearing the locket the night she disappeared.

It was now obvious why Jude had gone to great lengths to keep the contents of the bag secret. The evidence was indisputable.

I recalled a conversation I'd overheard between Jude and Shaun. Their words had bothered me initially, but now that I could put them into context, they chilled my blood.

I'm in charge, Ace. I brought you along to do one job; stay focused on that.

Followed by Jude's disturbing response: *We've been working together for almost a year. Think of everything I've done for you.*

A year ago, Lauren Huntsman vanished. Had Jude been involved? Had he murdered her? Was that his job description—killing?

Had Jude charmed Lauren first, like he had charmed me?

My head began to reel. A sour, sick feeling tickled the back of my throat. As I remembered kissing Jude, I felt like I'd been doused with ice water. I remembered lying beneath him, trapped by his body, the closeness of him almost overwhelming. I remembered his hands under my shirt, stroking—everywhere. I'd shivered then, and I shivered now. I felt dirty. What if he'd planned to seduce me, then kill me?

I never should have trusted him.

I was still rattled five minutes later, when I finished shoving Lauren's belongings and Jude's supplies into my backpack. I looked everywhere for Calvin's map, but Jude had taken it with him. Never mind the map. I knew Idlewilde was less than four miles from here, on the other side of two glacial lakes connected by a narrow strait. The water would be frozen, and I could cross the strait on foot. I was scared to hike the forest alone, but I couldn't stay any longer. I had no way of mending the canvas bag. Jude would know I'd found his secret. And it would change everything.

I hefted the backpack onto my shoulders. I meant to leave quickly, but something caused me to pause outside the entrance to our hideaway.

My insides squeezed at the sight of the crushed branches that had served as our bed. I thought of the many subtle ways Jude had helped me during the past few days, especially when Shaun was alive. He'd deflected Shaun's anger and encouraged me when I'd been on the brink of despair. He'd tried his best to make me comfortable. Was someone capable of such kindness also capable of such savagery? Did I really believe Jude could have killed Lauren Huntsman?

My mind traveled back to the evidence. If I tried to make

excuses for Jude now, I really was suffering from Stockholm syndrome. I'd tricked myself into believing I knew him. I'd looked past the hardened criminal and invented a romantic tale of a tortured hero in need of redemption. What a grave error in judgment.

No more excuses. The evidence was truth.

I walked hurriedly in the opposite direction from where I'd seen Jude go. He had the map, but I had the supplies. He was an expert tracker, but he wouldn't last long without water, blankets, a fire starter, and headlamps. Plus, I was counting on him being gone a while longer. Last time, it had taken us hours to hunt for food. If I got enough of a head start, I could beat him to Idlewilde.

From there, I'd call the police. And tell them Lauren Huntsman hadn't drowned in a lake. She'd been brutally murdered, and I had a pretty good idea where they could find her remains.

CHAPTER TWENTY-SEVEN

The mountains had never felt more hostile or inhabitable. A freezing cloud pressed down through the trees, painting the landscape in a strange casing of ice. The dense forest blocked out the sunlight, creating a dank darkness where twisted silhouettes of winter-bare trees played tricks. I saw skeletons with reaching arms and flashes of scowling faces in their marred gray trunks. A bitterly cold wind shrieked over the ground, kicking up snow like a frenzied herd of ghostly horses. The evergreens swayed uneasily, as if they knew something I didn't.

A hand snatched at my coat and I whirled around with a gasp, only to find a gnarled bush with thorny, untamed branches hooked in the fabric. Untangling myself, I swallowed nervously. I hurried forward, blindly beating away the cold, wet branches. With every step, I felt eyes on my back. The fog licked my skin, and I gave a convulsive shudder.

Bears and wolves. I thought of them as I slogged over the snow that last night's wind had swept into steep, formidable drifts. Each peak reminded me of a wave, frozen in icy whiteness a moment before it crested. The endless drifts and gloomy vapor made visibility difficult, so I kept my compass at my hip, consulting it constantly. Every now and then, the chilling wail of wind caused me to stop and glance over my shoulder, the hairs on my body raised.

Soon my muscles cried out in exhaustion. My last meal had been yesterday, and I felt weak and disoriented with hunger. It was too easy to imagine shutting my eyes against the lashing wind. But I knew if I rested, my thoughts would slide into a dangerous dream. One I'd never wake from.

My gloves were wet. My boots and socks too, the ice making my toes and fingers feel brittle enough to snap off. I flexed my hands, pumping blood to warm them. I rubbed them together, but I didn't know why I bothered. Eventually the pain would dull to an itchy numbness, and then I wouldn't feel anything. . . .

No. I was grateful for the sharp, stinging pain. It meant I was awake. Alive.

The snow and rocks slipped out from under my feet. When I failed to catch my balance, it was my backside that ended up wet. Each time, it took longer to drag myself upright. I dusted the snow off my clothes, but this too seemed pointless. I was already damp and shivering.

As I crested one wooded slope, another rose up behind it. And another. Behind the dense gray clouds, a bleak orb of sunlight made a slow trail across the sky. It reached the height of its journey, then began to sink toward the west. I'd been walking all day. Where was Idlewilde? Had I missed it? I didn't know whether to press on or circle back.

Degree by degree, my hope whittled down to despair. I wasn't sure the mountain would ever end. I dreamed of stumbling across a cabin, any cabin. I dreamed of thick walls and a hot fire. I dreamed of escaping the gale-force winds that ripped and chafed.

Out here, there was so much to escape. Wind and cold. Snow. Starvation.

Death.

CHAPTER TWENTY-EIGHT

The night Calvin taught Korbie and me how to play the Ouija board was the first night I ever remember being completely alone with him. There may have been other times, but that night I remember feeling like we were the only two people in the world. I loved Calvin Versteeg. He was my world. Every look he gave me, every word he spoke in my direction, felt forever etched on my heart.

"I have to pee! It's coming ouuuut!" Korbie giggled, yanking up the tent zipper. "I'm not gonna make it to the bathroom. I might have to pee on your shoes, Calvin!"

Calvin rolled his eyes as Korbie hopped dramatically from one foot to the other, cupping her crotch. He had left his tennis shoes outside the tent entrance, right next to my flip-flops. Mr. Versteeg never let us wear shoes inside the house. I doubted he cared about the tent getting dirty, but by now it was habit: no shoes inside.

"Why do you put up with her?" Calvin said to me, after Korbie stumbled out. We could hear her shrieking hysterically as she raced across the yard toward the cabin.

"She's not so bad."

"She's seriously short on brain cells."

I didn't want to talk about Korbie. Calvin and I were finally alone. I could have touched him; he was that close. I would have given anything to know if he had a girlfriend. How could he not? Any girl would be lucky to go out with him.

I cleared my throat. "You don't really believe ghosts use the Ouija to communicate with us, do you? Because I don't," I added with an eye roll, hoping I sounded sophisticated.

Calvin picked up a blade of grass one of us had tracked in, and began peeling it lengthwise into curling green ribbons. Without looking at me, he said, "When I think about ghosts, I think about Beau, and where he is now."

Beau had been the Versteegs' chocolate lab. He had died the previous summer. I didn't know how—Korbie wouldn't say. She cried for a whole week after he was gone, but refused to talk about him. When I asked my brother, Ian, how dogs died, he said, "They get hit by a car. Or they get cancer and after a while you have to put them down."

Since Beau died suddenly, it wasn't cancer.

"He's buried in my backyard at home," Calvin told me. "Under the peach tree."

"Under a peach tree is a good place to bury a dog." I wanted to wrap my arms around him, but I was scared he'd push me away.

My greatest fear was that he'd walk out and I'd lose my chance to really connect with him.

I scooted closer. "I know you really loved Beau."

"He was a good bird dog."

I placed my shaking hand on Calvin's knee. I waited, but he didn't jerk free or shove me away. He looked directly at me, his green eyes glassy and hurting.

"My dad shot him."

I hadn't expected that. It didn't fit with the picture in my head. I'd always imagined squealing tires and Beau's crumpled, broken body in the road. "Are you sure?"

Calvin gave me a cold look.

"Why would your dad shoot Beau? He was the best dog." It was true. I'd begged my dad for a dog. I wanted a chocolate lab like Beau.

"He was barking one night and the Larsens called to complain. I was asleep, but I remember the phone ringing. My dad hung up and shouted for me to put Beau in the garage. It was after midnight. I heard my dad, but I fell right back asleep. Then I heard the shots. Two of them. For a minute, I thought my dad had fired his rifle in my bedroom, the noise was that loud. I ran to the window. My dad kicked Beau to make sure he was really dead, then left him there. He didn't even lift him into a box."

I put my hand over my mouth. It was hot and stuffy in the tent, but I started shivering. Mr. Versteeg had always intimidated me, but now he seemed to transform into a frightening monster in my eyes.

"I buried Beau," Calvin said. "I waited until my dad went to bed, then I got a shovel. I spent the whole night digging. I had to lift Beau into a wagon, that's how heavy he was. I couldn't carry him by myself."

Knowing Calvin had to bury his own dog made me want to cry.

"I hate my dad," Calvin said in a low voice that gave me goose bumps.

"He's the worst dad ever," I agreed. My dad would never shoot a dog. Especially not for barking. Especially if I loved it.

"Sometimes I wonder if Beau's ghost is around," Calvin said. "I wonder if he's forgiven me for not putting him in the garage that night."

"Of course he's around," I said, trying to give him hope. "I bet Beau's in heaven right now, waiting for you. He's probably got a tennis ball in his mouth so the two of you can play fetch. Just 'cause you die doesn't mean you stop existing."

"I hope you're right about that, Britt," he murmured in a quiet, vengeful tone. "I hope when my dad dies, he goes to hell and suffers there for eternity."

CHAPTER TWENTY-NINE

At dusk, I saw chimney smoke rising above the treetops. I had walked the whole day without food or water and, delirious, I plodded heavily toward it. When the cabin loomed out of the swirling snow ahead, I thought it must be a mirage. It was too beautiful to be real, with its gold-burning windows and a puff of gray smoke twining up from the chimney.

Staggering to keep my balance as the winds toyed with me, I trudged toward it, mesmerized by the idea of warmth and rest. As I came up the slope of the snowed-under driveway, I gasped at how expertly my mind deceived me. Idlewilde towered before me in grand detail.

Icicles as thick as my arms hung from the gables, which were pitched one after another, replicating the glacial mountain peaks in the backdrop. Snow, inches deep, frosted the roof. I stared at the cabin hungrily.

A man's shadowy form crossed the expansive bank of windows. He gazed absently out at the yard, tipping a mug to his lips.

Calvin.

I heard myself say his name, a frozen, strangled sound. And then I was stumbling toward the cabin. I slipped and scrambled through the snow, never pulling my eyes from the door. I was terrified that if I looked away for even a moment, Idlewilde and Calvin would vanish into the growing dusk.

I pounded on the door, my frozen hands feeling like they would shatter. Wincing and crying, I scratched ineffectually at the thick wood door. I drove my boots against it, sobbing Calvin's name.

The door opened and Calvin stared at me. For a long moment, there was no recognition on his face, only confusion. All at once, his eyes sprang open in shock. "Britt!" He tugged me into the cabin, wasting no time taking off my pack and stripping off my wet coat and gloves.

I was too exhausted to speak. The next thing I knew, he'd carried me into the living room and stretched me out on the sofa next to the fire. I was dully aware of him searching my pockets, possibly looking for some clue to where I'd been. Finding nothing, he pried off my boots and massaged my feet. He bundled me in warm, dry blankets, and fit a hat snugly over my head. Then came a litany of questions that jumbled in my frozen brain.

Can you hear me? How many fingers? How long outside? Alone?

I tilted my chin up, gazing into his green eyes, reassured by their competence. I wanted to climb into his arms and weep while he held me, but I didn't know how to make my body move. A tear dripped down my cheek, and I hoped Calvin understood the words I was too tired to say. We were together. Everything was going to be okay. He'd take care of me.

Calvin slapped my cheeks. "Can't fall asleep."

I nodded obediently, but sleep dragged at me. He didn't understand. I'd used all my energy getting here. I didn't have any left. I had to sleep. I'd been outside, walking and freezing, while he was here at the cabin. Why hadn't he come looking for me?

While I faded in and out of awareness, Calvin left the room several times, always returning swiftly to poke and prod at me. I faintly noted him sticking a thermometer under my tongue. On the next trip, he nestled warm water bottles near my armpits and tucked what felt like a heating pad around my lap. He ordered me to drink a mug of herbal tea and even offered me some candy, but I shook my head. They could wait. I wished he'd leave me alone long enough to let me sleep soundly.

". . . stay with me, Britt."

I can't, I thought back, but the words dissolved inside me.

He grasped my head, forcing me to look directly in his eyes. "No sleep. Not . . . leave alone. Focus . . . me." His words sounded muffled, like they traveled down a long tunnel before reaching me.

Oh, Cal.

I sighed, trying to squirm out of his grip. He slapped my cheeks again. With a deeper pang of annoyance, I wished he would stop bothering me. If I'd had the strength, I would have shoved him away.

BECCA FITZPATRICK

"Let go," I slurred irritably, batting weakly at his hands.

"Keep . . . fight. Stay . . . me. Warm you up."

He grasped my shoulders, shaking me incessantly, until what little patience was left inside me snapped and I lashed out in anger. "Stop, Cal, leave *alone!*" After the words exploded out of me, I sagged back on the sofa, breathless and exhausted. But fully awake.

Bent over me, Calvin relaxed. He smiled, stroking my cheek affectionately. "That's more like it. Get as angry as you want, if that's what it takes to keep you conscious. I'm not letting you sleep until your temperature climbs above ninety-six."

"Says who?" I sniffed weakly.

"Really? You're going to argue with me now?" Cal's eyes softened, and he smoothed my damp hair off my face. Reaching under the blankets, he clasped my hand, squeezing hard, like he was terrified he's lose me if he let go. "I was so worried about you, Britt. Korbie told me everything. I know about Shaun and Ace."

I blinked a few times, thinking I must have misheard. My brain muddled through this new information at a lagging pace. "Korbie?"

"She's here. Upstairs, sleeping. I found her at the cabin. They left her to die, Britt. I found her just in time. She had no food. She's going to make a full recovery, but this isn't over. They tried to kill my sister and my—my girl," he finished, his voice cracking slightly. "If anything had happened to either of you—" He broke off, turning his face away, but not before I saw his eyes burning with rage.

Calvin had found Korbie. Of course he had. Cal was Cal. He loved Korbie, and he loved me. He would do anything to keep us safe.

But if I was his girl, and he loved me, why hadn't he gone back out to look for me?

I pushed myself upright against the pillow. My limbs were uncoordinated from the cold, but that didn't stop me from fighting to free myself from the blankets. "I have to see Korbie."

"In the morning," Calvin assured me. "I only found her today. She was bad off, panicked and delusional, and she hurt herself— she tripped on the stairs and bruised her back and elbow. She wouldn't let me touch her, kept screaming at me and calling me Shaun. I gave her a sleeping pill to help her relax. She needs a good night's rest. Same goes for you—can I get you a pill? My mom left her prescription up here last summer, and it hasn't expired yet."

"No, I just want to see Korbie."

Calvin tried to lower me back onto the sofa, but I struggled against him. I had to see Korbie. I needed to see for myself that she was okay.

"All right, you can see her," he relented, "but let me bring her to you. You should rest. I'll make you some dinner and then go get her." He dragged his hands down his face, but not before I saw his eyes moisten. "I thought the worst, Britt. I thought it was a miracle I'd found her, and I'd never be lucky enough to find you too. I thought— My life— Without you—"

Tears streamed down my face, and a knot swelled in my throat.

Calvin loved me. Nothing had changed. At that moment, it was so easy to forget the pain and heartache of the past. I forgave him completely. This was it—our fresh start.

"I'm scared, Cal." I scooted closer to him. "He—Ace—is out there." I didn't bother calling him Jude; explaining the name change would only complicate things.

Calvin nodded curtly. "I know. But I won't let him hurt you. As soon as the roads clear, I'm getting you and Korbie out of here. We'll go to the police and tell them everything."

I shook my head, indicating there was more. "Ace killed . . ." I licked my lips. I hadn't expected the words would be so difficult to say. It was hard to admit Jude had killed Lauren Huntsman, because it pointed glaringly to my utter lack in judgment. I'd trusted Jude. I'd kissed him. I'd let his hands explore my body, the same hands that had ruthlessly slayed an innocent girl. It was appalling and humiliating. If there was one event in my past I wished I held the power to go back and change, that was it. Failing to see Jude's revolting true character.

"Shh," Calvin murmured, gently pressing his finger to my lips. "You're safe with me. You lived through a nightmare, but it's over. I won't let him hurt you. He's going to pay for taking you hostage. He'll go to prison, Britt. You'll never have to see him again."

I tried to let Calvin's confidence console me, and forced myself to push aside the memory of Jude's searing, rousing kiss. Whatever had happened between us, it was a lie. He had deceived me; I had to remember that. Any lingering feelings I might have for him were based on the lie, and I had to cut them out, like a cancer.

"Ace murdered a girl up here in the mountains and I have evidence." There. I'd said it. And while it hurt, it was the right thing to do. I wasn't going to protect Jude. "He killed Lauren Huntsman. Look in my backpack—the evidence is there."

Calvin stared at me, his expression clouded with disbelief. "He killed—Lauren?" he stammered, clearly as startled as I'd originally been.

"She disappeared from Jackson Hole last year. Do you remember? It was all over the news." I felt relieved to pass the weight of Jude's secret to someone else.

"I remember," Calvin answered, still looking shocked. "Are you sure?"

I shut my eyes, feeling light-headed and weary again. "Look in the backpack. Everything needed to prove his guilt is there. Lauren's locket, her diary, and a photograph confirming he stalked her before he killed her."

Calvin nodded, obviously shaken. "Okay, I'll do it; just lie back and take it easy, you hear?"

Calvin went to the window and gazed out on the snowy woods surrounding Idlewilde. He cupped one hand behind his neck, squeezing methodically. I could tell he was uneasy, and that made the knot return to my chest. Calvin had not known we were going up against a killer.

"Do you have my map?" he asked without turning around. "Korbie told me you took it. I'm not mad, but I need it back."

"No, Ace has it. He's out there looking for me, Cal. I took the evidence that proves he killed Lauren Huntsman. He isn't going to let me get away. Idlewilde is marked on the map. I think he's going to come here."

"If he does, he's not getting in," he answered grimly.

"With the map, he'll be able to cover a lot of ground quickly without worrying about getting lost." I could have kicked myself for giving Jude the map. What a careless mistake. What had I been thinking, to trust him so easily?

"What weapons does he have?"

"He's unarmed. But he's strong, Cal. And smart. Almost as smart as you."

Calvin strode to the desk across the room and opened the top drawer. He took out a handgun and inserted a loaded magazine before shoving it into his belt. I knew the Versteegs kept guns at Idlewilde; Mr. Versteeg had a permit to carry concealed weapons, and Calvin had grown up hunting.

His eyes locked on mine. "Almost as smart."

CHAPTER THIRTY

Calvin brought me chicken broth and bread for dinner. Then he went to wake Korbie. When I saw her appear at the top of the stairs, I couldn't help myself. I hastily set aside the tray holding my dinner, tossed off my blankets, and ran for her. The groggy, drugged glaze in Korbie's eyes cleared as she saw me racing up the steps toward her. By the time I threw my arms around her, Korbie was already sobbing loudly.

"I thought I was going to die," she gasped. "I thought you were dead for sure."

"Nobody's dead," Calvin said, and I could practically hear him roll his eyes at our emotional display.

"I didn't have any food," Korbie explained to me. "They left me in that cabin to die. And I would have, if Calvin hadn't found me."

"Of course I found you," Calvin pointed out.

I said, "Ace told me he left you two granola bars and a canteen, though, right?"

A quick, guilty glance at her brother revealed that Korbie had left that part out. "Yes, but it was hardly anything! Not enough to last two days. Besides, the granola bars were stale and I had to force myself to eat them."

For once, Korbie's melodrama didn't bother me. I hugged her harder. "I'm so glad you're alive and safe."

"Calvin and I tried to call the police, but the phone line is down and Calvin's cell phone isn't getting service," Korbie informed me. "So Calvin's going to find Shaun and Ace himself and bring them in. Citizen's arrest, right, Calvin? They're on foot and Calvin's got a snowmobile. I told Calvin their plan is to get off the mountain and hijack a car, and he's going to go out first thing tomorrow and patrol the roads. They're not getting away with this."

"But Shaun—" I began dazedly.

"I'll use whatever force I have to to detain them," Calvin said. "One thing's for sure. They're not leaving the Tetons—unless they're tied in the back of my SUV."

I blinked at Calvin. Why was he talking like Shaun was alive? He shot Shaun and burned the body. I'd watched him do it.

"Calvin found the snowmobile abandoned by the roadside, wasn't that lucky?" Korbie went on. "It had the keys left in the ignition and everything. There was a radio in it, and Calvin thinks the snowmobile probably belonged to a park ranger. He tried to use the radio to call for help, but it had been destroyed."

"Lucky," I murmured in agreement, a faint chill passing down my spine. Calvin took the snowmobile from the ranger patrol cabin. So why wasn't he correcting his sister? Why was he lying?

Was Calvin going to pretend like he hadn't killed Shaun? Surely the police would understand. Shaun was a criminal. And anyway, Calvin shot Shaun in self-defense.

Only he hadn't.

As Jude had reminded me too many times to count, Shaun had been unarmed when Calvin pulled the trigger.

I went to bed numb, but not from cold. Calvin had monitored me closely all evening, and true to his word, had refused to let me sleep until my body temperature crept into a safe range. Even though I'd watched Calvin check the door locks, I was scared of the dark, and of what—who—might try to come in while I slept. Jude was out there in the forest. And while a bolted door might slow him down, it might not stop him. His future depended on destroying the evidence that proved he was a murderer. I had a hunch, right now, that Jude was feeling *very* determined.

Calvin put me in the bear-themed bedroom on the second floor at the top of the stairs, the same room I had slept in on my previous visits to Idlewilde. Mrs. Versteeg had given each of the bedrooms a theme, and mine had a four-poster log bed with a bear-patterned quilt, a faux bear rug, and framed photos of bears on the walls. One photo was of a mother black bear playing with two cubs, but the other portrayed a roaring grizzly, fangs bared. I suddenly wished I had Korbie's room, with its fishing theme. I didn't want to remember last night's encounter with the grizzly . . . or what had followed, under the tree, with Jude.

I lay in bed, listening to Calvin pace downstairs. He kept the TV off, tuning his ears to any strange sounds. He'd also shut off the interior lights, but left the outside ones blazing like spotlights on every entrance into the cabin. No one, he'd vowed to me, would approach the cabin without his noticing.

As I felt myself drifting off, a knock sounded on the bedroom door.

"Cal?" I cried out, bolting to a sitting position and clutching the sheet to my chin.

He cracked the door. "Did I wake you?"

I exhaled, relieved. "No. Come in." I patted the mattress beside me.

He kept the light off. "Just wanted to make sure you're okay."

"I'm a little scared, but I feel safe with you." As skilled and determined as Jude was, Calvin had him beat. If Jude found Idlewilde, if he tried to break in, Calvin would stop him. These were the words I told myself.

"No one is getting in," Calvin assured me, and it comforted me that like old times, he knew how to read my thoughts.

"Do you have an extra gun?" I asked. "Do you think I should carry one, just in case?"

The mattress dipped as he sat beside me. He was wearing a ratty red-and-black Highland High School Rams sweatshirt. I'd borrowed the sweatshirt countless times last year, taking it to bed with me so I could breathe in the warm, salty scent of Calvin while I slept. I hadn't seen Calvin or his sweatshirt since he left for Stanford eight months ago. It struck me as odd that he hadn't replaced the sweatshirt with one from Stanford. Maybe he had and it was in the wash. Or maybe he wasn't ready to let go of the past, and those who'd meant the most to him. It was a comforting thought.

Calvin asked, "Do you know how to use a gun?"

"Ian has one, but I've never fired it."

"Then you're better off without it. Britt, I owe you an apology—" He stopped himself, dropping his eyes to his lap and exhaling slowly.

I could have smoothed over the silence with one dismissive or witty remark, but I decided not to jump in and save him. I deserved this. I'd waited a long time to hear these words.

"I'm sorry I hurt you. I never meant to hurt you," he said, his expression crumpling with emotion. He turned away, hastily swatting his tears. "I know it seemed like I ran off as fast as I could, like I couldn't leave town, and you, fast enough. Believe it or not, I was scared to go to college. My dad put a lot of pressure on me. I was scared of failing. I felt like I had to cut myself off from home and start building my new life right away. I had to impress my dad. I had to show him I deserved the tuition money, and he'd given me a damn thorough checklist to make sure I was measuring up," he added bitterly. "Do you know what his last words to me were before I left? He said, 'Don't you dare get homesick. Only pussies look back.' He meant it, Britt. That's why I didn't come home for Thanksgiving or Christmas—to prove I was a man and didn't need to run home when things got tough. That, and I didn't want to see him."

I took Calvin's hand and squeezed it. To cheer him up, I lifted his chin and gave him a mischievous smile. "Remember how we made that voodoo doll when we were kids, and pretended it was your dad, and took turns stabbing a pin into it?"

Calvin snorted, but his voice remained toneless. "I stole one of his socks from his drawer, and we stuffed it with cotton balls and drew his face on it with a black marker. Korbie took the pin from my mom's sewing box."

"I don't even remember what he did that made us so mad."

Calvin's jaw clenched. "I missed a free throw during my seventh-grade basketball game. When we got home, he told me to start shooting baskets. He wouldn't let me in the house until I'd made a thousand free throws. It was freezing out, and I only had on my jersey and shorts. You and Korbie watched from the window, crying. When I finished, it was almost bedtime. Four hours," he murmured to himself despondently. "He let me freeze out there for four hours."

Now I remembered. Calvin had come inside at last, his skin mottled and chafed, his lips blue, his teeth chattering. Four hours, and Mr. Versteeg hadn't once stuck his head out the front door to check on his son. He'd sat in his office clicking away on his laptop, his back to the window that looked out on the hoop in the driveway.

"You'll thank me for this," Mr. Versteeg had said, clasping Calvin on his frozen shoulder. "Next game, no air balls. You'll see."

CHAPTER THIRTY-ONE

"I'm sorry your dad was so hard on you," I told Calvin, lacing my fingers through his to show him I was on his side.

He hadn't moved from my bed. Stiff-shouldered, he glared at the wall as if he were seeing his unhappy childhood projected onto it like a movie. The sound of my voice seemed to break his trance, and he shrugged. "Was? He's still hard on me."

"At least you were able to escape to California this year," I offered optimistically, with a soft, playful tug on his sleeve. I remembered Calvin once praising me for being able to stir him out of his dark, pensive moods with a simple joke or a kiss. I now felt obligated to show him some things never changed. "The distance must have helped. His beating stick only reaches so far."

"Yeah," he agreed blandly. "I don't want to talk about my dad. I want things between us to be like they used to be. Not between me

and my dad," he clarified quickly. "Between us. You and me. I want you to trust me again."

His words struck me with unseen force. Our conversation came uncannily close to the one I'd envisioned on the drive up to Idlewilde, days ago, before I knew the danger in store. I'd fantasized that Calvin wanted me back. I'd vowed I wouldn't soften until he'd fully paid for hurting me. But I didn't feel vindictive anymore. I wanted to let him love me. I was tired of games.

Calvin cupped my chin, nudging my face close to his. "I thought about you every night in my dorm. I imagined kissing you. Touching you."

Cal, dreaming about me. Miles away, in some small room I'd never visited. Cal, sharing my secret fantasy. Wasn't this what I'd wanted?

Playfully, he grabbed me by the scruff of my neck and gathered me onto his lap. "It feels right to be with you. I want you, Britt."

Calvin wanted to be with me. It should have been a romantic moment, I should have felt music in my heart, but my mind kept traveling back to everything I'd just gone through. Hours ago, I'd arrived on his doorstep freezing to death. I wasn't fully recovered. Why did he want this now? Wasn't he concerned about me?

"Is this your first time?" Calvin asked. "It only hurts a little." His mouth curved against my cheek. "Or so I'm told."

I had always wanted Calvin to be my first. I'd spent my childhood fantasizing that someday I would walk down the aisle and meet him at the altar. My first time would be on our honeymoon, on the beach, after dark, with the waves tugging at our bodies.

Calvin knew I wanted to wait. So why was he pushing me now?

"Say you want me, Britt," Calvin murmured.

Absurdly, I could think of everything but a response. Calvin wasn't guarding the cabin doors. Were we safe? Did I want this?

Calvin kissed me harder, batting my pillow out of the way as he pinned me against the headboard. His hands seemed to be everywhere at once: rucking up my nightshirt, kneading the soft flesh at my hips, stroking my thighs. I sank back on my rear and drew my knees up, trying to slow him down long enough to think, but he laughed softly, interpreting the gesture the wrong way.

"Playing hard to get. I like that." He advanced on me, kissing me with a short, painful grind of his mouth. My heart beat faster, but it had nothing to do with excitement. The word "no" bubbled up in my throat.

Suddenly I saw Jude's dark eyes flash before mine. The image was so real, it was like he knelt in front of me, not Calvin.

I tore away as if I'd been shocked. Staring at Calvin, I wiped my mouth dry with the back of my hand. All traces of Jude had vanished, but I continued to blink anxiously at Calvin, terrified Jude's face would reappear. Did I feel him close by? Was that possible?

I cut my gaze to the door, half expecting to see Jude stride through it. Bizarrely, I almost hoped he did. He'd stop Calvin.

No. I flung the thought from my head with self-loathing. I did not want Jude. He was a criminal. A murderer. Thinking he cared about me was a lie.

Calvin grabbed for me with an impatient groan. "Don't make me stop now."

I scrabbled over the edge of the bed and landed on my feet. I wanted Calvin out of my room, and Jude out of my head. "No, Calvin," I said firmly.

He reeled me roughly into his embrace. "I'll be a gentleman." His lips fumbled over mine.

"No."

My voice finally broke through his dreamy expression, and his face clouded with incomprehension. "You acted like you wanted this," he said accusingly.

Had I? I'd invited him in, but I wanted to cuddle, to talk. I hadn't asked for this. "This isn't about your boyfriend, is it?" Calvin groaned, plowing his hands through his hair. "Everyone cheats in high school, Britt."

Like you cheated with Rachel? I wanted to ask.

"I won't tell," he promised. "And you sure as hell won't tell. So where's the harm?"

It dawned on me that Calvin didn't realize Mason from the 7-Eleven wasn't my real boyfriend. Nor did he realize that that Mason was the same Mason, or Ace, who'd abducted Korbie and me. He'd missed that entire story unfolding.

Now wasn't the time to tell him. Calvin acting this way, jealous and scary, made me worry about what he might try next. He'd killed Shaun. Lied about it. And now he was in my bedroom, pushing me further than I wanted. Being with him now felt different. Something had changed, but I couldn't put my finger on it. Except to say that in eight months, he seemed to have forgotten everything about me.

"You're not going to say anything?" Calvin said angrily. "You're kicking me out, just like that?"

"I don't want to argue," I said quietly.

Calvin rolled off my bed, his sharp green eyes studying me a few beats longer. "Sure, Britt, anything for you," he said, in a bland voice that I interpreted as a little bit defeated, a little bit disappointed.

CHAPTER THIRTY-TWO

I woke to a chilly draft. I'd forgotten to close the drapes before drifting off. Padding to the window, I tugged the knot loose on the tiebacks. Since I was up, I stood at the window a moment, peering watchfully at the woods. I wished I could pinpoint Jude in the vast darkness. He was out there somewhere, coming for me, I was sure of it.

An arched alcove led to a Jack-and-Jill bathroom I shared with Korbie, and I went to the sink to splash water on my face. My muscles were sore from the long, arduous hike to Idlewilde, and when I glanced at my reflection, I saw with alarm that I looked awful. My skin was as bleached as driftwood, and every bit as gray. Dark smudges ringed my eyes, and my hair, dull and matted, hadn't been washed in days.

Unnerved by the sight, I put my back to the mirror. I stood

a moment on the cold tile floor, debating. Then I cracked the door leading to Korbie's bedroom. Leaving the lights off, I walked silently to stand over her bed. She slept on her stomach, her deep, rhythmic snoring partially muffled by her pillow. The urge to smooth her hair overcame me, but I knew Calvin would never forgive me if I woke her. Instead, I crawled into bed beside her and cried silently.

I'm so sorry, I thought at her. It was my idea to come to the mountains. I never meant to hurt you. Not now, or when I dated Calvin. I wish I'd told you about us. It was wrong, to keep it a secret.

Calvin and I had dated for less than six months. Since I'd known him my whole life, and had been in love with him for most of it, I guess it felt longer than that. He had always been a part of my life, even when we weren't an official couple.

I'd wanted to make him happy, and that's why I'd agreed to keep our relationship secret. But deep down, it had hurt that he'd been unwilling to publicly call me his girlfriend. It had hurt too to lie to my friends, especially Korbie, especially since Calvin was her brother. To make myself feel better, I'd told myself that relationships were about compromise. I couldn't have everything I wanted. That was part of growing up and accepting that the world didn't revolve around me.

And then Korbie found out. It happened at her pool party, last summer. The same pool party where Calvin kissed Rachel. Calvin and I had agreed beforehand that we would treat the pool party like any other occasion. He'd hang out with his friends, and I'd hang out with mine. If our paths crossed, we'd acknowledge each other, the same as we'd done for years, but flirting of any kind was off-limits.

I bought a one-piece black swimsuit with side cutouts for the party. The other girls would be wearing bikinis, and I wanted to stand out. I knew Calvin would be watching. Before the party, I changed into the swimsuit in Korbie's bedroom, and the moment she saw it, I knew I'd picked the right one.

"Smokin'," she said, with that desirable mix of admiration and envy.

Korbie had invited me over an hour early to help her finish setting up, so we put on our cover-ups and headed for the kitchen. I told her I had to use the bathroom, but I slipped down the hall to Calvin's room. I grabbed a piece of paper from his printer and scribbled a quick note, one that I'd been editing in my head for hours. I hadn't come up with the perfect lines yet, but I was out of time.

Tonight, when you see me stroke my arm, it means I'm thinking about you. And when you see me dip my toes in the pool, I'm imagining we're alone in the pool and I'm sitting in your lap while you kiss me.

XOXO,
Britt

Before I could chicken out, I folded the note, tucking it half-way under Calvin's pillow; then I hurried to meet Korbie in the kitchen.

It wasn't until right before the guests started showing up that Korbie marched outside to where I was raising the table umbrellas, and waved the note angrily in my face.

"What's this?"

"I—it's just—" I stammered. "Where did you get that?"

"On Calvin's pillow, where do you think?"

"You weren't supposed to see it." I'd been dreading this day for months. I'd had plenty of time to prepare my apology, but at that moment, words failed me.

Korbie burst into tears. She dragged me across the yard, behind the lilac hedge. I'd never seen her so upset. "Why didn't you tell me?"

"Korbie, I'm so sorry." I really didn't know what to say. I felt awful.

"How long have you been together?"

"April."

She wiped her tears away. "You should have told me."

"I know. You're right. What I did was wrong, and I feel terrible."

Korbie sniffled. "Did you keep it a secret because you thought I'd get mad?"

"No," I said truthfully. "Calvin wasn't ready to tell people."

"Do you think he's using you?"

I felt my face turn red. Why did she have to ask me that? On a night when I was already feeling insecure about me and Calvin? "I don't think so. I don't know," I said miserably.

"If you had to choose between us, you'd choose me, wouldn't you?"

BECCA FITZPATRICK

"Of course," I said quickly. "You're my best friend."

Korbie dropped her eyes and took my hand. "I don't want to share you with him."

Little did Korbie know, she wouldn't have to share me much longer. When Calvin took off to Stanford, it marked the beginning of the end of us.

I closed the memory and returned my mind to the present. I didn't want to leave Korbie's bed, but Calvin would be making his rounds soon, so I pulled her blankets to cover her shoulders, and shut the door behind me on my way out.

I was halfway to my own bed when my brain registered something not quite right in the corner beside the armoire. The large, human form blended like a shadow, hugging the wall, and before I recovered my breath, he sprang at me, wrestling me flat onto the bed and drowning my cry of alarm with his ice-cold hand.

"Don't scream—it's me, Jude," he said.

I convulsed harder, showing him that his announcement did little to mollify me. Managing to get my knee up, I aimed for his groin, but fell a few inches short, giving him a hard jab to his thigh.

Jude's gaze fell briefly on my intended mark, and he cocked his brows ironically as he returned his attention to me.

"Close call," he breathed. To prevent any further risks, he swiftly climbed on top of me, flattening me with his large, wet, and very cold body. However he'd gained access to Idlewilde, he hadn't been inside long; snow clung to his coat, and his dark facial stubble glistened with melting ice.

I protested the crushing weight of his body with an angry exclamation, but with his hand sealing my mouth, I doubted Calvin could have heard it even if he were standing in the hall with his ear pressed to the door. A more likely scenario was that he was downstairs pacing between Idlewilde's front and back doors, oblivious that the danger had already made its way inside.

"Surprised to see me?" Jude asked, bending close to keep his voice from carrying. He smelled the same way I remembered, of goose down, pine sap, and campfire. Only, the last time we'd lain this close, I'd been far more ignorant and therefore willing. "But not half as surprised as I was when I came back to camp this morning to find you gone. You should have told me you were leaving, and saved me the trouble of killing a rabbit for you."

There was a controlled anger in his tone that made me squirm inwardly. I didn't want to believe Jude would hurt me. Then again, he'd killed Lauren Huntsman. He was an expert at concealing his true character. Most psychopaths were. It reminded me of neighbors of convicted serial killers, who always exclaimed, "But he was such a nice man!"

"You're not going to scream, Britt," Jude informed me in that same quiet, lethal tone. "You're going to hear me out. And then you're going to tell me where you put the things you stole from me."

For one moment, my anger overrode my fear, and without thinking, I arched my eyebrows defiantly. *Is that what you think, you psychopath?* I inwardly raged at him. *Take your hand off and I'll scream so loud your ears will snap off!*

"Have it your way," Jude replied to my outraged wriggling. "I'll do the talking, and you can listen. And your friend downstairs can continue to stare stupidly out the living room window. Like I'd march up under the spotlights he's got fixed on the grounds and wave hello."

At his insult to Calvin, I bucked wildly with indignation. I prayed Calvin would come check on me and blow a hole directly between Jude's hateful eyes. But maybe it was better this way. Maybe it was good that Jude underestimated Calvin. I couldn't wait to see the shock on his face when he realized he never should have crossed Calvin. If Jude had come here to kill me now that I knew he'd murdered Lauren Huntsman, it would ignite a fire in Calvin. Jude would see.

"You said you trusted me, then went through my personal belongings. You should have asked me to explain myself before jumping to conclusions and running off," Jude said, his voice cool and pissed. "Then again, I'm not sure you ever cared. I misjudged you, Britt. Excellent marks for getting me to lower my guard—not many get to claim that achievement. You played me hard. Did you intend to go through my stuff all along? Or was your seduction act to ensure I'd help you to Idlewilde? Well, you wasted your time," he said, his tone growing angrier. "And threw away your self-respect. I told you I'd get you here, and I meant it."

I looked directly in his eyes and jerked my chin in a haughty nod. *That's right. I was faking. The kissing was an act.* It felt good to think the words at him, to not give him the satisfaction of thinking I ever cared, especially if this was it, the end of my life.

Only, my eyes filled with tears, and this ruined the brazenness of my attack. I tried to turn my head away before he saw, hating the idea of displaying weakness now. I couldn't decide if I was crying for fear of my life, or because Jude's words had ripped open a wound. Last night under the tree wasn't an act. I'd made out with him because I'd wanted to. I'd trusted him. And the betrayal, the truth about who he was, hurt like my heart was being wrenched in two.

"Crying now too? You're a better actor than I guessed," Jude snorted bitterly. "Cry yourself dry—I'm not letting you go, Britt. Not after I went to the trouble of tracking you down. I'm not leaving until you give me back what you stole. Now, where are they?" he demanded, shaking me roughly. "Where are the locket and diary?"

I shook my head emphatically. I panted hard through my nose, glaring at him to communicate my message. Never before had I wanted to curse so vehemently; a slew of the worst and foulest words I could think of flashed across my mind, and I only wished I had the great satisfaction of spitting them in his face.

"Where are they?" he growled again, grinding me harder into the mattress.

I squeezed my eyes shut, thinking this was it. He had one hand clasped over my mouth, the other braced behind my head. With one rough twist, he could snap my neck. My breath came in short, dire pants. I knew it was shameful to wait until now to pray, but I was desperate. *Dear God, comfort my dad and Ian after I'm gone. And if this is the end, please let Jude do it swiftly, and not draw out the pain.*

When nothing happened, I dared open my eyes. Jude leaned

over me, his harsh, raging features crumbling. He shook his head, self-disgust and weariness etched in his expression. He let go of me, grinding his palms into his bloodshot eyes. His shoulders sagged, his whole body trembling as he broke down, silently crying.

He hadn't killed me. I wasn't dead.

I lay on the bed, unable to do anything but cry alongside him. My shoulders shook in great, silent heaves.

"Did you kill her?" I asked.

"Do you think I did?"

"You had her belongings."

Bitterness edged his words. "So now I murdered her? Was it easy to jump to the conclusion, to condemn me as a murderer, or did you wrestle with your judgment a bit first? Given what we shared last night, I hope you spared a couple minutes to weigh my character."

"I saw Lauren Huntsman's dad on the news. He was adamant she would have been wearing the locket the night she disappeared."

"She was."

I swallowed hard. Was it a confession? "What were the handcuffs for?"

Jude cringed, and I knew he'd hoped I'd forgotten about them. But how could I? What kind of normal person carried handcuffs?

"Did you handcuff Lauren?" I continued. "So she couldn't get away? To make her powerless?"

"You think I'm capable of terrible things, you've made that clear," Jude said, his tone halfway between jaded and fatigued.

"But I'm not the bad guy you've made me out to be. I'm trying to do the right thing, which is why I'm here now. I'm trying to catch the *real* bad guy. And to do that, I need Lauren's belongings."

More cryptic explanations. I was getting tired of them. I didn't know what to believe. I only knew that if I made the mistake of trusting Jude a second time, I was not only a fool, but probably dead. He could be tricking me . . . only to kill me and eliminate me as a witness.

"Who was Lauren to you?"

Jude rubbed his hands over his face, and they shook as he did. He bent over, hunching his shoulders and ducking his head, almost like he was being assailed by memories—invisible, bewitched objects that flew at him with painful force.

"I didn't kill Lauren," he said in a flat, toneless voice. He sat on the edge of the bed, staring at the shadowed wall. Even in the low light, I could see his eyes were vacant. "She left a message on my phone hours before she disappeared. She told me she was going drinking, and I knew she was baiting me, like she'd done a hundred times before. She wanted me to stop her. My plane had just touched down in Jackson Hole when I got the message, and I wanted to shower and grab something to eat; I was sick and tired of dropping everything to come rescue her. So I ignored her call. For once, I wanted her to clean up her own mess." His breath caught and he looked up at me with hollow, tortured eyes. "Lauren was my sister, Britt. I was supposed to take care of her, and I failed her. Not a day goes by that I don't imagine how things would have been different if I hadn't been so selfish."

Lauren was his sister?

Before I could sort it out, Jude went on. "The police gave up on finding her, but I never did. I had her diary, and I pored through it for clues. I went to every bar, club, pool hall, and hotel in Jackson Hole that I thought she might have visited. My family had been vacationing there for a week before I arrived, so I knew she'd had plenty of time to make her way around. People must have seen her. Someone had seen *something*. Though I criticized the police for not making any headway, I had a resource they didn't—my family's money. I paid people to talk, and one person, a bartender, remembered seeing Lauren leave his bar with a cowboy. The bartender later leaked to the news that Lauren was seen leaving Silver Dollar Cowboy Bar with a man in a black Stetson, which infuriated me, because I didn't want to tip off the man I was hunting for.

"Based on the bartender's description, I knew I was looking for a man in his early twenties, slim, average height, broken nose, blond hair, blue eyes, and possibly wearing a black Stetson. Then I went back to that same bar every night for weeks, until at last Shaun came in. He matched the description. I learned his name and ran a background check, and found out he'd recently moved to Wyoming from Montana, where he had a record of misdemeanors—petty theft, simple assault, and disorderly conduct. I was pretty sure I had my man.

"I quit college, left my friends and family, moved to Wyoming, and made it my full-time job to earn Shaun's trust. I created a false identity and committed petty crimes and hustled his enemies to prove myself to him. I would have done whatever it took to get Shaun to confide in me. I believed eventually he'd confess to killing Lauren. And then, once I knew for sure he'd done it, I'd murder him. Slowly," he added in a cold, menacing tone, a flicker of black fire burning in his eyes.

I had recovered sufficiently to scoot backward across the bed—silently, so Jude wouldn't notice. It was a sentimental and convenient story. Maybe Jude realized threatening me wasn't working, and was trying a new angle. His story also didn't explain the locket and the stalkerish photograph. Lauren's parents were certain she was wearing the locket when she died. Jude must have been there when she was killed. He'd had to have removed it from her body. Carefully, I swung one foot off the bed, but the floor gave me away. It creaked under my weight.

Jude turned as if startled. I froze. I could scream now, but before Calvin could run up, Jude would have time to land a forceful, deadly blow on my head and slip out the window.

"Keep going," I urged him gently, trying to keep the nervousness out of my voice.

To my astonishment, Jude blinked, and in an almost trance-like manner obeyed my request. "Killing Shaun, if he'd murdered Lauren, was my endgame. He had started bragging about some of his crimes, like blackmailing wealthy married women with pictures he took of them when they were drunk. A little longer, and I was sure he'd tell me about Lauren.

"And then he robbed the Subway and shot a cop. Shaun was freaked out—I'd never seen him so afraid. He knew we were in trouble. As he sped away, he was so panicked, he hit a girl crossing the street. I don't think he even saw her. His reaction should have caused me to reconsider the likelihood that he'd killed before, but I didn't want to be wrong about him." Jude squeezed above his eyebrows, his expression tightening with pain. "I'd been hunting for Lauren's killer too long to go back to square one.

"After Shaun shot the cop, we were forced to go on the run. To make matters worse, you and Korbie showed up at the cabin we were hiding in. Instead of making your safety my priority, I was furious that you'd screwed up my plans. It was like I wasn't even human. The bloodthirsty rage was in control, driving me to get Shaun's confession. Everything had narrowed to that one target. If he'd killed her, I was going to return the favor to him, and if there were consequences for me, damn them. I knew I'd go down for it, but it seemed right. I wanted to die. I'd failed Lauren and didn't deserve anything less."

Jude planted his elbows on his knees and bowed his head, weaving his fingers together at the back of his neck. He was closer to the door than me, but if I continued toward it in small, quiet steps—

"When you and I teamed up to make it off the mountain alive, something happened to me. I came out of the rage. For the first time in months, I had someone other than Lauren's ghost to hold on to. I wanted to be there for you, Britt. I told myself I was worth more alive than dead. I had to keep fighting, because you needed me. And when we kissed . . ." He wiped the backs of his hands over his eyes.

I stopped abruptly. I hadn't expected him to reference me with such emotion. Out of nowhere, I was seized by an aching squeeze. I swallowed, fighting the sweet, dangerous memory of last night. I could not go back there. I knew it, but I wasn't strong enough to fight it.

I shut my eyes briefly, feeling the rising wave of longing. I recalled with hungry brightness the smoothness of his bare skin, the shimmer of firelight on his dark features. I could still feel his slow, deliberate caresses. He knew how to touch me. His hands were forever burned into my skin.

"So it meant something to you too," Jude said quietly, studying me with eyes that were now wholly present.

I didn't know what the kiss meant to me. And I couldn't sort it out now. I didn't know if I believed Jude's story. What kind of person quit college to finish work that should have been left to the police? Even if Lauren was his sister, I wasn't sure it justified his extreme measures. And the crimes he'd committed to earn Shaun's trust, were they justified? If he really wanted justice, he would have given Lauren's diary and locket to the police, and trusted the system.

"How did you get Lauren's locket?" I asked.

"I found it in Shaun's truck right after we took you hostage. I went to get your gear from the Wrangler, but first I broke into Shaun's truck and ransacked it. I knew it might be my only chance to see what he was keeping in there. I found Lauren's locket in a metal box under his seat. I also found Lauren's picture. There were pictures of other women too, but all I could focus on was that I finally had what I was looking for. Proof he knew Lauren. Proof he targeted her, watching and photographing her for days before he made his move.

"I had to sew the locket and picture, along with the diary and handcuffs I already had, into a canvas bag I could keep hidden from Shaun. That took time, which is why I was late getting back with the gear."

I still didn't know if I believed him. Jude had already proved himself extremely clever and smart. What if he were tricking me now? "If I tell you where the diary and locket are, will you swear to hand them over to the police?" I asked.

"Of course," he said impatiently. "Where are they?"

I watched him intently, trying to divine the slippery thoughts darting behind his eyes. He seemed almost too greedy, and it made me uneasy.

"I don't have Lauren's things," I said finally. "I gave them to Calvin. And you don't have to swear anything, because he's going to turn them over to the police for you."

Jude's face went white with fear.

In that next unbalanced moment, my heart started to pound. His reaction could only mean one thing. Guilt. Of course he'd come here to trick me and get Lauren's things back. He was a criminal mastermind. He'd cooked up an elaborate story that made him appear tragically heroic so that I'd drop the evidence in his lap like an obedient child.

I stepped away from Jude.

He shook his head, bewildered, as if he couldn't believe his lies were unraveling and I'd figured it out. "You shouldn't have given them to Cal—" he began.

A rap at the door caused us both to swivel to face it. Jude's bewildered expression dissolved. He leaped off the bed, crouching silently in the darkness beside the door, hands bared to fight. He wasn't carrying a weapon; he would fight with his fists if Calvin came through the door.

"Britt? Just making sure you're okay," Calvin called softly to me.

Jude's dark eyes cut to mine, and he shook his head once. He wanted me to send Calvin away.

There wasn't time to think. I hardly knew Jude. To trust him was quicksand. Calvin was solid; he had always taken care of me. Torn, I looked desperately between the door and the figure beside it poised to spring. My head was telling me to trust Calvin, but my heart wanted me to believe Jude.

One word from me, and Calvin would either go away or barge in. In the end, it was my hesitation, my silence, that betrayed my uncertainty to Jude.

And prompted Calvin to enter.

CHAPTER THIRTY-THREE

Calvin's arm shot up in reflex to deflect the blow Jude swung at him as Cal thrust through the doorway. Still, the impact caused Calvin to stagger back a step, nearly losing his footing. Jude didn't wait for him to find it; he lunged for Calvin, his fists clenched so tightly I could see the veins in his neck straining against his skin. But Calvin had drawn his gun before flinging the door inward, and it was ready and aimed as he fired at Jude.

The bullet tore through Jude's shoulder. Miraculously, after one convulsive jerk, he continued to propel himself forward, advancing on Calvin with almost superhuman determination. He staggered three more steps before Calvin backhanded the gun across Jude's face, the strike pitching him violently onto his back.

Jude lay utterly still, a pool of liquid spilling out beneath his shoulder. I was so shocked, I couldn't find my voice. I gawked in disbelief at Jude's lifeless body. Had Calvin killed him?

Calvin gazed down at his opponent with a certain twisted admiration. That is, until recognition dawned.

"What's he doing here?" he demanded, clearly identifying Jude as Mason from the 7-Eleven.

"You killed him!" I exclaimed in breathless horror.

"He's not dead." Calvin nudged his foot into Jude's rib cage. "I didn't aim to kill. And I used a small-grain bullet to minimize the damage. But this is that guy from the gas station. Your boyfriend. What's he doing here?"

"You—shot him," I stammered, my mind still reeling.

"'Him' meaning Ace, short for Mason, got it. Mason, the guy who abducted you and who now has my map. I take it he's not really your boyfriend?" he commented dryly.

"If we don't do something, he's going to bleed to death!"

"Quiet or you'll wake Korbie," Calvin chided me, walking a slow circle around Jude's body, keeping the gun trained on him as he did. "He's in shock. Help me tie him up before he comes around."

"Tie him up? He needs a hospital!"

"We have to keep him detained until we're able to contact the police. We're making a citizen's arrest. Once he's tied up, I'll treat his injury. Don't look so scared. What's the worst that could happen?"

"He could die."

"Would that really be so bad?" Calvin continued, in a mild voice that struck me as far too calm, even for Calvin. "He left Korbie in a cabin to die, and he forced you to guide him through the freezing mountains. You nearly died, Britt. And now we have evidence proving he killed a girl last year. Look at him. He's not a victim; he's a murderer. He forced his way inside the cabin tonight with the intent to kill you, and probably me and Korbie too. I shot him in self-defense."

"Self-defense?" I echoed, shaking my head in bewilderment. "He wasn't armed. And we don't know for sure he was trying to kill us."

But Calvin wasn't listening. "Go to the garage and bring me the rope. It's on a shelf to the left of the door. We have to restrain him before he becomes conscious."

I saw the logic in Calvin's plan, but my feet stayed rooted to the spot. I couldn't bring myself to tie up Jude, who appeared near death. The blood had drained from his face, which reflected more ghost than man. Were it not for his short, shallow breaths, he would have looked at home in a coffin.

I tried to sway myself to Calvin's line of thinking—Jude deserved this—but my heart kept holding me back. What if he did die? He didn't deserve that. The idea of him gone forever slashed me to pieces. I had questions, so many questions, and now I might never get answers. I couldn't believe this might be the end to our story. We'd never had a chance to set things right, to come to an understanding.

Calvin paused in his inspection of Jude long enough to look across the room at me with an expression of exaggerated patience. "The rope, Britt."

I left the room, shaking.

Calvin was right. I couldn't be emotional about this. We had to arrest Jude.

In the garage, I stretched up on my toes to pull the rope off the highest shelf. I hesitated, once again wondering if it was really necessary to tie Jude up. It wasn't like he could run off. As I fiddled with the rope in my hands, I saw a rust-brown stain matted into the fibers. Blood. I wrinkled my nose, wondering if Calvin had used the rope previously during a hunting expedition. The dried blood flaked off under my fingernail. Was it sanitary enough for tying a man with an open wound?

I put the rope back on the shelf and grabbed another one from behind it. After a quick check, I determined that though dusty, it was cleaner than the first.

Upstairs, Calvin had closed the bedroom door. I opened it, and was immediately overwhelmed by the sour stench of fresh blood. Calvin had thrown a few towels on the floor to keep from slipping on it, and had managed to haul Jude onto the bed, where the sheets were already darkening with red.

Reluctantly, I handed him the rope.

Calvin searched hastily through Jude's pockets for weapons. Finding nothing, he knotted Jude's wrists to the posts of the headboard. He repeated the maneuver, securing Jude's ankles to the footboard. Jude lay stretched in the star formation of an eighteenth-century prisoner about to be drawn and quartered.

"Now what?" I asked, trying to quell the sickening wave inside me.

"I stop the bleeding and we wait for him to wake up."

Not a half hour later, a loud, cursing growl stirred me from where I dozed on the living room sofa with my head in Calvin's lap. I didn't remember slouching sideways onto him, but I must have, because not a moment after the pained swearing carried down from the bedroom at the top of the stairs, Calvin jumped to his feet, depositing me roughly on the leather couch cushion.

He was already striding toward the stairs. "Don't come up," he told me, tossing a warning glance over his shoulder. "I want to talk to him alone."

There was an edge to Calvin's voice that made me shift uneasily. If he roughed up Jude, it wouldn't look good when the police arrived. And they would arrive. Not tonight, but maybe tomorrow. With luck, the sun would melt the snow on the roads enough that we could go for help.

I knew Calvin wouldn't like it if I second-guessed him, but he wasn't thinking logically. His anger had obviously taken control. He'd killed Shaun, and I was scared he'd do the same to Jude. He couldn't cover up both murders. The fact that he was acting like he could, only proved he was in over his head. I had to help him step back and think clearly.

"Calvin," I said. "Don't touch him."

Calvin halted on the stairs, squinting down at me with his jaw clamped fiercely. He held himself so rigidly, he reminded me of chiseled stone. "He hurt my sister. And he hurt you."

"He didn't hurt me."

Calvin scoffed. "Are you hearing yourself? He kidnapped you. He marched you through the freezing mountains like a prisoner."

How was I supposed to convince Calvin—without sounding brainwashed—that Jude had saved my life? Jude had treated me humanely. He'd promised to help me to Idlewilde, when it would have been easier for him to leave me to freeze in the woods and make his own escape. Even after I'd given him the map, he'd stayed with me. If I hadn't run off, he would have stayed with me to the end, I was sure of it.

"Stay out of this," Calvin said. "You've been through a lot, and you're not thinking clearly."

"I've been through a lot, Calvin," I said, jabbing a finger at my chest. "I know what happened out there on the mountain. And I'm asking you to leave him alone. Let the police deal with him."

He studied me with his head cocked slightly to one side, baffled. "Why are you protecting him?"

"I'm not. I'm asking you to let the police handle this. That's what they're there for."

"He kidnapped you, Britt. Do you hear me? What he did was illegal and dangerous. It shows a complete lack of respect for human life. He thought he could get away with it. He used you, and he'll keep on using people like you unless somebody stops him."

"People like me?" I echoed incredulously.

Calvin flapped his arms impatiently. "Helpless. Naive. You're just the kind of girl guys like him prey on. And he is a predator. He detects weakness and incompetence the same way a shark smells a single drop of blood from a mile away."

Heat surged into my face. Shaun and Jude hadn't abducted me because of my incompetence. In fact, the whole reason Shaun had picked me over Korbie was because he believed I was a strong, capable backpacker. Because I was clever enough to convince him that Korbie had diabetes, and should be left behind.

I leaped to my feet. "You are so stupid, Calvin. You think you know everything. Maybe you should ask why Shaun and Mason took me with them but left Korbie in the cabin."

"Because Korbie isn't half as submissive or helpless as you," Calvin said decidedly. "You've floated through life expecting your dad, Ian, even *me*, and probably a lot of other guys I don't know about, to come to your rescue. You can't do one thing for yourself, and you know it. Mason and Shaun looked at you and saw an easy target. A gullible girl with low self-esteem. Korbie never would have stayed with them as long as you did. She would have fought. She would have run."

"I ran!" I protested.

"I'll tell you why they picked you," Calvin informed me calmly, which only made my temper burn hotter. I couldn't stand his cool composure, or the patronizing look in his eyes. In that moment, I wondered what I'd ever seen in him. He was so wrong for me. I'd spent eight months of my life mourning a self-important, egotistical jerk. The irony of it was, Calvin had spent the past eight months trying to escape his dad, but he couldn't see what I could. He was transforming into his dad. It was hard to tell if I was talking to Calvin right now or Mr. Versteeg. "Because they wanted to exploit you. Some guys—guys like Mason—get off exercising power over girls. It makes them feel invincible. He needed you so he would feel in control."

I made a furious sound of disagreement. Calvin wasn't describing Jude. He'd never tried to control me. Shaun, yes. But not Jude. Calvin would never believe me, but out there on the mountainside, I hadn't relied entirely on Jude. He hadn't let me. I'd survived because he'd trusted me to stand on my own two feet. I'd grown up more in the past few days than I had in four years of high school.

"And I'm the stupid one?" Calvin finished simply.

"Shut up," I said, my voice shaking with anger.

"No one's blaming you, Britt. He brainwashed you. If you could see outside yourself and look at this from a legitimate perspective, you'd stop trying to make excuses for a criminal. You've stood up for him at every turn. If I didn't know better, I'd think you have a secret crush on him."

Whatever I'd expected, it wasn't that. I opened my mouth to argue, but I had no defense. I felt my face growing hot. The blush worked its way above my collar, tingling the tips of my ears. Calvin saw it, his superior expression slipping. His brows tugged together in puzzlement, and then a shadow darkened his face. For one moment, I feared he'd guessed my secret, but he shook himself, clearing away any disgust or betrayal I might have imagined seeing brew behind his eyes.

"I want ten minutes alone with him," he said flatly, and climbed the stairs.

I dropped onto the couch, hugging my knees and rocking back and forth, suddenly cold, despite the fire burning a few feet away. A strange fog hung in my head. If only I could think. I had to stop Calvin from going too far. But how? Korbie might be able to convince her brother. But she was drugged and sleeping, and Calvin would lose the last of his temper if I woke her. Even if I did manage to wake her, I doubted she would feel like going to the trouble of helping Jude. She knew him as Ace, one of two men who'd left her to die.

Feeling restless, I jumped to my feet again and paced the kitchen. If I couldn't take my mind off what was happening in the room at the top of the stairs, at least I could keep my hands busy. I tidied the kitchen and took the trash out, throwing it in the bin outside the kitchen's back door. When I lifted the lid, I was surprised to find several other bags of trash at the bottom. By the smell of the garbage, the bags had been there for weeks. As far as I knew, the Versteegs hadn't stayed at Idlewilde this winter. It seemed impossible that Calvin could have produced this much trash in the couple days he'd been here. Had the Versteegs forgotten to carry their trash out with them the last time they were here, at the end of summer? It was very uncharacteristic of Mr. Versteeg. He hired a cleaning service after every trip, leaving the cabin spotless.

Frowning, I went back inside and opened the kitchen cabinets. They were fully stocked. Mostly with junk food, mostly with Calvin's favorite foods. Lucky Charms cereal, beef jerky, donuts, Ritz crackers, and crunchy peanut butter. I knew Mrs. Versteeg had sent her assistant up the previous weekend to drop off boxes of food for Korbie and me, but I could plainly see those boxes from where I stood. They were still in the entryway hall where they'd been deposited, untouched.

It didn't make sense. Why would the Versteegs leave the cabin fully stocked during the winter when they hadn't intended to make any trips up? If I didn't know better, I'd think someone had been living here all these months.

A strange chill crept up my spine. There were more things that didn't make sense. Things that had been bothering me under the surface for a while now. Right before Calvin had killed Shaun, he'd said, "I've seen you around," but how could that be? Jude had said that Shaun moved to Wyoming about a year ago, and Calvin had spent most of the past year at Stanford. When would he have seen Shaun?

An impossible suspicion fluttered in my mind, but I swatted it away. I could not doubt Calvin. I *would* not doubt him. What was wrong with me, that I was thinking the worst of him? I didn't have any reason not to trust him.

But that's exactly what I found myself looking for next—reasons. Explanations. Proof that this alarming idea brewing in my head was completely illogical.

In the living room, I shuffled through the papers on the desk for signs that someone had been living at Idlewilde recently—utility bills, recent mail, magazines, newspapers. I found nothing.

The bathroom was a different story. There was a pinkish ring in the toilet bowl, indicating it had been used but not cleaned. The counter and sink were dirty with dried toothpaste. Water had splashed onto the mirror above the sink and never been wiped away. I *knew* Mr. Versteeg would have paid to have the cabin cleaned before the family closed up Idlewilde at the end of last summer. Someone had been here after Labor Day. Someone had been here over the winter. I swallowed thickly. I didn't want to think who.

Back in the living room, I went through the desk drawers more thoroughly. One piece of paper in particular caught my eye. It was a pay stub from Snake River Rafting Company. The check had been cut on September 15 of last year, and made out to Calvin, weeks after he supposedly left for college.

I shut my eyes, trying to sort through the horrible, half-formed suspicion pounding at the back of my brain. Cal? No, no, no.

Macie O'Keeffe, the rafting guide who'd disappeared last September, had worked for Snake River Rafting. Was that how Calvin met her? Was she the reason Calvin had stopped calling me and eventually broke up with me? Had they dated, quarreled, and one night after their shift, had he . . .

I couldn't finish the thought. I couldn't think it. Cal had been away at school for eight months. He couldn't have killed Macie last September—he couldn't have killed *anyone*.

I pinched the bridge of my nose to fend off a dizzy spell. The moment felt unreal, as convoluted and visceral as a nightmare. How could Calvin be a killer?

I dug more frantically through the drawers. I lifted out a rumpled flyer with the bold letters MISSING! printed across the top. I smoothed away the creases over Lauren Huntsman's smiling face. The hole at the top of the flyer led me to believe it had been nailed to a tree or telephone pole. It made sense that search parties had combed Jackson Hole, and the surrounding area, looking for her. All those people hunting tirelessly for a missing girl, and Calvin had taken the flyer as a keepsake.

A keepsake of what he'd done.

It was true, I thought dazedly. He'd been hiding at Idlewilde. No wonder he'd tried to dissuade Korbie and me from coming on this trip. His secrets were here.

His lie seemed to yawn open, swallowing me whole. Calvin, a liar. Calvin, a stranger.

Calvin, a killer.

CHAPTER THIRTY-FOUR

I had to get Jude out of Idlewilde.

I had to get all of us out of the cabin. We weren't safe with Calvin.

Calvin.

The horrible crimes he'd committed—oh, God, let them be a mistake. There had to be an explanation. He must have had a reason. I was missing some vital piece of information. I wasn't too late to help him.

At the top of the stairs, I found the bedroom door cracked. Calvin's voice carried through it as he spoke to Jude, his voice choked with fury.

"Where's the map?"

He sat on the mattress beside Jude, his back turned to me. In the low flicker of light from the candle on the nightstand, I could see Jude shivering violently, causing the ropes that kept his arms and legs pinned straight to quiver. Calvin had bandaged Jude's shoulder, but that was the end of his service to him. Cal had opened the window; the draft rushed under the door, wrapping around my ankles. In a matter of minutes, the room would be as cold as the wintry air outside. I had the sickening feeling that this was only the beginning of the suffering Calvin had in mind to inflict.

"Why so interested in the map?" Jude's voice was weary with pain. His breathing came in short, uneven rasps.

Calvin laughed softly, harshly, and it made my scalp prickle. "You don't get to ask questions."

Peering through the door crack, I watched Calvin tip the candle over Jude's unbuttoned shirt. Jude let out a sharp gasp that trailed into a low, pained groan.

"Once more, where is the map?"

Jude arched his back, straining to free himself, but it was no use; the rope was industry-grade. "I hid it."

"Where?"

"You really think I'm going to tell you?" Jude fired back, his defiance admirable considering he was at Calvin's mercy and had to be in a great deal of agony. Admirable or not, it was the wrong thing to say. Calvin tipped the candle a second time, wax dripping onto Jude's bare chest. His entire body stiffened before he uttered another moan. Sweat glistened along his temples and into the grooves of his neck, but the rest of his body continued to convulse in shivers.

"Three green dots on the map," Jude panted hoarsely. "You forgot to label them."

This time it was Calvin's spine that went rigid. He didn't respond, but the deep rise and fall of his shoulders told me he was upset by Jude's comment.

"Three green dots, three abandoned shelters, three dead girls. See a connection?" Jude's hardened intonation made it clear he wasn't asking a question.

At last Calvin found his voice. "So the kidnapper is trying to pin a few murders on me?"

"One of the green dots on your map marks a trapper's hut where Kimani Yowell's strangled body was found by hikers. The other two dots mark abandoned cabins. While we're on the subject of theories, here's another. I don't think Kimani's boyfriend murdered her, and I don't think Macie O'Keeffe was killed by drifters along the river where she worked as a rafting guide. And I don't think Lauren Huntsman got drunk and accidentally drowned in a lake." Jude's voice caught as he spoke his sister's name. Swallowing, he disguised his emotion with a piercing black look. "I think you killed them, then dumped their bodies where they wouldn't be found."

Calvin did not speak. His back rose as his breathing came faster; he was still trying to gather his words.

"What kind of idiot killer creates physical evidence against himself?" Jude asked.

"Have you shared your theory with Britt?" Calvin finally said, almost achieving an ordinary voice.

"Why? How far are you willing to go to keep your secret? Would you kill Britt, if she knew?"

Calvin shrugged. "Doesn't matter. Britt would never believe you over me."

My whole body seemed to tighten. I pressed back against the wall, vibrating with fear. I felt sick. This wasn't the Calvin I knew. What had happened to him?

"Don't count on it. I've got a pretty convincing story," Jude said. "At first I thought Shaun was the killer. When you shot him, my first reaction was despair—I'd lost the one person who could give me answers. My second reaction was to wonder why you killed him. It came out of left field. You could have tied Shaun up and left him for the authorities, but instead you shot him. You didn't even flinch. I knew it wasn't your first time killing. It made me suspicious of you, but I didn't know anything for sure until I saw the Cardinals ball cap you gave Britt. And your map."

The ground slid out beneath me. My legs were shaking. I had to get out of the cabin. I had to go for help. But the thought of going back into the bitterly cold forest, so dark and haunted, made my blood race. How far would I make it? One, maybe two miles? I'd freeze to death before the sun rose.

"Who are you?" Calvin asked, intrigued. "You're not law enforcement—you'd have a weapon and a badge." He rose to stand over Jude. "What are you?"

In one convulsive movement, Jude flung himself up, the muscles in his good shoulder and neck bulging as he strained against the ropes, which held tight. The bedposts began to creak under the stress. The sound seemed to rally Jude, who squeezed his chest more forcefully, attempting to draw his wrists together and snap the bed frame. Calvin heard the noise too, and scrambled to return the candle in his hand to the nightstand, trading it for the more immediately threatening gun at his hip.

He leveled the gun at Jude and commanded, "Lie still or I'll punch another hole in you."

Ignoring him, Jude tugged harder on the ropes, his face screwed up in exertion and raw hatred, sweat pouring freely down his face. The bedposts protested with a higher wail of bending wood, and Calvin fired a warning shot into the air.

Jude sagged against the mattress, his breathing coming in shallow, ragged pants. He gave a guttural moan of misery and his limbs flopped uselessly into the same sprawled star formation.

"You're a coward," he told Calvin. "No wonder your dad tried so hard to make you succeed—he knew he had nothing to work with. He didn't have to worry about Korbie, she knows how to get what she wants, but you must have been a severe disappointment. You were never going to make it. Your dad knew it. Deep down, you've always known it too."

Calvin's back went up. "You don't know me."

"There's not a lot to know."

Calvin shoved the gun in Jude's face. His whole body shook. "I can make you stop talking."

"You killed those girls. You killed them. Say it. Stop hiding and man up. This is what it feels like to be a man, Calvin. Admit what you did."

"Why do you care if I killed them?" Calvin spat wrathfully. "You don't care about people. You left my sister to die."

Jude's answer was hardly audible, it was spoken with such quiet lethality. "If I'd known Korbie was your sister, back when I had my chance, I would have kept her alive long enough to make sure you were present when I slit her throat."

A muscle in Calvin's jaw leaped in anger, his finger tightening on the gun's trigger. "I should kill you right now."

"Before I've told you where the map is? Wouldn't advise it. I figured out that you killed those girls before I hiked here. I needed insurance that even if I failed to kill you, the death penalty wouldn't. Wyoming uses lethal injection. I'm not a man of many regrets, but I'll be sorely disappointed I won't be there to watch you lose your bowels when they strap you to the table. I put that map where it will be found by authorities. That's the one thing you can count on."

"You're lying." Calvin dismissed the threat immediately, but there was a wavering in his voice that hinted at worry.

"You searched my clothes. You know I didn't bring the map with me. Why else wouldn't I have it, unless I knew I couldn't risk it falling back into your hands, because I knew what the map really marked—the grave sites of your victims." Jude managed to keep his tone cool and level. But his body, racked by shivers, and the sheen of sweat on his pale, clenched features revealed he was in agonizing pain. A wide crimson circle spread across the sheet beneath his wound.

"I'll give you a choice," Calvin said finally. "Tell me where the map is, and I'll kill you with a bullet to the head. Keep chasing me in circles, and I'll draw out your death as slowly and creatively as I can."

"I'm not talking. If you kill me, quickly or slowly, I have the assurance that you're up to five counts of first-degree murder, and there's no chance in hell you're escaping the death penalty with that kind of blood on your hands."

Calvin's eyes slid over Jude in curious assessment. "Who *are* you?" he asked again, with something almost like amazement.

Jude raised his head off the pillow, his eyes reflecting a brilliant, savage light. "I'm Lauren Huntsman's older brother. The last guy you should have crossed."

Calvin's composure faltered, but he recovered quickly. Flinging his head back, he managed a spirited laugh. "What's this? You assume that I killed your sister, and now you're here for—what? Retribution? This is a *vendetta*? Let me guess. Mason isn't your real name. You clever bastard," he added, with a strange mix of admiration and disgust.

In the hallway, I leaned against the wall to hold myself up. I'd made a horrible mistake. Jude had been telling the truth. He'd quit school to avenge his sister's death. I remembered him mentioning how close he was to her, how she had meant everything to him. Of course he wanted justice for her. I wondered if his parents knew. I wondered if his friends knew. What lies and excuses had he told them when he left? I was beginning to sense the enormity of his mission. He had given up everything to hunt down his sister's killer, and now he was about to give up the last thing he had. His life.

Because Calvin would never let him leave here alive.

Calvin shrugged, businesslike. "I guess *The Godfather* was right. Blood is blood and nothing else is its equal."

Jude shut his eyes, but not before I saw him grimace with emotion.

"I won't stop until I have the map, you have to know that," Calvin said, strolling around the bed, stopping on the far side. He lifted his eyes, staring directly toward the door I hid behind.

I froze. It was dark in the hall. I was sure he couldn't see me. He continued to stare my way, but I was positive it was a blank, unfocused stare; my silhouette couldn't be distinguished from the shadows behind me. He tucked one arm against his chest and rubbed his jawline more vigorously, a look I knew meant that he was weighing his next move.

When Calvin's eyes shifted back to Jude, I took my chance. I walked silently down the hall, and down to the kitchen. I checked the phone. No dial tone, like Korbie had said. Either the storm had brought down the lines or Calvin had cut them.

Calvin had left his cell phone on the counter, but I couldn't get a signal. I rifled through the kitchen drawers, looking for a gun. Nothing. In the living room, I sifted through the desk drawers, but Calvin had already removed the gun. Growing more desperate and panicked, I looked under the couch cushions. I nearly hurled the last cushion against the wall in frustration. Calvin's dad collected guns. There had to be several in the cabin. Rifles, handguns, shotguns—where were they?

I hurried over to the antique trunk pushed against the far wall,

BECCA FITZPATRICK

thinking it was my last hope. Lifting the lid, I looked in, my heart fumbling.

At the bottom of the old, grooved trunk lay a small pistol. With shaking fingers, I pushed it into a pocket of my pj's.

I rose to my feet, feeling the weight of the gun drag at me. Could I shoot Calvin? If it came down to it, could I kill the sweet, vulnerable boy who was always at the mercy of his father—the boy I'd fallen in love with? Our story began years ago, and his life was so deeply woven into mine, it was impossible to find two separate threads. Who was this warped, damaged version of Calvin? I felt him slipping away, growing cold to me, and the loss slashed me to the core.

Turning, I found him standing behind me.

CHAPTER THIRTY-FIVE

"Looking for something?" Calvin asked.

It took me too long to find my voice. "A blanket. I was cold."

"There's one draped over the back of the sofa. Just where it always is."

"You're right. It is."

I stared into the dark pools of his eyes, trying to glean some hint at his thoughts. Did he know I'd overheard everything? His gaze slid from my face to my hands, and back again. He was watching me just as closely.

"Did you kiss him?" Calvin asked.

"Kiss who?" I asked. But I understood him perfectly.

"Did you kiss Mason?" Calvin repeated, eerily quiet. "When you were in the forest alone with him, did you sleep with him?"

I wouldn't let him unnerve me. Trying to act as normal as possible, I gave him a bewildered look. "What are you talking about?"

"Are you a virgin or not?"

I did not like the probing, fixated glow in his eyes. I had to change the subject. "Can I make you a cup of coffee? I'll go start the—"

"Shh." He rested his index finger on my lips. "The truth."

The glow in his eyes was pent-up energy, waiting to be unleashed, and despite my mustering of defenses, I felt my courage crumbling. I chose to stay silent, knowing Calvin hated an argument. He wanted the final say, always.

Calvin wagged his head in disappointment. "Oh, Britt. I thought you were a good girl."

It was this self-righteous declaration that drew out my anger. For one brief moment, it eclipsed my fear. How dare he judge me. He'd killed three girls! Everything I'd ever hated about Calvin suddenly seemed heightened: his faults, his superiority, his superficial charm, his insincerity—and most of all, the detached, insensitive way he'd ended our relationship. Disturbing hints of his darker side that I'd always known, yet somehow ignored. He hurt people. I'd just never guessed how good he was at it.

"What I did with Jude isn't your business."

The corners of Calvin's mouth pinched downward. "It is my business. He hurt you and Korbie, and I'm trying to make him pay. How do you think it makes me feel when you side with him? When you go behind my back and help him? It hurts, Britt. And it pisses me off."

His hands curled into tight balls, and I drew back a couple

steps. He squeezed them open and closed in a methodical, absent way. I had seen Mr. Versteeg do the same thing, and it had always been Korbie's and my clue to hurry from the room and huddle together in perfect silence at the back of her closet, where he wouldn't find us.

"While I was out there in the forest, cold and hungry, searching nonstop for you and Korbie, you were flirting with some guy you don't even know, letting him shove his tongue down your throat, keeping him warm at night, showing him *my* map"—he punctuated the word by pounding his fist to his chest—"leading him here to *my* house"—*pound*—"putting *my* sister in harm's way"—*pound*—"Do you know what my dad would have done to me if Korbie had died in that cabin? Died on *my* watch? You're so concerned about Mason, Jude, whatever the hell his name is, but what about me? You led him here, you screwed me over, you gave him the map— You *screwed me over!*" he shouted, his face a dark, throttled red, his lips contorting with rage.

I pulled the pistol out, aiming it at his chest. My hands trembled, but at this range, nerves or not, he'd be hard to miss.

Calvin's face blanked at the sight of the gun.

"Don't come any closer." I hardly recognized my voice. The words came out solidly, but the rest of me teetered on the edge of hysteria. What if Calvin didn't listen? I had never shot a gun before. The cold metal felt foreign and heavy and frightening nestled in my fingers. Sweat slicked my palms, making my grip more clumsy.

A smile inched into Calvin's eyes. "You wouldn't shoot me, Britt."

"On your knees." Blinking hard to correct my reeling vision, I tried to focus on Calvin. He slanted left, then right. Or maybe it was the room spinning.

"No. We're not going through this charade." Calvin spoke with smooth authority. "You don't know how to handle a gun, you said so yourself. Look—your thumb isn't clear of the hammer, which will pop back abruptly when you fire and injure your hand. You're nervous, and you're going to jerk the trigger and it will throw off your aim. The sound of the shot will startle you, and you'll drop the gun. Save us both the trouble and put the gun on the floor now."

"I will shoot you. I swear I will."

"This isn't Hollywood. It's not easy to hit a target, even from this distance. You'd be surprised how many people miss this shot. If you fire at me, it's over. Someone will get hurt. We can stop that from happening. Hand me the gun, and we can work this out. You love me and I love you. Remember that."

"You killed three girls!"

Calvin shook his head adamantly, his cheeks flushing. "Do you really believe that, Britt? Do you think that little of me? We've known each other our whole lives. Do you really think I'm a cold-blooded murderer?"

"I don't know what I think! Why don't you explain it to me? What did those girls ever do to you? You had everything going for you. You're smart, good-looking, athletic, rich, and you had a free ride to Stanford—"

Calvin wagged his finger at me. I could see his frustration in the lines around his pinched mouth. His whole frame began to shake, and his face darkened again. "I had nothing! Stanford rejected me. I never got in! You don't know what it's like to feel powerless, Britt. I had nothing. They had everything. Those girls—that was supposed to be me! That should have been me," he echoed wretchedly.

"That's why you killed them? Because they had what you wanted?" I was horrified. Horrified and sickened.

"They were girls. Girls beat me, Britt. How could I live with that? My dad never would have let me hear the end of it. It was bad enough at home, how he'd turn everything into a competition between me and Korbie, and rig the rules in her favor. She could have sat on her butt and it would have been enough to beat me. My dad didn't expect anything from Korbie, because she's a girl. But he expected everything from me."

There was no remorse in Calvin's voice. I wanted him to sound sorry and scared. I wanted him to admit that he was broken. But he didn't blame himself. He felt threatened by the girls he'd killed. Humiliated by them. I thought of the rope in the garage, dried with blood. Kimani Yowell had been strangled. Had Macie and Lauren been as well? He hadn't only killed them—he'd made it personal. He'd used his hands. It was never about them. It was about him.

"You killed Lauren while we were dating! Would you have killed me if I'd gotten into a better school?"

His eyes snapped to mine. "I never would have hurt you."

"I trusted you, Cal! I believed you were the one. I wanted to protect you and make you happy. I hated how your dad treated

you, and even when you took your anger at him out on me, I never blamed you. I thought I could make you better. I thought you were a good person who just needed to be loved!"

"You can still trust me," he said, missing the point completely. "I'll always be your Cal."

"Are you even hearing yourself? People are going to find out about this. You could go to prison. Your dad—"

Calvin's hands knotted up tightly again. "Don't bring him into this. If you want to help, leave him out of it."

"I don't think I can help you anymore!"

His eyes flashed, but behind the quick anger, I saw deep sadness. "I was never good enough. Not for him, not for you, especially not for him. He would have killed me, Britt. If I'd told him I didn't get into college, he would have killed me rather than deal with the humiliation. So I had to lie to everyone about Stanford and hide here at Idlewilde. I didn't want to, and I definitely didn't want to kill Lauren. I didn't plan her death. I was hiking one night and came across Shaun taking pictures of her. She was wearing a Cardinals ball cap and something in me snapped. She was wasted and that only made me angrier. Stanford had accepted a drunk, but not me. I wanted to take Stanford from her, but I couldn't. So when Shaun went to the toolshed, I took . . . her life."

"Oh, Cal," I whispered, looking at him with pity and disgust. Shaun must have come back from the shed to find Lauren dead; he must have panicked and hid her body in the toolbox. He'd taken her locket, knowing it was valuable, something Cal would have overlooked—money had never been an issue for him. Now that I knew the full story, it was easy to see how Jude had mistaken Shaun for the killer.

But Cal was the killer. My expression turned revolted.

Calvin saw the way I looked at him, and something inside him seemed to break. His face transformed into a cold, untouchable mask. In that instant, he truly seemed to become someone else. I had never seen him look so hardened or unfeeling. He took a step toward me.

"Don't come near me, Calvin," I said shrilly.

He took another step.

My shoulders ached from holding the gun upright for so long, and I realized I'd locked my elbows and was losing feeling farther down, in my hands. At the realization, they began to shake in earnest.

Calvin advanced again. Another step and he'd be close enough to take me down.

"Stay back, Calvin!"

Calvin rushed at me, and in that upended moment, it was instinct that propelled me to act. I squeezed the trigger, jerking the gun forcefully like Calvin had predicted. A hollow click filled the air, and Calvin stuttered at the noise, the whites of his eyes bulging around his green irises as he tripped onto one knee in shock.

Had I shot him? Where was the blood? Had I missed?

Laughing with quiet menace, Calvin stayed on his knee an extra moment before rising to his full height. There was a coldness in his eyes that robbed me of breath. There was nothing of my Calvin left. He looked exactly like his dad.

I squeezed the trigger again. And again. Each time, a dull, empty click slapped my ears.

"Damn unlucky for you," he said, ripping the gun out of my hands. He grasped me roughly by the elbow, dragging me across the room toward the front door. I dug in my heels and wrenched from side to side. I knew what he was going to do next, because it was the worst possible way he could hurt me. I wasn't wearing a coat. I wasn't even wearing boots.

"Korbie!" I screamed. Would she hear? If she didn't stop her brother—

"Calvin? What's going on?"

Calvin jerked around, startled by the sound of his sister's voice on the stairs. Her sleepy gaze flickered between her brother and me.

"Why are you hurting Britt?" she asked.

"Korbie." Tears fell down my face. "Calvin killed those girls. The girls who went missing last year. He killed Shaun. And who knows who else. He's going to kill me too. You have to stop him."

Calvin spoke calmly. "She's lying, Korb. Obviously she's lying. She's delusional, a completely normal reaction to the hypothermia and dehydration she suffered out there in the forest. Go back to bed. I've got this. I'm going to give her a sleeping pill and put her to bed."

"Korbie," I sobbed. "I'm telling the truth. Check the kitchen cabinets and the garbage bin out back. He's been living here all winter. He never went to Stanford."

Korbie frowned, eyeing me like I'd lost my mind. "I know

you're pissed at Calvin for breaking up with you, but that doesn't mean he's a killer. Calvin's right. You need sleep."

I made a frantic sound and tugged fiercely against Calvin's grip. "Let me go! Let me go!"

"Come here, Korbie," Calvin said, gritting his teeth as he wrestled me more securely into his hold, "and help me get her into bed." Squashing his mouth to my ear, he hissed, "Did you really think my sister would go against me?"

"Go for help! Get the police!" I yelled to Korbie. With growing panic, I watched her descend the stairs.

"It's okay, Britt," she said. "I know how you feel. I felt the same way when Calvin found me at the cabin. I was dehydrated and I saw things that weren't real. I thought Calvin was Shaun."

"Get the police!" I screamed. "For once, just do what I say! This has nothing to do with me and Calvin!"

"Pin her legs together," Calvin instructed his sister.

Korbie knelt down beside me, and that's when Calvin slammed the butt of the gun against the base of her skull. Without a sound, Korbie sank to the ground.

"Korbie!" I yelled. But she was out cold.

"When she wakes up, I'll tell her you kicked her in the head," Calvin grunted, dragging me toward the front door.

"You won't do this to me!" I shrieked hysterically, fighting to free myself. His arms, locked around me, seemed to grind into my bones. "You won't hurt me, Calvin!"

Calvin opened the door and thrust me onto the porch. I tripped over the threshold, sprawling hands-first into the snow.

"Stay close," he said. "Mason doesn't care about his own life, but maybe he cares about yours. I'll call you back in after he tells me where he hid the map."

"Cal—" I begged, throwing myself forward at his feet.

He shut the door in my face.

Through a haze of disbelief, I heard the dead bolt roll into place.

CHAPTER THIRTY-SIX

I rose to my feet, dusting snow off my pj's. My mind waded through a black fog of shock, but on some deeper level, I mechanically processed my next crucial moves. I needed to keep dry. I needed to find shelter.

I eyed the edge of the dark forest, where the towering wall of trees swayed in the wind. The woods seemed alive, haunted; they seemed to be stirring uneasily.

My palms were scraped and bleeding from my fall. I stared at them blankly, thinking they couldn't be my hands. This couldn't be happening to me. I couldn't be out in the cold again, facing death. Calvin would not hurt me this way. I squeezed my eyes shut, then opened them, trying to flush out the fog and return to reality—because this couldn't be my reality.

I gazed up at Idlewilde. Seen from the outside, it had transformed. Instantly, it had become as sprawling and foreboding as the mountains around it, as cold and impenetrable as a castle carved from ice. I pounded my fists on the windows, gazing hungrily at the warmth inside while the wind whipped through my pj's and the cold boards of the porch sucked heat through my soles.

I could not see Calvin. My eyes traveled to the door at the top of the stairs. The door had been open when Calvin threw me out, but it was closed now. All at once, reality did return. Behind that door, Calvin was giving Jude his options: Reveal where the map is hidden. Or let Britt freeze to death.

I'm going to freeze to death, I thought. Jude won't tell Calvin where the map is. He wants Cal to go down for his sister's murder. He's willing to give up his life, and mine, for it.

The gravity of this thought startled me out of my paralysis. Jude would not come to my rescue. I was alone. My survival depended solely on me.

I didn't know how long I had. An hour at most. My internal temperature would continue to drop, and I knew too well what would happen next. I'd lose the use of my hands and feet. If I walked, my steps would be slow and uncoordinated. Then the hallucinations would start. With no accurate picture of my surroundings, I would begin to see things that weren't real. I would dream of a roaring fire, and sit contently by it to warm myself, when in reality I would be lying in the snow, slipping deeper into a sleep that I would never wake from.

Clenching my teeth against the icy burn of the snow melting

through my socks, I ran across the front yard. I rounded the cabin, the wind immediately blasting me. My eyes watered and my brain screamed in shock. Ducking my head, I struggled forward toward the ditch.

The ditch. It was as much a part of Idlewilde as the cabin. Korbie and Calvin had introduced me to it on my first visit, years ago. Mr. Versteeg had installed a footbridge over the deep ditch that ran along the back edge of the property, creating a shady nook beneath the trestle that Calvin had christened, unimaginatively, "the ditch." Dragging a large square of carpet into the basin of the ditch, Korbie had given the ditch a touch of warmth, and Calvin had nailed flanks of wood to make a ladder to hoist us safely in and out. The last time I'd come to Idlewilde with the Versteegs, Korbie and I had discovered Calvin's cache of cigarettes and adult magazines hidden under a flap of the carpet. In exchange for our silence, Korbie and I had blackmailed Calvin for fifty dollars apiece. What I'd give to go back and rat him out.

As I climbed down into the ditch, my heart sank to find it offered almost no relief. The carpet fibers were stiff with frost, and the wind could not be fooled; it surged after me, tormenting me with wintry gusts.

It hurt to draw breath, every inhalation washing me in a deeper wave of cold. I felt completely alone. I could not call my dad for help. I couldn't drag Ian to my aid. As for Jude, he was tied to a bed and suffering through torture by Calvin. I had to build a fire, but the enormity of the task overwhelmed me. If I failed, there was no one to save me. I was utterly and truly alone.

BECCA FITZPATRICK

Leaning back against the ditch, I began to cry.

While I cried, a strange memory unfolded: I was very young, and dashed outside barefoot one wintry day to play tag with Ian and his friends. My feet felt blisteringly cold on the sidewalk, but I couldn't bring myself to leave the game even for a minute to go inside for shoes. Instead, I pushed the cold out of my mind and played on. I wished I felt that way now. Absorbed in any distracting task that took my mind off the raw, penetrating, relentless cold.

Dig for dry twigs around the trees. I heard Jude's voice slip into my thoughts.

I can't, I thought back bleakly. *I can't walk on the snow; I have no shoes. I can't dig in the snow; I have no gloves.*

Pine pitch. It burns like gasoline, remember? Jude's voice persisted.

And waste what little energy I have hunting for it? I returned.

I ran my trembling hands over the rigid carpet fibers, wondering how long it would be until I was like them. Frozen solid. It was while staring despondently at them that the idea pushed into my mind: *Cal's cigarettes.*

I peeled back the edge of the carpet. There, nestled into a matted patch of brown weeds, were a carton of cigarettes and a book of matches from Holiday Inn. Cold, but dry. There was a chance they'd light.

This small victory propelled me to act. As agonizing as it would be to run over the snow to find kindling, I had to. I threw together a hurried plan before I talked myself out of it.

I could build a platform using the firewood Mr. Versteeg kept stacked near the kitchen door. I'd seen a fallen bird's nest near one of the trees; it could be broken down to form kindling. Pine cones and tree bark too. And I would scrape pine sap from the trees with my fingernails.

Gritting my teeth against the cold, I climbed out of the ditch and staggered into the wind. It slapped me with each icy blast. Stumbling forward one soaked foot at a time, I constricted my focus, until my thoughts consisted of only one thing: I would gather what I needed for a fire, or die trying.

I stopped battling the intolerable cold. I was freezing, and I accepted it. I put my energy into clawing my brittle fingers into the snow drifted around the trees, scavenging for bark, pine cones, twigs, and dry needles. Stuffing every treasure into my pockets, I paused only to shake feeling back into my fingers. Then I went back to work, scraping, clawing, digging.

With my pockets full, I ran in broken steps to the ditch. My hands and feet worked slowly. Even my brain lagged, churning thoughts like it was a rusty gear grinding reluctantly into motion.

I knew building a platform was the first step, but picking out the proper pieces from my scavenged resources was immensely difficult. I could feel my concentration slipping away. Shivering, I used my fists to nudge the larger logs together.

I was growing tired quickly. My hands trembled with cold, and with great deliberation and frustration, I tried to prop the twigs into a tepee. After several minutes, I'd successfully braced six or seven of the twigs upright. I broke apart the bird's nest and carefully wedged the tinder between the wobbly legs of the tepee. My knuckles bumped one of the sides, and the structure collapsed. With a cry of despair, I sank forward on my knees, sucking on my fingers to thaw them.

I started over. One twig at a time, I uprighted the tepee. This time, I fared better. It wasn't perfect, but I hoped it was enough. Striking a match between the flaps of the matchbook, I watched a small trail of smoke drift upward. Again and again I struck the match, until it was wasted. I drew a new match, and tried again. And again. My hands shook uncontrollably. If one of the matches didn't light soon, I was afraid I'd lose my ability to squeeze the match between the flaps, creating the necessary friction. Already my left hand was too stiff to manipulate.

"Damn," I said wearily.

And then I had the idea of striking the match against a rock. I didn't know why it hadn't occurred to me sooner, except that I could feel my good judgment fading rapidly, my fingers not the only part of me too numb to work. Thankfully the bridge overhead had kept the rock dry. Sluggishly, my brain struggled to process each command.

Rock. Match. Strike. Hurry.

It was with something of a shock that I watched the match sizzle to life. I stared at the dancing flame, eyes watering with tears of amazement. With extreme care, I set the flame against the tinder. Slowly it began to smoke, then burn. After a few seconds, the fire grew to eat the kindling. When the logs also began to ignite, I pressed my hands to my face with a sob of relief.

A fire.

I was not going to freeze to death.

CHAPTER THIRTY-SEVEN

Huddling close to the fire, I rubbed feeling back into my fingers. It was tempting to think I could rest now, but I knew the clock was ticking. I could not sit here through the night—I had to get Jude out. I'd made it over one hurdle, but I was not done.

I shuddered as I thought about what was happening within the walls of Idlewilde. Calvin wouldn't stop until he had the map. He would know how to hurt Jude, how to wear him down. If I waited much longer, I feared it would be too late.

And then my plan came to me. I straightened in surprise. Jude had found a way inside Idlewilde without using the front or back doors. Whatever access point he'd used, I had to find it.

Savoring the heat one final moment, I braced myself for the impending cold, then scrabbled out of the ditch. Running along the perimeter of the cabin, I made my way from window to window, trying to pry open the glass. One of them had to be unlocked. It was the only way Jude could have gotten in. And then, as I rounded the side of the cabin, I saw Jude's access point. A basement window had been broken.

I lowered myself into the window well. The tools he'd used lay at my feet: a large stone and a piece of firewood. Jude had used the stone to break the glass, and the wood to knock free any shards gaping like teeth from the frame.

I drew up a mental blueprint of Idlewilde. The bedroom at the top of the stairs was on the opposite side of the cabin. Jude must have scouted the cabin for some time, determined Calvin's and my positions, and forced his way inside as far from us as possible, to minimize the chance that we would hear the glass shatter.

It had been a wise plan. It also meant that I had to cross nearly every room in the cabin to reach Jude, without first being discovered by Calvin.

I darted through the chilly darkness of the basement. At the top of the basement stairs, I eased the door open, peering into the kitchen. The lights were off, and I scurried through the kitchen and into the dining room, hiding at the edge of a wall as I surveyed the living room. I could see Korbie on the sofa. She was still unconscious, but Calvin had covered her in blankets. Of all of us, Korbie was the safest. Despite what Calvin had done to her, I didn't think he could ever bring himself to kill his sister. Which meant I would get Jude out, go for help, and then come back for her.

My coat and boots were near the front door, and I grabbed them before climbing the stairs to the second floor, my footsteps making soft creaks that seemed deafening to my ears. At the door at the top of the stairs, I listened. Nothing. I opened the door.

The stench of blood and sweat hung in the air. The candle flickered on the nightstand, casting dim light on the motionless figure on top of the mattress. Jude's arms and legs, though tied, were relaxed, and his head lolled to one side, cradled on his good shoulder. For one terrifying moment, I thought he was dead. But as I stepped closer, his chest rose shallowly. He was asleep. Or passed out. Given the amount of blood on the sheets, I guessed it was the latter.

I hurried to the bedside, drawing back the sheet. The window had been shut, but a cold draft clung to the air. I didn't want to send him into another shivering spell, but I had to stir him awake. At the removal of the sheet, however, I felt a sickening wrench. The cause of the blood-dampened sheets came into full view.

The gory picture was enough to make my insides revolt. I threw my hand over my mouth, stifling the urge to be sick. Red, painful-looking welts and blisters dotted Jude's chest. But the marks on his body did not compare to the swollen lumps around his eyes, or the raw, split skin at his cheekbones. A bag of bruised skin puffed up like a small purple balloon around the now crooked bone at the bridge of his nose. His breathing came in soft, wheezing spurts, further proof that his nose was broken. Only his mouth had been left untouched, but of course Calvin wouldn't want to damage it, I thought bitterly. He needed Jude to talk. He needed the map.

"Britt?"

At the sound of Jude's feeble voice, I clasped his hand tightly. "Yes, it's me. You're going to be okay. I'm here now. Everything is going to be okay," I finished determinedly. No need to alert him to his condition by a horrified wavering of my voice.

"Where's Calvin?"

"I don't know. He could come back at any moment, so we need to hurry."

"Thank God you're safe," he murmured. "He let you back inside?"

"No. He would have let me die." My voice sounded thin. "I came in through the basement window."

"Tough, determined Britt," he sighed wearily. "Knew you'd find a way."

I'm not tough, I wanted to tell him. I'm scared and afraid we're both going to die. But Jude needed me strong right now. I would be strong for him. "How bad off are you? Do you need a tourniquet?" There was a shocking amount of blood still seeping from the bandage around his shoulder. I had learned how to apply a tourniquet at camp, but I wasn't sure I remembered how to do it correctly. Jude would have to instruct me.

"No," he said hoarsely. "It was a graze. Just like he wanted."

I stared at him. "He has good aim," I said at last.

"Most killers do."

I couldn't bring myself to laugh at his joke. "There's another cabin a mile away. With any luck, someone's home. If not, we can break in and use the phone to call the police." I was proud of the confidence I'd managed to force into my voice, but a worry clouded my brain. Jude was in no condition to walk. Especially in bitterly cold temperatures.

Even though every plane of his battered face was drawn taut in pain, Jude managed to turn his head, finding my eyes. "Have I told you how amazing you are? The smartest, bravest, most beautiful girl I know."

His murmured endearment brought on a fresh surge of tears. I wiped my nose on the back of my hand, nodding enthusiastically, trying to show him confidence. My true feelings—despair, hopelessness, and fear—I pushed out of my mind, not wanting him to read them in my eyes.

"We're going to get out of here," I said, tugging at the knots at his wrists. I untied them first, sucking in a sharp breath at the sight of the raw marks chafing his skin, then moved to his ankles, one of which was grotesquely swollen to the size of a tennis ball.

"Britt," he breathed, closing his eyes, and I realized with alarm that his energy was dwindling quickly. "Leave me. Go get help. I'll wait here for you."

"I'm not leaving you with Calvin," I said firmly. "Who knows what he'll do to you. I might not make it back in time."

"I can't walk. I hurt my ankle trying to free myself. I think I twisted it. Don't worry about me. Calvin told me he wouldn't be back for a while."

He said it so convincingly, I was tempted to believe him. But I

knew Jude too well. He'd given up on saving himself. His smooth assurance was intended to make certain I got out before Calvin returned. Which, I had no doubt, would be soon. Calvin would not leave Jude alone for more than a handful of minutes.

"I'm going to make a sled out of the sheet. I'll drag you out of here."

"Down the stairs?" Jude said, shaking his head. "I'll never make it. Go get help. Calvin left a gun in the bedside table. Take it with you."

I opened the drawer and slid the gun into my pocket. I hoped I didn't have to use it, but I would shoot Calvin if I had to. This time I would not hesitate.

"Let's get your boots on," I said, sliding his left foot into a boot as gently as I could. He sucked in a sharp breath as the boot slid over his swollen ankle, then went utterly still. His eyes shut, and this time they did not reopen. His breathing fell back into a shallow, uneven rhythm.

He'd passed out.

I felt dizzy, unprepared for such a bad stroke of luck. But I wasn't going down without a fight. I would get Jude out of here. Dragging him inch by inch if it came to that.

I buttoned his shirt and shoved his right foot into the other boot. Grasping his legs, I pulled him toward the edge of the mattress, hardly gaining a few inches. I made more progress when I hooked my fingers into the waistband of his jeans and jerked backward, throwing my weight into it. At last I untucked the corners of the fitted sheet under him, and lugged him off the bed in a series of exhausting heaves and tugs. His body fell to the floor with a heavy thunk, and for the first time, I was grateful he'd passed out. He hadn't felt a thing.

Jude moaned.

Hadn't felt anything consciously, anyway.

Sweat drenched my face and I strained to pull him across the floor. I glanced behind me at the doorway warily, knowing Calvin was somewhere beyond it, but there was no other way out. I could not drop Jude safely out the second-floor window.

I took a moment to tug on my own boots and coat.

Inhaling deeply, I drew one last steadying breath.

Then I opened the door.

CHAPTER
THIRTY-EIGHT

I scanned both ways down the hall. No sign of Calvin. Peering over the banister, I checked to see that he wasn't downstairs, either.

Where had he gone? To look for the map on his own?

I dragged Jude into the hall. Surveying the steep wooden stairs, I realized Jude was right: There was no way I could safely get him down. The sheet would not provide enough padding against the sharp edge of each step, and I didn't have time to saddle his back to a pillow.

"Wake up, Jude," I whispered, kneeling beside him and slapping his cheeks firmly.

He stirred, muttering incoherently.

"We're going to climb down the stairs together." Even with his twisted ankle, if I shouldered some of his weight, and he put the rest on his good leg, together we could hobble down the stairs.

"Britt?"

His head rolled to the side, and I patted his cheeks harder to rouse him. "Stay with me, Jude."

He flinched at my touch. Mercifully, his eyes cracked open. I pinned his face between my hands and gazed intently into his eyes, wishing I could transfer some of my energy into him.

"Go, Britt. Before Calvin comes back." He flashed a brave smile.

"I won't go anywhere, I promise."

I cradled Jude's head in my lap. I stroked his damp hair, my hands trembling as I did so. I had to convince him that he could do this. His talk frightened me. He was giving up, and I could not do this without him. "We're a team, remember? We started this together; now we have to finish it."

"I'm holding you back. The reality is, I might not make it."

"Don't talk like that," I said, hot tears slipping down the back of my throat. "I need you. I can't do this alone. Promise me you'll stay here with me. You're going to stand up. We're going down the stairs together. On the count of three."

Jude's face softened, the way I imagined a body slackens right before death. Right before the pain ends, when rest is in sight. He slumped in my lap, looking paler than before.

I swiped at my tears with the backs of my hands. I'd have to think of another way out.

And then an idea came to me. I rolled Jude over so he was lying facedown. Hooking my elbows under his shoulders, I dragged him headfirst toward the top step. His legs, trailing behind him,

would drop against the steps as we descended, but better them than his spine.

I walked backward down the steps, one at a time, panting heavily. He had to weigh close to two hundred pounds. Fortunately, carrying him this way I was able to distribute most of his weight to the stairs. Unfortunately, I might reopen his shoulder wound and cause him excruciating pain. As awful as that would be, I had to get him out, and worry about the damage I caused later. It was better that I injure him than leave him for Calvin to kill. At the bottom of the flight, I took advantage of the smooth hardwood floors to slide him to the front door.

Opening the door, I hunched my shoulders against the icy whipping of the wind. Calvin's SUV was parked in the snowed-in drive. He hadn't left. My eyes flicked anxiously to the forest as I tried to guess where he'd gone.

As if to punctuate my thought, a geyser of snow shot up near my feet, and a moment later I heard the piercing clap of a gunshot. Swearing, I dragged Jude faster toward the cover of the trees.

Four more staccato bursts of gunfire. Gritting my teeth against the heavy drag of Jude's weight, I heaved him toward the trees. The minute I crossed into the shadows of the forest, the bullets stopped.

"Britt?" Jude uttered softly.

I fell to my knees beside him. Sweat bathed his face, and his bloodshot eyes darted wildly around. "Where is he? Where's Calvin?"

"In the trees on the other side of Idlewilde. I saw the bursts of light from his gunfire. It's too dark for him to see us. He'll have to get a lot closer if he wants a clear shot."

"If he's smart, he'll come for us now. He can't see us, but we can't see him, either. It gives him the perfect opportunity to sneak up and take us by surprise." Jude thought only a moment. "You said there's a cabin a mile away. Go to it—"

"I'm not leaving you alone."

He stared at me. Alarmed, he pushed himself up to sitting. "Of course you're leaving. This is your chance. It's not a great one, I'll give you that, but it's the best one you're going to get. The longer we wait, the greater the likelihood Calvin will get close enough to take a shot, or take you from me."

Without thinking, I grabbed him and kissed him.

He'd hunched his good shoulder against the cold, or maybe to battle the pain, but I felt him loosen at my touch. I expected him to try to push me away, to try to talk reason into me, but he needed me as much as I needed him. We were facing death; that was the cold hard truth. Down to the final minutes, we weren't going to waste them. This wasn't about desire. It was hot, urgent need. A reaffirmation of life. Jude gathered me roughly against him. If I was making his injury worse, he didn't seem to care. He kissed me back hungrily. We were alive. Never more so than in the face of death.

"I'm sorry I didn't believe you," I choked out. "I was wrong. I made a huge mistake. I believe you now. I trust you, Jude."

Relief shone in his eyes. "You're sure I can't talk you into running to that cabin?" he asked, pressing his forehead against mine.

He panted softly, but I didn't think from pain. He seemed jolted back to life, rallying to the fight. There was a determination in his expression that no amount of pain could hold back.

I shook my head no, short of breath myself. His kiss had worked like a shot of adrenaline. If I was scared, it was outweighed by a reason to live. And that reason was looking me straight in the eyes.

CHAPTER THIRTY-NINE

"Calvin won't kill me until I've told him where the map is," Jude mused coldly. "He thinks he has to find it before a park ranger, or someone in law enforcement, does."

"Where is the map?"

"When I came back from hunting this morning and found you gone, I knew you'd hiked to Idlewilde. I knew Calvin was a killer and I had to get to you as soon as possible. I didn't have time to hike to the ranger station and leave the map there. So I left the map under our tree. I bluffed to Calvin. No one will find the map without help. And even if they do, they won't know what it reveals. They're just as likely to throw it away as turn it over to a park ranger. But I'm not going to let Calvin believe that's a possibility. We have to make sure he feels the threat of being found out. Britt, I'm going to see to it that you get out of here alive. You'll have to show the police where the map is."

"We're both getting out of here alive," I corrected him firmly.

"Calvin could shoot you, to eliminate you as a witness," Jude continued without answering me, "but I don't think he will. You're his last bargaining chip—if you're killed, he knows I won't give up the map. His plan is the same as before. To use you to try to force me into talking. Which is why we're staying together and going after him. We'll try to catch him from behind, and I'll disarm him. After that, it's just a matter of holding him until we can turn him over to the police."

"What if he catches us from behind?"

Jude merely glanced at me, but I knew the answer. We had a fifty-fifty shot, at best, of taking Calvin down.

Jude gave me a rough kiss. I felt warm and reassured as he held me tightly, and I wished he'd never let go. I wished we could stay here, holding each other, and somehow it would be enough.

"We don't have to go after Calvin," I suggested softly. "We can hike to the cabin down the road and call the police. It's the safer thing to do."

"He killed my sister," Jude said. "I'm not running. I'm bringing him to justice. Give me the gun."

The dark shadows brewing at the back of his eyes worried me. I touched his sleeve. "Jude, promise me something. Promise me you won't kill him."

His eyes cut sharply to mine. "I've spent the last year driven by the idea of killing him."

"He doesn't deserve to die." I wasn't in love with Calvin anymore. But I'd known him my whole life. I'd seen the good and the bad. It was too late to help him, but I didn't want to destroy him either. He was Korbie's brother. My first love. There was too much history.

But most importantly, I didn't want Jude to become like Calvin. A killer.

"He deserves worse," Jude said.

"He thought killing was the answer. I want to prove there's another way."

"You're asking me to let the man who murdered my sister live," he said tightly.

"He'll be in prison. For a long time. When you think about it, that's not really a life. Please promise me."

"I won't kill him," he said darkly at last. "For you I won't. But I want to."

I handed him the gun, hoping I wasn't making a mistake.

Jude checked that the gun was loaded. "When this is over, I'm going to give Lauren a proper burial. With family and loved ones. She deserves that."

I dropped my eyes to the ground. "The dead body in the storage room. The girl was wearing a black cocktail dress. I think—I think she was Lauren."

Tears glistened in Jude's eyes. He gazed up at the black sky, blinking them dry. He had known it was her from the moment I'd told him I'd found the body, but it was only now that his shoulders trembled and his breathing quickened. He'd kept his grief bottled up, because he'd needed to stay strong. For me. He couldn't have protected me if he'd been focused on her.

"She's forgiven you, Jude. You have to believe that. She chose to go drinking. She chose to leave with Shaun. What happened to her after that is inexcusable and horrific, and I'm not saying she deserved to be killed, because she absolutely didn't—no one deserves that—but at some point, she had to stop relying on you to save her, and learn to save herself." I spoke from the depths of my heart. In more ways than I could ever express to Jude. It had taken being with him to see how dependent I was on my dad, Ian, and Calvin. Jude had helped me see that I needed to change. He'd been with me as I took those first scary steps. And now it was up to me what I did with this newfound strength and independence.

Jude made a hot, tormented sound deep in his throat. "If only I could forgive myself. I keep asking myself why Calvin did it." He wiped his eyes on his sleeve. "I want to know why, because in my mind, there has to be a logical explanation, when in reality, there is nothing logical about the mind of a cold-blooded killer."

"Calvin resented Lauren because she got into Stanford and he didn't. He spent his whole life being led to believe by his dad that girls are somehow inferior, and it killed him to think that someone under him had achieved more." As I said it, it hit me how flimsy a reason it really was. It made Calvin's violence that much more senseless.

Jude stared at me. "He killed her because she got into a school she didn't even want to attend?" He shook his head in a disgusted and pained manner. "That's why he took her Cardinals hat?"

"What do you mean?"

"The Cardinals ball cap Calvin gave you. It was Lauren's. The yellow splatter on top—not mustard but paint. I was with her when it happened. We painted her bedroom yellow together. Yellow with black stripes," Jude said in a measured tone, but I saw the anguish in his eyes. "Calvin took the hat as a symbol that he'd triumphed over her and taken back what was rightfully his."

The hat wasn't even Calvin's. I'd spent the past year holding on to it, clinging to it, because I wasn't ready to let go of us. I'd thought the hat was his, and I needed to feel him close. But I'd been holding on to something that wasn't real. It hurt, but in a strange way, it also made it easier to let go of him for good.

Suddenly Jude turned his face toward the sky. "Do you hear that?"

I strained my ears, picking up the distant drone of a motor. It was coming this way. "What is it?"

"A helicopter."

"The police?" I breathed, not wanting to hope too soon.

"I don't know." He faced me. "Someone could have found your abandoned car and called it in. They could be looking for you and Korbie." He paused. "But I find it hard to believe they'd send a chopper up after dark and in this weather."

"It's them." I told myself it had to be. I couldn't bear the thought of it not being someone coming to help us. I buried my face in Jude's good shoulder. "It's the police. Or search and rescue. They're going to find us. We're going to be okay."

I sensed his wariness in the rigid, uncertain way he held himself. At last he stroked my hair soothingly, but his voice was heavy with doubt. "Even if we see their spotlight, we can't run into the open and flag them down. I don't know if Calvin will shoot at us with witnesses looking on, but I don't want to take any risks. Until we've got Calvin, we stay hidden in the trees, understood?"

We paced through the deep snow, weaving through the trees, making a wide path around the back of Idlewilde. Even though Jude limped only a stride ahead, I felt alone. The forest was dismally black. Anything could be lurking out of sight. I felt the eyes of the trees on me. Was Calvin watching us?

Suddenly I heard the soft crunch of footsteps behind me. I whirled around just as Calvin sprang lithely through the snow, running in a crouch at me.

"Jude!" I cried out.

Jude whipped around, aiming the gun at Calvin. Calvin stopped in his tracks, leveling his own gun at me. We stood at a standstill.

"If you shoot me, I'll shoot her," Calvin told Jude.

"You can hear the helicopter overhead," Jude said. "It's a police chopper. It's over, Calvin. They found the map. They're coming for you. You're going down."

"That's a surveillance chopper," Calvin said dismissively. "Probably search and rescue. Someone must have found Britt's car in the road and called it in. They can't see us down here. Nice try, but I'm not scared."

"You're scared all right," Jude said. "Not of being apprehended, but of never measuring up. You're scared of failure. It's why you pick the targets you do. What kind of man gets off controlling defenseless girls? I'll tell you: no man. Is it frustrating to realize you're not a real man, Cal?"

I drew a sharp breath. Was he trying to set Calvin off?

"It's going to feel good to kill you," Calvin said through gritted teeth.

"Sure it will," Jude replied in that same unworried voice. "I'm wounded, and that's what you like, isn't it? An easy target."

A slow, scheming smile spread over Calvin's features. "I took my time with them, especially Lauren. Every kick, every squirm, every flash of panic in her eyes—I drew all these out, feeling invincible with all that control and power," he went on, knowing how to unnerve and rattle Jude best. "I only wish I could have heard her screams, but I tied the rope around her neck so tightly, not a single noise came—"

Jude's eyes burned black fire, and then everything happened quickly.

Jude lunged at Calvin, attacking his gun hand. He seized control of Cal's wrist and chop-blocked the gun away. He finished his assault with a brutal thrust to Cal's face, sending him faltering backward, howling and clutching his nose.

"You broke my nose!" Calvin swore viciously.

Jude picked up Calvin's gun and aimed it at him. "Count yourself lucky. There are two hundred and five other bones in your body that I'd like to break. Hands on your head."

Face blanching, Calvin uttered a shaky laugh. "You wouldn't shoot me. Britt, you won't let him do it. I know you."

"Don't talk to her," Jude snapped. "You don't deserve to talk to her. You're a worthless bastard who never deserved to live."

Calvin seemed to absorb this, blinking over and over. He

shook his head, his eyes empty and unfocused. "You're not the first person to tell me that."

"How did you find the girls?" Jude asked harshly. "You must have researched them somehow."

"Calvin worked with Macie as a rafting guide," I said. "He must have killed her when he learned she was going to Georgetown in the fall. And Kimani went to Pocatello High, our rival high school. He knew she was expected to go to Juilliard. Everyone in town knew."

"My dad will kill me," Calvin said, speaking in a cloud of disbelief. "I can't believe the old man won."

Whatever he said next was swallowed up by the roaring *whump-whump* of the helicopter blades. The sound grew so loud, I thought the helicopter must be passing directly overhead. I didn't care what Jude said; if a spotlight came anywhere near me, I would run into the open and alert the pilot to our position.

Calvin tipped his head toward the black dome of sky overhead. His expression shifted from disbelief to understanding. A shadow of defeat crossed his face, a helpless, gloomy, almost boyish look.

He put his wrists together, extending them toward Jude. "Go ahead. Tie me up." His voice cracked and he started crying. "Better show my dad I can take my punishments like a man now."

At that moment, I felt my heart break. I wanted to wrap my arms around Calvin and tell him it was going to be all right, but it wasn't. Nothing was all right. He wasn't all right. This warped, damaged version of him was beyond help. I wondered what Mr.

BLACK ICE

357

Versteeg would say when he found out what Calvin had done. Would he feel responsible? I didn't think so. He would shun Calvin, wanting to distance himself from his son's disgrace.

Jude twisted Calvin's arms behind his back.

I started crying too. I felt hollow and uprooted inside, but I didn't think I was sad. Or maybe I was. Sad because I had loved Calvin, and I didn't understand how the boy I'd loved had grown into someone so brutal and destructive. Sad because I would have done anything to help him. But now I wasn't sure anyone could have helped him.

"Where are Lauren's belongings?" Jude said. "Where did you put them?"

"In the ditch behind Idlewilde," Calvin answered with soft resignation.

"I was just there," I said. "I didn't see them."

"There's a loose board on the underside of the footbridge." Calvin's shoulders were slumped, his chin tucked against his chest. "If you wiggle it free, there's a hollow space up there. I put everything in an envelope."

It was so unlike Calvin to help us, even though he realized he was cornered and there was no way out. Had it taken defeat to change him? Before I could untangle Calvin's motivations, Jude ushered me toward the cabin with a jerk of his chin.

"Let's tie him up first."

Inside Idlewilde, Jude shoved Calvin into one of the kitchen chairs. I went upstairs to get the rope Calvin had used to tie Jude, and together we secured Calvin's wrists to the chair. He didn't

struggle. He sat unmoving, eyes blank, staring into near space.

He said, "I guess this proves I was never good enough. Not good enough to be the guy you wanted. Not good enough for Stanford. Not even good enough to get away with murder." He laughed, a choked, forlorn sound. "Too bad I wasn't born a girl. Korbie's been getting away with murder her whole life."

Jude turned to me. "Show me the ditch."

CHAPTER FORTY

Jude and I knocked on every board under the footbridge. We double-checked our work. But each board was nailed tight.

"He lied," Jude said. "There's nothing here."

"Why would he lie?"

Jude and I looked at each other. And then we bolted for the ladder, hoisting ourselves out of the ditch as fast as we could.

I made it to Idlewilde first, racing into the kitchen where we'd left Calvin tied to the chair. My feet stopped working at the sight of Calvin swinging idly by the neck from the kitchen chandelier. Behind me Jude cursed, and rushed forward, uprighting the tipped chair below Calvin's twitching feet, jumping onto it to cut down the body.

"Knife!" he ordered.

I grabbed one from the drawer and Jude snatched it out of my hand, sawing viciously at the rope. The last fibers snapped apart and Calvin fell to the floor, limbs sprawled.

I probed his neck for a pulse. Nothing. I tried his wrists, then went back to his neck, pushing my fingers against the stubble under his throat. At last I felt a weak but steady beat. "He's alive!"

Jude gazed down at Calvin's open but vacant eyes. Both pupils were fully dilated, making his eyes appear almost entirely black. A slurred, blubbering noise slipped past his lips. Clear fluid drained from his nose.

"I don't think we got to him fast enough," Jude said, kneeling beside me and gently turning my head away.

Tears filmed my eyes. "What's the matter with him?"

"Brain damage, I think."

"Is he going to be okay?" I asked, crying harder.

"No," Jude answered truthfully. "No, I don't think he is."

Time seemed to expand, slowing down to a crawl, and as I watched Calvin's body convulse on the floor, a tidal wave of memories surged through me. They say that when you're about to die, your life flashes before your eyes. They never tell you that when you watch someone you once loved dying, hovering between this life and the next, it's twice as painful, because you're reliving two lives that traveled one road together.

One blink later, time contracted, snapping me back to the kitchen. I remembered why the deafening clap, clap, clap of a helicopter thundered overhead. I remembered why my hands and feet throbbed with cold, why Jude's blood was streaked across my coat sleeves.

I grabbed Jude's hand and together we ran outside, squinting against the gale-force winds blowing down from the helicopter hovering over the clearing behind Idlewilde.

"It looks like a private helicopter," Jude yelled at me above the engine's whine.

"That's Mr. Versteeg's helicopter!" I cried back.

"I see two search and rescue volunteers on the ground and one man with a rifle." He pointed at the shadows at the far end of the yard, directly below the chopper. "They must have rappelled down."

Two figures swaddled in red, and wearing white helmets, darted across Idlewilde's snowy lawn. I recognized the man behind them, the man carrying the rifle. Deputy Keegan. He and Mr. Versteeg hunted elk together every year in Colorado.

I cried out in relief, waving frantically. They couldn't hear me over the helicopter, but they had flashlights. They would see us any second now.

"You'll tell the police about Calvin," Jude said urgently. "You'll show them the map."

Hot tears of joy streamed down my face. It was over. The nightmare was finally over. "Yes."

Jude said, "I'm sorry I have to do this, Britt."

Then he grabbed me from behind and pressed Calvin's gun into my hairline above my ear. Using my body as a shield, he dragged me backward, away from the search and rescue volunteers and Deputy Keegan, who hustled through the snow toward us.

"Stay back or I'll shoot her," Jude yelled.

A sick feeling climbed up my throat, but I managed to croak, "Jude? What are you doing?"

"I said stay back!" Jude shouted at the men again. "I'm holding Britt Pheiffer hostage, and I will shoot her if you don't do exactly what I say."

A spotlight glared down at us from the hovering chopper, momentarily blinding me. The whirling blades gusted snow off the branches, and I raised my arm to block it. Why was Jude telling them I was his hostage? We should be running toward them, not away.

Jude hauled me into the forest, his arm latched painfully across my chest. He weaved erratically through the trees, but the spotlight found us easily. It also made visible the bold contrast of Jude's red blood splattered on the pristine snow at our feet. His wound was bleeding more heavily.

The deeper into the forest Jude dragged me, the more crowded the trees became. It was hard to tell where one tree ended and the next began. The spotlight stuck to us, but with difficulty. Under the thick cover, Jude was able to dodge into the pilot's blind spots, behind boulders and under fallen trees, and each time we reappeared, it took longer for the helicopter to pick up our trail.

Jude yanked me against a large pine tree, crushing us into the shelter of its branches. I was pinned with my back to Jude's chest, feeling his breath pant in my ear. There was a startling amount of blood at our feet. Given his injuries, I knew he was on the verge of collapse. He wouldn't make it much farther before he either passed out from blood loss or went into shock from the excruciating demands he was placing on his weakened body. I was amazed he had the strength to drag me, let alone himself, over the rough terrain.

The white glare of the spotlight swept frantically over the ground, then darted off in the wrong direction.

"What are you doing?" I cried. "The gun isn't even loaded—I saw you empty it after we tied up Calvin. You told them you're holding me hostage. You're making things worse. We have to go out there and tell Deputy Keegan everything—how you saved my life, and that you were only with Shaun to find Lauren's killer."

"When I tell you to, I want you to run as fast as you can toward him. Run with your hands raised and visible, and scream your name over and over, do you understand?"

"Why?" I asked him, starting to cry. "Why are you doing this? They'll hunt you down. They'll take you into custody, if they don't shoot you first!"

"They were already going to take me into custody." Jude grabbed my arm, forcing me through the thick, knee-deep snow, behind another pine tree. "Do me one favor. Don't mention Jude Van Sant. Tell them my name is Mason. Korbie's story will match yours. You were taken hostage by two men named Shaun and Mason, tell them that."

"Because Mason doesn't exist anymore."

Jude brushed his hands over my wet cheeks, drying them. "Yes. I'm leaving Mason here in the mountains," he said softly. "He finished what he came to do."

"Will I see you again?" I choked.

He pulled me to him. He ground a rough kiss to my mouth, making it last. I knew right away that it was a good-bye kiss. I was losing Jude. I didn't want to let him go. This wasn't Stockholm syndrome. I had fallen in love with him.

I peeled off my coat. "Take this at least." I slid it over his shivering shoulders. It fit comically tight, but I couldn't bring myself to laugh. Nothing about this was funny. There was so much I had to say, but there were no words for a moment like this. "I'll tell them you're headed to Canada. I'll tell them you're planning to hide there. Will that help?"

Jude stared at me with stark gratitude. "You'd do that for me?"

"We're a team."

He gave me one final hug. "Now run," he said, shoving me into the open.

I staggered forward into the deep snow, thrown off balance. As soon as I had my footing, I whirled around.

He was gone.

Not a moment later, the spotlight bathed me in a cone of blinding light. I could hear a man's voice speaking commands through an overhead PA. It was Mr. Versteeg. The two search and rescue volunteers rushed in from the trees with Deputy Keegan. I raised my arms and started running toward them.

I yelled, "My name is Britt Pheiffer. Don't shoot."

CHAPTER FORTY-ONE

A gentle rain drizzled on my bedroom window, falling slantwise under the streetlights outside. At least it wasn't snow.

Ten days had passed since I'd been flown off the mountain in Mr. Versteeg's helicopter. I'd learned that a park ranger had found my Wrangler abandoned on the roadside and notified the county sheriff's department, who'd then notified my dad and Korbie's parents that we'd never made it to Idlewilde. Without waiting for the sheriff to organize a search, Mr. Versteeg had immediately hired two search and rescue experts, and had flown his helicopter up to look for us. I wondered if Mr. Versteeg would have been as anxious to get up to Idlewilde had he known what he'd find.

After I'd been treated at the hospital for hypothermia and dehydration, I'd given my full report to the police. I'd told them where they would find Calvin's map. I'd explained where they'd find Lauren Huntsman's remains. Mr. and Mrs. Huntsman had flown out to retrieve their daughter's body, and the event had been broadcast by every local news station. I did not watch it. I could not see the Huntsmans and not be reminded of . . . him.

I had not talked to Korbie since that night at Idlewilde. Her cell phone was turned off, and I wasn't even sure she and her parents were in town. The lights at the Versteeg home were turned off too. Or maybe that was to deter the news reporters camped on their lawn.

I did not know what I would say when I saw Korbie again. I had told the police about Calvin. She saw it as a betrayal, I knew. Her entire family did. Because of me, Calvin's secrets had flooded into the open.

As for Jude, I did not allow myself to wonder. He'd escaped into the forest bleeding and battered and without sufficient clothes. He faced exposure, starvation, and capture. His odds of survival were minimal. Would a hiker stumble across his frozen body weeks from now, and then I'd hear about his death on the news? I shut my eyes hard and emptied my mind. It hurt too much to wonder.

I went downstairs for a bedtime snack, glad to find my brother, Ian, leaning against the kitchen counter chewing a peanut butter sandwich. Ian and I usually fought, but he'd been uncharacteristically sweet to me ever since I'd come home, and I was actually looking forward to his company tonight.

Ian slathered peanut butter on another slice of bread, folded it in half, and crammed the whole thing inside his mouth. "'Ont 'un?" he grunted.

I nodded, but took the jar and knife to make the sandwich myself. Ian eyed me with open astonishment as I spread peanut butter smoothly over the bread.

"You actually know how to make one?" he said.

"Stop being melodramatic."

"Dad told me you did your own laundry today. Is it true?" he asked, widening his eyes in feigned wonder. "Who are you and what have you done with my sister?"

I rolled my eyes and boosted myself onto the counter. "In case I haven't said it lately, I'm glad you're my big brother." I patted him affectionately on the head. "Even when you do insult me."

"Want to watch a movie?"

"Only if you brush your teeth first. It's so gross when your breath smells like peanut butter and popcorn."

He sighed. "Just when I thought you'd changed."

We flopped onto beanbags in front of the TV and Ian clicked it on. The ten o'clock news was in full swing.

A female reporter said, "Calvin Versteeg is being held on four counts of first-degree murder and two counts of attempted murder at the Teton County Detention Center. Sources tell us that Versteeg will most certainly be found incompetent to stand trial. He suffered severe brain damage during an attempted suicide shortly before his arrest and is expected to be committed to a state mental hospital for appropriate treatment."

"Do you want me to turn it off?" Ian asked, with a worried glance at me.

I motioned for him to be quiet and leaned forward, focusing

intently on the video feed that the station had briefly switched to. It was airing footage of Calvin being pushed into the detention center in a wheelchair. News reporters and camera crews pushed as close to him as the police would allow, taking photographs and thrusting microphones at him, but my eyes traveled to a man on the outskirts of the crowd.

He was wearing a goose-down parka and dark-wash jeans that appeared brand-new. My palms started to sweat. His head was tipped down, shielding him from the cameras, but he almost looked like . . .

The reporter continued, "Versteeg graduated from Pocatello's Highland High School last year and told family and friends that he was attending Stanford University this year. Stanford's admissions office confirmed that Versteeg applied to the school, but was not accepted. Calvin Versteeg's father, a CPA, and mother, an attorney, have not given a public statement on their son's arrest and did not return our phone calls. We interviewed Highland High School senior Rachel Snavely, who attended school with Versteeg since elementary school. She said, 'I can't believe Calvin killed those girls. He wouldn't hurt anyone. He was, like, such a great guy. I went to a pool party at his house last summer. He was the perfect gentleman.'"

"You can turn it off now," I said, rising to my feet in a daze.

Ian clicked the remote. "Sorry you had to see that. Are you okay?"

I walked to the window. I pressed my hand to the glass, searching the dreary darkness of the street outside, praying I'd see a figure in the shadows gazing intently back at me.

I didn't see him, but he was out there somewhere.

Jude was alive.

❄

That night I was either too hot or too cold.

At six I woke up tangled in my blankets. I gave up on sleep and went running. I had too much adrenaline, too much restless energy. The sky was overcast, threatening more rain. It reflected my mood uncannily.

I ran through the park, pumping my arms hard, trying to leave Jude behind. He wasn't coming back. He'd done what he set out to do. His life as Mason was over. Right now he was probably on a plane back to California to resume his life as Jude Van Sant. I was no longer in the picture.

I knew it was illogical to be angry with Jude. He'd kept his promises to me. But my heart was in too deep for me to be logical about him. I needed him now. We were a team. I felt cheated knowing we'd never go driving with the windows down, singing to the radio at the top of our lungs. We'd never sneak out to a late-night movie and hold hands in the dark. We'd never get in a snowball fight. After everything we'd been through, didn't I deserve to know him during the good times too?

It wasn't fair. Why did he get to leave on his terms? What about what I wanted? I tore my earbuds angrily from my ears and bent at the waist, catching my breath. I wasn't going to cry over him. I felt nothing. I was certain I felt nothing.

Once I was able to put him out of my head, I'd realize these feelings weren't real. We'd been trapped together in horrific circumstances, and because of this shared experience, I'd formed a powerful attachment to him. One of these days I'd remember that night under the tree and laugh at myself for thinking I cared about him. If I chose to remember that night at all.

I rounded a bend, and a man stepped into my path. I stopped in my tracks. It was early, the morning shadows blotting the tree-lined trail ahead. He wore a leather bomber jacket and he had a duffel slung over one shoulder, like he was about to board a plane.

My mouth had gone dry and my hands were trembling. He'd cleaned up. New clothes, and a trip to the barber. But despite the fresh shave, he didn't look harmless. Small cuts still nicked his face, and the bruises weren't completely healed. In the low morning light, he looked dangerous.

His jacket fit snugly around his muscled shoulders, and I shivered as I remembered what their smooth contours had felt like. I remembered that night under the tree in vivid detail. I remembered the taste of Jude's kiss, and the way I'd felt warm and safe in his arms.

I wanted to run and fling myself into his arms now, but I held my ground.

"You came back," I said.

He stepped closer. "It took me four days to get off the mountain. I didn't let myself stop walking, afraid I'd freeze if I rested. I used your coat as a bandage, so thanks for that. At the bottom of the mountain, I found a store with an ATM outside, and got enough cash to hide in a hotel until I was rested. After that, the plan was to get on a plane to California. I was ready to close this chapter of my life and go back to being Jude Van Sant. I didn't think there was anything stopping me." His eyes pierced mine. "But I kept waking up at night, haunted by a familiar face."

"Jude," I said, choking up.

He came forward and clasped my hands. "You kept my secret. I can't thank you enough."

"I know why you did what you did."

"Lauren deserved justice. So did Kimani and Macie, but not everyone would have agreed with how I went about getting it. Shaun took you and Korbie hostage, shot and wounded a police officer, and killed a game warden—and I was with him when he did it. It would have come out during the trial that I was living a lie, and I was smart enough to get away with it. A normal person has every reason to be scared of someone like me. They'd lock me away."

He was right. I knew he was. I also knew he'd taken a huge risk in coming here. I didn't let myself hope what it meant for me—for us—that he'd risked discovery and capture to see me.

"What now?" I asked. "What about us?"

Something in Jude's eyes changed. He dropped his gaze. Right away, I knew I had read him wrong. I wasn't going to get the answer I wanted. He was going to break my heart. "We've been through something intense and now we have to adjust to life going back to normal, even if it is a new normal. You need to be a regular high school student. This is your senior year. It's an important time. You should be celebrating with your friends and planning your future. I have to go home. I need to grieve with my family."

He was cutting me off. This was the end of our story. Four whirl-wind days. That was all I got. And I shouldn't care. Because these feel-ings weren't real. In the cold, relentless mountains, Jude had helped me stay alive. I was confusing my gratitude to him for something else. The unsteady beat of my heart when I thought of losing him stemmed from an irrational fear that I still needed him.

"I don't want to mess this up," Jude said, searching my eyes. He wanted to make sure I was okay. That he wasn't hurting me. I couldn't let him know that my heart felt like it was being severed in two. How could I be hurting so badly when the connection between us was imaginary?

"Here's my number," he said, handing it to me. "If you need to talk, call anytime, day or night. I mean it, Britt. I can tell you think this is a brush-off, but I'm doing what I think is right. Maybe I'm wrong. I'm probably going to regret this. But I have to do what I think is best, even if it isn't easy."

Of course it was a brush-off. And why not? The nightmare that had brought us together was over. Jude was right. It was time to go our separate ways. "No, it's fine. You're right. I'm glad you came to say good-bye," I said quietly. "And I'm sorry about Lauren. I wish her story had ended differently."

"Me too."

Not knowing what else to say, I reinserted my earbuds. "I should probably finish my run. It was nice knowing you, Jude."

He looked sad, distressed, and helpless to do anything about it. "Good luck in life, Britt."

I ran away from him, biting my lip and holding in the sob quivering in my chest. The minute I rounded the next bend and was out of sight, I sank to my knees and stopped fighting.

I cried myself empty.

One year later

EPILOGUE

"Road trip!" Caz, my college roommate, squealed. She pumped her arms in the air, the hot May breeze flapping her bouncy red hair around her face. Caz was from Brisbane, Australia, and reminded me of Nicole Kidman in that old movie BMX *Bandits*. Same poodle hair, same adorable accent.

We had just finished our freshman year at Pierce College in Woodland Hills, California, and we were experiencing the meaning of freedom firsthand. I'd sold back my textbooks, passed my apartment's cleaning check, and skipped my way out the door of my last final. Good riddance, honors chemistry.

My current list of worldly cares had been whittled down to one thing: having fun, fun, fun in the hot California sun.

"Neither of you have ever driven PCH?" Juanita, our other roommate, asked from the backseat of my Wrangler. She had her nose in her iPhone, furiously texting her brand-new boyfriend, Adolph. I think he was her first. Caz and I had barely convinced

Juanita to come with us. She was afraid after two weeks apart, Adolph would change his mind and dump her. I could talk all I wanted about insecurities and female independence, but I knew what it felt like to find love and lose it. "Just tell me where you want to stop along the way, and I'll dispense information of historical or social importance for each landmark or destination. There's Hearst Castle, Zuma Beach, Wayfarers Chapel—"

"We don't want to stop!" Caz exclaimed. "That's the point. We want to get as far away from here as possible. We want to drive forever!" She let out a holler that sounded like *wheee-hooo!*

"We've rented an obscenely expensive shack near Van Damme State Beach for two weeks, and the deposit is nonrefundable, so you can't drive forever," Juanita pointed out practically. "Whose idea was this again?"

"Britt's," Caz said. "She's from Idaho and the beach is a big deal. Cut her some slack. She usually spends her summers competing in potato-throwing contests on the farm."

"And don't people from Brisbane spend their vacations hooning in utes?" I quipped.

"Bogans have *way* more street cred than rednecks," said Caz, grinning.

"There's a great aquarium in Monterey," Juanita said. "We could stop there for lunch. You might appreciate it, Britt. Though it's likely too academic for *certain* individuals' tastes. Heaven forbid we actually learn something."

"School's out! No learning!" Caz protested, drumming her fists enthusiastically on the dash.

"I've heard you can harvest abalone at Van Damme State Beach," I said, trying to sound nonchalant. I was such a faker. I knew about harvesting abalone at Van Damme. I'd saved up my pennies working as a campus janitor the past semester, and now I was going to blow them on a two-week beach rental. All because I wanted to eat my first abalone roasted over a campfire, the authentic way.

Of course, what I really wanted was to see Jude.

"Yes, harvesting abalone is very popular at Van Damme State Beach," Juanita said. "But it can be very dangerous, especially if you don't know what you're doing. I wouldn't recommend it."

"I think we should try it," Caz announced.

"Go ahead," Juanita said, eyes glued to her phone. "I'll sit on the beach and watch you drown from the safety of my towel."

"You know, that would be a good motto for your life," Caz said, brushing her hand through the air like she was affixing an imaginary banner there. "Sit back and watch."

"And your motto would be 'Fall headlong into disaster'!" Juanita exclaimed.

"Especially if disaster is tall, dark, and gorgeous," Caz said, holding her hand up to me for a high-five.

"Guys," I said. "This is supposed to be fun. No more arguing. Close your eyes. Breathe in the air. Think happy thoughts. And give me your phones—I'm locking them in the glove box. No complaints. Caz, round them up. Here's mine."

After the phones were stowed, Caz and Juanita relaxed into

their seats and I drove the breathtaking stretch of coastal highway, with its twisty, cliff-hugging turns and sharp drop-offs that plunged into foamy white waves. The road's narrow shoulders reminded me of the switchback-riddled mountains of Wyoming, but the similarities ended there. I squinted through my sunglasses at glittering turquoise waves rolling as far as the eye could see. A high, blazing sun beat down on my worshiping freckles-be-damned skin. And the smell of the air. Blooming trees, baked pavement, and the cool, clean tang of sea mist. Nope, this definitely wasn't Wyoming.

I tried to take it all in, but I could not ignore the inevitability of where this road led. With every passing mile, I was being swept closer to him. If I wanted to see him, this was my chance. My heart leaped with excitement, then plunged with dread. What if he had a girlfriend? What if she was beautiful and smart and *perfect*?

I could call him. I had his number. I'd dialed it so many times during the last year, but something had always stopped me on the last digit. What would I say? We didn't exactly have a normal friendship or relationship, so "What's up?" had never seemed right. And "I miss you" felt uncomfortably revealing. Or clingy and strange, like I was making a bigger deal out of our time together than four days warranted.

I wanted us to bump into each other randomly, I supposed. Like fate was telling us something. Renting a shack near his favorite beach was probably pushing fate's hand, but what if fate never pulled through for me?

I could get over myself and call him. Whatever. It was just a phone call. If he answered, I always had the option of hanging up. I had a new phone with a new L.A. area code. He couldn't trace the call to me.

Caz's head lolled against the door frame and her eyes were closed, and Juanita was stretched out in the backseat sleeping. Before I could talk myself out of it, I leaned sideways and dug my phone out of the glove box. I dialed his number. With each ring, I felt my nervousness slip away, and something else fill its place. Relief? Disappointment? At last, his answering service picked up.

"Calling home?" Caz asked, yawning and rubbing her eyes.

"A friend in the Bay Area. He didn't pick up. No biggie." I mimicked her yawn, hoping I sounded ho-hum.

"Friend or love interest?" Caz asked perceptively.

"Just some guy I used to know." It felt weird to talk to Caz about Jude. Freshman year, Caz had become so much more than a best friend to me. I'd told her things I'd never told anyone, not even Korbie. We had too many inside jokes to count. We shared groceries and didn't divvy up the bill, because it wasn't about keeping score. What was mine was Caz's. We didn't keep secrets, either. And when we fought, we never went to bed angry. We stayed up until we worked it out, even if that meant pulling an all-nighter. So I felt guilty now, knowing that I'd kept Jude from her. But I wasn't sure I was ready to share him with anyone. Maybe because I never really had him. Because I wasn't sure what we had was real. We'd never had a chance to figure it out.

"We're young, Britt." Caz kicked her heels up on the dash. "We've alive. Save being cautious for when you're dead."

I watched her with admiration and jealousy. There was a time when I was like Caz. Blown by the wind. Hands in the air. But last spring break, in the mountains, everything had changed. I had changed.

Caz drove the last half of the trip. Juanita took shotgun, and I sprawled out in the backseat. I had to sing along to the radio to keep my thoughts on track. If I wasn't careful, they wandered back in time, to that night under the tree, replaying the secrets Jude and I had shared, and other things we'd shared.

An hour before sunset, I saw a sign for Van Damme State Beach. I felt a nervous little flutter in my veins. What if he was at the beach now? Of course he wasn't. But he would be someday—the beach meant too much to him for him to stay away forever. I could write our names in the sand, something sentimental and totally cheesy, and maybe weeks or months from now, he'd walk over the same spot, and suddenly, unaccountably, think of me.

"Take this exit," I blurted without thinking.

Caz glanced at me in the rearview mirror. Our beach shack was a few exits north of here, by the bay. I could tell that she was about to tell me this, but she saw my face and made the exit.

As the car slowed, Juanita sat up and stretched her arms. "Where are we?" she asked groggily.

"We're going hunting for abalone," Caz said. *What's abalone?* she mouthed back at me.

"Sea snails," I answered.

"Ah," Caz said wisely. "We are hunting for sea snails, which may or may not be code for something else."

Caz parked, and I pushed out of the Wrangler and walked to the craggy cliffs and bluffs overlooking the ocean. My heart was beating ridiculously fast, and I was glad I had a moment alone to collect myself. Jude wasn't down there. I was getting worked up for no reason.

The sun's rays skimmed the surface of the water, shimmering a luminous silver. Sharp rocks dotted the shore and seagulls cried out, circling overhead. As I climbed down to the cove, I tried to picture Jude diving for abalone, at ease with the ebb and flow of the current tugging at his body. I never asked him how long he could hold his breath. Whatever his record, I had him beat. I'd been holding mine for a year.

Several minutes later, Caz scooted carefully down behind me. "Do you see him?"

"Who?"

"Abalone."

I made a face. "You are so dumb."

"How'd you meet him?"

"You wouldn't believe me."

"He was the pizza delivery guy. Your best friend's boyfriend. The pallbearer at your great-uncle Ernest's funeral. Am I getting warmer?"

More like he kidnapped me, held me hostage, forced me to guide him through the mountains in a blizzard, then saved my life, then I saved his life, we made out, and somewhere along the way I fell in love with him. Yup, that about summed it up.

"We don't have to talk about him," Caz said. "But if he broke your heart, I will rip out his soul and feed it to my family's pet pig, Big Ol' Pig."

"That's reassuring."

"You'd do the same for me."

"I don't have a pet pig."

"But I bet you have a pet potato," Caz giggled.

I slung my arm over her shoulder. "Can I talk you into a beach walk?"

We left our shoes on, walking along the gravelly sand, out of the tide's reach.

"Speaking of things I'd do for you," Caz went on, "if you left your ice cream on the counter, I'd put it back in the freezer. If you left your coat at home on a rainy day, I'd drive it to campus."

"Where's this going?"

"And if, say, you left your cell in the car and it started ringing, I'd answer it."

I stared at her for three whole seconds before understanding dawned. "You answered my phone? Who called?" A whirlpool swirled in my belly.

"Some guy. He'd missed a call from you earlier, but you didn't leave a message, and he didn't recognize your number, so he called back."

"What did you tell him?" I said, my voice creeping higher with panic. "Did you tell him my name?"

"I told him if he really wanted to know who the phone belonged to, he could come to Van Damme beach and find out for himself."

"You didn't!" I grabbed her elbow, propelling her toward the rocky cliff leading back to the car. "We have to leave. Did he say how far away he was? Is he all the way back in San Francisco? Stop dragging your feet, Caz!"

"That's the crazy thing. He said he's already here."

"He did not!" I said, my voice shrill.

"He had to dry off, and then he was going to meet us in the parking lot. I told him that's where he'd find us."

I could feel heat surge into my face. I was suddenly terrified I'd see him. And terrified I wouldn't. "We have to leave. We have to go, Caz!"

The rocks were too steep to climb, so I grabbed her hand and started running toward the softer sand dunes farther down the coast. I had to beat Jude to the parking lot. I'd interfered with fate, and this was my payback. Yes, I wanted to see him. But not like this. I didn't know what to say, I hadn't thought of the perfect words yet, and my hair was messy and windblown, and what if he wasn't alone? What if he was here with her?

What happened next was one of those long, endlessly long moments where time really does seem to slow. Caz and I were running down the beach, and she made some comment about the hot guy strolling our way, and she lifted the brim of her sunhat to fully appreciate his shirtless physique. My feet came to a stop. My brain switched off and I could only stare. In some distant place in my mind, I must have recognized him. I was staring at him after all. But I wasn't thinking anything. I was too shocked to have a single thought. He must have been feeling the same way, because he came up short in the sand. His eyes were taking me in, but the expression on his face was as surprised as it was disbelieving.

Jude's skin was damp and bronze, the tip of his nose starting to sunburn. His hair hung longer than before, and he slicked it back out of his brown eyes. He had one hand slung loosely in his pocket. There was something carefree and weightless in his posture, and it completely transformed him. Gone was the rugged mountain man with shoulders hunched against the cold, and raw, chafed hands. The guy standing before me was as relaxed and inviting as a well-worn pair of jeans.

His face warmed with a smile. "For a minute there, you had me stumped. A friend with an Australian accent—nice red herring."

I couldn't even answer. I stood there, trembling.

"Sorry I missed your call—I was in the water," he went on, walking toward me, and the smile on his face faltered, his eyes growing serious. Gone was the Jude who masked every feeling. I watched the play of emotion on his face as his eyes drank me in. It made my breath catch. He still felt something for me. It was written unmistakably on his face.

It was all I needed to know. My restraint left me. I ran and threw myself at him, jumping into his arms, wrapping my legs tightly around his hips, burying my face in his neck.

I kissed him. It happened so quickly and easily; the months apart compressed into days, minutes, seconds, a mere heartbeat. I brushed my lips over his mouth, his cheekbones, every inch of his strong, beautifully carved face.

"I can't believe it's really you." He tucked my hair behind my ear and caressed my cheek gently. "You look amazing."

I laughed. "A shower will do that. And food and sleep."

"Think I'll mosey along the beach and find my own abalone," Caz said, hitching her thumb up the coast and backing away with a goofy, delighted grin on her face.

"Caz, wait! This is Jude." I tugged him over by the hand. "Jude, meet my best friend, Caz."

"A pleasure to meet you," Jude said, shaking her hand formally. The gesture seemed to win over Caz, who beamed approvingly at him.

She stage-whispered to me, "If you don't want 'im, I'll take 'im."

"Can I buy you both dinner?" Jude smiled wider, pouring on the charm. "I know a great place, Cafe Beaujolais, not far from here. You can't come all this way and not try it. I won't take no for an answer. You're in my territory now, and it's my duty to wow you."

"Isn't that thoughtful of you," Caz said. "I already ate, but I know Britt skipped lunch and is surely starving." She was so full of it, I nearly giggled. I had stuffed myself on lobster in Monterey and she knew it. "Juanita and I will head over to the shack and check in. We'll see you . . . when we see you." She winked at me.

"You're staying nearby?" Jude asked me, his face lighting up.

"Beach rental. I threw darts at the map, and wouldn't you know, Van Damme was feeling lucky."

Jude's mouth curved into an astute smile. "I love a lucky coincidence."

Jude was right. Cafe Beaujolais was incredible. We sat outside on the patio and ate escargot, which Jude said would have to tide me over until he could catch me abalone. The sky was a deep, satiny purple, not quite black, and the stars were out. The air smelled lush and sweet. I'd kicked off my flip-flops and had my feet propped on Jude's legs under the table. He'd put on a white linen shirt for dinner, and was stroking my leg affectionately.

"Five stars," I said. "I think that's the best food I've ever had."

Jude smiled. There was a light in his brown eyes that I'd never seen before, not in the mountains. It was as if the hardened veneer had fallen away and I was seeing the real Jude. He was casual, genuine, open. He had a good heart. He was a good man. "I've got a few other places I'd like to take you. Give you the local tour."

"I'm in."

He reached across the table and laced his fingers in mine. "You have beautiful hands. I never got to see them before. You were always wearing gloves."

"I threw away everything I wore on that trip. Gloves, jeans, even my boots. Four straight days of wearing the same thing was enough for me."

"I threw away most of my things too. I kept my hat, though. You wore it, and I wanted one thing to remember you by. I'm a sentimental sap, I know."

"No." I felt suddenly shy. "It's . . . sweet."

Jude's brown eyes turned expressive and honest. "I came to Van Damme almost every weekend since I last saw you. It was a long shot, but I hoped you'd remember the spot. I'd come and sit on the rocks and look for you on the beach. Sometimes I'd walk the shore and see you out of the corner of my eye. I'd turn quickly, but every time it was a trick of the light." His voice thickened.

"I came back, again and again, hoping this time it would really be you. And then, today, when I saw you, and it really was you, I realized you were looking for me too. Because those four days in the mountains, they changed us. I gave you a piece of me. And you must have given me a piece of yourself, too, because you wouldn't have come here otherwise. You would have let go. I can't let go of you, Britt. And I don't want you to let go of me."

My eyes filled. "I came all this way to find you. Those four days weren't enough. I wanted to be with you like this. On a warm, lazy night. At a restaurant. Walking on the beach talking about stupid, meaningless things."

"I have a brilliant idea. Let's take a walk on the beach and talk about stupid, meaningless things."

I giggled. "You read my mind."

"See? I'm the perfect guy. You don't have to tell me what you want." He tapped his head. "I'm a male mind-reader. That's one in a million. A B-list superpower at the very least."

"Stop it. You're going to make me snort my drink."

He tapped his head again. "I already knew that."

I sighed happily. "This is the best night, Jude. Thank you."

"I make you snort your drink, and it's the best night of your life. You're easy to please."

"C'mon," I giggled again, hooking my flip-flops over my finger and grabbing his elbow. "People are staring. Let's go be idiots in private."

Caz had once told me that you know you're comfortable with another person when you can sit in silence and not feel obligated to make small talk. That's how Jude and I were now. We lay flat on our backs on the gray sand, staring at the glittering sky. The ocean air was cool and refreshing. I was picking out the constellations I knew. Mainly the Dippers. I was pretty sure I knew Orion's Belt, too. I saw two bright stars nestled close together, far from the others, and decided that was our constellation. It felt romantic to think that we could be forever. Our love, written in the stars.

"What are your summer plans?" Jude asked me.

"Get a job, visit my family." I turned my head to look him in the eyes. "I'm not thinking about that right now."

"Stay. Here, with me."

I rose up on my elbow, searching his face to see if he was serious. "What do you mean?"

"My parents are in Europe for the summer. We've got plenty of rooms at our house. Caz and Juanita are welcome to stay. And if you're worried about a job, I know a few people who are looking for interns. If that's too fussy, there's always waiting tables. I'm here to help."

"You'd let us crash at your place the whole summer?"

"I'm pulling out all the stops on this offer. If I do it right, I'm hoping it'll be too good to refuse."

I smiled. "That sounds sinister, Don Corleone."

Jude said tenderly, "I let you go last year, and while I don't regret giving you the time to figure out what you wanted, I always hoped you'd give me a second chance. Say yes. Say you'll give us a shot."

"I don't know," I told Jude, biting my lip to trap a smile. "Our

last vacation together ended disastrously. I have to ask: Will there be snow?"

A slow smile spread over his features. "Just endless beaches and sun. And me."

I lay in his arms, my leg sprawled on top of his, my head on his shoulder. His eyes were closed, but he was awake. His arm was draped around me, his other hand resting on my thigh. A smile of contentment curved his mouth.

It was late the following afternoon, and the beach was ours alone. The sun had slipped across the sky, its rays encroaching on our sandy bed beneath an umbrella. I nudged the towel up to shade my foot.

"You're thinking about something," Jude murmured, keeping his eyes shut.

"I'm thinking about you." I sighed happily, running my hand over his chest. Only the lightest scars from that night remained. I kissed them softly. To me they weren't imperfections, but a vivid reminder of that dark night we'd shared together. *After the darkness comes the light.*

"Interesting. Because I'm thinking about you."

I brushed sand from his bicep and laid my cheek on it. "Go on. What about me? Don't leave me in suspense. I'm not opposed to flattery."

He rolled sideways, stretching his long, lean body alongside mine. "If you weren't so beautiful, I might have to reprimand your big ego." He traced his finger idly down my nose. "I always mean to do it, and then you look at me, and I forget what it is I want to say, and all I can think is that if I don't kiss you, and damn soon, I don't deserve you."

"I am perfectly fine with this."

"If I don't watch myself, I'm going to spoil you. Your head will grow so big, we'll have to roll it down to the beach." He propped his elbow in the sand, looking at me directly. "You haven't given me an answer. Will you stay?"

My smile faded, and I pondered his question seriously. In a way the rest of the world wouldn't understand, four long days in the mountains with him, trusting my life to him, was all it took to know I was in love with him. If I had to do it over again to find him, I would.

I covered his mouth with mine. He tasted of saltwater, and it hit me how lucky I was. All summer, I could lie with Jude on the beach, dusting our bodies in sand, kissing the ocean from his lips, listening to the soft pound of waves lull us to sleep in each other's arms.

"I'll stay," I said. "I think you're worth the trouble of putting up with endless beaches and sun a little longer."

He grinned. "I'm worth it, all right. And just to prove it, I'll show you. Come here. . . ."